Praise for the novels of

"*The Naked Marquis* is a delicious combination of sweetness and sensuality, the literary version of chocolate cake . . . every page is an irresistible delight!" —Lisa Kleypas, *New York Times* bestselling author

"With a delightfully quirky cast of characters and heated bedroom encounters, MacKenzie's latest *Naked* novel delivers a humorous, sprightly romance."—*Romantic Times BOOK Reviews*

"A pure delight . . . filled with very lovable characters, and pe

Praise for *The Naked Duke*

"MacKenzie sets a merry dance in motion in this enjoyable Regency romp."—*Booklist*

"This is a funny, delightful debut by a talented writer who knows how to blend passion, humor and the essence of the Regency period into a satisfying tale."—*Romantic Times BOOK Reviews*

"Delightful Regency story of love and danger."—*The Best Reviews*

"*The Naked Duke* is a thoroughly enjoyable story with several wonderful characters."—*Romance Reviews Today*

"A well-written and enjoyable first novel. Ms. MacKenzie has a wonderful voice."—*The Romance Readers Connection*

"Debut author Sally MacKenzie has penned a marvelously witty novel. . . . Readers who enjoy a large dose of humor will love *The Naked Duke*. The characters are charming, and the pace is quick. It is the perfect book for a cozy winter retreat."—aromancereview.com

"If you like Regency-set romances that offer both humor and excitement, you should enjoy reading *The Naked Duke*. MacKenzie's voice is fresh and intriguing, her characterization is sound, she knows the period—and her villain is extremely nasty."—rakehell.com

"We just might have a new star in the making! This is definitely a new author that one should take a closer look at."—*Historical Romance Writers*

"Author Sally MacKenzie combines humor and suspense in her debut novel."—booksforabuck.com

"Sally MacKenzie's first novel, *The Naked Duke*, runs a range of emotions that will have you laughing out loud and then biting your nails in anticipation. . . . The characters were realistic, the story was fast paced and the love story of an American girl returning to her father's homeland to find love and happiness is straight out of a fairy tale."—*Fallen Angel Reviews*

PLEASE EXPLAIN

"Be that as it may, miss, you cannot entertain naked men in your room and not promptly attire your finger with an engagement ring."

Meg squeaked again. She was becoming a regular mouse.

"Robbie was *naked?*"

"Well . . . yes." Lizzie feared she would spontaneously combust from mortification. "In a manner of speaking, that is."

"Hmm." Lady Bea's eyebrows shot up to her hairline. "And how can a gentleman be naked *in a manner of speaking?*"

Lizzie would not meet the older woman's eyes. "It was dark."

The Naked Earl

SALLY MACKENZIE

ZEBRA BOOKS
Kensington Publishing Corp.
www.kensingtonbooks.com

ZEBRA BOOKS are published by

Kensington Publishing Corp.
850 Third Avenue
New York, NY 10022

All Kensington titles, imprints, and distributed lines are available at special quantity discounts for bulk purchases for sales
promotion, premiums, fund-raising, educational, or institu-
tional use.

Special book excerpts or customized printings can also be created to fit specific needs. For details, write or phone the office
of the Kensington Special Sales Manager: Attn. Special Sales
Department. Kensington Publishing Corp., 850 Third Avenue,
New York, NY 10022. Phone: 1-800-221-2647.

Zebra and the Z logo Reg. U.S. Pat. & TM Off.

ISBN-   978-0-8217-8075-6
ISBN-   0-8217-8075-1

First Printing: April 2007
10 9 8 7 6 5 4

Printed in the United States of America

Helen R. Stanton
September 4, 1917–May 23, 2006
I love you, Mom.

For Dad, who reads romance, and for Kevin, Dan, Matt,
David, and Mike, who don't.

Thanks to my writer pals (www.romanceunleashed.com)
for keeping me sane.

Chapter One

Robert Hamilton, Earl of Westbrooke, was a light sleeper. His eyes opened the moment his mattress shifted. He turned to see what had caused the disturbance.

Two very large, very naked breasts dangled in front of his nose. Damn! He looked up to see to whom they belonged. Lady Felicity Brookton. She gave him an arch look as she drew in her breath to scream.

Bloody hell.

He bolted from the bed and leapt for the window. There was no time for such niceties as breeches or shoes. Once Lady Felicity started her caterwauling, the entire house party would be banging on his door. He'd be securely caught in parson's mousetrap, condemned to face Lady Felicity at the breakfast table every morning for the rest of his life.

Could there be a more succinct description of hell?

He swung his leg over the sill and dropped down onto the roof of the portico as she emitted her first screech. The sharp surface cut into his bare feet, but the pain was nothing to the panic raging in his chest.

He had to get away.

Thank God he had scrutinized the view from his window when he'd arrived at Tynweith's house party.

He'd made a habit of looking for escape routes since the ladies of the *ton* had gotten so persistent. If they only knew. . . . Well, if he was forced to flee naked from his bed perhaps it was time to do something. A discreet rumor judiciously planted should deter most marriage-minded maidens. He glanced back at his window. Or perhaps they would be happy to have his money and title without having to pay for them in his bed.

He shivered as an early spring breeze rushed over the portico. He couldn't stand here like a nodcock. At any moment one of Tynweith's guests would respond to Felicity's screams, look out the window, and wonder what the Earl of Westbrooke was doing standing naked in the night. He snorted. Hell, all of Tynweith's guests would assume they knew exactly what he had been doing, and he'd be as securely caught as if he'd stayed between his sheets.

It was much too long a distance to the ground to consider jumping. He had not quite reached that point of desperation.

Felicity screeched again. Someone shouted. He scanned the other windows that faced the portico. There, at the end—flickering candlelight showed an open window. He sprinted for it, hoping the room's occupant was male.

Lady Elizabeth Runyon stood naked in front of her mirror, hands on hips, and frowned at her breasts. She tilted her head, squinting at them through her right eye and then her left. Bah! They were small, puny little lemons next to Lady Felicity's lush, ripe melons. No corset in England could make them more impressive.

She turned sideways, grabbing the bedpost to steady herself. Perhaps this angle was more complimentary?

No.

A gust of cool air blew in from her open window, sliding over her skin, causing her nipples to tighten. She covered them with her hands, trying to push them back into place.

She had an odd tingly feeling, as if a vibrating harp string ran from her breasts to her . . . her . . .

She took her hands off her body as if burned. She should put her nightgown back on and climb into bed. Pull the covers up to her chin, close her eyes, and go to sleep. She would if the room didn't swirl so unpleasantly when she did so. She grabbed for the bedpost again.

That last glass of ratafia had definitely been a mistake. She wouldn't have taken it if she hadn't been so bored. If she had to listen to Mr. Dodsworth drone on about his stables one more time . . . It was drink or scream. The man hadn't had an original thought—or any thought that did not involve prime bits of blood—since her come out three years ago.

She leaned against the bedpost. How was she going to survive another Season? Seeing the same people, hearing the same conversation, tittering over the same gossip. It had been exciting when she was seventeen, but now . . .

Was it possible to die of ennui?

And Meg was no help. Lud! She'd finally persuaded her friend to leave the weeds of Kent for the wonders of London, and Meg turned out to be as big a bore as Dodsworth. Her topic of verbal torture was horticulture. Shrubbery. Damn shrubbery. If Meg had her way, she'd spend every moment in the shrubbery—and not with a gentleman bent on seduction.

Lizzie scowled at the bedpost. She should have poured that last glass of ratafia over Robbie's head. That would have livened things up. Ha! She pictured the looks of horror that would have adorned the assembled *ton* if Lady Elizabeth Runyon, sister of the

Duke of Alvord, pattern card of respectability, had caused such a scene.

At least she would have gotten Robbie's attention. She'd wager next quarter's pin money on that.

She looked at her mirror again. It was very daring standing here naked. She straightened, letting go of the bedpost. Perhaps she should be daring this Season. Wanton, even. Playing by the rules hadn't gotten her what she wanted—*whom* she wanted—so she'd break them.

She put her hands back on her breasts. She sighed. The poor little things barely filled her palms—they would be lost in Robbie's larger hands.

Mmm. She half-closed her eyes, biting her bottom lip. Robbie's hands. His long fingers, his broad palms. On her skin.

She felt very daring indeed. More than daring— hot. She rubbed her thumbs over her nipples. The harp string started vibrating again. She licked her lips, arching her hips, spreading her legs slightly so the breeze might find and cool her where she most needed cooling.

What would it feel like if Robbie touched her *there*? Her hand slid down her body.

"My God!"

A male voice, hoarse and strained. She screamed as her eyes flew open. Robbie's reflection was staring at her in the mirror. Robbie's very naked reflection.

She spun to face him, grabbing the bedpost to keep from falling. The room shifted unpleasantly, then righted. She blinked. Yes, Robbie was still there, still naked, standing just inside her window.

She had never seen a naked man before, except in paintings or statues. She stared.

Art did not do reality justice. Not at all.

Then again, perhaps no artist had ever had a model quite as splendid as Robbie.

He looked so different from the civilized London

lord she had left downstairs. He was larger. Well, obviously, he could not have grown simply by shedding his clothes, but it certainly seemed as if he had. His neck, freed from yards of muffling cravat and concealing collar, was a study in angles and shadows. And his shoulders . . . How had they fit into his coat?

She never would have guessed he had hair sprinkled across his chest. Golden red hair dusting down to his flat stomach, then spreading out below his navel around . . .

Oh, my.

She'd never seen *that* in any artwork. The . . . appendage was long and thick and stuck straight out.

How did he hide it in his pantaloons?

Lizzie looked back at Robbie's face. It was far redder than his hair. Could he be injured? The blacksmith's thumb had swollen to twice its size when he'd hit it with his hammer. Had Robbie bumped this part of his anatomy climbing in the window?

"Are you in pain?" She glanced at her bed. "Lie down. I'll get a wet compress."

He made a short noise that sounded like a cross between a laugh and a moan and jerked around to slam her window shut, pulling the curtains tight.

"No, I'm not in pain. Where's your nightgown?"

"Are you certain?" His back was almost as beautiful as his front. She studied his tight buttocks. She would love to touch them. "You sound like you are in pain."

"Just tell me where your blood—blasted nightgown is." He turned back to her, jaw clenched, eyes focused on her face. "Better yet, just put it on. Now."

Lizzie did not care for the note of command in his voice.

"No. I don't want to. I'm hot." She flushed. "Very hot." Uncomfortably hot. And damp. Wet, really. She moved her hand down to be certain she wasn't dripping.

"God, no." He caught her before she reached her stomach. His fingers—thick, warm—encircled her wrist. She needed them somewhere else. Her breasts ached; her nipples had tightened into hard pebbles.

He shook her arm slightly. "Put on your nightgown." He sounded a bit desperate.

She shook her head. She could smell him now. She inhaled deeply. He smelled of Robbie. She giggled. Silly, but true. It was a musky, spicy scent, stronger now that it wasn't muffled by layers of clothing.

His eyes kept darting looks at her breasts. She felt them swell with his attention. She needed to rub them against the hair on his chest.

Who cared about a nightgown? She didn't want a nightgown. She wanted his body against hers. His skin on hers. Everywhere. She panted slightly. She was certain a puddle of need was forming at her feet.

She reached for him.

"Lizzie!" He grabbed her other hand, holding both wrists in a firm grip.

"Let me go." She jerked back. His grasp was gentle but unbreakable. Well, she knew how to get free. She had an older brother. She wasn't above telling a small lie if necessary. "You're hurting me."

He released her at once.

"Ah!" She lunged, but he caught her by the shoulders. "Lizzie, you're bosky."

"N-no, I'm not. I just want to touch you. Please? Just let me touch you." His arms were too long. No matter how much she stretched, she could not reach his body.

"I don't think that would be a good idea. Now put on your nightgown."

"*I* think it would be a splendid idea." She lunged again. No luck. "Why won't you let me touch you?"

"Because besides the fact that you appear to be thoroughly foxed, I'm certain there are going to be people at your door and quite possibly your window any moment now. You don't want them to find us like this, do you?"

She hiccupped. "Yes, I do." She lurched toward him

again. If she didn't feel his body against hers soon, she would cry.

Robbie gave an odd little growl. "You wouldn't say that if you were sober."

"Yes, I would." She stopped fighting and touched him where she could reach. The muscles in his arms were warm rocks. She could barely get her fingers around his forearm. She stroked his wrist with her thumb and saw sweat bead on his upper lip. She wanted to lick it off.

"I love you, Robbie. I've loved you forever."

His jaw tensed. "No, you haven't."

"Yes, I have."

He shook his head. "Hero worship. Calf love."

"No. Kiss me. You'll see."

He rubbed his face on his arm, wiping off the sweat. "There's no time for that, Lizzie."

"Yes, there is. Kiss me."

"Lizzie." His hands clenched on her shoulders, but gentled when she drew in a sharp breath. "Lizzie, please. If I'm found here, the scandal will be beyond belief. James will kill me."

"No, he won't. You're his friend."

Robbie snorted. "You're his sister. Trust me. He will kill me."

"I don't see why. He met Sarah naked, didn't he? How can he complain?"

"That's different."

"No, it's not."

"Yes, it is, and if you weren't so foxed you would see that. Now put your nightgown on."

"All right, but you'll have to let me go. I can't put it on with your hands in the way."

"True. Just don't—"

Robbie loosened his grip too soon. Lizzie closed the distance between them in one step and threw her arms around his waist.

"Lizzie!" He moved almost as quickly, dropping his hands to her hips, pushing them back.

She had forgotten about his swollen part. She didn't want to hurt him, but she so ached to feel his entire body against hers. What she could feel felt very, very good. Her hands played over his back, running up and down his warm, smooth skin. She pressed her cheek against his chest and heard his heart pounding. She found a drop of sweat trickling down between his nipples and licked it, running her tongue up the trail to his neck.

"Lizzie!"

"Mmm?" His hands on her hips were wonderful, but they were too still. She tried to wiggle, to encourage his fingers to roam. Perhaps she could show him the way. She slipped her own hands over his buttocks and around to his stomach, careful not to touch . . .

"Lizzie!" Robbie leapt back as if scalded.

"Did I hurt you? I'm so sorry. I didn't mean to." She glanced down and smiled in relief. "No, see—you're better. The stiffness and swelling are almost gone. You should be able to tuck your . . . um, well, you should be able to tuck *it* into your pantaloons now."

"*God*, Lizzie."

Lizzie frowned, looking up. Robbie's mouth was so tight a muscle jumped in his cheek. His eyes looked . . . haunted.

"Robbie, I—"

She jumped. Someone was banging on her door— and someone else was banging on her window.

"What . . . ?"

"Your company has arrived." Robbie grabbed her shoulders, turned her, and pushed her toward the bed. "Get your nightgown on."

Bloody hell. Lizzie was not moving quickly enough. And she was clearly half-seas-over. Did she grasp the seriousness of the situation? No. She was sitting on her bed, staring at him. Staring at a particular part of him.

At least she had stopped grabbing him.

More banging. Whoever was hitting the window might manage to break it if Lizzie didn't get her nightgown on soon.

He snuffed out the candle, leaving the room lit only by the banked fire in the hearth. Perhaps darkness would help her concentrate on the matter at hand.

"Put on your nightgown."

"Hmm?"

"Lizzie, you need to put on your nightgown *now*. You have to answer the door." He reached to help her—and encountered a soft breast.

"Mmm."

Good God, the girl was purring. If only . . . No, he wouldn't think of it. It was impossible. Completely im—

"Lizzie!" He tried to keep his voice down, though with all the door and window pounding, he could have shouted and not been heard over the din. "Lizzie—yikes!"

He grabbed her wrist and pulled her fingers away from where they had wandered.

"Did I hurt you? You're swollen again."

"Lizzie, just put your nightgown on and get the door. Please?"

She huffed and the small puff of air tickled over his stomach.

"All right. Will you touch me again after they are all gone? It felt so good."

Damn. He balled his hands into fists. He really would like to hit something. He tried to keep his voice calm.

"We'll see. Now be a good girl and put on your nightgown." Louder banging on the door and some muffled shouts. At least James wasn't here. He was at

Alvord, awaiting the birth of his second child. "Hurry. The door first. Try to look as if you've just woken up. And remember, I'm not here."

"Not here. Right."

He watched her take her first steps toward the door, then he jumped onto the bed, pulling the curtains closed.

Betty, Lizzie's maid, must sleep like the dead, he thought. Hell, she must *be* dead if this racket hadn't woken her. Of course, that was assuming she was in her bed at all. More likely she was with his valet somewhere. It was no secret those two would like to make a match of it. Collins had certainly hinted about it enough. Robbie was beginning to fear for his life when the man shaved him each morning.

Betty and Collins would be merry as grigs if he wed Lizzie. Well, he would be, too, but it would never happen. He sighed. When he had seen her, standing naked in front of her mirror, the candlelight making her skin glow, her hand sliding down her curves to exactly the place he most wanted to be . . .

He buried his face in the pillow. A mistake. He inhaled her scent and grew even harder.

He stifled a moan.

The door had swung open. Light and the babble of voices flooded the room. Only a miracle would keep him from detection.

He prayed for a miracle.

"He's here, isn't he? I know he's here." Lady Felicity Brookton, clad in a pistachio-colored dressing gown, pushed Lizzie aside and stepped into the room, holding a candle high. "Where are you hiding him?"

"Um." Lizzie blinked, staring out her door. Half the house party had assembled in the corridor.

"Someone is knocking at the window." Lady Caroline, the daughter of the Earl of Dunlee, maneuvered her ample bulk across the room and opened the curtains. "Oh, look! It's Lord Peter."

"Let him in." Lady Felicity peered inside Lizzie's wardrobe.

"Um." Lizzie wished she could think. That last glass of ratafia had definitely been ill-advised. Her head felt as if it were stuffed with cotton wool.

She couldn't let them find Robbie. He didn't want to be found. She watched Lady Felicity light all the available candles. How was she going to stop them? There were only so many places to look.

Lord Peter, dressed in his shirtsleeves and pantaloons, climbed in the window. "Saw him vault in here." He chuckled. "Hard to miss his lily-white as—" He coughed. "Ankles. His lily-white ankles. Hard to miss them in the dark."

"So where is he, Lady Elizabeth?" Lady Felicity glared at her.

"Um, he who?"

"Lord Westbrooke, of course. Didn't he just climb in your window?"

"Uh . . ." Lizzie's mind went blank.

"Lady Felicity, surely you cannot be suggesting that Lord Westbrooke would behave in such an inappropriate manner?"

Lizzie turned to see Lady Beatrice, her nominal chaperone for the Season. Thank God! Lady Bea would deal with this mess in short order.

Lady Felicity lifted her chin. "I only know what I saw."

Lady Bea lifted an eyebrow. "And what exactly did you see, miss?"

"I saw Lord Westbrooke leap naked out the window."

"I thought you said he came *in* the window."

"Not this window."

"Ah, the window in your room then? Correct me if I am wrong, but any man exiting your window would end as a rather unsightly corpse on the terrace. Or have you changed rooms recently? I thought your bedchamber was just a few doors down the hall from mine on the other side of the corridor."

Lady Felicity turned red. She opened her mouth as if to speak, but no words issued forth.

"Let's look in the bed, Felicity." Lord Peter left the window and reached for the bed curtains. "I'll wager Westbrooke is hiding between the sheets."

"Lord Peter!"

Everyone turned to stare at the petite woman who'd managed to push to the fore of the crowd. The Duchess of Hartford—Lady Charlotte Wickford before her marriage to the elderly duke—was not someone Lizzie would ever have imagined coming to her rescue. Charlotte hated her. Well, she really hated James, but James spent most of his time in Kent these days. Lizzie was a much more convenient target.

"What, your grace?" Lord Peter stood back, gesturing to the bed curtains. "Would you like to do the honors?"

Charlotte stared at him. He flushed and dropped his arm.

"If you won't do it, *I* will." Felicity grabbed a handful of cloth.

"Lady Felicity." Charlotte's tone stopped Felicity's hand before it had moved an inch. "Surely you do not mean to imply that Lady Elizabeth would entertain a man in her bedroom?"

Felicity looked at Lizzie's small breasts. Lizzie crossed her arms over them.

"Entertain? No. However—"

"However, if Lord Westbrooke should be so bold as to visit Lady Elizabeth in her room at night—if he were found in her bed—I assume he would do the gentlemanly thing and offer for her." Charlotte shrugged. "Her brother, the duke, would insist, wouldn't you say?"

Felicity paused, an arrested expression on her face.

"In fact, I imagine if Lord Westbrooke were indeed hiding behind those bed curtains, he'd be wed to Lady Elizabeth before the week was out." Charlotte smiled. "I'm certain you would want to dance at that wedding, hmm, Lady Felicity?"

Lady Felicity's hand fell to her side. "Uh. Yes. You're right. Of course. Lord Westbrooke would never invade Lady Elizabeth's room. I don't know what I was thinking."

"I know what you were thinking. You told me—"

"Lord Peter!"

Lord Peter frowned and turned to Charlotte.

"I believe we intrude on Lady Elizabeth's privacy." Charlotte smiled up at him as she ran her fingers over his shirt cuff. "It's time you went to . . . bed, don't you think?"

It was Lord Peter's turn to have an arrested expression. He stared down at Charlotte for a moment and then grinned.

"I believe you are correct, your grace."

"Of course I am." Charlotte glanced at Felicity. "I imagine you dreamt the event, Lady Felicity. Sometimes our dreams are so vivid, they appear real, do they not?"

Felicity tore her eyes off the bed curtains. "Yes. Yes, I'm certain you are right, your grace." She glanced back at the bed. "Sometimes my dreams do seem real."

"Exactly." Charlotte moved toward the door, Lord Peter at her side. "So sorry to disturb you, Lady Elizabeth." Her eyes drifted to the bed also. "I'm certain you are eager to get back to"—Charlotte smiled slightly—"sleep." She inclined her head. "You have depths I never suspected."

Lizzie watched the crowd disperse. Lady Beatrice was the last to leave. She looked at the bed and raised her eyebrows.

"Anything you would like to tell me, Lizzie?"

Lizzie looked at the bed, too.

"Um, no."

"You're certain?"

"Yes." Lizzie nodded. She was definitely certain. She did not want to discuss the evening's bizarre events with anyone. She was of half a mind that she, too, was the victim of a very vivid dream. "I'm a trifle out of curl. I think I will just go to bed."

"I see." Lady Beatrice addressed the bed in a very stern voice. "Well, I am more than certain the duke would eviscerate any man who played fast and loose with his sister's reputation—or harmed her in *any* way."

"Yes. I'm sure. Thank you. Good night."

Lizzie ushered Lady Bea out the door and closed it firmly behind her. Then she sagged against the solid wooden surface, puffed out her cheeks, and eyed the bed.

Could she have dreamt the entire sequence of events? Was it possible the evening was simply the product of overindulgence?

There was only one way to find out. She pushed away from the door and stepped toward the bed.

Chapter Two

"What *were* you thinking?" Charlotte drew Felicity into her room. Sometimes she wanted to shake the girl. If she were serious about catching Lord Westbrooke, she'd have to start using her head for something other than keeping her ears apart. Men were supposed to think with their nether regions, not women.

Felicity stopped just inside the door. "Aren't you expecting company?"

"Yes, thanks to you." Charlotte took a deep breath, repressing her annoyance. Perhaps it was just as well. She needed to get Lord Peter into her bed. The evening's drama had served to force her over her initial reluctance. She glanced at her watch.

"He'll be here soon." And gone soon, too, she hoped. "I told him I had to speak to you first." And she wanted to fortify her nerves with a sip or two of brandy.

"Peter's not a patient man."

Charlotte shrugged. "He's not a bright man, either. If I hadn't distracted him and reined you in as well, Westbrooke would be engaged now—and you would not be the woman sporting his betrothal ring. Have you never learned discretion?" She headed for her bureau. Why had she agreed to help Felicity trap Westbrooke?

The answer was simple. Trapping the earl for Felicity meant the Duke of Alvord's sister could not wed the man. Taking Westbrooke off the marriage mart might even send Lady Elizabeth into a permanent decline—and *that* would hurt Alvord.

Three years ago when Alvord had chosen an American interloper as his duchess, Charlotte had been livid. She'd been determined to marry a duke, and the only marriageable one available after Alvord wed had been Hartford—eighty-year-old Hartford. As she was walking up the aisle at St. George's to meet her decrepit bridegroom, she'd sworn to make Alvord pay. Now, perhaps, he would.

She waited for the thrill she always experienced at the thought of finally getting her revenge. It didn't come.

She felt nothing.

She jerked on the bureau drawer, pulling it open more forcefully than she'd intended. She caught it before it came out entirely and dumped her belongings onto the floor.

What was the matter with her? She took out her small silver flask and closed the drawer carefully. It was the house party. That was it. She'd been feeling on edge ever since she'd arrived. She should have known being around Tynweith would do this to her.

She uncorked her flask and breathed in the pungent scent of brandy.

No, the truth was, she had more pressing concerns on her mind than revenge.

Hartford was failing. He needed an heir. Time was running out.

An all-too-familiar knot formed in her stomach.

"Discretion wasn't part of the plan." Felicity flung herself into a chair by the fire. "I was *supposed* to be discovered in bed with Westbrooke. Who knew he'd take to the window?"

"You might have guessed. He's made an art of avoiding parson's mousetrap. He's made an art of avoiding *you*." Charlotte raised her flask to her lips, then paused. "Care for brandy?"

"No."

"Suit yourself." She took a long drink. The liquid was comforting, as always. She closed her eyes, savoring the warmth that spread through her chest.

If she didn't need Lord Peter's services so badly, she would have stayed in London.

"You'd better go easy on the drink. You'll be passed out before your paramour arrives."

"I'll be fine." She wished she could pass out, but Lord Peter would probably prefer a sentient partner. Not that her alertness would make any difference, if her experience with Hartford was a guide.

She sat on the chaise across from Felicity. "I wonder what Lady Elizabeth thought when Westbrooke appeared naked in her room."

Felicity snorted. "I'm surprised Miss Prunes and Prisms didn't scream loud enough to wake deaf old Mr. Maxwell in London. She is such a prude."

"I thought she was, too, but now I'm not so certain. She was as cool as ice when everyone was crowded round her, your hand on the bed curtains ready to open them wide. She never flinched. I would not have guessed there was a naked man in her bed." Charlotte took another sip of brandy. "Are you sure Westbrooke was there?"

"Yes, I'm sure. There was nowhere else he could be. Lord Peter followed him. He saw him go in that window."

"Hmm." Charlotte shook her head. "I just can't picture Lady Elizabeth greeting a naked Lord Westbrooke. Of course, her brother always acted very proper, and you know what everyone said about him."

"That he was a regular satyr." Felicity's mouth slid into a sly smile. "He seems content enough now to stay home with his wife."

"She's breeding again, you know." The anxious knot twisted in Charlotte's stomach again. She took a deep breath.

Lord Peter would solve her problem.

"I'd heard. That's why Lady Beatrice is acting as Lady Elizabeth's chaperone this Season—that and the fact Knightsdale's sister-in-law has finally been dragged to Town." Felicity picked up a miniature from an end table and studied it. "This looks like you."

Damn. She should have put that picture in a drawer.

"It is me."

"Do you make a habit of taking your picture with you? I would have thought your glass would suffice."

"It's not mine."

She watched Felicity's eyes widen, then quickly narrow. Charlotte bit her tongue. She should have lied.

"What do you mean, it's not yours? How did it get here?"

She shrugged. "Our host has an odd sense of humor."

Felicity's nose twitched like a hound scenting a fox. "But why does he have a miniature of you?"

"I have no idea. Perhaps you should ask him."

"Hmm." Felicity put the picture back on the table and picked up the porcelain shepherdess standing next to it. "Perhaps you should have chosen him to come to your bed."

"Oh, no. Lord Peter suits my purposes far better." Lord Peter was more than a decade younger than Tynweith, and more importantly, his family was known to produce males. He should give her a son. A daughter would not do.

"Are you going to tell him what your purposes are?"

"Perhaps. Perhaps not." Charlotte could not imagine

that conversation. "Probably not. There is no need for him to know."

"You're going to make him think you lust after his body when all you want is his seed?"

"I don't mean to make him think anything. Thinking is not required for the procedure."

Felicity laughed. "No, I suppose not."

"I am offering him some free sport—why should he complain?"

"True. And Hartford? Will you tell him?"

"Definitely not."

"Won't he be suspicious?"

"I don't see why. Most babes look the same—and I can't imagine he'll survive the child's infancy." God, she hoped he didn't. She hadn't thought he'd live this long. "If he does, Lord Peter's coloring is much like mine. He'll just think his little sprig resembles mama."

"Well, yes, but if a man doesn't plow the field, he can't plant a seed, can he?"

"That is not a problem."

"You mean he still . . . ?" Felicity's eyes widened and her mouth twisted up in a look of disgust.

"Yes, he still does." Every Thursday evening— except the last two Thursdays. He'd tried, but he had not been able to rise to the occasion.

Her stomach clenched. She sipped some more brandy.

If she were able to get with child during this house party, Hartford should not suspect a thing. He *had* been able to accomplish the deed three Thursdays ago. Her courses were not terribly regular. She could be increasing now for all she knew.

"I just thought . . . well a bit of younger seed may help the plant grow faster."

Felicity grinned. "At least the planting will be more enjoyable."

"Perhaps." Charlotte doubted it. The act of coupling was uncomfortable, messy, and embarrassing by its very nature. How could substituting the male change that? "I do hope Lord Peter will not want to make too much of a production of the thing. You told me he wouldn't."

"He won't. Peter has a reputation for being quick." Felicity laughed. "Very quick. A good man for a tryst at a ball. He can get the job done easily while sitting out a set—or even between sets if need be."

"Lovely." Charlotte closed her flask regretfully. Lord Peter should be arriving soon.

Felicity examined the shepherdess in her hands. "So, how am I to get Westbrooke's ring on my finger?"

"Perhaps you should target Lord Peter instead. He is a marquis's son."

"*Fifth* son." Felicity shook her head. "No, I definitely want Westbrooke's title and money."

"Well, if he really was in Lady Elizabeth's room, I imagine there'll be a betrothal by breakfast."

Felicity clenched the shepherdess. "There had better not be. Westbrooke is mine."

"Careful!" Charlotte sat up abruptly. "Tynweith might well be a bit possessive of his trinkets."

Felicity looked at the figurine in her hand, then put it carefully back in its place. "If he treasures the knick-knacks, why put them in the guest rooms?"

"I assume he harbors the mistaken impression that his guests are civilized."

Lizzie's hand shook as she lit a candle. At least the events of the night had cleared her head. She no longer felt muzzy with wine.

She eyed the bed. So far, no motion or sound had come from behind the curtains. *Had* she imagined the evening's odd occurrences? There was only one way to find out. She reached out to pull back the cloth.

"Eek!"

Robbie's hand twitched aside the curtain just as her fingers touched it. He glared at her.

"Shh! You'll get everyone back in here. And watch that candle. You don't want to set us both aflame."

"No." Lizzie already felt flames burning in some very odd locations. Her breasts and her . . . belly. Robbie might be glaring, but he was still naked. Her sheet covered him from the waist down, but his lovely neck, arms, and chest were exposed. The candlelight created interesting shadows begging to be explored.

She was very hot indeed.

Robbie turned away from her and tugged on the sheet. She watched his muscles bunch in his back and arms.

"Could you give me a hand here, Lizzie?"

"What?" Robbie needed a hand? Where? She would love to give him a hand—both her hands. She'd love to run them over his shoulders, down his back, under the sheet at his waist. . . .

He tugged again. "It's not coming loose."

"What?"

"Can't you say anything other than 'what'?" He jerked on the sheet once more. "This. The sheet. It's not coming loose. Could you pull it out at the corners? I'm going to have to borrow it to get back to my room."

"Oh. Yes. Of course."

Lizzie put down her candle and pulled the sheet free of the mattress. Robbie wrapped it around his waist and slid off the far side of the bed.

"I don't know why Charlotte came to our rescue, but I'm not complaining," he said as he tucked the ends of the sheet more securely around his waist. "It would have been extremely awkward if Felicity had opened the curtains and everyone had seen me in your bed."

"Uh." Lizzie wasn't thinking about their close brush with discovery. She was thinking about Robbie's chest and shoulders. About the muscles in his upper arms. About how she wished the sheet would slip free of his waist.

Would he jump again if she touched him?

She started moving around the bed.

He started moving toward the window, giving her a wide berth.

"I do apologize for disturbing your sleep."

"I wasn't sleeping." She flushed.

His face turned red, too. Obviously he'd remembered what she *had* been doing.

"Still, I apologize for invading your room. I was in desperate straits, believe me."

Lizzie reached for his arm, but he jerked it away. He tried to take a longer stride, tripped on his sheet, and caught himself on the wall.

"Why *did* you come to my room?"

He grabbed the windowsill and turned. "I wasn't coming to your room, Lizzie. I was fleeing mine. As I'm sure you guessed from all the commotion, I woke up to find Felicity in my bed—quite uninvited, I assure you. I had to exit quickly."

"So you went out the window?"

He shrugged, making the muscles in his chest move in a most intriguing fashion. "I had no choice. I'm certain Lord Peter was stationed in the hall ready to nab me at Felicity's first scream."

Lizzie nodded. "Felicity *is* rather determined."

"Determined!" Robbie ran a hand through his hair. His arm muscles bunched and shifted delightfully. "She's beyond determined. She's a bedlamite."

Lizzie bit her lip and clutched her nightgown to keep her fingers from misbehaving.

"Once I was out on the portico roof, I had very few options. Yours was the only open window. I was hoping it was Parks's. He got in late, after most people had retired."

"I know. His room is next to mine."

"Yes, well, I realized that rather quickly." Robbie leaned out the window and looked right and left.

"Would you have wed Felicity if her plan had worked?"

He looked back at her and frowned.

"I suppose so. I don't know. The thought is appalling. You can be sure I will find a way to secure my bedchamber door from now on." He sat on the sill and swung his legs over it. "I am sorry for all the, um"—his gesture encompassed the room—"commotion. I think—I hope—there will be no lasting repercussions."

"Repercussions?"

He shrugged.

A naked shrug was *definitely* more interesting than a clothed one.

"Rumors, that sort of thing." He looked everywhere but in her eyes. "I'm certain it will all blow over if we don't let ourselves get flustered by the gabble grinders."

"Yes. Of course. Certainly." Surely he didn't think she was as bad as Felicity? She would never try to trap him into matrimony.

"Good. Then I'll see you in the morning, shall I?" Robbie dropped down to the portico's roof. "Sleep well."

"Sleep well." Lizzie hung out her window, watching him mince back to his room. He took a longer step and his sheet slipped. She held her breath, but he caught it quickly, allowing her only a glimpse of the top of his muscled buttocks.

When he reached his window, his hands went to his waist. Was he going to discard the sheet? It would definitely be easier to climb in without it.

She hung farther out her window. Yes, he was opening it. . . .

He glanced back and saw her just as the cloth slid past his waist. He caught it.

She could have cried in frustration.

He waved.

She waved back.

He waited. It was clear he was not going to attempt to reenter his room while she was watching. She pulled back from the window. . . .

. . . And leaned out again. All she saw was the sheet slithering over the windowsill.

She sighed and shut the window, drawing the curtains closed. Now that Robbie was gone, she could think more clearly. She glanced at the mirror and flushed. In her high-necked white nightgown, she looked the perfectly proper virginal sister of a duke, but earlier. . . .

What had possessed her? She covered her face with her hands. Her cheeks were hot to the touch. Perhaps she was feverish. She had a brain fever, that was it. An alcohol-induced brain fever. She didn't know herself. She had never behaved in such a way before. She certainly had never entertained such feelings before.

She had not even known such feelings existed.

What could he possibly think of her?

Lud!

She blew out her candle and stared up at her bed canopy. The firelight filled it with shadows.

Was she compromised? No one had actually *seen* Robbie in her room, though Felicity, Lady Beatrice— no doubt the entire house party—must believe he'd been naked in her bed.

What if Felicity *had* opened the curtains? Then she would have been compromised—spectacularly compromised. Robbie would have had to offer for her— Lady Beatrice would not have let him out of the room until he had done so.

She turned over and buried her face in her pillow. She breathed in Robbie's scent.

He hadn't offered for her. He could have, once everyone had left.

She stretched out on her side and hugged her pillow to her chest. Perhaps he intended to offer tomorrow. Perhaps he simply felt a marriage proposal should be presented in more formal attire—or at least some attire. She rubbed her cheek on the pillow. She would have been glad to hear his offer naked. Very glad.

If he were going to offer. She shifted to her back again. Perhaps he had no intention of doing so. He had seen her, all of her. Clearly, he had not been impressed. He must prefer more buxom women—though he most definitely did not prefer Felicity.

Her head hurt. There was nothing she could do tonight. Perhaps everything would make more sense in the morning.

She certainly hoped so.

Robbie sighed with relief as soon as his feet touched the floor of his room. He shuffled over to check his door. It had a lock, but the key was missing.

"Collins!" No answer. His valet was not on the cot set up in his dressing room. Envy twisted his gut. As he'd suspected, the man was probably in a snug corner of Tynweith's estate cavorting with Betty, Lizzie's maid. Just as he'd like to be cavorting with Lizzie.

He pushed a sturdy chest in front of the door. That should do the trick until the key was located. Then he unwrapped Lizzie's sheet from around his waist and stuffed it in the bottom of his wardrobe. Collins could give it back to Betty tomorrow and then all would be well.

He hoped. What a nightmare. His heart had stopped when he'd seen the bed curtains bunch in Felicity's hand. If Charlotte hadn't stopped her. . . .

Bloody hell, if Felicity had opened those curtains, half the *ton* would have been treated to the sight of the Earl of Westbrooke naked in the Duke of Alvord's sister's sheets. The story would have spread like the Great Fire of London, and the scandal . . . ? God! The scandal would have been enormous. Bloody enormous. The *ton* would have buzzed with it for the entire Season. Next Season, too. And Lizzie's reputation . . . well, Lizzie would not have a reputation, unless. . . .

No, he would not think about that.

He inspected his bed for stray maidens, snuffed the candles, and climbed in. He'd been sleeping soundly before he'd had to flee over the rooftop. He'd been in the middle of a pleasant dream. He closed his eyes.

Damn.

He jerked them open and stared up at the bed canopy.

He could see Lizzie's naked body as clearly as if she were standing before him—the graceful line of her back, the generous curve of her buttocks, her long legs, her sweet breasts, her milky skin glowing in the firelight.

The blasted fickle part of him was hard as rock . . . now. It made a splendid tent in his blankets. But put a female between his sheets and the damn thing turned limp as stewed cabbage.

His shy little organ would not perform in the presence of company.

Once upon a time he'd been able to . . . well, twice. It was the third time that had created the problem.

He'd gone with some fellows to the Dancing Piper. He'd been hardly seventeen—it had been his first visit to a brothel. His other two forays into Venus's delights had been with Nan, a cheerful, uncomplicated country girl.

MacDuff had introduced him to Fleur. She'd had coal-black hair, startling blue eyes, and a lush figure. She'd been alluring, seductive, mysterious—everything Nan was not. He'd been flattered when she'd agreed to go upstairs with him.

He flung his arm over his eyes.

What an idiot he'd been, but then he'd not been thinking with his head.

She'd moaned and writhed more than Nan ever had. He'd felt extremely cocky in every way. When he'd climbed between her thighs, he'd thought himself the greatest bloody lover in England.

He rubbed his eyes with the heels of his hands. He couldn't rub away the memory. It was as clear as if it had happened yesterday.

She'd yelled, apparently overcome with need.

"Gawd, give it to me now!"

He'd hesitated. He was not so far gone in lust that he'd lost his mind completely. Something seemed off. Something *was* off.

The door flung open, and MacDuff and the other boys rushed in laughing. Fleur laughed, too, letting her legs flop, holding her sides. It had been a grand joke.

He had not seen the humor. He'd leapt off the bed, got tangled in the sheets, and fallen at MacDuff's feet.

"Fleur, lass," MacDuff had said, *"looks like we saved you from a wee little man."*

"Aye. Thankee kindly, my lord. From the size of him, ye'd think he'd carry a great sword, but ye'll see now he carries only a little dirk."

He'd been on his back, the sheets tangled around his feet, his tiny "dirk" exposed for the amusement of the assembled multitude. Covering it with his hands had only added to the merriment.

He clenched his jaw. The damn thing had happened more than a decade ago and still it haunted him. He'd not been able to mount a woman successfully since.

He turned over on his side and pounded his innocent pillow.

He was an intelligent man. He should be able to put the stupid incident in the past where it belonged.

A specific part of him refused to listen to reason.

Bloody useless appendage. It was a damn agent of torture, that was all. It had forced him to worship at Onan's altar too many times to count.

He snorted. If he'd been discovered in Lizzie's bed, Lady Beatrice would have cured him of his problem. She would have castrated him on the spot with the handle of her lorgnette.

He flopped onto his back and stared up at the bed canopy again. What was Lizzie thinking now? Surely she must have expected an offer.

At least the commotion in her room appeared to have cleared her head. She'd shown more restraint after everyone had left. Thank God! What would he have done if she'd touched him?

He knew what he'd like to have done. Taken her straight back to bed.

His ridiculous appendage leapt at the thought. He scowled down at the author of his misery. The miscreant had no shame. No one looking at him now would think he could not perform his bedroom duties.

He was going to have to take himself in hand, literally, if he hoped to get any sleep tonight.

Still, he would never have guessed Lizzie was so passionate. She had been so sweetly wanton. God, how he wished he were a normal man. . . .

The truth was, he would disappoint her if he came to her bed. He couldn't give her passion. He couldn't give her children.

She would want both—must want both. She needed a man—a husband—who would take care of her in bed and out.

He turned over on his stomach and buried his face in his pillow.

No need to use his hand to find relief. The thought of Lizzie in another man's arms deflated his uncooperative organ most efficiently.

Baron Tynweith paused in the darkened corridor to observe Lord Peter slip out of the Duchess of Hartford's bedroom.

Hmm. So Charlotte had started to play games, had she?

A flicker of pain flashed in his gut, but he doused it at once.

Lord Peter sauntered down the hall, apparently not caring who saw him. He did glance back when he reached his door. He froze for a moment, then grinned, his teeth flashing white in the dim light, and nodded at Tynweith before he went into his room.

Cocky.

Tynweith eased open his own door. He heard Grantley stirring in his dressing room. He did not relish seeing his sour valet right now, but he'd never get out of this damned coat by himself.

He shrugged. The stiffness in his shoulders was not due just to his coat's tight fit. He rubbed the line between his brows.

Lord Peter was little more than a boy. He would amuse Charlotte—if he did amuse her—only briefly. She was too canny to take him as a second husband once Hartford cocked up his toes. Short of a gruesome miracle, there was no hope of Lord Peter inheriting. His father, the Marquis of Addington, was barely sixty and still rode to hounds. The heir had six strapping boys and there was a plethora of nephews crowding the country. The Brants were legendary for producing males—the title had never passed out of the direct line.

And Charlotte would have to marry again, unless she was able to produce the next duke. Hartford's current heir was not inclined to be generous with her. Claxton had been rather vocal at the wedding—Hartford had threatened to horsewhip him if he didn't stop maligning Charlotte. He'd stopped his public tirades then, but not his private grumbling. No one in the *ton*, least of all Charlotte, had any doubt as to Claxton's sentiments.

No, if she were looking for Hartford's successor, she would not look to Lord Peter. He was merely a diversion.

Tynweith pressed on his temples. He did not want Charlotte to have diversions.

He'd worked hard to block the thought of her in bed with her wizened husband from his mind. Did he also have to expunge the image of Lord Peter's very unwizened body entwined with hers? The bloody boy was not much more than twenty.

Bah. The whelp was inexperienced. Only a boy—and boys focused only on their own pleasure. He wouldn't know how to satisfy Charlotte.

Not like Tynweith could.

He ripped off his cravat. Where the hell was Grantley? He wanted to get out of this coat, out of his eveningwear, into his bed.

He snorted. What he really wanted was to get into Charlotte's bed.

He balled up the cravat and threw it at the dressing room door. The damn cloth opened in flight and fell limply to the floor.

Surely he would have heard if Charlotte were taking lovers. A juicy piece of gossip like that would have had all the old tabbies—and most of the younger ones—in alt. Lord Peter must be her first.

The ache had moved to the back of his head. He'd have Grantley mix up a powder.

Why the hell was he having this bloody house party anyway? He must have been drunk as an Emperor when he'd hatched the notion. He didn't give a rat's ass for any of the over bred cod's heads cluttering his estate.

"My lord."

"Grantley. Get me out of this damned coat, man."

"Yes, my lord."

Another reason to curse his guests. He couldn't wear his comfortable old coats and baggy breeches with the *ton* invading his house. A pox on all of them.

Well, not Charlotte. *She* was the reason he had invited this plague of idiots. She'd been restless.

He'd noticed—and had hoped to tempt her to some dalliance.

Damn Lord Peter.

"You heard about the disturbance this evening, my lord?"

"What? Oh, if you mean the confusion in Lady Elizabeth's room, yes, Flint told me." Tynweith paid the butler well. One of his duties was to keep his master informed of everything that happened on the estate.

"Her grace came to Lady Elizabeth's defense."

"Yes, I heard. Interesting. I would not have thought the duchess harbored any warm feelings for the Duke of Alvord's sister."

Grantley twisted his thin lips into a more supercilious smirk than usual. "I believe her grace was assisting Lady Felicity."

"Oh?"

"The duchess pointed out that if Lord Westbrooke was found in the room, he would be obliged to wed Lady Elizabeth."

"Ah. And Lady Felicity would prefer that *she* be the next Lady Westbrooke."

Grantley nodded. "One of the upstairs maids observed the woman slip into Lord Westbrooke's room shortly before the incident." Grantley's nostrils flared as if they had encountered an unpleasant odor. "The maid believed Lady Felicity had not been invited to share the earl's bed."

"I'm certain she had not. Westbrooke's been studiously avoiding her since her come out." Grantley pulled off the blasted coat and Tynweith sighed in satisfaction, rolling his shoulders. "Perhaps I should not have lingered in my study. I seem to have missed a very entertaining tableau. Do you suppose Westbrooke was actually cowering in Lady Elizabeth's bed?"

"Certainly, my lord. Lord Peter followed him and saw him climb in the window."

"Climb *in* the window?"

Grantley smoothed the coat's lapels. "Yes. From the portico roof." His mouth pursed so tightly it resembled the sphincter of another orifice. "Unclothed."

"Naked? The Earl of Westbrooke was capering over my portico roof naked?" Tynweith choked on a laugh. He really had missed an interesting series of events.

"It would seem so, my lord. Will you require anything else this evening?"

Charlotte.

Tynweith bit his lip. Surely he hadn't said that aloud, had he? No, Grantley's expression had not changed—it was still his habitual, mildly dyspeptic frown.

"No, that will be all."

Grantley bowed. "Very well. Pleasant dreams, my lord."

God, the man was annoying. He'd have gotten rid of him years ago if he weren't so good at what he did.

And he was not going to have pleasant dreams. He was going to have hot, sweaty dreams of Charlotte—Charlotte whom the wags now called the Marble Duchess.

She wasn't cold. He knew there was passion in her. He sensed it. She just had not yet found the right man to bring it out. He'd bungled the job all those years ago in Easthaven's garden. He'd been too ardent—and too insignificant. If he'd been a duke, she'd have suffered his touch.

Well, she'd gotten her duke—a randy old codger. Better Hartford, though, than Alvord. Hartford would not live many more years—perhaps not even many more months.

He climbed into bed and blew out his candle.

When the duke died, Tynweith planned to be the first in line for the duchess's hand.

Would she have a mere baron this time? He smiled

up at his bed canopy. Yes. He meant to have her panting for him.

He was going to get into Charlotte's bed during this
house party, even if he had to drag Lord Peter out.

Chapter Three

"Up early, Westbrooke?"

Damn. Robbie's appetite fled. He wished he could do likewise.

"I might say the same of you, Lord Peter. I did not think to see you before noon." He'd hoped not to see anyone. He did not care to make idle conversation. He chose some toast and eggs from the sideboard and took a seat at the table.

Lord Peter grinned. He had obnoxiously white, straight teeth. "You wouldn't find me up so early in the normal course of things. Usually can't abide mornings." He cut a large bite of beefsteak, speared it, and pointed the bloody morsel at Robbie. "I just had an, um, especially stimulating evening, as I'm certain *you* can understand." He popped the meat in his mouth and chewed vigorously, waggling his brows in a knowing way at the same time.

God. Robbie stared down at his plate. The eggs looked distinctly unappealing. He broke off a corner of toast instead.

"There is something invigorating about balancing the body's humors, don't you agree? Not that I enjoy bloodletting, of course. But other methods of ridding oneself of excessive fluids can be quite enjoyable."

Robbie grunted. The toast was dry as dust. He poured himself some tea.

Lord Peter took a swig of ale and then leaned close, dropping his voice. "I highly recommend married women, Westbrooke, for adjusting one's humors. No need to worry about pulling out at the most interesting moment. Much tidier and pleasurable to deposit the fluids inside a female body, don't you know? And I'm certain it must be better for the female. Calms their nervous agitation."

"Lord Peter!" Robbie did not consider himself a prude, but he had no desire to hear what the other man had been doing with the Duchess of Hartford. He assumed it was the duchess. The only other married female at the house party was Lady Dunlee. He could not see the young lord mounting Lady Caroline's mother—and he assumed Lord Dunlee might lodge a strenuous objection to such an attempt.

"I offered to withdraw, of course. Wanted to be a gentleman about it. But the lady insisted I remain throughout the proceedings."

"Perhaps it would be more gentlemanly not to discuss the experience."

Lord Peter frowned and straightened. "I'm not one to bruit my conquests about. I thought we could speak man to man. It's not as though you were languishing alone in your bed last night. Just thought I'd give you some friendly advice for when you're ready to fish in other streams."

"What?"

Lord Peter rolled his eyes. "I saw you go in Lady Elizabeth's window, Westbrooke. I know you were naked in her bed." He took another swallow of ale. "Damn, I'd never have guessed the girl would behave in such a fashion. I always thought her a pattern card of respectability, and yet, there she was, cool as a cucumber, only inches from having her perfect reputation shredded."

He shook his head, then grinned. "Have you two been trysting for a long time?"

Robbie's right hand clenched into a fist. Lord Peter's straight nose begged to be broken. Red blood streaming down over his snowy white cravat would be an interesting contrast in color.

"I am not trysting with Lady Elizabeth."

"No? What do you call it then? F—"

Lord Peter did not finish his sentence. He was lucky to finish his breath. He might be on the verge of finishing his life.

Robbie twisted his hand again, pulling the man's cravat even tighter around his throat. Lord Peter's face turned an attractive shade of purple.

"Lady Elizabeth's reputation is spotless. She is a wonderful girl, and I will personally kill anyone who says—who hints—otherwise. Do I make myself perfectly clear?"

Lord Peter gagged and nodded.

"Excellent. You will not be tempted to forget that, will you?"

Lord Peter shook his head no.

"I'm so glad we understand each other." Robbie let the man go. "Now, if you'll excuse me, I seem to have lost my appetite. I believe I will go for a stroll."

He left Lord Peter gasping like a trout in a fisherman's basket.

"Wake up, slugabed."

"Uhh." Lizzie turned on her side and pulled her pillow over her head. Did Meg have to shout? "Go away."

"I will not. It's past noon—you should be up and dressed."

Lizzie heard Meg open the window draperies. Light tried to get past her bed curtains. She burrowed farther into the bedding.

"What happened in here last night?"

"Nothing. Go away."

"There were too many people clustered around your door for 'nothing.' I think I was the only member of the house party not milling around in my night-clothes in the corridor. The noise woke me from a very pleasant dream."

"I'm so sorry." Lizzie moved the pillow away from her mouth far enough to be heard distinctly. "Now *go away!*"

"Not until you tell me everything that happened." Meg had always been a stubborn busybody.

"Nothing happened." Lizzie's head started to throb. "Not that you care. I could have been murdered in my bed."

"You *will* be murdered in your bed if you don't tell me everything. When you said the *ton* lived on gossip, I didn't realize you intended to feed them their main course." Meg threw open the bed curtains and yanked the pillow away.

"Ohh." Sunlight pierced Lizzie's head like shards of glass. She covered her eyes with her arm.

"And here comes Betty with your morning chocolate—even though it's no longer morning. Perhaps it will help you feel more the thing."

The thick, overly sweet scent enveloped Lizzie.

"Meg." She swallowed. She scrambled into a sitting position. Her mouth was watering, but not in a pleasant sense. "I think I'm going to be . . ."

Meg took one look at her and dove for the chamber pot, shoving it into her hands seconds before the previous night's turbot *a la Anglaise* made an unfortunate reappearance.

"Apparently Lady Elizabeth doesn't care for chocolate at the moment, Betty," Meg said.

"Oh, my lady, let me get ye . . ."

Lizzie looked up at her maid, got another whiff of chocolate, and bent over the chamber pot again.

"I think it's best if you just take the cup away."

"Yes, Miss Meg. I'll do that right quick. I'm sorry—"

"Just a moment." Lady Beatrice's strident voice cut through Betty's apologies.

Lizzie groaned. She leaned her head against her bedpost. Lud! The woman looked like an old bruise in her puce and pomona green dressing gown.

"How long has this been going on, miss?"

"Uh?" Why did Lady Beatrice have to speak so sharply? And she was scowling at her. "What?"

Lady Bea's nose wrinkled, and she pointed at the chamber pot. "That. How many times have you cast up your accounts?"

What an odd question. "Twice." Lizzie felt her stomach lurch. "So far."

"That is not what I meant."

Lizzie's head felt as if a blacksmith were hammering horseshoes against the inside of her forehead, her mouth tasted like a barnyard floor, and her stomach.
. . . She gripped the chamber pot more tightly. Best not to think about her stomach. Suffice it to say, she was completely incapable of playing guessing games this morning. She looked to Meg for help.

"What *do* you mean, Lady Bea?"

Lady Bea put her hands on her expansive hips.

"What I mean is how *long* has this been going on? How many days has Lady Elizabeth been sick?" She frowned at the chamber pot and turned to Lizzie's maid. "Betty? Can you give me an answer?"

"It was the chocolate, my lady." Betty held up the cup in her hand. "The smell set her off. She was fit as a fiddle last night."

"Really? She is sensitive to odors?" Lady Beatrice puffed up like her cat, Queen Bess, did when faced with a canine intruder. "The smell of chocolate made her . . ." She grimaced.

"Yes, my lady."

"I see. Then let me rephrase my question yet

again." Lady Beatrice bit off each word. "How many *mornings* has Lady Elizabeth greeted the day hunched over that, that receptacle?" She gestured at the chamber pot. "This type of malady usually manifests itself in the morning, does it not?"

"My lady!" Betty drew in a sharp breath. "I don't know what ye mean."

Lizzie didn't know either, but she wished Lady Bea would take her riddles elsewhere—along with the increasingly offensive chamber pot. She looked hopefully at Betty. For some reason her maid's cheeks were bright red.

"So your mistress has not been shooting the cat regularly before breakfast?"

"Of course not, my lady."

"There's no 'of course' about it. I sincerely doubt Lord Westbrooke is a eunuch."

"*What?*" Lizzie sat up abruptly, causing the contents of the chamber pot to slosh dangerously. Robbie a eunuch? She didn't completely understand the specifics but—the image of Robbie as he had appeared the night before flashed into her mind. No sultan would put such a man in charge of his harem.

Betty's face had turned a dark purple, rivaling the puce in Lady Bea's gown.

"Ye can't mean—"

"I most certainly can. Surely the rumors flying through this house party have reached your ears—wherever those ears were resting last night."

An uncomfortable silence greeted this statement. Lizzie squeezed her eyes shut. Lady Bea could not be suggesting . . .

Her stomach twisted again. Sarah had been queasy in the mornings with her pregnancies.

The room started to spin. Someone—Meg?—took the chamber pot from her hands and pushed her head down between her knees.

Surely she could not be with child? There must be

more to the process than merely touching hands or the entire female populace would be increasing. True, Robbie had not been wearing gloves. . . .

A slightly hysterical giggle bubbled up in her chest. No, he had not been wearing gloves.

"Lizzie!" Lizzie cringed as Meg's voice hissed in her ear. "What *have* you been up to?"

Lizzie grunted. Perhaps if she closed her eyes and kept them closed, everyone would go away. She buried her face in her hands for good measure. This was a dream, that was it. A bad, bad dream. She would wake up in a few moments, shudder, and get on with her day.

"Don't think you can hide from me." Meg's voice was still buzzing in her ear like an annoying insect. "I mean to find out exactly what happened in here last night."

"Mmphft."

Meg laughed. "And don't think you can hide from Lady Bea, either. She looks very determined."

She sounded very determined also.

"You may go, Betty, but I shall have more to say to you later. And take that disgusting chamber pot away—*far* away—and dispose of it."

"Yes, my lady."

Lizzie kept her face in her hands. She heard Betty leave the room. There was a long pause. She began to wonder if the gods had smiled on her and she'd been left to suffer in solitude. Well, not complete solitude. Meg had not left her place on the bed next to her. But perhaps Lady Bea had departed?

She lifted her head cautiously. No. Lady Beatrice was still there, scowling at her.

"Would you like to explain what exactly is going on, Lady Elizabeth?"

Oh dear. She felt as if she were fourteen, being called on the carpet by her brother for some infraction.

No, that was ridiculous. She was twenty years old, a

woman grown. This was her fourth Season. A lady of her age and experience did not need a chaperone, and certainly should not be cowering in fear of a dressing-down. Lady Bea was more of a companion really, an older woman to satisfy society's strict notions of propriety.

Lizzie straightened her spine, took a sustaining breath, and looked Lady Bea in the eye.

Her stomach clenched immediately. She dropped her gaze to stare at her hands.

"Uh. I think . . . I believe . . . I'm just not accustomed to . . ."

"I should hope you are not accustomed to such activities, miss. I can't imagine what your brother will say. The least you could have done was gotten Westbrooke's betrothal ring on your finger before you got his—"

"Lady Beatrice, I believe you are laboring under a misapprehension."

"Oh? And what would that misapprehension be? Are you prepared to tell me that Lord Westbrooke has nothing to do with your current malaise?"

"Yes. Definitely. It is all my own doing." Lizzie cleared her throat. "Last night, well, I believe I had one glass of ratafia too many."

"Hmph."

Lady Beatrice stared at her, most directly at her stomach. Lizzie placed her hands over that area and tried to breathe slowly.

"You are *positive* your current indisposition has nothing to do with a certain lord?"

"*Yes!*" Lizzie took another deep breath and struggled to recover her composure. "Yes, indeed. Most assuredly. Lord Westbrooke's presence—"

Meg made a very unusual noise, something between a squeak and a whoop. Lizzie and Lady Bea both turned to stare at her. Meg grinned back at them.

"So Robbie was actually in your room last night, Lizzie? I had heard the rumors, but I hadn't believed them. How splendid! Not that I'm really surprised, though I would have thought he'd have chosen a more conventional setting for his proposal. When is the wedding?"

"Uh."

"Yes, miss, when *is* the wedding?" Lady Bea frowned so that her brows met over her nose. "While it is fortunate that Lord Westbrooke apparently restrained his animal urges, the fact remains that he was here in your bedchamber."

Lizzie studied her fingernails. "Robbie did not propose."

"*What?*" Meg's voice squeaked with indignation. "What do you mean, he didn't propose? He *must* have proposed! You've loved him forever. And he loves you. How could he not have asked you to be his countess? Why else would he have sought you out in your room?"

Lizzie blinked at Meg. Robbie loved her? Where had Meg gotten that notion? Lizzie had hoped—prayed—for years that he did—that he would—but when she was being completely honest with herself, she had to admit he didn't treat her much differently than her brother did. Meg must be confusing that brotherly sentiment with the kind of love Lizzie wanted—romantic love. Kisses-and-wedding love.

"He didn't seek me out, exactly. His being here was more of an accident."

"An accident? How could Robbie have come to your room by accident?" Meg scowled. "Surely he wasn't looking for some other lady's room?"

Lady Bea snorted. "Fleeing more like—and from his own room. It is too bad Lord Needham won't rein in his daughter, but then that would require him to drag himself out of his brothels and gambling dens, wouldn't it? Lady Felicity is far from the dirtiest dish in the Brookton cupboard."

Lizzie nodded. She reminded herself of that fact whenever she wanted to strangle the other girl. The Earl of Needham was a large pill for any prospective suitor to swallow. True, the earl's vast wealth had to make marriage to his daughter more palatable, but the embarrassment of having a father-in-law in trade—and such a trade—had made many a man choke on his proposal. It didn't help that Felicity refused to consider any matrimonial applicants below her father's rank.

"Be that as it may, miss, you cannot entertain naked men in your room and not promptly attire your finger with an engagement ring."

Meg squeaked again. She was becoming a regular mouse.

"Robbie was *naked*?"

"Well . . . yes." Lizzie feared she would spontaneously combust from mortification. "In a manner of speaking, that is."

"Hmm." Lady Bea's eyebrows shot up to her hairline. "And how can a gentleman be naked *in a manner of speaking*?"

Lizzie would not meet the older woman's eyes. "It was dark." *After Robbie snuffed the candles.* "I really didn't see. . . ." *Enough.*

Lady Bea narrowed her eyes. "Immaterial. He was naked and in your room. He has to wed you. I am astounded that he did not propose the moment the door closed behind me. If word of this gets out—"

"Word won't get out."

"Word *always* gets out. Granted, only Lord Peter saw Westbrooke enter your window, and I suppose it could be argued he was mistaken since no one actually witnessed the earl with you, but still, as they say, where there's smoke, there's fire."

Meg nodded. "And Felicity will stoke the flames."

"No, I don't believe she will in this case." Lady Bea arranged her ample form in the upholstered chair by the fireplace. "She clearly wants Westbrooke for herself—just as he clearly does not want her. I expect he will offer for you this morning, Lizzie, so you must get dressed and go out. One would hope that he would address me first, as I am your chaperone, but given the fact that he has known you since infancy and is one of your brother's closest friends, I doubt he will stand on ceremony."

Lizzie rubbed her suddenly wet palms on her nightgown.

"Do you really think he will offer for me?"

"How can he not? He has compromised you quite spectacularly. Of course he will offer. He is probably searching the estate for you now."

The thought of Robbie looking for her made her feel amazingly better.

Damn.

Robbie dodged behind a topiary bear. He'd taken a brisk walk around Lendal Park, searching for his equilibrium. He still had a number of days to live through this blasted house party. He couldn't be trying to strangle Tynweith's guests every time they mentioned Lizzie's name—though Lord Peter had done far more than that. He forced his fists to relax. Every time he thought of the scene in the breakfast parlor, he wanted to hit something, preferably Lord Peter's face. He would love to reorder his features. He would be doing the women of the world a favor, making Lord Peter's countenance reflect the ugliness of his character.

He'd hoped to make it back to the house without encountering anyone wishing to discuss last night's unusual activities, and here was Lizzie, not twenty feet away, examining an oddly shaped bush. Sunlight filtered through her thin muslin gown, outlining her long legs.

God. He rubbed suddenly damp palms on his breeches. Muslin should be outlawed or at least restricted to darkened areas, free of revealing sunbeams.

He had not slept well. He'd been haunted by dreams of Lizzie's white skin, her lovely small breasts and delicate pink nipples, her golden hair—*all* of it, curling over her shoulders, around her breasts, sweeping the curve of her lower back . . . and the separate patch nestling between her thighs.

He was going to spill his seed in Tynweith's blasted garden if he didn't think of something else immediately.

Escape. That was it. He needed to get back to his room undetected. He'd chosen this route because it went through one of the less popular gardens—Tynweith had actually discouraged the ladies from exploring it, telling them it was not suitable for their finer sensibilities. Why hadn't Lizzie taken the hint and avoided the place?

He would just have to choose a circuitous route to his room. He peered around the other side of the bear.

Double damn. Lady Felicity, hands on hips, scanned the hedges. Her nostrils flared.

God, was she a hound that she could sniff him out?

What was so bloody attractive about the shrubbery today? This garden was sadly overgrown. The bear he was hiding behind, for instance. It definitely needed a trimming. Just look at . . .

Robbie's jaw dropped. The bear was not a bear at all, but a very large woman. A very large, very enceinte, very naked woman doing some very odd things with her bushy fingers.

Tynweith's gardener was clearly demented. Well, Tynweith had an odd kick to his gallop as well. Why Lady Beatrice accepted this house party invitation was beyond him.

Felicity was headed his way. He felt a sudden affinity for Odysseus, forced to sail between Scylla and

Charybdis. Well, it was clear who the six-headed monster was. And really, he'd be happy to be sucked into a certain whirlpool.

He left the shelter of the obscene bear woman.

"Lizzie." He kept his voice low. Felicity probably had preternatural hearing. "Walk with me, will you?" He grabbed her elbow and tried to hustle her away from disaster.

"Robbie!" She smiled widely up at him. "Have you been looking for me?"

"Uh . . ." He smiled back, thinking quickly. Clearly the answer was supposed to be yes. She would not be happy to hear the truth—that he had wanted to sneak past her. "Actually, I didn't expect to find you here. Didn't Tynweith discourage you ladies from exploring this garden?"

She shrugged. "I suppose he did. I got a bit lost and wandered in the wrong direction, I guess. But I found you." She grinned.

God, she was beautiful, especially when she was practically glowing up at him like this. But he couldn't stand here admiring her. Felicity would find them in a moment. True, Lizzie's presence would put paid to any compromising plans Felicity might harbor, but he didn't care to spend any time in that she-devil's company.

"Yes. Well. Tynweith was correct. This is not an appropriate place for you. Come along."

Lizzie didn't move.

"This *is* a very odd garden. Can you tell me what this topiary is designed to depict? I've been studying it for the last five minutes and I cannot puzzle it out."

"Oh, for—" They were running out of time. He could almost feel Felicity breathing down his neck. He looked at the bush. "It's a dog."

"Well, yes, I discerned that. But what's it doing? What's that part there?"

"That? That's, uh, that's . . ." *Bloody hell!* "That's not

something you should be looking at. Now come along." He tugged on her elbow again, and this time she came with him, though she kept looking back at the lascivious vegetation.

"Why are you in such a hurry?"

"Shh. Felicity is just on the other side of that hedge."

"Not anymore."

"Blast!" Sure enough, Felicity was back by the pregnant bear creature. She was looking the other way—perhaps she had not seen them yet. There was a slight break in the foliage just up ahead. "Hurry."

Robbie dragged Lizzie through a gap in the hedge. She tripped on a root, and he caught her against his chest, holding her tightly and turning so her dress would not draw Felicity's attention to their hiding place.

They were in a small bower with just enough room for two people to stand close together. Very close together.

Robbie breathed in Lizzie's light, lemony scent mixed with sunlight and vegetation. Her body was so soft against his. Her breasts. Her thighs. His hands smoothed over her bottom, pulling her toward him. He wanted her close. His palms moved up her sides, slid to her back.

Her arms were now wrapped tightly around his waist, and—God!—her fingers were tracing the curve of his buttocks. Then they slid up under his coat.

He was panting.

"Lizzie." He put his mouth close to her ear—he couldn't risk Felicity hearing him, could he? He brushed his face against her hair, sweet and silky. It would be a sin not to taste her throat, he was so close.

She tasted of sun and salt. Soft and feminine.

Lord, did she purr? She tilted her head, giving him room to kiss the spot behind her ear.

Was she panting also?

"Lizzie . . ."

"Mmm?"

Christ, her lips . . . they grazed his chin, his cheek, and then her mouth found his.

He was going to die. His head, his heart, his groin were going to explode.

Her lips were so soft. They welcomed him, promising heaven—and he was a dying man, desperate for salvation. He ran his tongue along their seam. She whimpered, opening for him.

He had known Lizzie forever. He had loved her as long. But he had lusted for her only since her come out and never quite like this. This was a mistake, a terrible mistake. He was starting something he could never finish; promising things he could not give.

It made no difference. He could no more stop his plunge into her warm, wet mouth than he could stop breathing.

Actually, he could stop breathing.

But he could not stop kissing Lizzie. Felicity could have marched into this private bower with Lady Beatrice and all the *ton*—even James, Lizzie's brother—and he would not have, could not have stopped. She tasted of life, of hope, of all that he wanted and could not have.

His lips left hers and moved down her throat. He loosened the neck of her gown.

"When," she breathed as he ran his tongue into the crease between her breasts.

"When will . . . ohh." She made a breathy little noise as his fingers skimmed over her skin and dipped down to free her breast from her corset.

"When will we . . ."

His mouth found her nipple. She shuddered.

"Oh, don't stop. Please don't stop."

He grunted. He was incapable of any more coherent response. He flicked her nipple with his tongue, and then had to cover her mouth with his when she squeaked.

God, this *was* heaven—or as close to heaven as he

could ever hope to get. He wanted her naked. He wanted his hands, his mouth, on her from her throat to her ankles. He wanted to see her, to taste every inch of her.

His mouth found the pulse at the base of her throat.

"R-Robbie."

She was moaning. Good. Could he make her squeak again? He touched her nipple and heard her breath catch.

He could.

"R-Robbie . . . when . . . Oh. Oh, do that again."

She pressed closer. Her belly cradled his hardness. She rubbed against him. Heaven. If only . . . no, he wouldn't spoil things by pining for what couldn't be. He would enjoy the present moment.

It was a very good, a splendid moment.

"Do what again, love? This perhaps?" He cradled her breast with his hand and kissed its nipple.

"Oh, yess . . ." She put her hands on his hips and pulled him closer still. "When . . . ohh . . . when . . . will . . . we . . ."

"Hmm?" He moved to lave the other nipple. She arched back, giving him more room to explore, pressing her hips even tighter against his.

"Don't . . . stop." Her hands pressed into his buttocks. She twisted against him. Could he bring her to satisfaction just by fondling her breasts? It was a challenge he was happy to undertake.

"Robbie . . . what are you *doing*?"

The last word came out in a squeal.

"Shh." He had never felt so powerful, so alive. "Not so loud. We don't want to attract attention." Thankfully, Felicity must have moved on. If she heard them, found them . . . well, if he wasn't more careful, Lizzie was going to find herself chained to him for life.

"I don't mind."

"Hmm? What don't you mind?"

"I don't mind if we attract attention."

"Lizzie, sweetheart . . . the scandal."

She smiled up at him, her eyes glowing. "There won't be a scandal, Robbie."

"There won't?" She must be more drunk with lust than she'd been with ratafia the night before. Her face was flushed, her hair was coming out of its pins, and her breasts . . . her breasts were completely, beautifully exposed. He traced a circle around one nipple and watched it pucker in response. "You look rather scandalous to me."

She rubbed against him. "I feel very scandalous." She ran her hands up his waistcoat. He watched her pink tongue moisten her lips and bent to capture that tongue again.

She giggled and pulled back before his mouth touched hers. "There won't be any scandal because we're betrothed."

He felt the blood drain from his face. He felt limp—everywhere. He couldn't wed Lizzie. She was passionate. She would want children. She would not want a useless excuse for a man.

Despair, all too familiar, choked him.

"Aren't we betrothed?"

He hated seeing that lost look in her eyes, but he would hate more the disgust and pity he would see on their wedding night when he had to admit he was incapable of consummating their union.

He tried to smile, tried to sound blasé.

"I'm sorry—did I propose?"

The sting of her hand hitting his cheek actually felt good.

Chapter Four

She hated him.

Lizzie strode up the path to the house. She wanted to cry. She wanted to scream. She was afraid she would do both if anyone spoke to her.

"You don't look happy."

It was Meg.

"I'm not."

"What happened?"

Lizzie shrugged and kept moving. It was quite impossible to get any words past the huge lump in her throat.

Meg fell into step beside her. "Did you see Robbie?"

Lizzie nodded.

"Do you want to talk about it?"

She shook her head. She most definitely did *not* want to talk about it. She lengthened her stride.

Unfortunately, Meg lengthened hers as well.

"Surely he proposed?"

"Gaa."

"He didn't? How could he not have?"

Excellent question. How could he not have? He should never have taken such liberties with her person if he were not going to offer for her immediately. Ha! Immediately? He should have offered for and *married* her before he touched her in such a way. He had had his hands on . . . Her breasts throbbed in memory. Her breasts and . . . She flushed and bit her lip. She would not think about the other part of her that throbbed.

And it was not just his hands! His mouth. His tongue.

She swallowed a moan. Oh, lud—she would go mad. She was so angry. That was it. Anger was making her stomach feel so peculiar. Achy. Shivery.

She was so angry she was panting.

She had to get to her room.

"Are you all right, Lizzie?"

"I . . . I really need . . . to be alone, Meg."

"Oh, Lizzie."

The sympathy in Meg's voice stabbed through her.

She would not cry. Not now. Felicity, Charlotte—anyone could see her. She would not give them the satisfaction of witnessing her distress.

She walked even faster.

Meg must have decided she needed solitude, because by the time she reached her room, she was alone. She shuddered with relief as she shut her door—and then she shuddered into tears.

What had happened in the shrubbery?

She ran her hands up over her stomach to her breasts. She wanted to strip off her clothes and touch her own skin. Something was definitely wrong with her. It was not only anger that pulsed deep inside her. It was something else, something dark and bewildering.

What had Robbie done to her? His kisses had caused this problem. Each touch of his lips, of his hands, had wound something inside her tighter and tighter like a spring, until . . . until what? She didn't know.

She really did feel like screaming.

If she had only waited, if she had kept her tongue between her teeth—she shivered—between *his* teeth—she felt certain he would have done something, taken her to some point of release, and she wouldn't feel so . . . upset.

She went to the window and leaned her forehead against the glass. She looked out over Lord Tynweith's estate, but she saw only the shaded bower.

Why hadn't he offered for her? Certainly Lady Bea had expected him to do so. What would the older woman say when Lizzie had to tell her she was not betrothed?

Dear God, she had thrown herself at the man, literally. Well, technically she'd tripped, but that made no difference. A proper lady would have pushed herself away the moment her person encountered a hard, muscled male form.

Very hard. Very muscled. Very male.

He had felt so good. And when he'd wrapped his arms around her, she had felt as if she had come home.

She drew in a deep, shuddery breath.

For years she had wanted Robbie to hold her. She had dreamt of it. Prayed for it. And then, when it had actually happened . . . dear heaven! She had attacked him like an animal.

Could she have behaved more inappropriately? She'd clung to him, let her hands wander all over him. She pressed her head harder against the glass. She had actually touched his . . . pantaloons. Felt the curves, the muscles, of his . . .

She flung away from the window and threw herself onto her bed.

He had been there just hours before.

She muffled her mouth with her pillow.

He must be thoroughly disgusted with her. That's why he hadn't offered for her. She was worse than Lady Felicity. Lud! She had paraded herself—her naked self—in front of him with no shame last night. And then today . . . Could she have begged more desperately for any of the shocking things he had done?

He would never offer for her.

She turned over, staring up at the bed canopy.

Would he really never offer for her?

Tears pooled at the corners of her eyes and ran down the sides of her face. She turned over again, wiping them on the counterpane.

What was she to do? She loved Robbie. She had not lied last night. She *had* loved him forever. He was nine years older than she. When she was very young, he had seemed tall and gangly and godlike. James's other friends had ignored her, but not Robbie. He'd smiled at her and teased her. And then, when she was twelve and James went away to fight Napoleon, Robbie had come regularly to check on her and Aunt Gladys. Her father certainly could not be bothered to come down from London to see how they went on. But Robbie came.

By the time she was fourteen and James returned, she was irredeemably in love.

She was *supposed* to marry him. He was her brother's closest friend—well, his closest unmarried friend. She had turned down countless proposals these last three years because she knew she was supposed to wed him. She would live at Westbrooke and her children would play with their cousins at Alvord, with little Will and the new baby that was due soon. It would be perfect.

Why had he suddenly looked at her that way in the garden—with his London society face? And spoken to her in his society voice—that all-knowing drawl? She had felt like a worm.

Lud, and then she had slapped him! She had left the red mark of her fingers on his cheek.

She buried her head under the pillow.

Someone knocked on her door.

"Go away."

"No."

It was Meg again. Lizzie did not want to see anyone, even Meg.

"Go away."

"No." The doorknob rattled. "Lizzie, listen. I saw Lady Bea. I have to talk to you. Let me in before someone notices me standing out here muttering."

Lizzie glared at the door. "No. I want to be alone."

"No, you don't." Meg poked her head into the room. Lizzie sat up and threw her pillow at her.

"Hey! Is this appropriate behavior for the Duke of Alvord's sister?" Meg closed the door and scooped up the pillow from its landing place near the foot of the bed. She flung it back and grinned. "You used to be better at throwing."

"I used to be a lot of things."

Meg's smile dropped into a frown. "Lizzie . . ."

Lizzie could not bear the pity in Meg's eyes. She turned over on her stomach.

The mattress tilted as Meg sat down. Lizzie shrugged away her hand.

"Go away."

"But I have good news. Lady Bea says the story of Lord Westbrooke's nocturnal visit has died. No one is talking about it—not the duchess, not Lady Felicity, not even that fat sow, Lady Caroline. Apparently Lord Tynweith took it into his head to scotch the rumor. Lady Bea actually saw him examine Lady Dunlee through his quizzing glass as if she were a particularly noxious species of insect when she had the temerity to mention it to him."

Lizzie grunted. Meg's cheerfulness was salt in her wounds.

"What is the matter, Lizzie? You should be happy. Aren't you relieved there will be no gossip about last night's events?"

"No. I don't care. My life is ruined."

"Lizzie! It can't be that bad."

"Yes it can."

"Well, I don't see how, unless . . ."

Silence. Meg wasn't supposed to be silent. She was supposed to say something to make things better. Lizzie shifted onto her side and glanced up. Meg had a very peculiar expression. Lizzie leaned up on one elbow.

"Why are you looking at me that way?"

"I just can't . . ." Meg turned bright red. "So, you mean . . . But you told Lady Bea. . . ." Her hands fluttered at Lizzie's middle. "So, last night, in your room . . . Robbie did . . ." She clasped her hands together finally. "You know."

"I don't know. I have no idea what you are getting at." Lizzie dropped back down and covered her face again. "And anyway, last night was nothing compared to this afternoon."

"This afternoon!" Meg grabbed Lizzie's hands and pulled them away from her face. "You mean he actually . . . In the daylight? Out of doors?!"

"Yes." Lizzie flushed and turned away. Meg didn't have to look so very shocked.

"And he didn't offer for you? After doing . . . that?"

"No, he didn't." The words came out as a wail.

Meg patted her on the shoulder, but she was clearly distracted. "I just can't believe Robbie would be so heartless."

"Well, believe it." Lizzie shrugged off Meg's ineffectual hand and sat up. Robbie should definitely not have done what he did, but he wasn't the sole participant in the activity. She could have stopped him. Should have stopped him.

She should have had a colossal fit of the vapors.

No, no matter how much she would like to think of Robbie as a beast, she just couldn't do it. She sighed. "I'm certain it was mostly my fault."

"Ridiculous! He is much more experienced than you. He knew what he was doing. I just can't believe he would do it without offering for you."

"Neither can I." Lizzie was wailing again. She covered her mouth with her hands and flopped back on the bed. "I was so sure. . . . I would never have done . . . would never have let him. . . ." She shuddered. "I thought he meant marriage."

"Of course you did. Anyone would. I still can't believe. . . ." Meg shrugged. "How could you have guessed Robbie had this side to his personality?"

No, how *could* she have guessed? Robbie had never given a sign of it before, and she had spent many hours in his company. The most he had ever done was kiss the air above her hand. He had never even kissed her cheek, let alone her lips.

Well, if she were completely truthful, she had been the one to introduce that activity, though she had had no idea of where it would lead.

Perhaps that was it. Perhaps men did turn into beasts when given suitable provocation.

She closed her eyes. She had not been behaving like a lady. What lady ran her hands over a man's pantaloons, especially while they were still on the man's body?

Perhaps Robbie had felt he was only being courteous to an elderly spinster.

Her breasts throbbed as she remembered his mouth on her nipples.

He didn't have to be *that* courteous.

"Don't worry, Lizzie. We'll tell Lady Bea. She'll tell your brother and he will insist Robbie marry you."

"No, I don't want Robbie that way. I don't want to be married to a man who doesn't want me."

"I thought the problem was that he *did* want you." Meg patted her shoulder again. "Chances are it was just the thought of marriage that frightened him for a moment. Many men have an irrational fear of matrimony, but once the knot is tied they settle down quite nicely. A bit like a horse being broken to bridle."

Meg's words did not lighten the leaden feeling in

Lizzie's stomach—if anything, they added a stone
or two.

"I really don't think—"

"No, don't think. The deed is done. You have no
choice—nor does Robbie. I'm sure he'll realize that—
most likely he has already realized it. If he hasn't, your
brother will help him see the situation quite clearly."

"Perhaps." Lizzie stared up at the bed canopy. She
did not relish having a bridegroom who needed a
pistol at his back to pronounce his vows.

Meg shifted on the bed. "There is one thing. . . ."

"Yes?"

Meg shifted again. Lizzie was beginning to get sea-
sick from the mattress rocking. She sat up. Meg was
staring down at her hands, her face distinctly red.

"What is it, Meg?"

Meg addressed her hands. "I know I shouldn't ask
you, especially now, but I've been wondering ever
since I overheard two of the maids at Knightsdale. I
thought about asking Emma, but I just couldn't bring
myself to do so."

Lizzie waited. Meg pleated her skirt.

"Yes?" Lizzie could not imagine a subject Meg was
too hesitant to ask her sister. Really, she could not
imagine a subject Meg was hesitant to ask anyone.
Meg was not shy. "What did you want to ask me?"

Meg turned even redder.

"Does it hurt?"

Lizzie frowned. She must have missed some part of
this conversation.

"Does what hurt?"

"*It.*" Meg stopped torturing her skirt and looked directly at Lizzie. There was annoyance as well as embarrassment in her eyes. "I do not understand why
women keep unmarried ladies in ignorance of such
things. You would think they would want to be certain
we understood the procedure. I'm certain men know
all the details as soon as they are out of short-coats."

"What *are* you talking about?"

"What Robbie did to you in the garden. Did it hurt?"

It was Lizzie's turn to blush. "No." The activity had certainly evoked many sensations, but pain was not one of them. "No, of course it didn't hurt."

Meg nodded. "I didn't think it could, else why would so many women consent to participate in the deed? Well, I suppose they want children—"

"Children!" Surely what she had done with Robbie in the garden did not lead directly to children, did it?

"Yes, children." Meg frowned at her as though she were an idiot. "And I assume since it didn't hurt, there was no blood?"

"Blood! Why would there be blood?"

"Because he breached your maidenhead, of course."

"What?" Lizzie did not like the sound of "breaching." It brought to mind James's stories of storming fortresses on the Peninsula.

"So Sarah hasn't told you anything either?"

"Of course not. Those discussions are reserved for the night before one's wedding." Lizzie shifted position. "What, um . . ." She cleared her throat. "What does a man use to do this breaching, do you know?"

Meg's eyebrows shot up. "Don't you? You were the one with Robbie in the shrubbery."

"There was no breaching going on in the shrubbery." Unless a tongue counted? But surely there was nothing constituting a maidenhead in one's mouth.

"What *was* going on in the shrubbery?"

"Just tell me what a man uses to do this breaching."

"His male organ."

"His male organ? What exactly do you mean?"

"Well, I've never seen one in the flesh, of course, but I've seen plenty of naked statues."

"Well, yes, so have I."

Meg nodded. "The male organ is that little dangly

bit in the front. I know it looks very odd, but I don't suppose all those artists would have made it up, do you? Especially since they were all men. They must know what they've got in their breeches."

"Oh." Lizzie remembered quite clearly Robbie's naked physique. She swallowed a large lump in her throat. There was nothing little or dangly about Robbie's bit. "And the maidenhead?"

"It protects your womb, of course."

"Of course." Lizzie pressed her knees together. "And so you think the dangly bit somehow gets, um, into that area?"

"Yes. Haven't you noticed the animals around Alvord?"

"No. Definitely not." Lizzie was certain watching such behavior was extremely inappropriate. Meg had spent too much time in the fields, looking at plants and, apparently, other things. "There was no such activity going on between me and Lord Westbrooke in the shrubbery."

"So what *was* going on?"

Lizzie gestured vaguely with her hand. "A bit of kissing. A little cuddling. Absolutely no breaching whatsoever."

"Oh." Meg blinked at her, and then grinned. "Well, if no breaching occurred, your life is not ruined. You've been somewhat indiscreet, yes, and if word of your activities gets out, you'll certainly be compromised, but since Robbie is the only witness to your indiscretion, you should have no worries."

"No worries?" Lizzie contemplated smothering Meg with her pillow. "How can you say that? I've loved Robbie forever."

"Well, yes, I understand that. And I really did think he loved you, but if he won't offer for you—you are sure about that?"

"Of course I'm sure. I'm not completely beetle-headed." No, not completely beetle-headed, just beetle-headed enough to have spent the last six years or more in love with a man who didn't care the snap of his fingers for her. Beetle-headed enough to turn down marriage offers from a duke, two marquises, and an assortment of earls, viscounts, and other men because she was certain Robbie would ask for her hand eventually.

She could not fool herself any longer. If Robbie'd had any intention of wedding her, he would have spoken today in the shrubbery. He would not have looked horrified and then hid behind his society manners.

She bit her lip and squeezed her eyes closed. She would not cry.

"Well, if you are quite certain," Meg said, "I suppose there is little to be done about it. Unless you want James to force Robbie to wed you? He could, you know."

"No!" Lizzie leapt off the bed and wrapped her arms around her waist. "No, I do not want James to compel Robbie. That would be horrible."

"I agree. A reluctant bridegroom would not be pleasant." Meg pushed back a strand of hair that had fallen over her eyes. "You could try to make him jealous, of course. Sometimes men don't realize they are interested in a woman until they think they can't have her."

"How do you know that?"

Meg shrugged. "I observe more than plants. And unlike you, I have not had my attention focused solely on one gentleman."

"I have not been focusing solely on Robbie."

"If you say so."

"Does Emma know you've been studying biology as well as botany in the neighboring fields?"

Meg grinned. "Just the biology of lower animals, Lizzie. I have not come upon any examples of human biology."

"I should hope not."

"But I have observed human social behavior in detail, especially since Emma married and decided finding me a husband was one of her goals in life." Meg wrinkled her nose. "I have been to more dinners and dances in the last three years than I can count. The prospect of another minuet with old Mr. Ruttles was enough to get me to come with you to London."

"Mr. Ruttles is showing interest in you? Surely not! The man must be seventy."

"Seventy-four last November," Meg said. "And you'll be happy to know that his gout is much improved."

"I will?"

"Indeed. I actually have quite the stable of admirers. Besides Mr. Ruttles, there is Mr. Gordley, Mr. Farrell, and Mr. Nunn."

"Meg! That's terrible. Not a one of them is under sixty. Why didn't you come to London before?"

"Because Emma hadn't gotten so persistent before. And when Charlie was born, she got distracted for a while. But now that she's increasing again, she is even more determined to see me happily settled with my own children."

"That's understandable."

"No, it's maddening."

Lizzie grinned. "All right, it's maddening. You will just have to find yourself a husband this Season." She sat back down next to Meg. "Now about making Robbie jealous . . . I'm not certain I want a man who is only interested in me because he thinks someone else wants me."

"No, no—you're missing the point. Yes, there are men like that, and if Robbie turns out to be one of them, you will have to discard him. In this case, our goal is merely to wake him up. Make him realize what he really wants."

"Wake him up?"

"Yes. From what I have observed, men are very simple creatures. They may be able to fight battles and build canals, but when it comes to emotions, they are hopelessly inept. They go along merrily eating and sleeping and fornicating until something—or someone—interrupts them."

Lizzie did not care for the thought of Robbie happily fornicating. And shouldn't the events of last night and this afternoon have served to wake him to his love for her, if he harbored any love at all? Still, she did not want to give up her dream of marrying him until she had exhausted every possibility.

For the first time since she'd left Robbie in the garden, she felt some hope.

"All right, though I have to say, Meg, that after our interlude in the shrubbery, I would have thought Robbie would be as awake as he could be."

"You have a point." Meg clasped her knees, pursed her lips, and rocked back on the bed. "But you have not yet introduced the threat of losing you. In fact, if you don't mind my saying so, it sounds as if you've been very, um, accessible."

Lizzie blushed. "Well, perhaps."

Meg nodded. "Robbie may need to face the real possibility that you will wed another man before he is prompted to take matrimonial action. Or he may be a special case—I cannot guarantee success."

"Yes, of course." Lizzie chose not to think about failure. She had already contemplated that unpleasant possibility and she did not like the heavy feeling it created in her stomach.

"At least you will be able to move beyond your current state of uncertainty. You've lingered there far too long." Meg sat up straight. "So, we need to come up with a plan to upset Robbie."

Lizzie frowned. "You didn't say anything about upsetting Robbie."

"Lizzie, you have not been paying attention. He needs to think you will wed another man. If that doesn't upset him, you must wash your hands of him.

As you say, he's had ample opportunity to discover you stir his animal instincts. If that is all he feels for you, you will never get him to come up to scratch. He can exercise those instincts with women of easier virtue. At least I hope their virtue is easier."

"Meg!"

"You would not be the first lady to mistake passion for love and fall for a scoundrel." Meg frowned. "I understand some men won't pay for what they can get for free, but I wouldn't have thought Robbie would be one of those men."

Lizzie flushed. "You mean—"

"If a man thinks he can get a woman into bed without a wedding ring, he will be happy to do so. Though Robbie must know he cannot do that with you, even if you were willing. James would not stand for it." Meg chewed on the edge of her thumb. "It is a puzzle."

"Yes." It was more than a puzzle. It was a stomach churning nightmare. "So what do you suggest?"

"First, you need to keep your distance from Robbie. If he should try to initiate any of the activities from the shrubbery, you must decline firmly."

"Of course. There is no danger he will be allowed any such liberties again."

"Good. It would be best if you do not spend any time alone with him."

"But—"

"No. This is important. If he has feelings for you, we want them frustrated, so no tête-à-têtes, understand?"

"Very well. Not that I expect he will initiate any."

"You never know. And you will have to enforce this policy yourself. Lady Bea will be no help—she is not the strictest of chaperones. In fact, she's more likely to urge you into Robbie's arms than out of them."

"I really do not need a chaperone."

"Hmm. An adequate chaperone would have kept you from your encounter with Robbie in the bushes. Be certain to stay out of Tynweith's gardens."

"Of course."

Meg nodded. "Right. Then at the same time you are frustrating Robbie by keeping your distance, you must convince him you are in danger of contracting another alliance. He must expect that anyway after his recent behavior. You most certainly do not want to give him the impression you are pining for him."

"All right." That was going to be difficult, since she *was* pining for him. "In whom am I supposed to be interested?"

"Whoever would most annoy Robbie. Unfortunately, you do not have a wide selection at this house party." Meg grinned. "How about Mr. Dodsworth?"

"Mr. Dodsworth! Have you spoken to Mr. Dodsworth?"

"Well, no. It is rather difficult to squeeze a word into the man's equine monologues. I have listened to him, however."

"Really?"

Meg's grin widened. "For a few moments. I have become adept at appearing fascinated by a gentleman's conversation while thinking of something else entirely. It's all in the gaze. If you fix your eyes on the man and nod occasionally, he thinks you are hanging on his every word. I'll be happy to teach you the trick. It's what got me through many an interminable dinner party."

"Well, Robbie would never believe I was interested in Mr. Dodsworth."

Meg laughed. "True. Perhaps Lord Peter? He is quite the Adonis."

Lizzie wrinkled her nose. "And he knows it. No, he is much too beautiful for my tastes."

"Then how about our host, Lord Tynweith?"

"Too old. He must have close to forty years in his dish." Lizzie was not enthusiastic about approaching any of the men at the house party—well, she was not enthusiastic about approaching any man other than

Robbie. She must get over her reluctance. "Perhaps Mr. Parker-Roth would do."

"Who is Mr. Parker-Roth?"

"One of Robbie's friends. He's here—he just arrived late."

"Well, if he is Robbie's friend, he will not do at all."

"He won't? Why not? He may not have a title, but his family is old and wealthy."

"That's not the problem. If Mr. Parker-Roth is a friend, Robbie will either feel he is a good match for you and step aside, or he'll know the man would never steal a woman he wanted and not feel threatened. We want Robbie worried. We want to provoke him to action."

Lizzie contemplated the action she would most like Robbie provoked to. She straightened her spine and forced herself to contemplate Meg's plan instead.

"I'll try."

"Splendid." Meg stood and smoothed her skirt. "You should begin immediately. It is time to get ready for dinner. Choose one of your more revealing gowns."

Dinner? Lizzie hugged herself tightly. "I don't believe . . ." How could she sit down to the same table with Robbie? "I have a slight headache. I think I'll have a tray sent up to my room."

Meg glowered at her. "You can't hide in your room, Lizzie. Lady Dunlee, Lady Felicity, the duchess—they will all remark on your absence."

"Let them." The thought of seeing Robbie again made Lizzie's stomach heave. She would not be able to swallow a morsel.

"Absolutely not. They are dying for the opportunity to gossip about you. You cannot allow them that pleasure. You must act as if nothing out of the ordinary has occurred."

The thought of facing those harpies further unsettled her stomach.

"I'm not certain I can."

"Of course you can. You have to. I will be there to lend you my support and Lady Bea"—Meg paused, and then shrugged—"Lady Bea will be there also. We can only hope she has not imbibed too much brandy."

"I shall certainly avoid the ratafia."

"I would hope so." Meg headed for the door. "Remember, choose one of your most revealing gowns."

"Meg . . ."

"No, Lizzie. Stiffen your spine. Think of it as a game, if you must. Or a punishment. It sounds to me as if Robbie deserves a little suffering after his behavior in the bushes."

"Well, yes." Robbie should definitely not have behaved as he had. He'd probably not given it a thought after she left him—at least once his face had stopped stinging.

"I believe the azure blue silk would be just the thing—and perhaps I will have Betty make an strategic adjustment or two."

Chapter Five

"She's in the garden, my lord." Flint cleared his throat. "The *special* garden."

"Ah. Thank you, Flint. And she's alone?"

"Yes, my lord."

"Splendid."

Baron Tynweith strolled down the broad gravel walk, past the knot garden and the parterres. The trees and bushes were neatly trimmed into spheres, cones, and pyramids. He had been told his garden was too symmetrical, too unnatural. Too French. He didn't care. It pleased him. He enjoyed the feeling of order—of control, perhaps—that the straight lines and sharp angles gave him.

He passed under an arch of honeysuckle and ivy and into the topiary gardens. He ignored the plantings on the right. They were his father's and grandfather's. He had left them unchanged. Amazing, really. He had been so angry when he had inherited, it was a wonder he had not taken the entire estate to hell.

He turned to the left, walked between two high hedges, and entered the special garden.

He cringed now to look at it. What had he been thinking?

He knew what he'd been thinking. The moment the

last shovel of dirt had hit the coffin of his carping, overbearing, perfectionist father, he'd set out to insure the dead man never stopped spinning in his grave. The topiary garden was an obvious target. For the last ten years of his life, the old bastard had spent every waking moment supervising the gardeners, making certain they trimmed the fanciful shapes—the horses and dogs and women—exactly as he wanted.

Tynweith grimaced, looking at an especially fanciful arrangement of a dog, a horse, and a woman. He suspected Jacks, his head gardener, also harbored some anger toward his father. He'd been quite delighted, after he'd recovered from the shock, to fashion this twisted mirror garden.

He found Charlotte observing a leafy tableau featuring two women and a snake.

"Admiring the foliage, Duchess?"

She gasped and spun around to face him.

Damn, she made his blood quicken. She'd been a debutante when he'd first met her. It had been his first Season as baron, his first Season free of his father. He had been wild.

He'd seen her the moment he'd walked into Easthaven's ballroom. She'd been standing by the door to the garden, next to her beak-nosed mother, staring out at the crowded room, not talking to anyone. She'd looked so small, so blond, so self-possessed. So cold. The wags had dubbed her the Marble Queen before she'd risen from her first curtsy.

He'd wanted her.

He'd gotten Lady Easthaven to make the introductions. The Duchess of Rothingham had wrinkled her nose at a mere baron approaching her daughter—well, it was also possible she had heard of his rapidly deteriorating reputation—and would have denied him a dance if she could have. But Charlotte had said yes before her mother could say no.

He still didn't know why she'd agreed. She had

hardly spoken to him. Hardly touched him. Yet he could hardly keep from dragging her out into the darkened garden.

He'd seen an exotic mix of fear and passion behind her controlled façade. It fascinated him. Drew him. He told himself that she presented a challenge, and he could no more turn down a challenge than he could stop breathing.

He had managed to get her into the garden, but he had shown little finesse. Well, no finesse. He had jumped her like the animal he was and she had slapped him soundly.

She was eyeing him nervously now. "I'm looking for Lady Felicity."

"Hmm. An odd place to look. I thought I'd made the point of mentioning this part of the gardens is not suitable for the fairer sex."

Charlotte flushed slightly. "I took a wrong turn."

"Well, since you are here, may I show you around? Unless, of course, your maiden sensibilities will be offended."

"I am not a maiden, my lord."

"No, you aren't, are you? Then I need not send for the hartshorn."

She stared back at him, her cold society face firmly in place. The corners of her mouth twitched up briefly in her bored half smile. "I have my vinaigrette handy."

"Ah, that is a relief. Then I don't need to mind my manners, either."

A flicker of alarm lit her eyes as he placed her hand on his arm.

"I understand you saved one of my guests from certain ruin. Quite kind of you to exert yourself."

Charlotte covered her mouth with one gloved hand as she yawned delicately. "It was nothing."

"Still, I thought you hated Lady Elizabeth."

"My lord, hatred is by far too exhausting an emotion."

"Really? I'm delighted to hear it. I feared you hated me, also."

That got her to glance at him. She would have removed her hand from his arm, but he would not release her. She shrugged.

"I am here, am I not? I could easily have declined your invitation to this house party had I harbored a strong aversion to your company."

"I had wondered why you accepted." He steered her past one of Jacks's more inspired creations involving a naked woman and a ram with remarkable horns—and other startling endowments. Charlotte paused, her attention caught.

"I do think my gardener has a special talent, don't you? Warped, perhaps, but still, remarkable."

"Um." Charlotte stared at the figures. Her small pink tongue darted out to wet her lips.

So, she liked it, did she? Interesting. He had always suspected she had untapped depths.

"Actually, my dear, I believe you accepted my invitation so you could have a little fun while your husband was elsewhere." He stroked her fingers. "While the cat's away, you know."

She tried to snatch her hand back. He kept it on his arm.

"I assure you, Lord Tynweith, 'a little fun' was not my intention."

"No? I saw Lord Peter leaving your room last night—very late last night."

Charlotte shrugged. "I do not believe you'll tattle to Hartford."

"No, you're right. I won't tell your husband." He turned his attention back to the shrubbery. "I can't imagine Lord Peter could entertain you for more than an evening. Frankly, I can't imagine the boy could entertain you at all."

Charlotte was studying the leafy woman's bound hands. "Entertainment is not important, my lord."

Her eyes flicked over at him, then fastened on the shrubbery again. "As I'm certain you realize, I do not find such activities entertaining at all. Necessary, but not entertaining."

"Necessary?"

"Of course. It is the only method I know of to become pregnant. My husband needs an heir."

"Ah, so you plan to present him with a cuckoo." He steered her toward more foliage in flagrante delicto.

"Believe me, Lord Tynweith, my husband is diligent on his own behalf. Any child may well be his. I'm just looking for some insurance. The men in Lord Peter's family are prolific. They also, without exception, manage to produce males."

Tynweith guided Charlotte between two closely spaced hedges. The tour could wait. He had more pressing business to attend to.

"Where are we?" Charlotte frowned. "There is nothing to see in here."

Tynweith rubbed her shoulders. "Let me help you, Charlotte."

"My lord!"

"Shh." He laid his finger gently over her lips. "I believe that a woman greatly increases her chances of conceiving if she enjoys the coupling process."

"Well, I shall just have to hope that your belief is in error."

"Charlotte, Charlotte." He bent to whisper in her ear. "Do you not see that there is another possibility?"

She moved her head away from his mouth, but did not try to break his hold.

"What do you mean? What other possibility?"

He moved his lips over her forehead, barely touching her skin.

"You only need to find the right man, sweetings. The man who will make your heart quicken." He brushed his mouth over the sensitive spot just behind her ear and smiled when he heard her indrawn breath. "The man who will make your breasts swell and your nipples harden to tiny pebbles." He ran his fingers over her bodice. "The man who can make you hot and wet and ready. Who can prepare your field so when he plows it and sows his seed, the plant will take root and flourish." His mouth hovered over hers. She did not pull back. Her cheeks were nicely flushed.

"I don't know what you are speaking of," she whispered.

"I know you don't. Let me show you. Let me come to your bed tonight."

"Lord Peter—"

"Send him away. Tell him you are indisposed. He is a boy, Charlotte. He cannot satisfy you."

"I—"

He rubbed his thumbs over her jaw. "Did he make you pant with need, love, so that you begged him to take you? Were you so desperate to feel him inside you that you were weeping, here"—he touched her eyes—"and here." He ran his hand down the front of her dress to the top of her legs.

She was panting now. He smiled.

"And when he finally took pity on you and came into you, did he give you what you wanted? Did he tease you and stroke you there until your body shattered and clenched around him? Or did he climb into your bed, spread your legs, and ram into you, finding his own release, but leaving you . . ."

"Bored." She whispered. "Relieved he was done."

"I would never bore you, Charlotte."

"You were rough in Easthaven's garden."

"That was seven years ago. I was an idiot. Ignorant. I knew only hunger. I hadn't learned patience." He touched his mouth to hers. "And you were just a virgin."

She still didn't know how to kiss. Her lips were motionless beneath his. He licked them.

"We can have so much more fun now," he murmured

and then let his tongue find its way into her sweet, wet mouth.

She stood quietly in the circle of his arms, her hands against his waistcoat, not pushing him away, but not pulling him closer. Patience, he reminded himself. She doesn't know the passion inside her yet. Waken it slowly.

He ran his hands over her soft bottom and then released her.

"Shall I come to your room tonight, Charlotte?"

Her eyes were not quite in focus. She stared up at him; then she blinked and stepped back.

"May I come, Charlotte? Will you let me into your bed and into your body? Will you let me make you scream with pleasure?"

"I . . ." She flushed, swallowed, looked away. When her eyes met his again, her society face was back in place. "No, Lord Tynweith. I am sorry, but I find I must decline your kind offer. Now, if you'll excuse me?"

She stepped out of the shrubbery and began to walk sedately away. In a moment, though, she had picked up her skirts and her pace. She was almost running.

Damn. He struggled to bring his body back under control.

He'd gone too quickly with her again. But he'd felt her response to him. She had softened for a few moments in his arms. He had felt her heat.

She wasn't a virgin. She knew the mechanics of coupling. And she certainly wasn't held back by loyalty to her husband—she had already handed him his horns. So what *was* holding her back?

She had let that sprig of the Marquis of Addington's tree under her skirts. Was that it? Did she still worship rank above all else? Not that Lord Peter had any rank at all. His title was merely courtesy. The man was a commoner. *He* was the peer, but apparently in Charlotte's eyes, a mere baron could not compare to the son of a marquis, even a fifth son. His blood was not blue enough to mix with hers.

Well, there were other women at this blasted house party. He would get over his fascination with the cold-blooded bitch.

He glanced down to be certain his clothing was in order before he returned to the house. Something gleamed in the grass. He picked it up. A lady's brooch, a pretty trinket of diamonds and emeralds in the shape of someone's initials. EMR. Elizabeth Runyon? He thought her middle name was Marie. What had Lady Elizabeth been doing in this secluded bower in his special garden? And with whom had she been doing it?

Puzzles. He put the brooch in his pocket. Solving puzzles could be quite an enjoyable activity.

"I haven't heard an engagement announcement, have you?"

"What?" Charlotte hoped Felicity hadn't noticed her startle. She was never so completely oblivious to her surroundings. Tynweith had definitely upset her, and she did not like the feeling. She had not liked it seven years ago, either.

The man was a menace to her carefully cultivated peace of mind. She usually avoided him. Why had she let herself come to Lendal Park? She was an idiot.

No, not an idiot. Desperate. Time was running out. Hartford was failing. If he died before she was increasing. . . .

She took a deep breath. She needed a glass of brandy.

She had to get pregnant *now*. Hartford's current heir, an obnoxious grandnephew, hated her. She didn't blame him—if she got her wish, she'd keep him from getting the title and all the wealth and land that went with it.

He would certainly not treat her kindly if he became duke.

She should have at least one child by now. She'd been submitting to Hartford's attentions for three full years. She'd wed only weeks after the Duke of Alvord had married his American, and *she* was in imminent expectation of delivering her second child.

Taking Lord Peter to bed *had* to work.

Or was Tynweith correct? Did enjoyment increase one's chances of success?

Impossible. How could she enjoy such an embarrassing, uncomfortable act? Yet she had felt . . . odd just now, just as she had all those years ago in Easthaven's garden. Hot and . . . unsettled. Wet between her legs, exactly where—

"Charlotte! Where has your mind gone?"

It had happened again. She could not allow herself to let down her guard like this.

"What? I'm sorry—my attention wandered."

Felicity gave her a pointed look. "I should say so. I asked what you thought about the lack of an announcement."

"An announcement?" She really needed to be alone in her room with her brandy flask. Charlotte quickened her step through the broad formal garden. "What announcement?"

"*Lack* of announcement. Lord Westbrooke and Lady Elizabeth's engagement, of course. I haven't heard a word, have you?"

"No."

"Don't you think that is interesting?"

"No."

"You don't? You were the one who said we should expect an announcement this morning, weren't you? Westbrooke was in Lady Elizabeth's room last night. Naked."

"He wasn't seen. For some reason Tynweith has chosen to stop any rumors." Charlotte slowed as they approached the house. She'd like to tell Felicity to go away. A halfway perceptive person would discern she wanted to be alone.

Felicity was not perceptive in the slightest.

"I still don't understand what happened last night." Felicity frowned. "I was quite taken aback when Westbrooke bolted from his bed. I've been told I have a lovely pair of tits. I expected him to stay around long enough to admire the scenery. The way he leapt from the window, you'd have thought all the hounds of hell were after him."

"Shh!" A footman had seen them and opened the door. Charlotte nodded at him. Felicity stopped and ogled the man. The girl was impossible. Charlotte tugged her toward the stairs.

Felicity laughed. "I never took you for a prude, Charlotte." She snickered. "Lord Peter did not find you overly prudish, either. At least he told me he had no complaints."

Charlotte stumbled on the first step.

"Surely Lord Peter did not. . . ." She swallowed. "Do I understand that Lord Peter discussed . . ."

"You *are* a prude! I never would have guessed."

Charlotte noticed the footman was looking in their direction.

"Keep your voice down. I am not a prude. I am merely surprised that a man would discuss his sexual affairs with an unmarried woman to whom he is not related in any way."

Surprised and ill. How could Lord Peter have told Felicity what had occurred between them? And to say he had no complaints! Of course the idiot had no complaints! He'd gotten what he'd come for—several times, in fact. She was the one who had complaints. The man was as inept as Hartford. At least he was quicker about it. It had taken all of thirty seconds each time. She only hoped it had done the job.

Perhaps she'd been too hasty in turning down Tynweith's offer.

Felicity shrugged. "We are friends." She grinned. "Good friends. Very good friends. Actually, I would have said Lord Peter had the best arse in England until I saw Westbrooke's."

"You've seen Lord Peter's ar—" The footman was still loitering by the door. "You've seen Lord Peter's armor?"

"What?"

She grabbed Felicity's arm again and hurried her up the stairs.

"When did you see . . . no, I don't want to know."

"Yes, you do—and it was just last week."

"You really should not talk of such subjects where you can be overheard."

"I won't be overheard. Everyone is getting ready for dinner."

"The servants aren't."

Felicity laughed. "Who cares about servants?"

Charlotte looked away. She had never cared growing up, that was true. But now, after spending three years with Hartford. . . . The servants were the only people who seemed to have some compassion for her—or was it pity? Whichever, it made little difference. They had some feeling for her, though it had taken her a while to unbend enough to see it.

And the truth was one disgruntled servant could hang all one's dirty laundry out for society's inspection. She needed to keep the servants on her side, especially if her plan worked and Lord Peter's seed took root. She didn't want whispers flying through the *ton* prompting speculation as to the baby's paternity.

She headed down the corridor toward her room. Unfortunately, Felicity kept pace with her.

"We really should be getting ready as well."

Felicity shrugged. "There's no rush. We have plenty of time. I wanted to talk to you before we went down, anyway. We had agreed to meet, remember?"

"Yes. I was looking for you in the gardens earlier."

"In the gardens?" Felicity sniggered. "Tynweith has some interesting gardens, doesn't he?"

Interesting was one adjective, though not the one Charlotte would have chosen.

"They *are* rather unusual." She cleared her throat. Was Felicity impervious to hints? "I find now is not a good time to talk, however." Now she wanted to shut her door firmly and take a few deep breaths.

"Why?"

Charlotte avoided Felicity's eyes.

"I'm a little tired. I would like to lie down for a while before dinner."

"Something happened in the gardens, didn't it?"

"No, nothing happened." At least nothing she would ever tell the other girl about. Lord Peter might think his amorous encounters common news, but she did not.

Felicity gave her an arch look. "I saw Tynweith out walking."

"It *is* his estate. I imagine he walks about it frequently."

"He was headed toward the gardens. Did he find you?"

"Do you think he was looking for me?"

"He definitely appeared to be looking for someone."

"Perhaps he was searching for his head gardener." Charlotte reached her door. "Felicity, this really is not a good time for our chat."

"Nonsense. It won't take long. You'll have plenty of time to nap." Felicity pushed past her into her room. "You need to help me plan how to capture Westbrooke. I want him securely hooked before this house party ends."

"Not that it's any of my business, of course, but won't Westbrooke be a trifle annoyed on your wedding night when he finds no blood on your sheets?"

"Oh, he'll find blood."

"Pig's blood? Get him drunk and then pour a little where it's needed?"

"Or a lot." Felicity laughed. "One of my friends spilled the whole vial. She was terrified her new husband would catch on. Instead he thought he'd injured her. He bought her a new carriage and matched grays in apology. But don't worry, I'll have no need to resort to such tricks. I *am* a virgin—technically." She grinned. "Surely you know there are many amusing games to play that leave a maidenhead intact."

Charlotte could not imagine any. Did not want to imagine any. There was nothing faintly amusing about anything connected to the procreative process. Embarrassing, messy, painful, yes. Amusing, no.

Except for those few minutes in the shrubbery with Tynweith. . . . But that experience had not been amusing, either. She did not care to feel hot and unsettled.

She was right to avoid him. Definitely, she had made the correct decision in denying him her bed. She reached for her brandy, opened the flask, and took a long drink.

"Thirsty?"

Charlotte shrugged and wiped her mouth as delicately as she could with her fingers. She settled on the chaise—it was clear Felicity was not leaving until they had their discussion.

"I don't know how I can help you."

"I'm sure two heads are better than one." Felicity sat down. "What happened to the miniature?"

"I put it away. As you said, I've no need to look at myself."

"Are you certain Tynweith didn't find you in the gardens?"

"I thought we were talking about Westbrooke."

"Right." Felicity gave her a searching look. Charlotte took a sip of brandy and looked calmly back at her. She'd had years of practice hiding her feelings, first with her mother and then with Hartford.

She must remember that. She would not allow Tynweith to upset her. She could not let the untidy emotions he caused affect her behavior.

Felicity shrugged and leaned forward. "Westbrooke was definitely naked in Lady Elizabeth's room and yet there's been no betrothal announcement. What can it mean?"

"Perhaps that if you do manage to catch Lord Westbrooke in a compromising position, he will not marry you."

"Or perhaps it means I will have to catch him in a *very* compromising position." Felicity smiled. "That opens some intriguing possibilities."

"Such as?"

Felicity tapped her chin with her index finger. "It will have to be something very public. I want plenty of witnesses, especially if Westbrooke is not inclined to do the right thing."

"Yes, you will do better if his honor is compromised as well." Charlotte looked at the door. Perhaps if she poured the rest of her brandy over Felicity, the girl would leave.

"Exactly. Something shocking, too. Very shocking. A kiss won't be enough." Felicity sighed. "I do think if I'd been found in his bed last night, I'd be betrothed this morning. I would not have made Lady Elizabeth's mistake. I would have been certain everyone saw us together. If only I'd moved a little more quickly. If I'd screamed a second earlier. . . ."

"Timing is everything." Charlotte looked at her watch. "And it is definitely time for you to leave."

Thankfully, Felicity rose.

"I can see you are determined to be no help. Well, Lord Andrew arrives tomorrow. He is always full of ideas."

Charlotte tried not to look too relieved as Felicity closed the door behind her.

Chapter Six

"My lord, it is time to dress for dinner."

"I know, Collins."

Robbie stared out at the gardens. How was he going to face Lizzie? God. He still saw her, her smile fading; the light dying out of her eyes; the bewilderment; the pain.

How was he going to face her? What could he say to her? He could not tell her. . . .

Shame pulsed deep in his gut.

He could not tell her his secret. Better she hate him than pity him.

"My lord."

"Yes, I'm coming." He swallowed his annoyance. Collins was only doing his job. He had to go down to dinner. He could not hide in his room. Gentlemen could not claim the "headache," even when one's head was actually pounding hard enough to split one's skull.

"You do seem a bit down pin, my lord, if I may say so."

Robbie grunted. Collins was a master of understatement. He could not remember ever feeling so low. Even after the disaster at the Dancing Piper, he had not felt this heavy, energy-sapping melancholy.

When Lizzie had left him in the shrubbery, he'd

walked Tynweith's estate again. Bloody hell, he must have traversed every damn inch of the place. If the baron had been thoughtful enough to provide a handy cliff, he might have thrown himself over the edge.

No. He stared at his reflection as Collins fussed with his linen. He wasn't that desperate, not yet. Almost, but no—he would not let himself go down that road. Death was a coward's way out. He hoped to God he wasn't that spineless.

"I heard about the, um, bumble broth last night." Collins handed him a cravat.

"Did you? A pity you weren't here." Robbie wrapped the muslin around his neck. "Perhaps you could have prevented Lady Felicity from inviting herself into my bed. That, by the by, is one of your duties—ascertaining that no females get lost in my sheets."

Collins had the grace to blush. "She had not arrived by the time I left, I assure you, my lord. If I had suspected she would be so brazen, I never would have, um. . . . Well, I would have stayed here. I would not have let her cross the threshold."

"Yes, I'm certain you would have done battle with her and kept her out. I am hoping a sturdy lock will accomplish that task as well. The door does have one—you are to persuade Tynweith's butler to give you the key before I retire tonight."

"Yes, my lord. I'm certain that will not be a problem."

"I hope not, or you *will* have to remain to guard my slumbers. I do not want to go capering naked over the portico roof again."

Robbie finished tying his cravat and stood. Collins held his coat. Clearly the man had something on his mind.

"Yes? What is it, Collins?"

"About last night, my lord." The man looked down and brushed the coat's lapels. If there was any dust on the cloth, Robbie couldn't see it.

Robbie swallowed a sigh. He had hoped to avoid

any detailed discussion of the previous evening. It appeared that was a vain hope. He had employed Collins as his valet for almost ten years. He knew the man. If there was something on his mind, it was going to come out eventually. Might as well get the unpleasantness over with.

"You have something to say about last night?"

"Happens I do, my lord." Collins cleared his throat and straightened. "Betty told me Lady Elizabeth was feeling poorly this morning."

"I'm not surprised—she was drunk as an Emperor last night. Shot the cat, did she?"

It was a wonder she hadn't cast up her accounts when Lady Felicity and Lady Caroline had burst into her room. Their entrance had certainly unsettled his stomach.

He would definitely need to keep a close eye on her for the duration of the house party if overindulgence in spirits had such a notable effect on her behavior. She could have given London's top courtesans lessons in seduction last night. Just the memory made his useless organ stiffen.

She'd been exceedingly bold in Tynweith's garden as well, and she'd been sober then. What was the matter with her? A chill settled in his gut. Had someone slipped an aphrodisiac into her wine? He would not put any trickery past some of Tynweith's guests. Or Tynweith himself. A man who cultivated a garden of obscene vegetation was not a man to be trusted. Hell, the blackguard probably grew some potent herbs on his estate. He would have to ask Parks.

For now he would watch Lizzie. He would dog her every step. She was safe as long as he was with her. But alone—any of the bounders at this house party might take gross advantage of her. Lord Peter, for example, the rutting bastard. He'd wager Lizzie would not have kept her virginity if Lord Peter had encountered her in the shrubbery.

Damn. Just the thought made his heart pound and a red haze veil his eyes. He'd kill any man who took advantage of Lizzie. She was so sweet, so generous, so responsive. If only he were capable. . . .

"Yes, my lord."

Robbie blinked. He'd forgotten Collins was in the room.

"Betty did say Lady Elizabeth had a severely unsettled stomach. She blamed the ratafia for her condition, but Lady Beatrice thought . . . at first she suspected . . . that is, she believed you had visited Lady Elizabeth in her chamber."

"Get to the point, man."

"Lady Beatrice thought perhaps Lady Elizabeth was increasing."

The thought of Lizzie growing heavy with his child caused a jolt of pure lust to shoot through him. The feeling was followed immediately by an aching emptiness that made his head spin. If only it were true. He would give anything. . . .

He forced his mind away from the matter. He had learned a long time ago that no amount of wishing or praying or bargaining with God made a thimbleful of difference.

"That is absurd."

"Well, yes, my lord. Of course it is. A woman does not exhibit signs of breeding immediately after one night of pleasure. And I know you have not been frequenting her bed before this."

"Collins!"

The man stepped back in alarm. Robbie struggled to get hold of his temper. "I have not been frequenting Lady Elizabeth's bed."

"I know, my lord. Haven't I just said so?"

Robbie took a breath and counted to ten.

"I did not frequent her bed last night either." He paused. That was not completely truthful. "That is, not in that way."

"My lord?"

"Damnation. The point is, Collins, there is no way that Lady Elizabeth could be increasing. The necessary activity did not occur."

Collins looked disappointed, for God's sake!

"Why didn't it, my lord?"

"What do you mean, why didn't it? Lady Elizabeth is a gently bred young woman who also happens to be the sister of one of my closest friends. Why would you think I would take such advantage of her?"

"My lord, I meant no disrespect. Lady Elizabeth is also a young woman who is clearly in love with you. Betty is certain on that point. And you care for her, do you not?"

"Yes. No." Robbie wanted to smash something, perhaps Collins's face. But it wasn't his valet's fault that he was defective. "I do care for Lady Elizabeth, but not in that way."

Collins just stared at him.

"Well, not exactly in that way. You don't understand. The notion is absurd. I cannot wed Lady Elizabeth."

"But why is it absurd, my lord? You are almost thirty. You need to produce an heir. Lady Elizabeth would agree in a heartbeat to wed you—Betty says her mistress has turned down other offers, waiting and hoping for yours. There's no other lady you prefer, is there?"

"Collins . . ."

"And I know—well, at least I think—you do not prefer men, but even if you did, you would need to overcome those feelings to get an heir."

"Collins!" Robbie felt as if someone had kicked him in the stomach. "I do not prefer men."

"I didn't think you did." Collins shifted position, holding Robbie's coat up almost as a shield. "My lord, I am sorry to be so bold, but I am waiting for your proposal as well. Betty and I would like to marry. If you wed Lady Elizabeth, we will be able to do so easily. If you don't . . . well, neither of us wishes to leave our employers, but. . . . You see the awkwardness of the situation?"

"Yes, Collins. I do understand. I'll speak to Lady Elizabeth."

"So you will propose?"

"No. I will discuss your situation with her during the house party. We will find a solution to your problem."

"But what about *your* problem, my lord? Will you find a solution to that as well?"

Robbie shrugged. His problem had no solution. "Perhaps. Now it is almost time for dinner. Are you going to stand there holding that coat all evening or are you going to help me into it?"

"Help you into it, of course, my lord."

Collins held the coat out and Robbie slipped his arms into its sleeves. He would put on his society clothes and his society smile and his society charm. He straightened his cuffs and looked in the mirror one last time.

"You look complete to a shade, my lord."

Robbie nodded. Indeed. Lord Westbrooke always looked all that was proper. He forced a smile.

Lord Westbrooke always had a joke. Lord Westbrooke was always amusing. Lord Westbrooke was the master of inane chatter, of the bon mot.

Society had no inkling of how miserable the witty Lord Westbrooke really was.

"You look beautiful, Lizzie," Meg said. "Doesn't she look beautiful, Lady Bea?"

"Are you sure I don't need a fichu?" Lizzie studied her reflection. Betty had been a bit too zealous in altering this dress. There was a shocking expanse of skin exposed. Her poor little breasts were almost popping out. "Perhaps a shawl?"

"Pshaw!" Lady Bea examined Lizzie's chest through her lorgnette. Lizzie clenched her hands to keep them from flying up to cover the area under inspection. "Leave the shawl and other drapery in your room."

Lady Bea was not a proponent of excessive modesty. Lizzie eyed the plunging neck of the older woman's coquelicot dress. At least a large rope of diamonds, emeralds, and rubies covered much of the wrinkled and dimpled flesh. With the bunches of lime green ribbons festooning the red cloth, she looked like a very ripe apple hosting an inchworm soiree.

Lady Bea winked at Lizzie. "That dress is just the thing to bring Westbrooke to his senses." She chuckled. "*All* his senses."

"Um." Lizzie flushed. After her interlude in the shrubbery, she wanted Lord Westbrooke to keep his offensive senses to himself. "I believe a fichu would be perfect. Betty, could you get my favorite brooch for me?"

Lady Bea pointed her lorgnette at Lizzie. "Timidity never won any battles, missy, or any husbands."

"So you are saying society's dictate that unmarried women be meek and well behaved is humbug?" Meg asked, grinning.

"Of course. Most of those asinine rules were conceived by dried up old maids."

Lizzie looked at Meg. She appeared to be biting her tongue as hard as Lizzie was. Surely Lady Bea, with over sixty years of unmarried life in her dish, would qualify as an old maid.

"I still can't believe that idiot has not yet offered for you, Lizzie. It's not as if there is anything standing in his way." Lady Beatrice frowned. "I never thought he was such a cod's head."

"We have a plan to make Lord Westbrooke come up to scratch, Lady Bea," Meg said. "Lizzie is going to make him jealous. We thought he might need a goad to get him moving toward the altar."

"Hmm. Some men respond better to a carrot."

"A carrot?" Lizzie asked.

"A taste of what they will get if they step into parson's mousetrap."

Lizzie flushed. Robbie had already had a large taste of that.

"A kiss here; a cuddle there. They get a craving for you. An addiction. It takes over their bodies—especially a prominent part of their bodies—and their minds. You become all they can think of. You invade their dreams. Finally, they are willing to do anything to have you—even become a tenant for life." Lady Bea sighed, then frowned. "Just be certain you get a ring on your finger before you give Westbrooke, or any man, much more than a taste, Lizzie."

"My lady, I can't find the brooch." Betty had Lizzie's jewelry case open and a worried look on her face. "When did ye last wear it?"

"I had it just this afternoon, Betty. Are you sure it isn't here?"

"As sure as I can be, my lady. It's the brooch with yer initials ye'd be wanting? The one Lady Gladys gave ye for yer come out?"

"Yes, that's the one. I know I wore it this afternoon."

"Could it have come off somewhere? Ye did say the clasp was weak. Ye were going to get if fixed when ye got back to Lunnon."

"Yes, but the clasp wasn't *that* weak. I can't imagine—"

Lizzie flushed. Maybe she could imagine. There had been a significant rearranging of her dress in the shrubbery. It was possible the brooch had become detached at that point.

It was too late to go looking for it tonight. It would be safe where it was. No one else would be making use of that odd little bower in that even odder garden.

"Never mind, Betty. I'll find it in the morning."

"And you don't need it tonight." Lady Beatrice headed for the door. "Come on, before all the brandy is gone."

* * *

"So what exactly happened last night, Westbrooke?"

"Nothing." Robbie watched the door to the drawing room. Where was Lizzie? He took a sip of brandy, smiling slightly. He would wager she would avoid the ratafia tonight.

Lady Felicity hadn't made an appearance either. He knew not to hope she'd left the house party so soon. Collins had best procure a key from Tynweith's butler. He wanted the door to his room securely locked before he climbed into bed tonight.

"Nothing? Then how do you explain the wild story my valet told me this morning? Something about you cavorting naked in Lady Elizabeth's room. Not quite your style, I would have said."

Robbie glanced at his friend Parks—John Parker-Roth. The man kept a straight face, but his damned eyes gleamed behind his spectacles.

"Why didn't you come out and gape with the rest of the house party, Parks? Your room is right next door. Didn't you hear the commotion?"

"Certainly. And I did poke my head out when I got up to pour more brandy. Didn't look as though another body was required in the corridor. I had better things to do than gawk and gossip."

"Had your nose in some plant book, did you?"

"Repton's *Fragments on the Theory and Practice of Landscape Gardening*. Shall I tell you about it?"

"God, no."

Parks laughed. "It's not too technical. There are quite a few pictures."

"Pictures of shrubbery." Robbie remembered a certain section of shrubbery and flushed. Parks's gaze sharpened. The man never missed a thing.

"Hmm. I wonder what is so embarrassing about shrubbery? Take care or your face will be as red as your hair."

"Stubble it, Parks. And my hair is brown."

"No, *my* hair is brown. Yours is red."

"Oh, for God's sake! We've had this stupid argument ever since Eton."

Parks's face grew serious. "Yes we have, but you've never missed your sense of humor before. What's wrong, Westbrooke?"

"Nothing. I'm just not nine years old any longer."

"No, you're almost thirty—two months younger than I, if I recall correctly. *Did* something happen in Lady Elizabeth's room last night?"

"No. No, everything is fine. I'm tired, that's all. Slightly blue-deviled. My apologies for being a bore." Robbie took another swallow of brandy—and almost sprayed it over Parks's cravat.

"What *is* the matter?" Parks took out his handkerchief and dabbed a few stray droplets from his waistcoat.

"*That* is the matter." Robbie gestured at the drawing room door. Lizzie had just arrived.

"What? Oh, I grant you Lady Beatrice's attire is somewhat alarming, but I thought you'd be used to it by now. She has been on the Town for an age and her taste in clothing hasn't changed."

"Not Lady Bea." What was the matter with Parks? The man wasn't usually a clod pole.

"No?" Parks studied the women, then shrugged. "If this is a riddle, Westbrooke, I'm afraid I can't answer it. Who is the beauty, by the by?"

"Lizzie, you dolt!"

Parks turned back to stare at Robbie. "I know Lady Elizabeth, Westbrooke, and she does look especially fine this evening. That shade of blue is very complimentary." He glanced back at the women. "But I was referring to her companion." He grinned. "Not Lady Beatrice—her *other* companion."

"That's Meg." Robbie had barely noticed the color of Lizzie's dress. His eyes had focused on its bodice. Or lack of bodice. What had Lizzie been thinking? Her perfect breasts mounded up so any dissipated rakehell could easily imagine what they would look like naked. Her nipples were almost exposed, for God's sake.

"Meg?"

"What?" Robbie glanced impatiently at Parks. "Oh, Miss Margaret Peterson. Sister of the Marchioness of Knightsdale. Vicar's daughter. This is her first Season, even though she's Lizzie's age. Couldn't tear herself away from Kent and the countryside. Obsessed with plants."

"Really? That sounds intriguing."

"Only to you." Robbie straightened his waistcoat. Someone needed to talk sense to Lizzie. Lady Beatrice obviously would not. He'd known the woman was a terrible choice for chaperone. "Come on. I'll introduce you."

"He's coming," Meg said.

"Yes, I see that." Lizzie took a deep breath. Calm. She must be calm. And daring. That was her new plan for this Season. Be daring.

"A good sign." Lady Beatrice nodded, sending her red and green plumes bobbing. "He was watching the door, waiting for your arrival. The man's obsessed. Don't know why he hasn't offered yet. Perhaps I'll have a word with him."

"No!" That would be all she needed, to have Lady Beatrice discuss Robbie's matrimonial plans—or lack thereof—with him in Tynweith's drawing room for the assembled *ton*'s amusement. "No, please. I'm certain that's not necessary."

"Well someone should light a fire under that young man's arse."

"Lady Beatrice!" Lizzie glanced around. No one was tittering or staring at them. "Please keep your voice down."

"Hmph. Don't know why I should. Man needs someone to tell him what's what."

"No, really." Lizzie tried to keep her own voice down, though it was hard to know how softly she spoke, mortification was throbbing so loudly in her ears. "It's quite all right."

"Perhaps your dress will inspire him. Remember to lean toward him when you talk. Let him see what he can't have until he marries you."

"Uh." The memory of Robbie's touch made Lizzie's breasts throb. "Yes. No. Didn't you want some brandy?"

"Yes, I did. You might want something, too. You look a trifle"—Lady Beatrice examined Lizzie's face and neck—"hot." She raised one eyebrow, and suddenly Lizzie was certain Lady Beatrice knew exactly what she'd been doing with Robbie in Tynweith's garden. Exactly.

Impossible. An elderly virgin would not know of such things. Lizzie certainly hadn't known of them until Robbie'd demonstrated.

Lady Bea leaned closer. "Remember, Lizzie, it's a better notion to get a wedding ring—or at least a betrothal ring—before one gets"—she looked pointedly at Lizzie's stomach—"other things."

"Yes, Lady Beatrice. I mean, I don't understand—"

Lady Beatrice patted Lizzie's arm. "I'm quite certain you can puzzle it out." She started to walk away, then paused. "And stay away from the ratafia."

"Yes. Definitely. Do not worry." Lizzie blew out a long breath as Lady Bea moved off to find the brandy.

"That woman is insufferable. How can you bear her, Meg? How can *I* bear her? I will never survive this Season with my sanity intact." Lizzie gripped her skirts. "Aunt Gladys was an unexceptionable chaperone. Don't you think she could have waited a year to retire to Bath?"

"Hmm?"

"Meg?" Lizzie glanced at her friend. Meg was

staring at the two men making their way across the
drawing room.

"Who's the man with Lord Westbrooke?" Meg's
voice sounded odd. Breathless. Her cheeks were
flushed.

"Mr. Parker-Roth." What was bothering Meg? Lizzie
examined Parks. He was handsome enough, she supposed, but he wasn't Robbie. He was a few inches
shorter and broader, with wavy brown hair, green eyes,
and spectacles. "You'll probably like him, Meg. He's
mad about plants, too."

"Oh."

"I do hope you'll manage to be more articulate
when you are introduced."

Meg glared at her.

Lizzie turned to find Robbie glaring at her as well.

"Where did you get that dress, Lizzie?"

"Good evening to you, too, Lord Westbrooke."
Lizzie turned pointedly to face the other man. "How
are you, Mr. Parker-Roth? I don't believe I saw you last
night."

Lizzie blushed the moment the words left her lips.
Had he been in the corridor with the rest of the house
party? Surely not—but his room was right next to
hers.

He smiled, but his eyes kept drifting to Meg. "No, I
arrived quite late. I had some business that needed
my attention before I left my estate."

"I see." All Mr. Parker-Roth appeared interested in
seeing was Meg. His eyes had strayed to her again.
"Have you met my friend, Miss Peterson?"

He grinned at her then, as if she were a prize pupil
who had finally hit upon the key question. "No, I
don't believe I have."

"Well, meet her then." Robbie sounded impatient.
"Parks, Miss Peterson; Meg, Parks."

"Parks?" Meg's voice was soft, almost shy.

"My nickname, Miss Peterson."

"Ah, for Parker-Roth."

"No, Meg—for greenery." Robbie laughed. "Parks is as keen on weeds as you are. Maybe keener. Actually, I think MacDuff did try to dub you Weed at Eton, didn't he, Parks? Lord Weed. You took exception and thrashed him soundly as I recall. Got a standing ovation."

Parks frowned. "I really don't think the ladies need to be treated to our boyhood tales of mayhem, Westbrooke."

Robbie shrugged. "No need to stand on ceremony with these ladies. I've known them both since they were infants."

"Well I have not. I'm certain Lady Elizabeth and Miss Peterson will think me a complete barbarian if I model my behavior on yours."

"You could never be *that* barbaric, sir."

"Very funny, Lizzie." Robbie turned to Mr. Parker-Roth. "Not to worry, Parks. As you see, Lizzie is inclined to be generous. If you want to impress Meg, just talk to her about your horticultural activities. I'd wager she would love to hear all about that book you were reading last night. What was it called? Garden fragments or something?"

Meg smiled. "Never say you have Repton's *Fragments on the Theory and Practice of Landscape Gardening*, Mr. Parker-Roth."

"Actually, yes."

"See, I knew you two would have something of interest to discuss—as I have something of interest to discuss with Lizzie. So, if you'll excuse us?"

Robbie took Lizzie's arm and moved her a step or two away. She dug in her heels and glanced back at Meg. Her friend was already in deep discussion with Parks. Obviously Meg was going to be no help in keeping Robbie at a distance.

"Step out into the garden, Lizzie. I want a word with you."

"I am definitely not going into any more gardens

with you, Lord Westbrooke. My last such excursion had very unsettling results."

Robbie flushed. "If you are going to throw yourself at men—"

"I *tripped*. I did not throw myself."

A muscle jumped in Robbie's jaw. "What do you call that dress, then, if not throwing yourself at men? It's indecent."

Lizzie wanted to cover her chest with her hands. She clenched them into fists instead. Who was Robbie to tell her how to dress anyway? If he wanted to dictate her attire he could offer for her.

"It is not indecent. My chaperone has no objections to it whatsoever. In fact she said it was quite the thing." What Lady Bea had actually said was it was just the thing to bring this fat-pated, buffle-headed idiot to his senses, but Lizzie wasn't going to tell him that. He didn't have any senses to be brought to, anyway.

Robbie's teeth looked as though they were clenched as tightly as her hands. "Lady Beatrice is not a suitable chaperone."

"Don't insult Lady Beatrice."

"I am not insulting Lady Beatrice." His jaw flexed. "She is a charming woman—just a mutton-headed chaperone, especially if she thinks a dress that displays your, um, *charms* for any man to ogle is acceptable attire for a duke's sister. People will think you are a member of the fashionable impure, a high-flyer, a—"

Lizzie was so angry she wanted to spit. She leaned forward—and watched Robbie's eyes drop to the neck of her dress. Someone was definitely doing some ogling.

He jerked his eyes away quickly.

"People are welcome to think what they will," she said. "I am certainly wondering what a certain person was thinking this afternoon in Lord Tynweith's shrubbery."

Robbie's ears turned bright red. "Keep your voice down. Lady Dunlee just looked this way."

"Do not worry. I do not intend to prolong this conversation." Lizzie took a deep breath. She was shaking, she was so incensed. "I do have one question. This afternoon I was wearing a brooch on the quite modest neck of my dress. I appear to have lost it. Did you happen to find it?"

"A brooch?"

"Yes. With my initials."

"No, I didn't find your brooch. Why would you think I did? Ask one of Tynweith's servants."

"I don't believe Tynweith's servants frequent the section of the garden where I lost it, though I may be mistaken. I seem to be mistaken about many things these days." Lizzie stepped back and pasted a false smile on her face. "Now, if you will excuse me, I believe Tynweith's butler is about to announce dinner. I'm sure you'll understand if I prefer a different escort. Present company has a deleterious effect on my appetite."

Lizzie was delighted to see as she left that Robbie's face was almost as red as Lady Beatrice's dress.

Bloody hell. Robbie stabbed his slice of venison as if the beast were still on the hoof. Lizzie was sitting on Tynweith's left and batting her eyelashes at the man while he peered down her dress.

"I had the oddest dream last night, Lord Westbrooke. I blush to tell you what it was. Perhaps you have heard a rumor or two?"

Robbie left the meat on his plate. He'd choke if he tried to consume it now—he was struggling to swallow Lady Felicity's whopper. Was she really going to pretend she had dreamt the entire bedroom incident? Did she think to persuade him that he, too, had been asleep when he'd stared at her pendulous breasts, leapt from his window, and scampered naked over Tynweith's roof?

"No, Lady Felicity, I can't say I've heard a word about your activities, real or imagined."

"No?"

"No." Robbie examined his plate. Nothing was appealing. Sitting next to Lady Felicity had definitely cost him his appetite. "How does one's dream become a rumor, may I ask? Who's to spread the tale of something that happened only in your mind?"

"Well, the activity wasn't confined to my mind, I'm afraid. The dream was so vivid, I thought it was real. I disturbed Lady Elizabeth and a few other guests, I regret to say."

"Oh?"

"Yes." She dropped her voice and leaned close. "Shall I tell you my dream? You played a role in it. It really was quite shocking."

"Um." Robbie eyed her sizable breasts nervously. It was an amazing feat of cloth engineering that they remained even partially covered. Her corset pushed them into such mounds her dress hovered just over her nipples. He could speak with authority on that. After last night's incident, he knew exactly where in the geography of her bosom the small mole now displayed for his inspection appeared. "I really don't believe that is necessary. In fact, I think I would much prefer not knowing." He tried to smile. "I do apologize for disturbing your slumber."

He might not have spoken for all the attention she paid his words.

"But it was so . . . stimulating." Lady Felicity's voice dropped even lower to a throaty whisper. "We were in bed, you and I. Naked. Completely naked. I could see your chest, your muscles . . ." Her eyes stripped him of coat, waistcoat, shirt, and cravat. "Everything." She met his eyes, then moistened her lips, licked them, really, before letting them slide into a slow smile. "It was the most wonderful dream I have ever had." Her eyes focused his mouth. "I don't suppose you had a similar dream?"

"No. Not at all. Definitely not." Could he get up now and leave the room? Claim a sudden case of nausea? It would be true. "Perhaps it was something you ate. Sometimes food or drink ingested right before bed can cause nightmares."

"Nightmares?" She tittered. "Oh, Lord Westbrooke, it wasn't a nightmare, I assure you."

For you. He nodded and prayed for deliverance. It came. Lady Dunlee, his dinner partner on his other side, apparently grew tired of Felicity monopolizing his attention. She tapped him on his arm.

"I haven't had the opportunity to talk to you, Lord Westbrooke." Lady Dunlee displayed her usual tight little smile. "I looked for you this afternoon, but I couldn't find you anywhere."

Because I was attacking Lizzie in the shrubbery. Robbie hoped his ears weren't as red as they felt. "You were looking for me, Lady Dunlee?"

"Of course. My dear daughter, Lady Caroline, missed you dreadfully these last weeks. I understand you traveled to your Scottish estate?"

Fled, more like. "Yes, Lady Dunlee. I did spend the last few weeks in Scotland. But I'm back now and intend to stay in England at least until the end of the Season." *Keeping an eye on Lizzie.* Damn. Lizzie was still flirting with Tynweith. The Duchess of Hartford, on Tynweith's other side, was looking extremely displeased. Her head was tilted politely toward Lord Dunlee, her neighbor on her right, but her eyes were fixed on Tynweith and Lizzie.

At the moment, Robbie was in complete charity with the duchess.

". . . and my dear daughter Caroline is also an extremely accomplished singer. I'm certain you must have heard her perform."

Only when I haven't had adequate warning. "Yes, Lady Dunlee. I believe I have had that, um, pleasure. Ulp."

Lady Dunlee's eyes widened. "Excuse me? What did you say, Lord Westbrooke?"

"Help." Robbie smiled at the woman while he grabbed Lady Felicity's hand under the table and removed it from his pantaloons. "Lady Caroline's talents always help the evening's entertainments."

Lady Dunlee nodded. "Indeed." She nodded down the table to where Tynweith's cousin, their hostess, sat. "You might mention to Mrs. Larson that you would enjoy some music."

"A splendid idea. I just might do that." *When hell freezes over.*

He turned back to Lady Felicity.

"Could you please keep your hands to yourself?" He kept his voice low, but tried to put enough emphasis into his whisper to convey his annoyance.

She pouted at him. "I thought you'd enjoy a distraction. Lady Dunlee does drone on so about her fat daughter."

He couldn't deny the truth of that statement.

"I have not given you permission to touch my person. It is shockingly improper." He must sound like some ancient chaperone, but really, what did a man say to a woman who had accosted him under the dinner table?

"Most men don't complain."

"How many men have you treated in such a manner?"

She shrugged. "I don't keep a tally. It helps pass a boring meal, don't you agree?"

"No, I do not." Anger made his voice rise above a whisper. "I prefer to eat my meal in peace without having to worry someone's fingers are feeling my—"

Thankfully, he noticed the silence before he completed his sentence. He coughed.

"That is *singers.* I mean to say, someone's *singers* are

feeling my lack of attention. I wouldn't want any of our talented ladies to think their musical abilities are not properly displayed and appreciated." He smiled at Lady Dunlee. She nodded carefully back at him. He sighed.

Hell had frozen solid.

"Mrs. Larson, Lady Dunlee tells me her charming daughter has a lovely voice."

Chapter Seven

Charlotte looked down at the food on her plate. The thought of putting even the smallest morsel in her mouth made her stomach rebel. She pushed the items around with her fork while she pretended to listen to Lord Dunlee.

"And then I told Lord Huffington . . ."

She tilted her head in his direction and smiled. Thankfully, the man was content to continue his monologue with only the slightest encouragement from her. He was probably delighted to hear his own voice for a change. Lady Dunlee did not impress Charlotte as a woman who listened to anyone but herself.

Tynweith was still staring down Lady Elizabeth's dress. Who would have guessed the girl was such a lightskirt? Perhaps now that her aunt had retired as her chaperone, her true character was coming out. Lady Beatrice was obviously not inclined to rein her in. The woman was too busy guzzling Tynweith's brandy.

The baron was showing *his* true character as well. Thank God she had refused his oh-so-generous offer to come to her bed. She speared a bite of venison and moved it to the middle of her potatoes *à la Hollandaise*. He had been so persuasive in the garden, acting as if he actually cared for *her*. She snorted. He didn't. He merely wanted a willing female. Anything in skirts would do. He was no different from any other man.

"Excuse me, your grace," Lord Dunlee said. "Did you say something?"

"Oh, no, my lord. A crumb tried to go down the wrong way. It's nothing. Please continue."

The man flushed. "You are certain I'm not boring you? Lady Dunlee does tell me I drone on at times."

Charlotte had a hard time believing that. She glanced at the woman who now had captured Lord Westbrooke's ear. No one could squeeze more than a word or two into any conversation with Lady Dunlee.

"No, really. Do continue."

She looked at Tynweith while Lord Dunlee's words flowed over her again. The baron had finally raised his eyes from Lady Elizabeth's breasts. He was now studying her lips.

He was welcome to her. Really, it was only courteous. If the girl was making the rounds of the house party, the host should have his turn.

She impaled the next bit of venison with such force her fork scraped against her plate. She took a deep breath and put her utensil down.

"Don't care for your food, Duchess?"

"It is fine, Lord Dunlee. I'm just not feeling quite the thing. A little tired, I believe. I think I'll retire to my room after dinner."

"A good plan, especially if Lady Dunlee foists my daughter on the company. She's a good girl, but she can't sing worth a farthing. I plan to sneak out to blow a cloud."

Lord Westbrooke's voice rose then. He was glaring at Felicity. "I prefer to eat my meal in peace without having to worry someone's fingers are feeling my—" He coughed.

Lord Dunlee made an odd noise, as if he were swallowing a laugh. Charlotte swallowed a sigh. Had Lord

Westbrooke never been seated next to Felicity at table before? She watched as the earl tried to extricate himself from his faux pas, cavalierly sacrificing all their ears for his cause.

"I do advise escape," Lord Dunlee whispered as they rose to adjourn to the music room.

"Thank you. I *am* tired." She happened to look down the table and catch Lord Peter's eye. He raised his brows and grinned.

Oh, God. Unless she missed her guess, this musical interlude meant Lord Peter would be visiting her sooner than she had expected. Well, perhaps then he would leave sooner, too.

She allowed Lord Dunlee to escort her to the stairs.

"Sleep well, Duchess."

"Thank you, my lord."

She so wished she were going up only to sleep. Unfortunately, she had unpleasant business to conduct before she could rest.

The thought of Lord Peter sharing her bed was extremely depressing. Last night she'd not looked forward to his arrival, but at least she hadn't dreaded it. To be truthful, she had wondered if the intimate exercises might be more pleasant with a younger man. And Felicity had raved about Lord Peter's bedroom skills. She smiled slightly. She knew enough not to trust Felicity's words completely, but she had hoped there was some truth to them.

There was not. The procreative process was uncomfortable and unpleasant no matter whom one invited into one's bed. While Lord Peter had been quicker than Hartford, he had also insisted on multiple encounters. The time wasted was probably the same.

She entered her room and headed immediately for the drawer with her brandy flask. She took a long swallow. The warmth of the liquid spread throughout her, steadying her nerves.

She hoped the time with Lord Peter had not been

wasted. She prayed his seed would take root. It had to. Time was not something she had a lot of. Hartford's skin had definitely had a gray pallor when she'd left him in London.

She took another drink. And then there was Tynweith. His words from the garden had been whispering in the back of her mind all evening. Was he correct? Did dampness and heat and need increase one's chances of conception? Did those things really prepare the field for a successful plowing?

Ridiculous. The tumultuous feelings she had experienced in the garden could not help. If anything, they must hurt. A quiet, stoic manner was best. It only made sense. Just as a seed planted on a still, calm day had a much better chance of growing than one tossed into a raging storm.

She took one last swallow of brandy as she heard a tap at the door. Lord Peter had arrived. She closed her flask and prepared herself to be stoic.

Tynweith cringed as Lady Caroline reached for a high note. It eluded her grasp for the fourth time.

They'd been doomed the moment Westbrooke had suggested singing. Lady Dunlee's calculating little eyes had lit up and she'd latched on to the earl's arm with an unbreakable grip. She was not to be denied. They must adjourn forthwith to the music room. There was no time for the gentlemen to enjoy their port. A musical feast awaited them.

Now Westbrooke had a prime seat, right in front of the performer and next to her proud mother. Served him right for inflicting this punishment on them all, but why Lady Dunlee thought the earl would be tempted to offer for her daughter after listening to this screeching was beyond Tynweith's comprehension. Any man wishing to preserve his hearing would flee at the first opportunity.

Tynweith grinned. Westbrooke certainly looked anxious to flee. He had consulted his watch several times already. He'd tried to be surreptitious about it, but he'd failed miserably. Lady Dunlee was glaring at him again. Perhaps she would decide he wasn't worthy of her talented child.

Perhaps that was Westbrooke's goal.

To add to his torture, Lady Felicity, who'd rushed to sit on his other side, had started whispering in his ear. The man was having a miserable time.

He was not the only one. Lady Caroline hit another wrong note, and Tynweith's hands twitched. He wanted so badly to cover his ears, but that would not be the mark of a gracious host. Mousy Miss Hyde, Nell's companion, was trying valiantly to accompany the girl on the pianoforte, but was not having much success. She cringed every time Lady Caroline made a mistake—which resulted in her hitting the wrong keys, adding to the cacophony.

Perhaps if he focused on something else, he would not notice the pain. He surveyed the rest of the music room. Most of his guests appeared to be more successful than he at ignoring the caterwauling. Lady Beatrice was talking to Flint, probably trying to persuade the butler to bring her more brandy. The woman must have a hollow leg—she could out drink most men of his acquaintance. Viscount Botton, an aging Lothario at least an inch shorter and easily half Lady Beatrice's weight, flitted around her like the annoying gnat he was. Tynweith frowned. It had really been too bad of him to invite Botton. He knew Lady Beatrice could not abide the man—few people could—but as Nell had said, he had to even out the numbers and Botton was at hand.

Nell sat with Sir George Gaston. It had been understood when she'd agreed to act as his hostess that the baronet would be invited. Larson had had the good sense to die and leave Nell a widow; Gaston was still waiting for his wife to be as accommodating. Lady Gaston was a shrew, prone to a variety of maladies that Gaston's presence exacerbated. She must be happy he frequented Nell's bed instead of hers.

Miss Peterson was in close conversation with Mr. Parker-Roth by the windows. Interesting. He didn't know Miss Peterson well since she was new to London, but Parks hadn't shown any interest in a female since Lady Grace Dawson had jilted him a few years ago.

Mr. Dodsworth was watching Miss Hyde. Poor woman. Perhaps it was a blessing she'd been coerced to play for Lady Caroline—it freed her from Dodsworth's grip. It did look as though she were the man's newest victim. Dodsworth had latched onto her before dinner, taking her aside to show her the wall of horse paintings Tynweith's father had commissioned George Stubbs to produce. Miss Hyde had followed him meekly—she couldn't say boo to a goose—and had stood next to him, her head moving in nervous little bobs, obviously agreeing with everything he said, until Flint had announced dinner.

His other guests, with the exception of Lady Elizabeth who sat at his side, had vanished. Lady Caroline's proud papa, Lord Dunlee, obviously knew his daughter's musical limitations too well. He'd gone out onto the terrace to enjoy a cigar.

Tynweith leaned back in his chair. If he were a good host, he would find a tactful way to bring this musical torture to an end.

He was not a good host. He was far too lazy. He contemplated following Lord Dunlee's example and vanishing. If he couldn't join him for a smoke, he could retreat to his study. He had some paperwork that needed doing.

Right. As if he could concentrate on paperwork.

Charlotte and Lord Peter were missing, too. Charlotte had pleaded fatigue after dinner and retired to her room. Lord Peter had disappeared as soon as

Lady Caroline opened her mouth to begin her auditory onslaught.

Were they in bed together already?

God! Lady Caroline screeched again. He glanced to his right. Lady Elizabeth looked almost as pained as he felt.

He'd expected her to sit next to Westbrooke, but no, she hadn't contested Felicity for that choice location. She had chosen to sit by him. He smiled at her. She smiled back with a funny little expression he presumed she thought looked coy.

Something unusual had definitely occurred between her and the earl. At every other gathering of the *ton*, Lady Elizabeth acted as if Westbrooke were the only male in attendance. Tonight, however, she'd had words with him in the drawing room. Then she'd come looking for Tynweith to take her in to dinner—and she'd flirted with him from soup to sweets.

It should have been a balm for his wounded pride, but he knew it was an act. She'd kept looking at Westbrooke when the man was looking at Lady Felicity. She had not been happy to see Felicity's head so close to the earl's. Tynweith chuckled. She would have been even less happy had she known where Felicity's hands were. Tynweith had had the dubious pleasure of sitting next to the girl at other dinner parties. He knew exactly where her fingers liked to roam.

"What is so humorous, Lord Tynweith?"

"Nothing appropriate for your ears, Lady Elizabeth." He leered at her. "Pardon me for entertaining such . . . private thoughts in your presence." He dropped his voice lower. "Though your presence, of course, provokes all manner of private thoughts."

She blushed and smiled uncertainly back at him, clearly uncomfortable. He almost laughed again.

It might be amusing to play with her. She had spent three Seasons in London, but she was still as naïve as the greenest debutante.

Was she finally going to do something to provoke Westbrooke?

Definitely amusing.

Perhaps they could help each other. He'd noticed at dinner Charlotte had not cared for the way Lady Elizabeth had flirted with him. Was *she* jealous? He smiled. He would love to make Charlotte jealous.

Of course, now she was upstairs, spreading her legs for Lord Peter.

Lady Caroline was drawing to a close, thank God. Ah, no. A pause only. He closed his eyes, trying to project the image of a man deep in musical admiration.

He should hate Charlotte, the little bitch. She was as bad as Felicity, chasing after titles or prestige or family connections.

But he couldn't hate her. He wanted her too much.

It was her contrasts that drew him. She was so cold-blooded and determined—and so terrified of passion. But he knew she was passionate—he had felt her response in the garden. It was a small flame now, flickering, close to dying, but he would blow on it and turn it to a raging fire. He grinned. Yes, he would love to blow on a number of things relating to the Duchess of Hartford. Blow and lick and suck and . . .

He clasped his hands over a revealing section of his pantaloons.

Could he use Lady Elizabeth to get into Charlotte's bed?

He looked at the girl. She batted her eyelashes at him. Perhaps. And if Charlotte still refused? Lady Elizabeth had fine blue eyes. They were almost the same shade as Charlotte's.

He could do worse. He needed a wife. If Lady Elizabeth had eliminated Westbrooke as a possible husband, she might be willing to consider him. She'd already turned down more attractive alternatives. The Duke of Easton, the Marquis of Benningly, the Earl of

Calder. Her list of rejected suitors sounded like a reading of Debrett's *Peerage*.

He wasn't getting any younger. He did not want to be an octogenarian like Hartford, still scrambling for an heir.

"Are you enjoying Lady Caroline's fine singing, Lady Elizabeth? We are so fortunate Lord Westbrooke brought her talents to our attention."

Lady Elizabeth snorted. "I don't know what possessed Robbie. He usually shows more sense."

She really was rather pretty. Slim with lovely small breasts. He eyed her dress. Very lovely breasts. She didn't usually display them so publicly.

She was much too tall, of course, but still, once the candles were snuffed, he could imagine she were Charlotte. He had done it often enough with whores. And she was welcome to picture Westbrooke in his place, if she liked.

The two of them, swiving imaginary lovers. Well, it was probably quite a common pastime in the *ton*. Once he had his heir, he'd be done with her, and they could go their separate ways. She'd be welcome to invite anyone she cared to into her bed then.

He fingered the brooch he'd dropped into his pocket right before he'd come down for dinner.

Then again, perhaps she was not as naïve as he thought. She had been in the secret bower with someone. Unlikely they'd only been discussing the weather.

Whom had she been with? Westbrooke was the obvious guess, but if it had been he, surely he would have offered for her, especially after the odd occurrence last night in her bedroom. And if not Westbrooke, then who? Did everyone but he have a willing bed partner?

Perhaps it was time to solve this particular puzzle.

"Would you care to see my conservatory, Lady Elizabeth?"

* * *

Lizzie stepped out of the music room with Lord Tyn-weith. Botheration! Robbie had not seen her leave. He was trapped between Lady Felicity and Lady Dunlee at the front of the room, his back to her.

"I don't show many people this particular room, you know."

"No?" Would Robbie even care she was gone? He hadn't noticed her flirting with Tynweith at dinner. He'd been too busy entertaining Lady Felicity. Lizzie's fingers had itched to take the girl's knowing expression and smash it into a nice big bowl of turtle soup. And then the idiot man had condemned them all to listen to Lady Caroline sing. He knew the girl had a terrible voice. She'd heard him liken it to a cat's in heat.

"No. Only *special* guests."

"Oh." There was an odd note in Tynweith's voice. She finally looked at him closely. There was an odd expression on his face as well. Almost a wolfish look.

Ridiculous. The man was close to forty years old. How dangerous could he be? Frankly, she had chosen to flirt with him rather than Lord Peter because of his advanced years.

His mouth slid into a smirk; his eyes examined her chest.

Perhaps his years were not quite advanced enough. Now that she considered the issue, Hartford had married Lady Charlotte when he was twice Tynweith's age.

"Actually, Lord Tynweith, I find I'm a bit fatigued."

"Really, Lady Elizabeth? Then the restful environment of my conservatory is just what you need."

"I don't think. . . ."

He had taken her hand and placed it on his arm. She felt muscle under her fingers.

He wouldn't attack a guest, surely? No, the thought was absurd. He was just trying to be outrageous. His house parties had a reputation for being a little fast. A little dangerous. For affording many opportunities for romantic trysts. It was one of the reasons she had accepted the invitation. She'd hoped to have a tryst or two with Robbie.

She had definitely not considered trysting with Lord Tynweith or any other gentleman.

She took a steadying breath. She had decided to be daring, hadn't she? Daring was not hiding in her room. She sent a sidelong glance at her host. If he turned slightly amorous, well, she needed experience.

Perhaps. He *was* almost forty years old. His hair was beginning to thin, he had lines around his mouth and eyes, and his waistline was expanding.

"Here we are."

He guided her across the threshold and closed the large wooden door behind them.

"Is that wise, Lord Tynweith?"

"Nervous, Lady Elizabeth?"

"No, of course not. I merely thought it would be more proper to keep the door open or at least ajar."

He grinned at her. He was definitely looking wolfish.

"Ah, but then this is not a terribly proper room."

"I see." She tried to keep her voice calm.

She examined her surroundings. Two candles in wall sconces lit the area—a landing, really—where they stood. There was not a great deal of space, just enough for a stone bench and two small tables. A few steps led down into a very leafy room. Occasional lanterns provided some light—and created many pockets of darkness. The walls were mostly glass—she could see the moon and the shadowy bulk of trees outside. She drew in a deep breath and smelled dirt and flowers and greenery.

"I don't see anything especially improper." She hoped her voice sounded confident. It was a little unnerving, being in this quiet, shadowy room with a man who had a reputation for giving parties that skated on the edge of propriety. And he definitely had some very improper bushes on his estate.

"No? Let me show you." He took her hand. She

considered protesting, but objecting now seemed a trifle missish. She should have refused to leave the music room with him. She should have—no. She was no longer a debutante. She was twenty years old. Experienced. Daring.

And the longer she stayed away from the music room, the greater the odds Robbie would notice.

She allowed her host to guide her down the stairs. The moment her foot cleared the last step, however, she moved away to examine a potted tree with broad, waxy looking leaves.

"Meg would love this room. Mr. Parker-Roth would, too. Has he seen it?"

Tynweith stood very close behind her. He was almost touching her. She could hear him breathing.

He was making her extremely apprehensive.

She reminded herself again she had decided to be daring. She reminded herself she was looking for experience.

She reminded herself he was old.

"I believe I said I invited only special guests to tour the conservatory. 'Special' does not include men."

"I see. *That* kind of special." She felt his breath on her neck. She shivered and pushed the leaves she was examining aside, slipping around the tree.

"Indeed." He followed her. She moved behind a bush with pink flowers. A vine tangled in her hair. She brushed it aside. Her heart was pounding, and her palms were beginning to perspire.

Perhaps she did not want experience. She could be daring another day. With another man. With Robbie. Daring with Robbie was much safer.

"I'm quite certain I'm not that kind of special, either."

"No? Perhaps we should see." He stepped around the bush and drew his fingertip across her collarbone. "This is a lovely dress, my dear. Much more enticing than your usual style."

"Thank you. I think." She put a bushy, needle-leafed plant between them. He was extremely agile for an older man. "Lord Tynweith, I believe you are operating under a misapprehension."

He reached for her again, but she dodged his hand.

"It was most certainly an error in judgment on my part to accompany you from the music room. Please accept my apologies. I'll just retire to my chamber now. Alone."

He smiled, shaking his head. "You're very good. If I didn't know better, I'd think you were a blushing little virgin."

"I *am* a blushing little virgin." She backed up. He followed her. "Well, not little, precisely." Lady Felicity's chest flashed into her mind. All right, so she was little in some areas. "But blushing certainly. And a virgin, most definitely."

"I thought Lord Westbrooke visited your bed last night."

She tripped on a root. He reached out to steady her, but she avoided his hand.

"Only in a manner of speaking."

"Really? Now I wonder what that means."

Lizzie had no desire to explain further. "I hate to be rude, but it is really none of your concern, my lord."

"True. Then let us not discuss Westbrooke. I agree he is a boring topic. Let's discuss your behavior at dinner instead. I was flattered to have so much of your attention."

"Uh, yes." Could she manage to reach the door and get out of this plant-infested purgatory? It would help if she could turn around, but she did not want to present Tynweith with her back. Better to keep an eye on him.

Or should she stand her ground and push past him? Could she cajole him into letting her go? Flirt with him even? She had seen many young ladies wrap men around their little fingers with skillful flirting and well-placed flattery.

No. Definitely no flirting. Her ill-advised attempt at that activity had landed her in her current predicament. And she felt no desire to try on Tynweith any of the cajoling tricks she'd used with Robbie the night before. Robbie was . . . comfortable. Safe. Oh, it was too hard to figure out with this stranger stalking her. She felt excitement and desire with Robbie, not nervousness or fear.

She was more than a little nervous at the moment.

Her posterior encountered a sturdy branch and she changed course, veering to the right. Tynweith stayed with her. He could easily close the gap between them, but he apparently preferred to taunt her.

Could she explain that her behavior had been designed solely to make Robbie jealous? It seemed exceedingly rude to say so.

"And then when you agreed to accompany me from the music room—well, you raised hopes I had never thought to entertain."

"Oh." She felt terrible now. She had not considered his feelings at all when she'd decided on this course of action. "I do apologize." She had to explain, no matter how embarrassing it was. She took another step backward.

She stopped. Something was poking her in the small of her back. Something pointed. A dagger?

At least Tynweith had stopped also. He wasn't going to force her to impale herself on the thing. She looked at him more closely. It was hard to see in the shadowy light, but she'd swear he had a gleam of mischief in his eyes.

She reached around behind her. The thing was rounded at the tip. She ran her hand up its length. It was smooth, and too wide to be a dagger or sword. A cylinder of some kind, with two ball-like objects beneath, attached to a statue.

"All right. I give up." Lizzie was no longer nervous. Annoyance was now her predominant emotion. Tynweith looked as if he would burst if he held his mirth in any longer. "I was never good at guessing games. What is it?"

"Look."

"You won't attack me if I turn my back on you, will you?"

"Of course not."

Lizzie hesitated. Tynweith folded his arms and lifted an eyebrow. He did not look threatening any longer.

She turned—and gasped.

She had backed into the very swollen male organ of a naked statue.

Where the hell was Lizzie?

Robbie stood in Tynweith's corridor and tried not to look like he wanted to murder someone, preferably Tynweith. Lizzie must have grown tired and gone up to bed.

Listening to Lady Caroline sing certainly was tiring.

So where the hell was Tynweith? The man was their host, damn it. He should not vanish in the middle of his guest's performance.

Robbie glanced over his shoulder and moved farther down the corridor. He had only escaped the ladies' clutches by hinting he had some business of a very personal nature to attend to. If they saw him loitering in the hall, they would become suspicious.

"Thank you, Lord Tynweith. I will definitely consider your proposal."

Proposal?! That was Lizzie's voice. She should not be considering any proposals from a rake of Tynweith's stamp. Where *was* she?

He hurried toward her voice. She must be close by. She had not been shouting. He had heard her quite clearly. Too clearly. Tynweith must still be with her. He would enjoy explaining to the man, with his fists if necessary, that Lizzie was not available for dalliance.

He turned a corner. There she was, standing far too close to Tynweith. The blackguard was holding her hand.

"Lizzie."

She startled and turned to him. Damned if she didn't blush. She looked guilty. He narrowed his gaze. Were there leaves in her hair?

What the bloody hell had she been doing with Tynweith?

He looked at the man. Tynweith lifted an eyebrow and smiled slightly. Self-satisfied devil. He would kill him right where he stood. Immediately. The man did not merit a challenge.

"Ah, Westbrooke. I see you survived your musical experience."

"You are holding Lady Elizabeth's hand."

Tynweith made a show of looking down. "Why, so I am. Do you object, Lady Elizabeth?"

Lizzie's eyes darted to Robbie and back to her hand. She flushed.

"No, Lord Tynweith. I do not object." Her voice got a little louder. "Lord Westbrooke apparently believes he is my brother, the way he meddles in my affairs."

Robbie saw a red haze. He wondered if his jaw might shatter, his teeth were clenched so tightly. "I do not think I am your brother."

Lizzie shrugged. "Chaperone, then."

"You need a chaperone. Lady Beatrice is totally in-competent for the task as evidenced by your presence here, in this shadowy corridor with *him*."

"Don't insult Lord Tynweith. He is our host—our generous, attentive host."

"Generous? Attentive? What kind of attentive?" In two seconds—less—he was going to plant his fist in

Tynweith's face. He'd so enjoy seeing that self-satisfied smirk erupt in blood.

"Lord Westbrooke? Are you there?"

Damn. Lady Felicity had tracked him down. Didn't she believe in giving a man a few minutes of privacy to visit the necessary? She sounded close. He glanced over his shoulder. She wasn't in sight yet.

"Perhaps you two would like a moment to discuss your differences?" Tynweith smiled. "I will be happy to deal with Lady Felicity."

Perhaps Tynweith wasn't such a bad fellow after all—though if he had harmed one hair on Lizzie's head, he would pay for it.

"Splendid. Come on, Lizzie."

Lizzie had turned very red. "I really don't think—"

"Lord Westbrooke?" Felicity's voice echoed down the corridor.

"I believe Lady Felicity is almost upon us." Tynweith gestured toward the door behind him. "You really have no time to waste."

"Right." Robbie was not risking another encounter with Felicity. He grabbed Lizzie's arm.

"Let me go!"

"Will you keep your voice down? Do you *want* Felicity to find us?"

"Perhaps I do. Perhaps I prefer Lady Felicity's company to yours."

"Perhaps you are lying. You can't stand Lady Felicity."

"Oh, so now you are telling me what I think?"

"Lord Westbrooke, where are you?"

Robbie looked over his shoulder again. Felicity must be just around the corner. In a second, she'd be on them.

"You may hide in the conservatory." Lizzie crossed her arms. "I am staying with Lord Tynweith."

"For God's sake—"

"Lady Elizabeth"—Tynweith interrupted Robbie—
"might you be losing sight of your, um, goals here?"

Lizzie turned red. "I can't take him in *there*." She
tilted her head at the conservatory door.

"And why not?" Suspicion and anger surged in
Robbie again. "You were in there with Tynweith."

"Westbrooke, you've run out of time."

Robbie looked back again. Damn. He saw Felicity's
slipper. In less than a second, the rest of her would
follow and he'd be well and truly caught.

He yanked Lizzie into the conservatory, shutting
the door on Tynweith's chuckle.

What would Robbie say if he saw Tynweith's statue?

"Let's sit here to talk." Lizzie pointed to the stone
bench on the landing.

"Is that where you sat with Tynweith?"

Lizzie felt her cheeks flush.

"I didn't think so. You were very hesitant to let me
in here. I want to know why." Robbie started for the
steps. Lizzie grabbed his arm.

"I'm certain you'd be more comfortable on the
bench."

"Lizzie, get it into your head that I am not sitting on
that blasted bench. Why don't you just show me what
has you turning five shades of red? I'm going to find
it anyway."

No. She could not show him Tynweith's obscene
statue. She would die of mortification.

"Am I red? It must be the heat." She fanned herself
with her free hand. "It's cooler up here. Come, sit on
the bench."

"No." He peeled her fingers off his sleeve and de-
scended the stairs.

Lizzie followed him. Could she stop him if she
grabbed hold of his coattails or would he just drag her
along behind him?

"There really is nothing of interest here, Robbie. Meg or Mr. Parker-Roth might enjoy spending some time studying the vegetation, but I never thought you had a keen interest in botany."

"I don't." He stopped and picked a leaf out of her hair. "And I didn't think you did, either. Apparently, I was mistaken." He let the leaf flutter to the ground and turned away. Thank God he was headed in the opposite direction from the embarrassing statue.

"What were you talking to Tynweith about?"

"Oh, nothing." Once she had convinced the baron that she did not want to engage in any amorous activities, he had proved quite rational. He'd proposed various plans to make their respective love interests jealous. Not that she approved of Lord Tynweith trying to make another man's wife jealous, of course. And some of his notions were rather distasteful. And risky. If they didn't prod Robbie to offer for her, she might well find herself compelled to marry Tynweith. She shuddered. Robbie turned back to face her.

"What's the matter?"

"Nothing." She was certainly not going to tell Robbie a word of her conversation with their host. "I have a chill."

"How can you have a chill? You just said you were over warm."

"Well, I was chilled just then." She knew how to end this conversation. "It's a female matter."

"Oh." Robbie flushed. "I see. Well." He clasped his hands behind his back and frowned. "You still haven't told me what you were talking to Tynweith about."

"He merely wished to return my brooch. He found it in the garden this afternoon."

"Oh? Where in the garden?"

"Where do you think?" How could the man mention the garden in that tone, as if he were accusing her of something? He was the one who had taken outrageous liberties without honorable intentions.

Maybe she didn't want to make him jealous. Maybe she would just strangle him with a handy vine. And now the man was glowering at her.

"You've been busy today, haven't you? Does James know you make a habit of entertaining men in the bushes?"

"What?!" God give her strength, she *was* going to murder him. "You are the only man I've visited the shrubbery with, much to my chagrin."

Robbie snorted. "Come, Lizzie, I am not a complete slowtop. You had leaves in your hair just now. You came to this very private location with our host—or are you telling me Tynweith forced you?"

"Of course not, but that doesn't mean—"

"Lizzie, if Tynweith just wished to return your brooch, he would have done so in the music room. Putting his hand in his pocket does not require this privacy. Putting his hand elsewhere, well . . ."

"Stop it!" She had to clasp her own hands together to keep from slapping him.

"But what I can't understand is why you didn't want to let me come in here. Tynweith is gone. What are you hiding?"

"I'm not hiding anything." Lizzie took a step toward the door. "Surely Lady Felicity has departed. I believe I will go up to bed."

"Just a minute. What's over here?" Robbie wandered down a path next to a large fern.

"Nothing." Lizzie followed him. She was safe. The offending statue was on the other side of the conservatory. "Will you come along? You are as bad as a terrier in search of a badger hole."

"I am not—oh."

"What?"

Lizzie pushed up next to Robbie.

"Oh, my."

Tynweith had more than one unusual statue in his conservatory.

Chapter Eight

"What are they doing?"

"Nothing." Robbie grabbed Lizzie's arm and started to turn her away. She resisted.

"They are obviously doing *something*." She studied the sculpture. The man might be the twin of the fellow she had backed into across the way. He had his hands on a woman's shoulders and his face was contorted in what looked to be pain. No wonder. The woman, crouched at his feet, had her mouth around the tip of his poor swollen, um . . .

"Is she *biting* him?"

"No, she is not biting him."

Robbie sounded very odd, as if he were strangling. Lizzie looked up at him. His cheeks were flushed. His ears were red. He would not meet her eye.

"How do you know? He looks like he's in pain."

"He is not in pain."

"Are you certain?" Lizzie examined the artwork again.

"For God's sake, Lizzie, it's only a statue. A tasteless, obscene statue. Tynweith should be drawn and quartered for exposing you to it."

"He didn't expose me to this one." The man did

have a very odd expression. She'd never seen anything like it. If it wasn't pain, what was it?

Robbie rubbed his forehead. "There are others?"

"At least one other. That's why I didn't want you to come in here. But this statue is much more interesting than the one I saw with Tynweith."

"It is *not* interesting."

"I think it is. I have never encountered an artwork like it." Lizzie thought about her tour of the garden that afternoon. "Hmm. On second thought, perhaps I have. Do you suppose Tynweith's gardener uses these statues as inspiration? I have to say, stone is a much better medium than vegetation."

"Lizzie!" Robbie took her firmly by the shoulders and turned her toward the main path. "We are leaving right now. I am sorry I didn't take your hint immediately and stay by the door. Why didn't you just tell me it was unwise to venture into the foliage?"

"I doubt you would have listened. You were quite determined, if you will recall."

Lizzie's thoughts strayed to their other excursion into the leafage. She had thoroughly enjoyed those activities—before the unpleasant ending, of course.

She slowed her steps.

Meg had told her to avoid any tête-à-têtes with Robbie, but she had not been given a choice this time. And after her experience with Tynweith, she doubted she could convince anyone she was interested in another man.

Lady Beatrice's plan was more appealing.

Could she cause Robbie to become addicted to her by giving him some kisses, some cuddling? This was a perfect location to engage in those activities. Once he was suitably addicted, he would marry her, and once the knot was tied, he would realize he belonged with her. He would be happy. It was just a matter of getting that thought through his thick skull.

So, where could she persuade him to repeat his

actions of the afternoon? Not on the landing—that would be too exposed if Tynweith should happen to come back. However, there were a variety of lovely shadowy places at hand, little nooks framed by potted trees and draped in flowering vines. Surely not all of them were occupied by inappropriate artwork.

"Look at that lovely flower, Robbie."

"I am not interested in flowers."

Yes, it was fortunate she had come to the conservatory with Tynweith. There was something about being presented with a real flesh and blood man in an isolated location that clarified one's thinking. The thought of being held against Tynweith's body, of kissing him—she shivered. Repulsive.

"Are you cold again? Perhaps you should consult a physician." Robbie turned red again. "I've never heard of, um, female complaints causing so many temperature changes. Are you quite certain you don't have a fever?"

"I do not have a fever." She stopped. Yes, being presented with a flesh and blood man in an isolated location definitely clarified one's thinking. She knew exactly what she wished to do with this particular specimen, and she'd found the perfect spot in which to do it. She tugged him in the desired direction.

"How do you know anything about female complaints? You don't have any sisters."

Embarrassment must have clouded his thinking. He went with her without a protest.

Tynweith was of the opinion Robbie *was* strongly attracted to her, and Tynweith was a male, after all. He should have a better understanding than any female of the mysterious workings of Robbie's mind. But then why hadn't Robbie offered for her? He'd had the perfect opportunity—several perfect opportunities— to do so. Tynweith had had no satisfactory answer to that question.

She would give Robbie another opportunity now

to offer for her—or at least to become more addicted to her.

"I don't know anything. It just stands to reason. If all females were prone to such temperature changes, they'd be donning and shedding their shawls constantly."

"Hmm." This was definitely the perfect spot for giving Robbie a teasing taste. And for taking a taste herself. A large broad-leaved plant shielded them from prying eyes. But how should she initiate the activity? She couldn't very well fall against him as she had this afternoon.

"I suppose you have a point. Perhaps you should feel my forehead. Is it unnaturally warm?"

He touched her with the back of his hand. She put her hands on his lapels. His body was so hard, so different from hers. She ran her fingers over the cloth. It was very much in the way. She wished she had his skin under her fingers instead. The cloth was rough; his skin had been warm and smooth. Wonderful. She drew in a deep breath. His musky, spicy scent mixed with the smell of flowers, leaves, and earth.

"No." Robbie's voice was slightly husky. "You feel quite cool to the touch."

"That's odd. I feel very hot. Perhaps you should feel my cheeks, too."

His hand moved down to cup her jaw, his thumb stroking over her skin.

She turned her head to brush her lips over his palm. She set her fingers to work on his waistcoat buttons.

"You are not overly warm." His voice was definitely husky.

"Are you certain? I think my temperature must be rising."

She spread his waistcoat open and ran her hands over his shirt. This was better. Not as good as skin, but better than the armor of his waistcoat. She could feel the strong beat of his heart, the heat of his body.

An odd, intense light flickered in his eyes. She

reached up to touch his lips, to trace their outline. He kissed her fingers.

She held her breath. She didn't want to startle him, to wake him from this fragile, seductive web she was trying to spin. *Come closer. Kiss me like you did in the garden.*

His head dipped toward her.

Closer. She tilted her face up, waiting. . . .

His mouth brushed lightly over her eyes.

"Mmm." She wanted to grab his head and hold it still, but she kept her hands flat on his chest and waited. He kissed her cheekbone, her eyebrow, her jaw.

Her lips felt swollen, throbbing. She needed to feel his mouth on them. She was ready to beg, but she stayed still. *Patience.* If she pressed him, she knew he would wake to the impropriety of their activity. He would push her away, rant at her, drag her back to Lady Beatrice.

She did not want to leave the conservatory until he was well and truly addicted.

His hands were moving. Down to her hips, over her seat, feeling her outline. More than her lips throbbed now. She felt hot and damp between her legs; her breasts ached; her nipples tightened. Still she stood quietly, letting him explore at his own pace.

His hands slid up her sides, over her back, to her neck. They cradled her jaw again.

She opened her mouth slightly, touching the tip of her tongue to her aching lips.

"Are you still warm?" His voice was a rough whisper.

"Yes." She whispered back. "Can't you feel me? I am very, very hot." She let her hands wander over his chest. He did not draw away. She slid them around to his back, down to his hips, watching his face. The odd light in his eyes glowed brighter. She stroked his buttocks and felt his muscles move under her fingers.

She felt a hard ridge against her belly, too, but she was careful not to rub against it. Poor man. He was swollen again. She did not want to hurt him. At least he did not act as if he were in pain. She smiled up at him.

"I'm getting hotter. And you? Are you feeling slightly warm?"

He grunted. Words appeared to have deserted him. No matter. His tongue was exceedingly eloquent without uttering a syllable. It swept through her mouth, stroking and teasing, filling her and then withdrawing.

Her knees melted, and she sagged against him. She hoped she didn't hurt his swollen part, but she couldn't help herself. He didn't flinch—that was good. She tilted her head back farther, resting against his chest, and opened her mouth wide to his invasion.

He shifted her so her front was no longer pressed against his body. One arm supported her, cradling her against his chest, while his free hand slid from her jaw, over her throat, to the neck of her dress. It hovered there, just grazing her bodice, teasing her. She arched her back, thrusting her breasts higher. Her nipples ached.

"Impatient, love?" The words whispered over her cheek.

"Yes," she breathed. "Please. I need . . ."

"This?" His fingers slipped under the fabric.

She wanted to cry with relief. She was very glad she had not bothered with a fichu.

"Yes. Oh, yes."

His hand cupped her breast, lifted it, stroked it. Then his finger circled her nipple—around and around without touching the aching center. His mouth left hers and moved to her forehead.

She was panting. Moaning.

"Please."

He chuckled. "Please what?"

"Please . . . touch . . ."

He did. He rolled the hard little nub between his thumb and forefinger.

"Oh!"

She was going mad. The ache between her legs was unbearable. She was hot and wet and . . . empty. She needed something, but she didn't know what.

Did Robbie know? Could he give it to her?

"Robbie." She tried to press herself against him, but he would not let her move. "Robbie, please."

"*Are* you feverish, love? Now you do feel hot, very hot. I think I might be able to help."

He bent his head and licked her nipple. Lud, it felt so good. And then he took her into his mouth and sucked.

"Robbie!" She twisted her hips. Why Robbie's mouth on her breast would make the emptiness between her legs throb was a mystery, but it did.

"Robbie . . ."

"Shh, love." He slid his hand down and cupped her ache through her skirts. "Is this what you need?"

"Yes." She closed her eyes. His touch felt wonderful, but . . . She arched her back, pressing against his hand. She needed something more, something just beyond her grasp. "Robbie, I . . . you . . . please."

His fingers moved, found the center of her need, and she shattered.

"Robbie!"

He captured her wail in his mouth.

Robbie had never seen a more beautiful sight. Lizzie was limp in his arms, her cheeks flushed, her eyes dazed. He held her close, stroking her hair, and grinned.

God, he felt wonderful.

He had never brought a woman to satisfaction before.

He wanted to do it again. He wanted to feel Lizzie's passion again, see her overcome with need, hear her moan with desire and gasp her release. He wanted to carry her up to his room, strip off her clothes, kiss every inch of her beautiful body, and then slide his length deep inside her.

It would be heaven.

Could he do it? Perhaps. He felt he could. If only there was a soft bed nearby. It was too far to go to his room. He would never last. He looked around. The ground was covered with sharp stones and dead leaves. There was no space here. Where else? The bench by the door was too hard. Too exposed. What if Tynweith came back? He knew they were here. He might check to see what was taking them so long. Or Felicity. She might find her way into the conservatory.

God, what if she walked in on them? What if she found him between Lizzie's white thighs, just as Mac-Duff had. . . .

Anxiety spiraled through him. His breath got short, his palms grew damp, his stomach roiled—and a very important part of him shrank. He closed his eyes, resting his forehead against Lizzie's hair. Damn it to hell. He was small and limp. Useless.

He swallowed, squeezing his eyes tightly together, clenching his jaw. He sniffed. Bloody hell. He would not cry. He had not cried for years, not since he'd realized his problem was not an aberration but a curse. He'd gotten used to the situation, God damn it.

It had never bothered him so much.

It should be different with Lizzie. He cared for her. He *loved* her.

Damn, damn, damn.

Anger made his voice sharp.

"Your gown is indecent."

"What?" Lizzie blinked up at him.

"Your gown. Look at it." He held her away from him. "Your breasts are exposed."

Her lovely white breasts glowed in the subdued light of the conservatory like rare flowers. Lizzie flushed and struggled to pull her bodice back up where it belonged.

"They were adequately covered before you got your hands on them." Her cheeks grew redder. She ducked her head and stepped away from him. "That is, I mean my dress was—is—perfectly acceptable. Definitely within the bounds of propriety."

"Ha!"

She stopped fussing with her clothing and glared at him.

"Don't take that tone with me, Lord Westbrooke. My gown is less revealing than most."

He didn't care about most gowns—he cared about this gown. He cared about these breasts and who might be looking at them.

"I saw Tynweith staring down your dress all through dinner."

"You did not! You were too busy flirting with Lady Felicity to notice anything."

"Don't be a ninnyhammer. And it was hard not to notice our host. He was just about drooling. It was quite the spectacle."

Lizzie exhaled a short breath. Her brows met above her nose, a deep furrow between them.

"You are a mutton-headed, jingle-brained nodcock." She finished with her bodice and tried to put her hair back in order. Somehow it had become severely disarranged.

"That is hardly helping. You look thoroughly compromised."

That earned him another hard look.

"Perhaps because I *am* thoroughly compromised. And I assume you are still not proposing?"

It was his turn to flush.

"Lizzie . . ."

"Lizzie what? Lizzie, would you make me the happiest of men and give me your hand in marriage?"

She paused, hands on hips, one brow raised.

"Uh, Lizzie . . ."

"No, of course not. It's Lizzie, thank you for the entertaining interlude. We will have to do it again the next time we find ourselves in some isolated flora." She poked him in the chest. "Well, don't count on it, Lord Westbrooke. I am finished frolicking with you in the foliage."

He heard the pain in her voice. He had never wanted to hurt her. He caught her hand, wrapped it in his.

"Lizzie . . ." He sighed. What could he say?

Her expression softened. "Is it that you prefer men, Robbie? Is that the problem?"

"God, no!" He dropped her hand as if it were a hot stone, stepping back so quickly he almost slipped on a loose pebble. She couldn't think—no, it was too revolting. He wanted to cast up his accounts right there on the nearest potted plant. Not that he was surprised she knew of such things—her cousin had had some very odd proclivities—but that she could imagine *he* felt that way—

God, he *would* be sick.

"You don't have to be embarrassed to tell me, Robbie. I'll keep your confidence. I just would like to know—"

"Lizzie." He couldn't bear to hear her say more. "No. Believe me, I am most certainly not attracted to men."

"I would not think less of you if you were."

"Well, I am not. Definitely. Without a doubt. Not the slightest. Wherever did you get such a notion?"

"Lord Tynweith suggested it as a possibility." She shrugged. "It made sense. I've never seen your name linked with a lady's in any of the London gossip columns, nor have I heard any rumors of a mistress."

"My God!" He hadn't considered this. If Tynweith thought it possible, how many others of the *ton* also wondered? Collins had mentioned it as well. Was everyone speculating, watching him? "You were discussing this with Tynweith? Are you mad?"

"No. I just . . ." She looked down at her hands. He could barely hear her, she spoke so softly. "I guess I only hoped. . . ." She paused, then looked back up, though her eyes only went as high as his chin. "So it is just that you are not attracted to *me*."

"No!" He hated hearing her voice waver with suppressed tears, hated the way her eyes shied away from his. "Surely our recent activities—and what happened in Tynweith's garden—prove I *am* attracted to you." He rubbed his forehead. How could he make her believe him? He could not tell her the truth. "It's just . . . complicated."

"So, explain. I have no pressing engagements—ha! Definitely no engagement." She sniffed, bit her lip, then frowned, crossing her arms under her breasts. "I think I merit an explanation, don't you?"

"Yes." She did deserve that. He had taken shocking advantage of her. It was wrong. He had to stop.

But he didn't want to stop. He never wanted to stop. How could he give her up now that he had tasted her passion?

He had to find a way. It was the only honorable course. She needed a real man, a man who could love her properly, who could fill her and give her children. She would not be happy with less. Even if she thought she wanted him, she would soon realize her mistake. She would become frustrated and bitter. He could not bear that.

"I'm waiting."

Perhaps he could explain without telling her everything.

"The problem, Lizzie, is that I can't marry anyone."

"What do you mean, you can't marry anyone? You don't have a secret wife somewhere do you, like Prinny's Mrs. Fitzherbert?"

"Of course not."

"Then I fail to see the problem. You *have* to marry. You're the earl. You have to produce an heir."

"No, I don't. I have an heir—my cousin."

"Robbie, Sarah is your only cousin."

"My only first cousin, but not my only cousin. You've forgotten Theobald."

Lizzie gaped at him, then snorted. "That idiot? It's whispered his wet nurse dropped him on his head. Surely you don't mean to turn over your estates to him?"

The thought did not make him happy, but there was no alternative.

"He's not that bad."

"Well, no, perhaps not *that* bad, but certainly bad enough. Did you know he is obsessed with snuff boxes? He has eight thousand, five hundred and forty-three in his London lodgings, and he would be delighted to show you each one."

Robbie chuckled. He would never have thought he'd find anything amusing in this conversation, but the image of Lizzie listening to Theobald hold forth about his snuff boxes was humorous. "Surely you have not taken the tour?"

"Of course not. It would be completely improper for an unmarried lady to visit a gentleman's lodgings. He told me about them at one of Easthaven's balls. *All* about them. I was actually happy to be rescued by Simple Symington, if you can believe it. It was the first time I was ever happy to see the fat old top."

"Perhaps Theobald's son will be better."

"He'll never have a son. Any woman foolish enough to marry him would die of boredom before she ever made it to her marriage bed. The butler would find her stiff among the snuff boxes, while Theobold, oblivious, described box one thousand four hundred and seventy-two."

Robbie smiled. "I see you do not care for my cousin."

"No one does, Robbie. You know it. You cannot leave the continuation of the Hamilton line to him."

"I haven't any choice, Lizzie. What I've been trying to tell you is that I can't marry—I have no need to marry—because I cannot beget children."

Lady Felicity stood in the shadows behind a bank of potted trees, watching Lord Westbrooke and Lady Elizabeth leave the conservatory. Westbrooke's waistcoat was unbuttoned; the neck of Lady Elizabeth's dress was crooked and her hair was falling down her back. They had obviously been doing more than admiring Tynweith's plants.

They were not behaving as lovers, however. They were barely touching, not looking at each other, not talking.

Interesting.

Had the experience been so unpleasant? Or so wildly erotic they were both stupefied?

She hoped the latter. If she had to have Westbrooke's heir, she'd like the planting to be some of the best carnal play she'd ever experienced. And she had experienced a lot—as much as she could and still be a virgin. Since she was exceedingly creative, that covered a lot of territory.

But if she wished to be the next Countess of Westbrooke—and she definitely did—she would have to deal with Lady Elizabeth. She did not care for competition.

Felicity frowned. *Was* Lady Elizabeth competition? She should be. She was unmarried and the sister of a duke who also happened to be the earl's good friend. And Lady Elizabeth and Westbrooke were obviously extremely friendly as well. Yet there was no engagement announcement. Why not?

If Lady Elizabeth wished to be the next countess, she needed to play her cards with more finesse. She needed to get Westbrooke to misbehave before witnesses if he were reluctant to come up to scratch.

Felicity stepped from behind the leafage. Her quarry and his companion had disappeared down the corridor. She was not about to give Lady Elizabeth advice on how to snare the elusive earl—she intended to catch him for herself.

She looked at the conservatory door. Another puzzle—why was Tynweith helping Lady Elizabeth? He must have known Felicity was looking for Westbrooke. She knew the earl had come down this corridor. She'd been right behind him. Yet he had vanished and in his place she'd gotten Tynweith. Tynweith who'd whisked her back to the music room, no matter how much she'd tried to drag her feet or get him to go on ahead alone.

Tynweith was not known for his philanthropy. So why would he help Lady Elizabeth? If he helped anyone, it should be Felicity. *She* was Charlotte's friend, and Tynweith appeared to have some connection to Charlotte.

What was it? Charlotte became very evasive when his name was mentioned. She was usually extremely frank, yet she would not say one revealing word about their host.

Well, the house party was still young. There was plenty of time to solve these mysteries—and compromise a certain earl. She had to think about that, what the trap would be and how best to bait it. The capture must be spectacularly public and unequivocal. She wanted no loopholes for Westbrooke to wiggle through.

She headed upstairs to bed. Alone, unfortunately. Lord Peter was probably still swiving Charlotte.

Felicity had considered inviting him to stop by her room afterward, but she had decided against it. He'd been too obnoxiously proud of himself yesterday for plowing a duchess. Well, Lord Andrew was arriving in the morning. He was entertaining. *Very* entertaining. He knew quite a number of inventive games.

Lady Felicity paused on the stairs and smiled. And he had asked for Lady Elizabeth's hand and been denied. He'd been rather bitter about that if she remembered correctly. Perhaps he would be interested to hear that lovely Lady Elizabeth was no better than she should be. He was known to be a mite vindictive.

Yes, Lord Andrew should turn out to be very useful indeed.

Chapter Nine

Robbie could not have children.

Lizzie didn't know how a man knew such a thing, but Robbie must know it. His voice had sounded tortured when he'd told her. She had wanted to cry.

She sat on the window seat in her room and leaned her head against the glass. It was still cool from the night. It felt good. She had a dull headache and her eyes were dry and gritty, as if there were sand in them.

It had taken her forever to fall asleep, and then she'd been haunted by bizarre dreams. Nightmares, really. She'd been looking for a baby, sometimes in the countryside, sometimes in the stews of London. She'd argued with so many people—with James, Robbie, some one-cyed hag with broken teeth. One time she'd actually held a baby boy, but another woman had snatched him out of her arms and vanished into the London fog.

She pressed her forehead harder against the glass.

Perhaps Robbie was wrong. How could he know for certain? He wasn't married. Maybe once he wed, he'd discover that he *could* have children.

But what if he were right? She squeezed her eyes tightly together, but that didn't keep the tears from leaking out.

Did she love him enough to give up hope of ever having a child?

She did not know.

She took a deep shuddering breath, wiping her tears with the back of her hand. Betty would be in at any moment with her chocolate. She had better wash her face. She did not want to explain why she had been crying.

As she got up, she glanced out the window. There were two people outside on the lawn. It was hard to tell from this distance, but it looked like Felicity was with a man. Not surprising. Lizzie just hoped the other girl would find a secluded spot before she did what it was rumored she usually did with men.

But who was her companion? He was too short to be Robbie, thank heavens, and too broad to be Parks or Lord Peter. Certainly Lord Tynweith would not be showing Felicity his gardens, would he? Who else was there? None of the other male guests would tempt Felicity from her bed—or into her bed, for that matter.

The man took off his high-crowned beaver and the mystery was solved. Black hair with a narrow white streak gleamed in the sun. Lord Andrew had arrived. "Lord Skunk" the *ton* called him for his hair, but Lizzie thought the nickname suited his personality as well. The man had offered for her once, even though she had given him absolutely no encouragement. She assumed he could not resist the gleam of her dowry. She had tried to be polite when she refused him, and she had tried to politely avoid him ever since.

She turned away to splash water on her face. It was going to be extremely difficult to avoid him here.

"Up early to greet me, Felicity? If I'd realized you were here, I would have come down yesterday and saved you the trouble of getting out of bed."

Andrew reached for her, but she stepped back.

"Not here in full view of the house."

"Why not?" He pulled off his hat and looked up at the building. "Never say you're turning shy?"

"No, of course not. But Westbrooke's room faces this direction."

"Ah, still trying to catch the earl, are you?"

"Of course." She turned and started walking down the lawn. Andrew fell into step beside her. "I could use your help."

"Really?" He leered at her. "It will cost you."

She did like Andrew. He was not overburdened with scruples.

"I expected it would." She stepped onto the wide gravel path and followed it though Tynweith's Frenchified garden, past the parterres and ridiculous bushy spheres and pyramids, under an arch. She turned left, passing between two hedges into the topiary garden. She knew exactly where she was going. She'd found this spot yesterday when she'd been searching for Westbrooke.

Andrew stopped to examine a topiary orgy. Well, hardly an orgy to her mind—if she discerned the sex of the trimmed bushes correctly, there was only one male and three females.

"Tynweith's gardener is quite inventive."

"Yes, I know. Come on, Andrew." She ran her hand over his forearm. "There's a place up ahead where we can . . . talk."

"Where our tongues can be busy, hmm? I'm ready for a very long, very deep discussion."

"Good." She wet her lips, noting the breadth of his shoulders, the muscles in his thighs. He was shorter than Westbrooke, but he seemed much larger. His nose, his hands, his . . . um. Excitement shivered down her spine, settling between her legs.

He looked like he should be lifting boxes on a dock, not wineglasses in aristocratic drawing rooms.

"Here we are." She stepped through some tall

hedges and walked over to the stone bench in the center of the grassy square. They were hidden from the house, but anyone happening through the gap in the hedge would see them. Another shiver of expectation skittered up her spine. Frolicking behind closed doors was so boring. The threat of discovery added spice to any encounter.

"Tynweith's damned bushes are quite inspiring, Fel. They give a fellow all sorts of interesting ideas." Andrew cupped her cheek with one hand and pulled down her lower lip. "I might have trouble deciding how best you can repay me."

She tilted her head so she could suck on his thumb.

"I packed the handcuffs and the switch when I heard you were coming."

"Did you?" His eyes got a very sharp, intent look. "Lovely. So what do you need me to do?"

A very bawdy answer popped into her head, but she repressed it.

"You know I plan to marry Westbrooke."

"All the *ton* knows it." He cocked an eyebrow. "And you know I'm not one of his intimates. If you're looking for someone to persuade him, I'm not your man."

Felicity sat down on the bench. It was still cold and damp with dew. It felt quite splendid against her heat. "I'll handle Westbrooke. I have a different job for you." She looked up at him. "It involves a woman."

"Does it?" He came over to stand beside her.

She put her hand on the front of his pantaloons and smiled. He was already hard.

"It might involve a rape."

His bulge leapt.

"Really? This sounds very interesting. Perhaps I should be paying you."

"Probably. I think you'll be delighted to rape this particular young lady."

"But will it leave me required to marry her?"

Felicity shrugged. "Most likely. However, she comes

with piles of money, and if you find her boring, I will be happy to entertain you."

He freed one of her breasts. She arched, making it easier for him to squeeze her nipple. She loved the feel of the sun and his fingers on her skin.

"Who is it? Lady Caroline? She is fat and ugly."

"No, not Lady Caroline." Felicity grinned. "You once offered for this lady."

"I did?" Andrew squeezed harder and she yelped. "Don't say it's Lady Elizabeth you want me to deflower?"

"You are so astute."

"God." He kissed her, thrusting his tongue all the way to her throat. "I would love to have that bitch under me." He grabbed both her breasts, kneading them roughly. "Your choice, Felicity. How do you want it? I'll give it to you any way you like."

Felicity started unbuttoning his pantaloons. "We should finish discussing the terms."

"I've heard enough. I'll be happy to take her wherever, whenever you like. On Almack's dance floor even, under the noses of all the patronesses."

"In front of her brother?"

Andrew's hands stilled. "Damn, don't ask that, Fel. He'd kill me before I'd breached her."

Felicity laughed. "No, I won't ask that. And I'm not certain she's a virgin, so don't be disappointed if there's no blood."

"No? That little Puritan's been spreading her legs for someone? I feel cheated. Who's she been swiving?"

"Westbrooke."

Andrew laughed. "Westbrooke? As far as I can tell, the man barely knows how to unbutton his breeches to piss."

Felicity finished unbuttoning Andrew's pantaloons and freed his lovely, thick length.

"He appears to have mastered the skill. I'm fairly certain he was in her room—in her bed—naked the night before last. And I saw him leaving Tynweith's conservatory with her last night. They both looked extremely untidy, as if they had been doing something besides admiring Tynweith's plants."

Andrew shook his head. "Fascinating." Then he sucked in his breath as Felicity sucked on him.

"The most fascinating thing is there has been no engagement announcement. I want it to stay that way—at least with regard to Lady Elizabeth. The only announcement I wish to hear is Westbrooke's name with mine."

He squeezed her breast. Ahh. If only Andrew were the eldest son—then he'd be heir to a dukedom. But he had three healthy older brothers. Only a fool would wager on his getting the title. She was not a fool.

She stroked the delightfully large organ in her hand. If one part of Westbrooke proved small and disappointing, she'd imagine the part that was not—his pockets. The music of jingling coins could get her through many a bedroom waltz.

"The house party is going to some ruins tomorrow—an old castle, I think Tynweith said. There'll be plenty of places to steal a few moments alone." She drew her finger from the sack between his legs to his tip. "It shouldn't take you long to get the deed done."

Andrew laughed. "Not long at all. Seconds, if need be. But I hope I have more time. I'd like to taunt her a bit. See if I can get her to scream. God, I'd love that. She was such a cold little bitch when she rejected my suit."

Felicity licked a salty bit of moisture from his tip.

"You can tease her today—that would be fun to watch."

"Yes." He rubbed her nipple between his thumb and forefinger. "I can think of many ways to make her uncomfortable."

"Don't overdo it. We don't want her so frightened she runs from your shadow."

Felicity took him into her mouth again. Did she want him here or in her bum? Both had their advantages.

Andrew had his hands in her hair now, holding her to him. Enough talk of Westbrooke and Lady Elizabeth. She pulled back. He held her a moment longer than she wanted and then let her go.

"You want it the other way, do you?" He pulled her up and turned her. She felt his erection pushing against her. "Aren't you afraid someone will find us?"

His hands were squeezing both her breasts. His fingers pinched her nipples. She gasped and leaned over.

"That's part of the fun. Ahh . . ."

She screamed her approval as Andrew grunted his release.

By the time Mr. Dodsworth came running to investigate the disturbance, they were sitting discreetly side by side on the bench.

"Lord Andrew, it's so pleasant to see you. What kept you in London?" Lady Caroline leaned forward, giving the man a better view of her plump breasts. Robbie watched him survey them briefly, then return to cutting the slice of ham on his plate.

"I had an engagement I could not break."

Lord Peter sniggered. "With *Le Petit Oiseau*, I don't doubt."

"The little bird?" Mr. Dodsworth took a swallow of ale. "Didn't know you were keen on ornithology, Lord Andrew."

"I don't believe Lord Peter was referring to a bird of the feathered variety, Mr. Dodsworth." Lady Beatrice scowled at the younger man. "I know your mother, sir. She would be most interested to hear what topics her son considers appropriate for polite conversation."

Lord Peter's ears turned red. "Your pardon," he mumbled to his plate. He shoved a roll into his mouth.

Robbie wanted to stand up and applaud. It was about time Lady Beatrice took on a chaperone's duties. If only she had been more alert last night. She should never have let Lizzie leave the music room with Tynweith.

He took a bite of his beefsteak. The meat might have been boot leather for all he could tell. Lizzie was seated next to Lord Andrew—Lord Skunk. An excellent sobriquet for the man, even if one ignored his unusual coloration. He sprayed a clinging stench of innuendo and malicious gossip wherever he went. Innuendo? Ha! Ofttimes he not only disseminated the tale, he authored it. Or worse, he was its leading actor. More than one unsuspecting debutante had been sent home to the country to try to clean his stink from her reputation.

Now the blackguard was leering at Lizzie.

Robbie scraped his knife across his plate and made Miss Hyde jump.

He had chosen a seat almost as far from Lizzie as possible. He'd hardly slept last night. The scenes from the conservatory—the sounds, the tastes, the textures—kept flashing through his mind. The silky smoothness of Lizzie's breasts; the rich taste of her mouth and the tang of her nipples; the smell of lemon and silk and skin; the quick little breaths and moans she uttered as his hands moved over her; the sweet wail of his name as she found her release.

If Felicity were sitting next to him now, playing last night's games, she would find the fall of his pantaloons ready to burst its buttons.

"Are you enjoying your visit, Lord Westbrooke?"

He looked at Mrs. Larson. She was smiling at him, but a frown etched a furrow between her brows.

"It has been agreeable, ma'am." Some parts had

been much more than agreeable—and some parts had been mortifying.

He had used Lizzie unconscionably in the conservatory. At least he had finally told her part of his secret. She'd looked as stricken as he'd imagined she would when she'd heard it. Surely now she was cured of her desire to wed him.

Good. That needed to be done.

He felt like puking.

"Are you certain?" Mrs. Larson touched his sleeve gently. "You look . . . well . . ." She sighed and glanced up the table. Her gaze settled on Felicity before she looked back at him. "I apologize for the events of the other night. Flint told me he gave your man the key to your bedchamber yesterday."

"Yes, thank you. Do not worry another moment, ma'am. I am well settled. The accommodations are perfectly satisfactory."

"I hope so."

Mrs. Larson turned to address Lord Botton on her other side. Robbie took the opportunity to look at Lizzie again. Surely she had the key to her door. He would make a point to ask her. She might need it. Lord Andrew was definitely leering.

Perhaps he had made the wrong choice in sitting so far from her. If he were closer, he could grab the man by the cravat and twist it until his face turned purple. One would think one's host might notice a guest misbehaving, but Tynweith's attention was all for his luncheon. He would only bestir himself if Lord Skunk threw Lizzie onto the table and disturbed the dishes.

"If I'd been fully aware of how charming the company was here," Lord Andrew was saying, "I would have forgone my appointment, I assure you." The man's eyes were focused on Lizzie's bodice.

Lizzie shifted slightly in her chair so she was closer to Sir Gaston.

At least today she had on an appropriate gown. Its

neck reached almost to her chin. The blackguard was not going to be able to ogle her lovely breasts. If he wished to scrutinize a bosom, he would have to limit his inspection to Lady Caroline's. Hers was the only one on display at the moment—well, hers and Lady Beatrice's, but elderly breasts . . . ah, the less said, the less thought, the better.

Well, and Lady Felicity's were available for inspection as well. He was certain Lord Andrew could see them in their entirety if he wished—Felicity was not shy about trotting them out. Of course, the man had probably already examined them quite thoroughly, many times.

Robbie glanced at Miss Hyde. She was nibbling on some carrots, darting glances at the company. He had tried to engage her in conversation, but every time he addressed her, her eyes got a panicked, hunted look. He'd decided it was kinder to leave her alone. And ignoring her made it easier to eavesdrop on Lord Andrew and Lizzie.

The blackguard leaned closer to Lizzie. She tried to move away again, but she had nowhere to go. Another inch and she'd be sitting in Gaston's lap.

"It is *so* delightful to see you again, my dear. Our paths have not crossed much recently."

"Very true." Lizzie's face was expressionless. Good for her. "And I am not your 'dear.'"

"No? I'm heartbroken. I've missed you so."

A small, slightly mocking smile creased her lips. "My lord, you are gammoning me."

"Not at all. I am quite anxious to renew our acquaintance." Lord Skunk displayed his own cold smile. "I don't intend to let this opportunity go to waste. We have a number of days to enjoy each other's company and, um, deepen our friendship, hmm? I look forward to getting to know you more"—his smile widened—"intimately."

Robbie half rose. He was going to murder the man here and now.

Mrs. Larson put her hand on his arm again.

"Ladies," she said, "who would like a tour of the house?"

Tynweith headed for his study. He needed to get away from his bloody house guests. Why had he invited them? He loathed house parties. He'd been an idiot to have one. An asinine, buffle-headed nodcock. How many more days till he could shut the door on the last guest and get back to his comfortable life? Four? God, it was an eternity.

He paused in the hall. Was that Dodsworth he heard? Damn! He stepped quickly behind a statue of Aphrodite. Yes, it was Dodsworth droning on about horse breeding to Sir George. Nell had probably asked the baronet to sacrifice some of his time to keep the man company. She knew *he* wasn't about to do it, even though it was his party. He waited until they had vanished into the back of the house to step out from his hiding place.

Things had reached a low point when a man had to cower behind the statuary in his own home.

He grimaced. He was certainly at a low point. Why had he thought he could get Charlotte into his bed? He was an idiot—and now he was stuck with a house full of idiots. His hand flexed. He would like to hit something.

Charlotte was ignoring him. She'd sat as far from him as possible at luncheon today. She'd barely looked at him. She'd spent the entire meal talking—or rather, listening—to that idiot Dodsworth inventory his stables. It hadn't been the topic that riveted her—he was certain Charlotte didn't give a rat's ass about horses. Nor was it the man. He wasn't overly vain, but there was no way any female could prefer stout old Mr. Dodsworth—stout, old, *boring* Mr. Dodsworth—to him.

After luncheon she'd vanished. He'd just spent the

better part of an hour searching his estate for her. Discreetly, of course. He didn't want her to think he was stalking her, even though he was.

He hadn't looked in her room, however. He hadn't had the nerve. Was she there, in bed with Lord Peter?

Bloody hell.

He wanted to strangle the man. Draw and quarter him. Castrate him with a dull knife. Chop his testicles up and feed them to his dogs. He'd almost cheered when Lady Beatrice had put him in his place at luncheon. One did not discuss the fashionable impure in genteel company.

He smiled at Miss Hyde as he passed her in the corridor. The little mouse ducked her head and scurried along as if she were afraid he was a cat. How could Nell bear to have her underfoot? Just seeing her put his teeth on edge.

No, to be truthful it wasn't poor Miss Hyde's fault his teeth were on edge. He'd barely slept last night. Every time he'd closed his eyes, he'd seen Lord Peter between Charlotte's lovely thighs. It was driving him mad.

Lord Botton popped out of the music room.

"I'm looking for Lady Beatrice, Tynweith. Can you tell me where I might find her?"

"Sorry, Botton, I have not seen her recently. You might look in the gardens. It is a fine day. Perhaps she decided to take the air."

"Right. Thank you. Interesting gardens you've got, don't you know?" The old roué winked.

"Uh, yes. Indeed. Enjoy them."

"Oh, I mean to—especially when I find dear Lady Beatrice." He waggled his eyebrows, then hurried down the hall.

Tynweith watched him go. The man was destined to be as frustrated as he. According to Nell, Botton's quarry had retreated to her room with a brandy bottle.

He shook his head. Lady Beatrice certainly was not

the best of chaperones. Of course, her charges were well past the age when they should need close monitoring. He'd encountered Miss Peterson and Mr. Parker-Roth in a sedate section of his gardens this morning. They'd been arguing about one of his plants. In Latin. At least that is what it had sounded like—he hadn't actually engaged them in conversation. He'd just nodded and kept walking. No need for a chaperone there.

Apparently Lady Elizabeth and Westbrooke weren't getting into any interesting trouble either. He'd thought when he'd left them alone in the conservatory last night there'd be an engagement announcement this morning, but no. They hadn't even sat together at luncheon.

He continued on toward his study.

There was definitely *something* going on between those two. When he could tear his eyes away from Charlotte, he'd watched them. The earl had been quiet, far from his usual witty self. He'd kept sending Lady Elizabeth longing glances—when he wasn't sending Lord Andrew murderous ones. And Lady Elizabeth had been most subdued as well.

What the hell had happened in the conservatory?

And what was Lord Andrew up to? If Nell hadn't spoken when she had at luncheon, Westbrooke might have tackled the man. Wonderful. A brawl among the beefsteak. Did he need to see that the two were on separate ends of the table at every meal? What an exhausting thought. He would put Flint in charge of it.

He had almost reached his study. Thank God. Peace—and the chance to mull over his options with Charlotte. It was clear he'd have to abandon his plan to make her jealous. Lady Elizabeth would not be convincing, and frankly he wasn't certain he would be either.

So how was he going to get into Charlotte's bed?

Perhaps he'd find the answer in his study.

What he found was Lord Peter lounging in his favorite chair, drinking his brandy.

"What are you doing here?"

"Testy, Tynweith?" Lord Peter grinned and took another swallow. "You don't sound like the gracious host."

Tynweith contemplated hitting him. He stepped into the room and closed the door.

"Pardon. I wasn't expecting to find anyone here. What *are* you doing in my study?"

"Just wanted a private word with you, that's all."

"Really?" His stomach clenched. Why would the man want to talk with him in private? They had nothing in common—except Charlotte. Surely the nodcock was not going to talk about her?

Lord Peter grinned. "As I think you've surmised, I'm doing the duchess some slight . . . service."

God, he *was* going to talk about her. Tynweith grunted and took the chair behind his desk. Best put some barrier between him and his unwelcome visitor.

"I felt sorry for her—stuck with that old man for a husband. Can't be pleasant. Shriveled up body." Lord Peter shuddered. "It's a wonder he can manage the deed, don't you think?"

Did the bloody idiot expect a response?

"I fail to see why you are discussing this with me."

Lord Peter continued as if he hadn't heard. "When she invited me to visit her bed, I didn't want to decline. She's not ugly, even if she is a little old."

Tynweith made a strangling sound. Charlotte old? She was only twenty-four—only a year older than this pup.

"You said something?"

Tynweith clenched his jaw. "No."

Lord Peter nodded and leaned forward. "You see the thing is I've had her two nights now and, well"— he took another swallow of brandy—"it's just not much fun. She lies there with her eyes closed, still as death, and lets me have at it. I tell you, it's like swiving a corpse—not that I've ever done such a thing, of course."

He chuckled. Tynweith just stared at him. He was now too angry to speak.

Lord Peter cleared his throat and looked away. "Frankly, I can't stomach another visit to her bed, but I don't want to offend her. As I said, I feel sorry for her—and she *is* the Duchess of Hartford. No use making her my enemy, heh?"

Tynweith gripped his hands so tightly together he wondered if he would break a bone. Killing the man was very appealing. He could strangle him in short order. Castration with his penknife would be even more enjoyable.

"You are telling me this, because . . . ?"

Lord Peter shrugged. "She mentioned you last night. I was eager for something to talk about. Casting around really, hoping to get something to spark the fires, as it were. Said I'd come up, and wanted to keep my word—she hadn't invited me for tea obviously—but I was having trouble, um, rising to the occasion, if you know what I mean. The first night had been a lark—and I never turn down bed games when I'm offered a chance to play. And it is a rare treat not to have to pull out—"

"Lord Peter!" Tynweith took a deep breath. He would not shout.

"Yes, well, she said there was something between you once. Ancient history, I think she said, but she didn't sound like she meant it. So I thought, as soon as I'd managed to come and knew I didn't want to come there again, that maybe you'd be interested in taking my place. For old time's sake, perhaps?"

What to say? Tell the whelp in no uncertain terms that a gentleman never discussed his conquests? But he was happy for the information—a specific part of him was rigid with delight. And even happier that

Lord Peter thought Charlotte still entertained some feeling for him.

"You will, of course, not repeat any of this. I am certain the duchess would not care to know she had been the topic of such a conversation. And Hartford most especially would not like to hear he had been cuckolded."

Lord Peter sat up straight. "Of course not. That's why I sought you out here, in private. Knew it was a topic of delicacy. Didn't want the thing bruited about." He leaned forward. "So, will you do it? Will you take charge?"

Tynweith nodded. "You can put your mind at rest on that score. Don't give it another thought. I will handle the duchess."

Lord Peter looked visibly relieved. He stood and straightened his waistcoat. "I believe I'll play least in sight so I don't have to explain anything."

"I understand. If the duchess should ask, I'll say you are indisposed. Shall I have a tray sent up for dinner?"

"I thought I might go off to the tavern in the village." Lord Peter grinned. "Find a bite to eat and a barmaid to satisfy my other hungers."

Tynweith nodded. He'd be happy to have the man elsewhere. "I hear Harriet is very accommodating."

"I thought you'd know. I'll be off then." He paused with his hand on the doorknob. "If you don't mind, I think I'll head back to Town in the morning. Wouldn't want to risk making her grace uncomfortable with my presence and, well, there's not much here to amuse me any longer."

"Of course. Shall I have your things sent on to the inn?"

"That would be splendid." He let himself out.

Tynweith hardly noticed the door closing.

So, Charlotte still had feelings for him, did she? But was Lord Peter a good judge? Doubtful. Still, she *had* responded to him in the shrubbery yesterday.

She had such an iron hand on her emotions—well, she had never had them fully awakened. He would love to waken them for her.

He leaned back in his chair. Tonight. He would go to her tonight. He would show her what could be done in bed between a man and a woman. It would be his pleasure.

He began to plan how exactly he would woo the Duchess of Hartford.

Chapter Ten

"Meg!" Lizzie grabbed Meg's arm as she walked past the library.

"What is it?" Meg stepped into the room and looked around. "Have you been hiding among Lord Tynweith's books all afternoon?"

"Yes."

"Whatever for?" Meg looked at Lizzie as if she had lost her mind.

Lizzie shrugged and glanced away. "I don't wish to encounter Lord Andrew alone, that's all. He made me extremely uncomfortable at luncheon." And she didn't wish to encounter Robbie, either. What could she say to him after last night? Especially since she still didn't know how she felt.

"What did Lord Andrew do?"

"Nothing so bad—just his usual unpleasant innuendo. But Robbie looked ready to attack him. Fortunately, Mrs. Larson stepped in with a distraction." Lizzie frowned. "Didn't you notice?"

"No. I missed luncheon."

Meg had an odd note in her voice. Lizzie looked at her more closely.

"That's right, you did." Was Meg blushing? Why would she be embarrassed about missing luncheon? It was an informal gathering. Many people skipped the meal. Hmm. Many people including Parks. "I don't remember seeing Mr. Parker-Roth at table either, now that I think about it. I don't suppose you know where he was?"

Meg's blush darkened. "We were examining an interesting plant specimen in Lord Tynweith's garden. We lost track of time."

"Oh? Was that the only thing you were examining?"

Meg examined her finger nails. "Of course. What else would we be looking at?"

What else, indeed? Give Meg an interesting plant specimen, and she was lost to all other considerations. A mere male had no power to distract her—yet she did look distinctly distracted.

"You didn't stray into the left side of the topiary gardens, did you?"

"Of course not. We did not venture into those gardens at all. I do not care for topiary work—it's plant mutilation, in my opinion. It draws people's attention away from the vegetation itself. If a man wants statues, he should hire a sculptor and leave the shrubbery alone."

"I see." Lizzie did not want to hear another of Meg's tirades on garden subjects. What she did want was to get away from Lendal Park and the house party. She felt extremely agitated at the moment.

"Meg, would you like to go for a walk? Perhaps we could preview the ruins we'll be visiting tomorrow. I've been told they are not too far."

Meg brightened. "Perhaps there are some interesting plant specimens there—maybe even remnants of the castle garden. I will go get my bonnet."

"Meg, we do not have all day to examine the plants, you know. You will be able to do only a quick survey. We have to be back before dark—and I do want to see the buildings."

Meg grunted in a fashion Lizzie took to be assent.

Soon they were walking briskly over the lawn. Lizzie smiled and lifted her face to the sun. It felt so good to stretch her legs. She thought better when she was in motion. Something about the repetitive action of putting one foot in front of the other freed her mind to consider thorny issues.

The thorniest issue at the moment was Robbie. Did she love him enough to give up motherhood?

She glanced over at Meg. The other girl was surveying the ground around them with keen interest.

"Meg, you won't desert me for a clump of weeds, will you?"

Meg tore her eyes away from the vegetation. "Of course not." She grinned. "Unless it is a very interesting clump."

"Meg . . ."

"All right. I promise to stick to you like a burr. I just hope I don't encounter any irresistible specimens."

Lizzie sighed—and then smiled. A small breeze tugged at her bonnet. She missed the rambles she used to take with Meg when they were girls. They'd walked for hours, all over Alvord and Knightsdale—until Meg's attention was caught by an interesting bit of greenery.

Why couldn't life be simple like that again? It wasn't as if she wanted something unusual. She just wanted what most women wanted—a husband, a home, children. Normal things. Everyday things.

She followed Meg up a slope. Trying to keep pace with her was making her breathless. She'd spent too much time in London while Meg had been wandering the fields of Kent.

Lud! She wanted to stay in Kent, too—to stay near her home, near James and Sarah and Will and the new baby. If she married Robbie, she'd still be close to them. But if she married another man, she might have to live in Cornwall or Cumbria or Cardiff. Lord Malden, her most recently rejected suitor, had his principal seat in Yorkshire far to the north. Lord Pendel, another former candidate for her hand, lived most of the year in Lancashire. If she'd married either of them, she'd not have seen her brother and his family for months.

Robbie was the perfect choice. Except he wasn't.

She walked faster, but she couldn't outwalk her thoughts.

Meg waited for her at the top of the hill.

"Meg, do you ever think of marriage?"

Meg laughed. "Of course I do. I let myself be dragged up to London for the Season, didn't I? It's a little hard to avoid the subject when you're surrounded by so many young misses scrambling to catch a husband."

"True." Lizzie stepped around a pile of horse droppings. "But doesn't it make you sad, the thought that you might move away from your father and sister?"

"Not really. In fact, after the interminable dinner parties Emma orchestrated for my matrimonial benefit last year, I'd consider myself blessed to be beyond her reach."

"You don't mean that!"

"Well, no, I suppose not—though if you'd asked me right after one of Emma's parties. . . ." Meg grinned and shrugged. "I don't worry about it. I'm sure I'll visit Emma from time to time. And I imagine I'll have my own children to keep me busy. That's usually the way of it, isn't it?"

"Yes." Surely Meg was correct. Lizzie had just never thought she'd have to consider moving away.

She had never thought she'd have to consider a life without Robbie. Could she do so?

Which was more important—Robbie or children? How could she decide? It was a terrible choice to make.

"Your stepmother, Mrs. Graham—I mean, Mrs. Peterson now—she never had children, did she? Does she regret that, do you know?"

Meg walked a moment or two in silence.

"I think she wishes she could have had children, but she is too wise to bemoan something she could not change."

"But if she had married someone else. . . ."

"Who's to know what would have happened? She may well have been barren. She assumed she was." Meg shrugged. "She loved Mr. Graham and had twenty years of happiness with him. Now she has my father and Emma's children to dote on. She's happy."

"True." But would *she* be happy? Lizzie did not know.

And if she would be happy, could she convince Robbie? He was not inclined to offer for her at the moment.

She and Meg walked along a path up through a small grove of trees. As soon as they came out into the sunlight again, Lizzie saw the ruins. The gray stone castle stood a little above them in the middle of a broad field. It was much smaller than Alvord. Its stone was dark with age and lichen, and one of the towers had lost a few of its crenellations.

"How old do you think it is?" Meg asked.

"Several centuries. It was built in 1372."

Meg laughed. "How do you know? Has Tynweith had some penny guide books printed up? I'll have to complain—I did not get mine."

"You'd only be interested if he were describing the local flora. No, I did not get my information from our host. Someone left a history of the castle on a table in the library."

"I would not have thought we had any avid students of history among our number."

"I'm not certain history was the topic attracting this reader, Meg."

"No? What then?"

"The book was marked at the page describing the castle dungeon."

"Really? I'd love to see a dungeon. It's not every day one gets the opportunity. Does Alvord have one? You've never shown it to me."

Was Meg daft? Lizzie stared at her friend. She was now trying to examine the raised castle portcullis.

Well, perhaps she was letting her imagination run away with her. Now that she considered it, there was no reason to attach any special significance to the fact the book was marked at a particular page. The reader might just have been called away for a game of billiards at that point. And really, she didn't know for a fact any of the present guests had been reading the history. It was possible Tynweith's staff wasn't terribly conscientious. The book could have been sitting out for weeks.

She took a deep breath. She was not going to worry—it was too beautiful a day. The sky was blue and cloudless, and the sun was warm on her face. She watched a hawk float high over the field. She would love to climb the battlements and look out over the countryside.

"Alvord did have a dungeon at one time," she said. "My grandfather turned it into a wine cellar."

"So this will be a treat for you, too."

Treat was not the description that came to mind, but she would try for some of Meg's enthusiasm.

"Right. A treat."

They passed through the gatehouse into a large courtyard. Weeds grew everywhere. Lizzie noticed Meg's eyes widen. She grabbed her arm.

"You promised to stay with me—stick to me like a burr, I believe were the exact words."

"But Lizzie . . ."

"No. If I let you go off among the greenery now, I won't see you again. Come on. You wanted to explore the dungeon, didn't you?"

"I'm willing to give that up."

"Well, I've conceived a burning desire to see the

view from the battlements." Lizzie tugged on Meg's arm. "Come *on*. You can look at the vegetation when we finish with the buildings. And we'll be back tomorrow with Mr. Parker-Roth. Then you can argue with him over every little leaf and flower."

"All right." Meg came along, but kept looking longingly over her shoulder. "I don't know why you are so keen on heights."

"And I don't know why you are so keen on weeds. Those are probably just the same things that grow at Lendal Park."

"Oh, I don't think so."

Lizzie pushed Meg through the door to one of the towers. It took a moment for her eyes to adjust to the dim light. The air was damp and chill. She shivered.

"Not much to see here," Meg said. She walked over to inspect a tattered tapestry hanging on one wall. "Looks like moths have gotten to this." She looked down at the floor. "And mice."

"Here are the stairs to the battlements." Lizzie crossed the leaf-strewn floor to where a dusty suit of armor guarded a set of steps and started up the circular staircase. Meg hung back.

"Are you certain you want to go up there?"

Lizzie stopped at the first turn.

"Yes." Suddenly she wanted desperately to be up on the battlements, high above the countryside. She had loved to go up on Alvord's and feel the wind in her hair. She needed that feeling of freedom now. "Come on."

"There are an awful lot of stairs."

"Meg, you cannot be dissuaded by a few stairs. You are not a delicate flower. You just hiked here from Lendal Park without tiring in the slightest. I could barely keep up with you."

"Well, I'm tired now."

"Meg . . ."

"Oh, very well." Meg climbed up after her. "This looks like something Mrs. Radcliffe would include in her novels. Are there ghosts, do you suppose? Do you hear any wailing or rattling chains?"

"Of course not. The history did say the castle was haunted, however. One of Lord Tynweith's ancestors lost his head, literally, and some of the former inhabitants of the dungeon have stayed on." Lizzie put her hand on the stone wall. The steps were uneven, worn down by centuries of use.

"Hmm. It's a shame Tynweith let the place go to ruin."

"You can't blame the present Lord Tynweith, Meg. Once the manor house was built, the family abandoned the castle."

"Why?"

"I assume because it was small and drafty."

"Small, drafty, *and* haunted."

"I imagine the small and drafty aspects were the most persuasive."

Lizzie reached the door at the top of the stairs that should open onto the battlements. She pushed. It did not move.

"What is it?" Meg crowded up behind her.

"Hold on. The door's stuck." Lizzie had climbed all those stairs—she was not going to be denied her prize. She put both hands on the door and shoved. Nothing.

"Perhaps if I help?"

"There's hardly enough room for me to stand here, Meg. With the curve, the top step tapers to nothing. If you try to stand on it, you'll tumble down to the ground and break your neck."

"I don't think—"

"I do. Give me a moment." Lizzie took a deep breath.

"Throw your shoulder into it."

"I intend to."

Lizzie threw herself against the door. Her shoulder

ached; the door remained closed. She tried again. Still nothing.

"We are coming back tomorrow with some sturdy men," Meg said. "One of them will be able to open the door. There's no need to bloody yourself today, Lizzie."

Lizzie had to admit defeat. "All right. Let's see if we can find the dungeon. If I understood the text correctly, it should be at the bottom of this tower."

They went back down, hugging the outside wall. Lizzie would hate to meet anyone coming the other direction—there simply was not room on the inner side of the stairs for a foot to fit securely. They passed the suit of armor on the ground floor and kept going.

"Are we almost there?"

"We're here." Lizzie stepped off the staircase to face another thick wooden door, much sturdier looking that the one at the top of the tower. "But I'm afraid we're out of luck again."

"Don't give up without trying." Meg stepped by Lizzie and grabbed the bolt that secured the door. She pulled. It slid back easily.

Lizzie and Meg stared at the door and then stared at each other.

"Tell me it's a good thing the door to Tynweith's dungeon opens easily," Meg said.

"Mmm, I don't think so. Are you certain you want to go in there?"

"No." Meg pushed on the door. It swung open without the slighted protest. "Hullo," she shouted. "Is anyone there?"

Silence.

"I'm not afraid of ghosts."

"I'm not afraid of ghosts either, Meg. I don't believe ghosts have any need to ensure doors are in proper working order. They just go through them, don't they?"

"True." Meg chewed her lip. "However it seems

poor spirited to come this far and turn back—no pun intended, of course."

"You have heard that discretion is the better part of valor, haven't you, Meg? As you pointed out just a moment ago, we will be back tomorrow with a number of sturdy men. Perhaps it would be wisest to put off this exploration until then."

"No. I'll be all right. You stay here. If I shout, run for help."

"Meg, by the time I make it to Lendal Park and back, you'll be murdered—or worse."

"Lizzie, there is really no fate worse than death." Meg stepped over the threshold.

"Meg!"

Lizzie grabbed for Meg's arm, but Meg had already moved beyond her reach. Should she follow her? Perhaps she should go upstairs and borrow the suit of armor's ax.

"Meg, what are you—what is the matter?!"

Meg was standing in the door to another chamber. Her face was white as death.

"It looks as if Tynweith's dungeon has been used recently."

Lizzie had been gone all afternoon. Robbie knew. He'd been looking for her.

Well, not looking *for* her precisely. He hadn't actually wished to speak to her. What could he say? He had said all he could last night. He'd just wished to ascertain she was safe.

He had not been able to do so to his satisfaction. It had made for a very unpleasant afternoon.

"You do not care for Arabians, my lord?"

He had no idea what Dodsworth was talking about. Something about horses and stables. The man had latched on to him during port and had not let go when they'd adjourned to the drawing room and the tea tray had been brought in. More than one of the other house guests had seen his predicament, smiled, and taken themselves quickly out of harm's way.

"Arabians are fine."

Dodsworth nodded. "I couldn't agree more. Why, just the other day . . ."

At least he was giving poor Miss Hyde a holiday. She was sitting by the fire all by herself, sipping her tea and looking as happy as a little mouse could look.

He would have been happier if Lizzie hadn't taken it into her head to walk over to the blasted ruins with only Meg as a companion. He'd finally asked Collins to ask Betty where she was when he couldn't find her. Why hadn't she thought to take a footman? He'd been all ready to set out after them when they'd finally returned.

He'd wanted to ring a peal over her then, but Lady Beatrice and Lady Dunlee had intercepted her before he could say his piece. He'd been choking on it all through dinner.

"I'm considering renovating my stables. Been thinking about it for a long time, actually, ever since I had the pleasure of viewing our Regent's striking edifice at Brighton. Built in the Indian style, don't you know. Breathtaking. I was in awe, I tell you."

Robbie grunted and took another sip of his brandy. Dodsworth had already launched into a detailed account of his architectural plans. His precious horses would be living like sultans.

How could the man not know he was a crashing bore? Obviously no one had told him. Would he even comprehend? It was tempting to try. Perhaps on the last day of the house party.

His monologue did have its benefits. No need to actually listen to him. A well placed nod here, an interested-sounding grunt there, and Robbie was free to pursue his own thoughts.

They were not pleasant.

Lizzie was certain to marry some day.

Now that he had firmly removed himself from her list of eligible suitors, that day might come sooner rather than later. Perhaps by the end of the Season. There were plenty of men who would be delighted to have her. She would be lost to him forever.

He had never felt so morose.

Better to feel angry. She was sitting on the settee by herself, just inviting any dirty dish to come join her. Lord Andrew took her invitation. The bounder sat right next to her. Damn if his leg didn't brush up against her skirt.

"Did you have a comment, Lord Westbrooke?"

"No. Sorry, Dodsworth. Brandy went down the wrong way."

Lizzie did not care for the company. The moment Andrew's arse touched the cushion next to her, she'd put on her haughty face, the expression that said "I'm the sister of the Duke of Alvord—keep your distance." She only looked like that when she was very nervous.

Now Lady Felicity had joined them. Lizzie's smile was more strained. She turned her head, as if looking for help. Meg was talking to Parks by the windows; Lady Beatrice was dodging Lord Botton on the other side of the room.

"Excuse me, Dodsworth."

"Don't you want to hear how I'm arranging the stalls, Lord Westbrooke?"

"Love to, but some other time."

". . . billiards," Lord Andrew was saying as Robbie came up to the group.

"I don't know. . . ."

"Don't know what, Lizzie?"

Felicity smiled up at him. "Lady Elizabeth doesn't know if she wants to play billiards, Lord Westbrooke. Can you persuade her?"

Lizzie sent Felicity a very annoyed glance. "I am not very adept at the game."

"Ah, Lady Elizabeth, don't let that concern you." Lord Andrew patted her hand. Robbie clenched his own hands to keep from grabbing the blackguard and throwing him across the room. "I would be happy to assist you."

"Lady Elizabeth is too modest," Robbie said. "Come, Lizzie, you know you are a more than adequate player."

She smiled then, a little of the tension leaving her face. "I did beat you last time we played, didn't I?"

"Yes, but only because I let you."

"Unfair, sir." She laughed. "Very well, I will play, but I insist on being your partner. I cannot give you the opportunity to claim your charity gave me a victory."

Lady Felicity frowned, but before she could speak, Robbie took Lizzie's hand.

"Agreed."

Lady Felicity was not going to concede without a protest. She touched his sleeve.

"Oh, Lord Westbrooke, I thought you could"—she smirked up at him—"play with me."

Not while I have breath in my body.

"Perhaps next time." He bit the inside of his cheek to keep from laughing at the girl's expression. He hoped Tynweith had a very large billiard table as he intended to put as much space as possible between himself and Lady Felicity. He offered Lizzie his arm.

Lord Andrew's demeanor gave no clue as to whether he was annoyed or indifferent.

"Don't pout, Fel. We can still have lots of"—the man's lips slid into a slow smile as he examined Lizzie's bodice—"fun."

Robbie would have been delighted to castrate the man with his cravat pin.

Chapter Eleven

Tynweith's billiard room would benefit from a few more candles. There were far too many shadows for Lizzie's tastes. She intended to stay as close to Robbie and as far from Lord Andrew as possible.

"Lady Elizabeth, would you care to go first?" Lord Skunk smiled in a decidedly oily fashion as he held out a cue.

"Thank you." She ignored him and chose her own stick from the rack. She wouldn't put it past him to offer her defective equipment.

She surveyed the billiard table. Thankfully it looked to be about the same size as the one at Alvord and in good repair. She was nowhere near as skilled a player as James or Robbie, but she wasn't truly terrible. She willed her stomach to stop fluttering. She just wished she knew how good her opponents were.

Her hands needed to stop fluttering, too. Her left hand shook so badly the cue bounced when she tried to line up a shot. She took a steadying breath. She should have let Lady Felicity go first.

"A little agitated, sweetings?" Lord Andrew murmured by her ear.

Lizzie gritted her teeth. *Sweetings?* She would like to take this cue and thrust it up his. . . .

No, she would express her displeasure by potting his ball.

She took another breath and tried to ignore the man. He was far too close to her. She wished he would step back. She looked at Robbie—he was busy fending off Felicity.

Well, the sooner she began, the sooner the game would be over—and as soon as the last point was scored, she was pleading the headache and fleeing to her bedchamber.

She lined her cue up, drew back, and—

"Eep!"

She hit the ball at an angle, missing Lord Andrew's completely and sending hers into the far pocket.

"Oh, dear." Lady Felicity giggled. "Too bad. That's minus three points." She moved the hand on the wall counter back past zero.

Lizzie glared at Lord Andrew. He lifted a brow and smiled slightly, then turned to get Felicity a stick.

"What happened?" Robbie asked quietly.

"Lord Andrew touched my—" Lizzie flushed. She glared at the man's back and whispered. "I'm certain he touched my, um, my skirt just as I took my shot."

Robbie also glared at Lord Andrew's back.

"Next time I'll come stand beside you to be certain the bast—um, blackguard keeps his hands to himself."

"Oh, Lord Westbrooke, would you help me with this shot, please?" Lady Felicity leaned against the table.

"Sorry, I'm certain that would be against the rules. Can't aid the opposition. Ask Lord Andrew for help."

Lady Felicity batted her eyelashes. "Please? This is just a friendly game. No need to be overly concerned with rules."

Robbie smiled. "Still, I must regretfully decline. Lord Andrew, would you like to help Lady Felicity?"

Lord Andrew grinned. "Do you want my assistance, Fel?"

"No." Lady Felicity's lower lip jutted out. If she weren't careful, her face would freeze in a perpetual pout. "I suppose I can do it myself."

She chose a shot that required her to lean toward Robbie, displaying her breasts to her best advantage. They swayed over the table, but stayed in their bodice—barely. Lizzie glanced at Robbie. He looked more disgusted than entranced.

"Ha!" Lady Felicity's ball struck Lizzie's, sending it into the side pocket. "That's two points for me."

"For us, Fel. We are a team, remember." Lord Andrew recorded her score. "Your turn, Westbrooke."

"Guard my back," Robbie muttered as he studied the table.

"With pleasure." Lizzie readied her cue to whack Felicity if she should encroach on Robbie's space.

Really, the girl had more arms than an octopus. She was constantly trying to touch some part of Robbie's person while he was shooting. Lord Andrew's attacks on her were slightly more discreet, but equally annoying. He'd brush up against her when Robbie was lining up a shot. She could tell it distracted Robbie—he was not playing well at all.

"I wish this cue were a sword," he murmured. "See if you can end this torture, will you? You're up after Andrew."

"They're at thirteen. All they have to do is pot the red ball and they'll have won."

"Haven't you noticed what they're doing? When they get close to sixteen, they take a penalty. See, watch Andrew."

Sure enough, the man sent the cue ball into a pocket.

"Too bad." Felicity moved the counter's hand back. "Two point penalty."

"I'd have to score a seven—a perfect shot."

"You can do it. You've done it before. Look, you're lined up perfectly to take Andrew's ball."

Lizzie nodded. "All right, I'll try. Keep him from bumping me."

"I shall be delighted to do so."

Lizzie concentrated on her shot. She needed to hit Andrew's ball and the red ball in one stroke, sending them both into pockets without potting the cue ball. Robbie was right. She could do it. She just needed to focus.

Lord Andrew was headed toward her. She felt Robbie move to intercept him. Robbie couldn't hold him off forever unless they got into a brawl. Lady Felicity started to walk around the table to reach Robbie.

She didn't have much time.

She focused her attention on the little white cue ball, the tip of her cue stick, and the angle she needed for the two to connect. She narrowed her eyes, held her breath, and took her shot.

It was beautiful. Lord Andrew's ball in the left side pocket, red ball in the far right corner pocket, cue ball hovering on the edge—and then rolling back to the center of the table.

"I did it!"

"Alleluia!" Robbie grinned and looked as if he would kiss her. He bent toward her, but stopped himself at the last moment.

Lizzie wanted to grab his head and pull his face down to hers, but he moved away too quickly. Good thing. Once the thrill of winning abated, rational thought returned. She looked around. Lady Felicity was glaring at her; Lord Andrew had a slight smile and a calculating look.

"That was"—what? Exciting? Entertaining? Horrifying?—"interesting," she said, "but I'm rather tired. Meg and I went for a long ramble this afternoon. I believe I'll retire for the evening."

"I'll escort you." Robbie had her hand on his arm before he'd finished his sentence.

"Yes, thank you. That would be lovely." She nodded to Felicity and Andrew. "Good evening."

She let out a long breath as soon as the door closed behind them.

"I'm glad that's over."

"You and I both." Robbie scowled down at her. "How could you have encouraged Lord Andrew like that?"

Lizzie felt her mouth drop open. "What?" A hot flush swept up her neck that had nothing to do with love or attraction. Robbie was glaring at her. The pompous nodcock was glaring at her!

She snatched her hand off his arm. If she'd still had a billiard cue, she'd have used it to knock some sense into his thick skull.

"Encouraged? *Encouraged*? How did I encourage him? As I remember, I was sitting by myself in Lord Tynweith's drawing room, minding my own business, when Lord Andrew approached *me*."

"Exactly. You should not have been sitting by yourself. You know the man is trouble. He was extremely offensive at luncheon. You should have been sitting with one of the other ladies."

"Lady Felicity, perhaps?"

Lizzie turned and started down the corridor to the stairs. She wanted to get to her room as quickly as possible.

The cod's head kept pace.

"No, of course not Lady Felicity. Meg—or Lady Beatrice. The woman *is* your chaperone, after all."

"I am twenty years old. I do not need a chaperone."

"You most certainly do need a chaperone. No, you need a keeper! What were you thinking, walking across the countryside with only Meg as your companion this afternoon?"

They had reached Lizzie's door.

"I was thinking I wanted to get away from mutton-headed nodcocks like you." She poked him in the chest. "I've managed to survive three full Seasons in London's ballrooms without serving the tabbies anything significant to chew on over their scandal broth."

"We are not discussing London's ballrooms; we are discussing this current, slightly scandalous house party. Tynweith's gatherings have a reputation. Frankly, I was shocked when I heard you'd agreed to come."

"Oh?" Lizzie grabbed her doorknob tightly to keep from slapping the supercilious expression off Robbie's face. "So kind of you to put aside your misgivings to attend." She opened her door and stepped into her room. "You should not have bothered."

"I had to come, Lizzie. James couldn't. Someone had to be here to keep an eye on you, to see that you don't get into trouble."

Anger pounded in Lizzie's temples. "I am not a child."

"Of course not. If you were, you wouldn't have to worry about rakes of Lord Andrew's stamp. I'm certain James would be appalled if he knew what was going on here."

Lizzie took a deep breath. She did not shout. "Thank you, Lord Westbrooke, for so kindly meddling in my affairs. However, I take leave to tell you I already have one older brother—I do not need another."

"You certainly need someone to keep track of you if you don't want to permanently ruin your reputation."

Robbie kept talking, but Lizzie stopped listening. She grabbed hold of her door with both hands and slammed it in the beef-witted, cork-brained cabbage-head's face.

He should be here by now. Charlotte consulted her watch again. It was past midnight.

She took a sip of brandy. She'd persuaded Flint to give her a bottle—her flask was running low.

Where was he? She hadn't seen him since luncheon. He hadn't been present at dinner.

She took a larger swallow of brandy. He had said he would come, hadn't he? Perhaps not in so many words, but surely it was understood.

She began to pace.

How was she to get with child if he didn't come?

A bubble of hysteria lodged in her throat. It was Thursday night. If she were home, Hartford would be paying her his weekly visit, fumbling under her nightgown.

How many more Thursdays would he be able to attempt the deed? His breathing had been labored last week and his skin had definitely had a gray tinge. And he had been unable to animate the relevant organ. It had flopped between her thighs like a dead fish.

She bit her lip. Time was definitely running out.

She heard a scratching at her door. Thank God!

"Finally. I thought you had forgotten, Lord—"

She looked at the man on her threshold. It was not Lord Peter.

"I'm delighted you are so eager to see me, Duchess."

"Lord Tynweith!"

What was the baron doing here at this hour? She had to get rid of him. She looked over his shoulder. Still no sign of Lord Peter.

"If you are looking for Addington's whelp, he will not be coming. He had another, ah, engagement. He asked me to take his place."

"What?" Lord Peter was not coming? He'd asked Lord Tynweith. . . . Charlotte felt her cheeks burn. Lord Peter had been discussing what he'd done . . . had been discussing her . . . with Tynweith?

"May I come in? I'd rather not stand here in the hallway. Someone might come along and wonder what I was about."

"Yes. All right. Come in." She definitely did not want any of the house guests—especially Felicity—speculating as to why their host was visiting her room at night. Frankly, she did not want to speculate herself. She trusted he would get to his point eventually. He always had in the past.

"Where is your maid?"

"Marie knows she is not needed."

He picked up the brandy bottle.

"Still drinking, Charlotte?"

"Yes." Surely he was not angry that Flint had been kind enough to supply her with her own bottle? "Would you like some?" She looked around the room. "I don't see an extra glass. Perhaps you could get one?" And she could lock the door behind him. He was making her very nervous. Her stomach was shivering in an extremely unsettling fashion.

He smiled. "I don't need a glass."

"You don't?" Was he going to drink directly from the bottle?

He approached her. She backed up—into her closed door. He put his hands on either side of her head.

Her stomach clenched. He was too close. She closed her eyes. She felt his breath on her cheek. It smelled of brandy, but she knew he wasn't drunk.

"Charlotte, love. You know I'm happy to help you. Happy and willing"—he kissed the corner of her closed eye, just a butterfly brush—"and able"—his lips skimmed the spot under her right ear—"and anxious, too, actually."

He spoke right above her lips. If she moved her head, tilted her chin just the slightest, their mouths would meet.

She kept her head perfectly still.

"Help me?" she whispered.

"Have a child."

Her eyes flew open. "You are joking."

"You know I am not. We spoke about it in the garden yesterday, remember?"

How could she forget? "Lord Peter—"

"—isn't here. I am." His lips pulled into a slow smile. "And I assure you, I possess the equipment necessary to accomplish the task. I am delighted—ecstatic—to put it at your disposal."

"Oh." She wet her lips. She saw his gaze sharpen, focus on her mouth. His eyes looked . . . hot.

In some odd manner, he was causing *her* temperature to rise. Precipitously.

It could not be healthy. She needed to put some distance between them.

Tynweith chose that moment to kiss her.

Oh dear.

His lips were gentle, slow, unlike Hartford's or Lord Peter's. Well, neither of them had bothered much with her mouth. One quick mashing of lips against teeth and they were off to more interesting territory, leaving her with an unobstructed view of the bed canopy.

This was different. Tynweith was in no hurry. He kept his hands on the door. The only part of him touching her was his mouth. He played with her lips, sucking, licking. And then his tongue slipped inside. It swept through her, filling her, stroking her.

She braced herself against the door, trusting it to keep her upright.

She had never felt this way before.

"Are your nipples hard little nubs, sweetings?"

They were.

"Is the secret place between your legs wet? Aching?"

It was. God, it was.

"Your body is ready for my seed, Charlotte. Shall I plant it now? Shall I give you a child?"

She was mindless with need. What was the matter with her? She felt ill, feverish. Out of control.

She did not care for this feeling at all. It was unsettling.

Frightening. She knew in her gut if she let Tynweith do what he wished, something important would change.

She should say no and send him on his way.

Her body was weeping for her to say yes.

She needed a child. If dampness was the key, she would conceive tonight.

She sighed, letting her resistance drain away.

"Yes," she whispered. "Yes, please."

"Then let me get this lovely dress off you. It is very much in the way, don't you agree?"

"My nightdress—"

"Is totally unnecessary. You are going to be naked, love. I am going to see every inch of your lovely body. I am going to touch every inch. Won't that be wonderful?"

No, it would be frightening. Or frighteningly wonderful.

Her body silenced her mind. She pushed herself away from the door—and felt his fingers on her dress. She stared at his cravat while he loosened her fastenings and let her clothing slip slowly down to her feet.

She closed her eyes. She was standing before him in only her stockings. She felt the cold air and the heat of the fire on her skin.

She had never been naked with a man before.

He touched her gently between her legs and she shuddered.

"Beautiful."

His voice was husky, strained. She looked at him. The heat she'd seen before had ignited. His eyes blazed—but still he didn't put his body against hers.

"I think it's time we went to bed, don't you?"

"Yes." Her knees were wobbling.

"Walk."

"I can't."

"You can. Please. For me. I want to watch you."

Hartford and Lord Peter had snuffed the candles and come to her in darkness. All the light, all the looking . . . She felt exposed. Shy.

"I'm skinny."

"No, you're beautiful. Perfect." He brushed his lips over hers and she felt another rush of dampness between her thighs. "I have lusted for you from the moment I saw you. I've pictured your body under mine with every woman I've mounted. I am dying to see how far my imagination has fallen short of reality."

"If it has."

"Oh, it has." He traced her lips with his finger. Her mouth felt swollen. It opened quite without her volition and he kissed it gently. "I was too rough in East-haven's garden, Charlotte. I will not be rough tonight. I will be slow and courteous." The corner of his mouth crooked up. "At least the first time."

"Oh." Usually she wanted the business over as quickly as possible, but strangely, she was not interested in speed at the moment.

She stepped away from him. She felt his gaze slide over her skin, touching her everywhere. Her nipples tightened. He smiled.

"Get into bed, Charlotte."

She nodded and walked the length of the room. He was just behind her. Still he didn't touch her.

She climbed up onto the mattress and reached for the bedclothes.

"No." His hand covered hers and then took the blanket and sheet from her, pulling them down to the bottom of the bed. "We don't need these."

"I'm cold." She wasn't, but she should be. She was naked. She tried to cover her breasts and her most private part with her hands.

His eyes laughed at her.

"You are? You'll be very warm in a moment."

"No, I—"

She stopped speaking. Tynweith was untying his cravat. He pulled it free and took her hand from her breast, looping the cravat loosely around her wrist.

"You must not cover your beauty, Charlotte." He tied the other end to the bedpost.

"What are you doing?" Her breath came faster, with fear as much as desire.

"Don't be alarmed. You can get free easily if you want. Try—you'll see."

She tried. Tynweith was right. "So why . . . ?"

"To remind you not to hide. To encourage you to trust me."

He slid one of her stockings slowly off her leg and tied her other wrist with it. Then he bent and blew over her nipples. She arched up. Still he would not touch her.

"I need to feel you. . . ."

He laughed. "Patience, love. You will feel me soon. Everywhere. On your skin—and in your body."

He removed his coat, his waistcoat, his shirt, slowly, methodically while he walked around the bed, looking at her. Occasionally he would bend over and blow on her skin, but he still would not touch her.

She was on fire. Her nipples ached; the opening between her legs throbbed. She had never felt this way before.

She had never wanted to see her lover's body before either. Why should she? Hartford's was shrunken and bony. Lord Peter's was like a Greek statue and just as hard and cold. But Tynweith's . . .

His chest was broad, but welcoming. Dark hair narrowed down to a line disappearing under the fall of his pantaloons.

The fall was bulging. She was actually happy to see that—she shivered with delight. The most delighted part of her wept with eagerness. Her hips arched and twisted on the bed.

"Now?"

"Not yet, love. I think you offered me some brandy, didn't you?"

"Forget the brandy. Take your pantaloons off."

Tynweith laughed. "Charlotte, how bold!"

She flushed. "I'm sorry, I—"

He bent over her, putting his finger on her lips. "No, don't be sorry. I want you to be bold." His eyes gleamed. "I should reward your boldness, shouldn't I?"

"Uh—oh!"

Tynweith flicked one of her nipples with his tongue. She lifted her back off the bed, offering him more.

"Again. Please."

"You don't want me to drink brandy from your navel?"

"No. Not now. Some other time. Take off your clothes."

He grinned slowly. "With pleasure."

Slowly, too slowly, he undid his buttons and slid his pantaloons over his hips and down his legs. She wanted to shout at him to make haste, she was burning for him.

Where had this new impatience come from? She shook her head on her pillow, wetting her lips. She could not think about it. She could not think about anything but seeing—touching—Tynweith's body.

Finally his drawers slid down, letting his hard length fall free.

"Ah." She thought about freeing her hands so she could touch it.

She had never found that organ attractive, but Tynweith's was beautiful—thick and long. Larger than Lord Peter's. Far larger than Hartford's. She wet her lips again, pulling on her bonds. She wanted to touch it, to stroke it. She was glad it was big. She was empty enough to take it all. She wanted it all now.

Should she touch him?

No. He was bending over her. He licked her breasts, sucked on her nipples. She arched, writhing. He kissed his way slowly down her body. She raised her hips to him, and he laughed, blowing on her heat.

"Anxious, love? Hungry for me?"

"Yes. God, yes. I need you."

"I am so happy to hear that."

Finally he brought his body over hers. She felt him heavy between her thighs, touching her entrance.

"Oh. Oh." She was panting. Burning. Aching. "Something is happening. I feel . . . I feel . . ."

"Empty? Needy?"

"Yes."

"Good. You are ready for my seed, then. Shall I give it to you now? Shall I fill you?"

"Yes." She almost sobbed the word. She twisted under him. He was teasing her still, hovering just outside her. "Please."

She slipped her hands free of her bonds. She had to touch him. She ran her hands over the muscles in his back down to his buttocks. She tugged on his hips, trying to bring him closer. "Now. Please."

"So impatient, my love." His words were breathy. "Have you never felt this wildness before?"

"No. Never. I want you *now*."

He chuckled, though his breath was coming quickly and his back was slick with sweat.

"Demanding, too, Charlotte?"

"Yes. Please. Now. Edward, I need you."

She saw through her madness that his face stilled. His eyes blazed into hers.

"God, Charlotte." His voice was rough. "God, to hear my name on your lips. I want to hear you scream it. Will you?"

"I . . ."

He teased her, flexing his hips, touching her entrance, brushing it, but not coming in. She arched up, but she could not capture him.

"My name, Charlotte. Scream it and I will come to you."

It was not hard to do at all. She felt like screaming in frustration.

"Edward!"

He was a man of his word. She sobbed as he surged into her. She started to come apart even as he entered. Her passage contracted around his hard length and her womb trembled as she felt his warm seed pulse into her.

"Charlotte." He kissed her slowly, his body heavy on hers. He was still inside her. She liked it. She liked his weight, his possession.

Surely this coupling had given her a child.

She was surprised she didn't feel more triumph. The job was done, wasn't it? Now Edward could leave and she could sleep.

She didn't want to sleep. She wanted to do what they had done all over again. She moved her legs against his and flushed.

"I still have one stocking on."

"Really? I am so sorry to have overlooked that detail. I shall just have to do better next time, hmm?"

He flexed his hips and she felt him growing hard inside her.

"Perhaps I had better try again now, do you think? They do say practice makes perfect."

She smiled. "Yes, please, Edward. Now would be splendid."

Chapter Twelve

"I've worked out a plan."

"Hmm?" Charlotte sipped her chocolate. She had not gotten up yet. She didn't want to. She wanted to pull up the covers and stay in bed all day, remembering the wonderful things that had happened here last night and this morning. Edward hadn't left until dawn.

"Charlotte, *will* you pay attention?" Felicity's tone was sharp.

Charlotte blinked. Felicity was glaring at her.

"I'm sorry. You said something about a plan?"

"Yes." Felicity pulled a chair up to the bed. "I've come up with a plan to compromise Westbrooke when the house party visits the ruins today." She smiled. "Or at the very least, I will remove Lady Elizabeth from the competition for his title."

"Oh?"

"What do you mean, 'oh'? This will give you what you've wanted, too, you know. Even if I don't manage to trap Westbrooke, Alvord's sister should be well and truly ruined. Lord Andrew is taking care of it. You'll finally have your revenge."

"Yes." Revenge was the furthest thing from her mind at the moment—unless it was revenge against Edward for what he had made her do the third time

he'd taken her. She hadn't wanted to do it, but he'd
been right. It had been very enjoyable.

Perhaps she could persuade him to take a tour of
his topiary gardens after they got back from this trip
to the ruins. Now that she was better versed in the amatory arts, she was certain she'd find the shrubbery
much more interesting. Inspiring even.

"Charlotte! Where *is* your mind?"

Charlotte flushed. "Your pardon. I didn't sleep well
last night."

The moment the words left her lips she felt her
flush deepen. She must be the brightest shade of
red. She glanced at Felicity. The other girl's eyes had
narrowed.

"If I didn't know better, I'd say you'd been engaged
in serious bed play. But you couldn't have been. Peter
spent a lusty night at the local inn last evening."

Charlotte felt a spurt of annoyance. "So that's
where he was."

"Yes." Felicity's gaze sharpened. "Did you find a
substitute?"

Charlotte put down her chocolate and threw back
the covers.

"You said you had a plan?"

Felicity gave her one more searching look and then
shrugged. "Yes. It is not terribly complicated. I believe
it should work like a charm. As I said, Andrew will take
care of Lady Elizabeth. Your job is to be certain Westbrooke pays a visit to the castle's dungeon—alone."

"How am I going to manage that?"

"He'll be looking for Lady Elizabeth. Tell him that's
where Andrew took her. He'll fly down the stairs." Felicity leaned forward. "And I will be waiting for him.
It should take me only a few minutes to set the scene,
then you are to come looking for us. Bring as many of
the house party as you can, but be sure to include
Lady Dunlee. She is a splendid gossip. I hope to have

a spectacle staged that will titillate society for many months, if not years."

"When am I supposed to accomplish this? Westbrooke might be suspicious if I try to send him off the moment his foot crosses the threshold."

"Tynweith is planning a picnic. After we finish the meal, I will go off. Wait a few minutes and then send Westbrooke after me."

"Very well." Charlotte could not find a scrap of enthusiasm for the plan, but she supposed she did owe Felicity something. "I will see what I can do."

Lizzie straightened her bonnet. She was waiting in Tynweith's entry hall with the other house party guests for the caravan of carriages to arrive and take them to the castle ruins. They were still missing Lord Andrew, Lord Peter, and Lady Felicity. Perhaps those three had found something more amusing to do. She could only hope. Whatever it was, it was probably depicted in Tynweith's obscene shrubbery.

She stepped behind a pillar to avoid Mr. Dodsworth.

This house party was a complete disaster. She should never have come. Perhaps she could persuade Lady Beatrice and Meg to leave early.

She glanced around the room. Meg was in close conversation with Mr. Parker-Roth.

Perhaps not.

She straightened her bonnet again. Shouldn't the carriages be here now? She'd prefer to walk, anyway. It was ridiculous to ride such a short distance.

Her gaze touched portly Lady Dunlee and Lady Caroline.

Well, perhaps carriages were not a terrible idea for some of the party.

She heard a noise on the stairs and glanced up. Another hope dashed. Lord Andrew and Lady Felicity were descending. At least Lord Peter was still absent.

Felicity caught sight of her and said something to Lord Andrew. He nodded and started toward Lizzie. She dodged behind another pillar. She did not want to spend time with Lord Andrew.

She found Lady Beatrice standing next to a statue of Aphrodite. The older woman looked delighted to see her.

"Come here, Lizzie, and pretend to be fascinated by some conversational topic, so Lord Botton will not approach me."

"He's talking to Miss Hyde now."

"Yes, poor woman. If I were of a more charitable disposition I might take pity on her. But I spent an entire hour with Botton last evening and my charity is depleted. It really was too bad of Tynweith to invite the little lecher."

Lizzie glanced over her shoulder. Lord Andrew was still coming her way.

"I do wish he had not invited Lord Andrew either."

"Is the boy becoming a nuisance?" Lady Beatrice raised her lorgnette and inspected him. He changed direction quickly and went to speak to Lord Dunlee. "Why aren't you with Lord Westbrooke, anyway? I believe he has just joined Meg and Mr. Parker-Roth."

"I . . . well . . . we are not on good terms at the moment."

"Really? Why not? I thought the whole point of attending this affair was to give you the opportunity to bring Westbrooke up to scratch."

Lizzie flushed. Had she been so obvious? "I'm sorry. You must be very annoyed with me for making you and Meg come."

"Well, I would have been if I'd known Botton would be here." Lady Bea laughed. "Don't castigate yourself, child. I had my reasons for wanting to get away from Town for a few days. And I don't believe Meg is complaining either. She seems quite taken with Mr. Parker-Roth."

"The carriages are here!" Lord Tynweith stood at the front door, grinning.

"Now I wonder what has happened to him," Lady Bea said. "I don't believe I've ever seen Tynweith so jovial."

"He does seem unusually happy." Lizzie glanced around. Felicity was looking at her now. "May I sit with you, Lady Beatrice?"

"Of course. Are you certain you wouldn't prefer to join Lord Westbrooke's group?"

Lizzie met Robbie's eye for a moment. He looked right through her. He was still as angry as she was over their argument.

"I'm certain."

"Come along then. We will see if we can rescue Miss Hyde."

God, he felt wonderful. Tynweith tried to stop smiling. Nell had already commented on his high spirits. Worse, Lady Dunlee had given him a searching look. If that gabble grinder got wind of the fact he'd visited Charlotte's bed, the story would be all over London within the week. Hartford would not be pleased. More, Charlotte would be distressed.

He would not have Charlotte distressed for the world.

She wanted any baby she might conceive credited to Hartford. Tynweith frowned. He didn't like that, but there was little he could do about it. She *was* married to the man. And really, if she were enceinte now, it would be difficult, if not impossible, to say for certain who the father was—he, Lord Peter, or Hartford.

Perhaps that was for the best. Still, he hated the thought of his son being raised as another man's. He should have given that more consideration before he'd climbed into Charlotte's bed.

No, it would have made no difference. He would not give up last night for anything.

Lady Dunlee was staring at him again.

"You are looking unusually merry this morning, Lord Tynweith. Have you some good news to share?"

He'd put an announcement in the *Morning Post* before he told Lady Dunlee any news, good or bad.

"I don't believe I do, ma'am, except that it is a beautiful day for an outing."

She peered at him through her lorgnette. "My lord, how can you say so? Just look at the horizon. Aren't those rain clouds?"

Lady Dunlee was correct. Sinister clouds loomed off toward the sea.

"Ah, but it is sunny here. The wind may well keep the storm at bay for hours—and I will have the carriages stand ready to whisk us back to Lendal Park at the first rain drop. Your lovely bonnet and gown are quite safe."

"I see." The enlarged eyes examining him held a puzzled look that was quickly replaced by a spark of excitement. He swore her nose twitched, as if she could smell the hint of gossip on his person. He half expected her to bay.

The hunt was on.

He tried to keep his face expressionless. "May I help you into this carriage?"

She examined him for another instant and then lowered her lorgnette.

"Thank you, my lord."

He helped her and Lady Caroline up the carriage steps. Lady Beatrice and Lady Elizabeth came next, dragging Miss Hyde with them.

"Shall I send Lord Dunlee to join you?" He was certainly not volunteering to climb into this rolling inquisition chamber himself. The trip to the castle would take no more than fifteen minutes, but that was more than enough time for an accomplished gossip such as Lady Dunlee to extract all his secrets.

"No, thank you," Lady Dunlee said. "We will do very nicely without him."

"Lord Botton, perhaps?"

"Have you lost your mind?" Lady Beatrice glared at him. "Don't you dare let that lecherous cod's head in here. And don't think to fob off that crashing bore, Dodsworth, on us either."

"Indeed." Lady Dunlee raised her lorgnette again. She and Lady Beatrice both inspected him as if he were a repulsive bug. Fine with him. He was merely trying to be a thoughtful host. He bowed and stepped back so the footman could close the carriage door.

He sighed with relief as soon as he heard the latch catch. Thank God. He would have to be very careful now that Lady Dunlee was on the hunt. He'd do his best to put as much distance as possible between them this afternoon.

He would have to put distance between himself and Charlotte as well. She was standing with Lady Felicity, waiting for Lord Andrew to help her into another carriage. He had purposely not gone to assist her. If Lady Dunlee saw the two of them together. . . . He was not certain he could hide his feelings when he touched Charlotte, even with so mundane a contact as taking her gloved hand to steady her on the carriage steps.

She glanced over, caught him watching her, and blushed.

Damn, it was a very good thing Lady Dunlee was already closed away in her carriage. He glanced back. Fortunately she was too well bred to hang out the window and gawk.

He would definitely need to stay far away from both women this afternoon. But this evening, after the house party had retired for the night. . . .

God, Charlotte had been just as passionate as he had hoped. Last night had been amazing. Perfect.

Each coupling had been better than the last. She learned so quickly, was so eager. By morning, she'd even begun to take the lead. He'd hated to leave her, but at least he could console himself that there was tonight and every night for the rest of the house party.

Nell touched him on the sleeve. "I think everything is in order, Edward. The servants have gone ahead and should be setting up for the picnic. Sir George and I will take Lord Botton and join her grace, Lady Felicity, and Lord Andrew in their carriage—I don't trust those three together. You can do your duty and ride with Mr. Dodsworth."

"Very well." He could tolerate fifteen minutes of horse talk. "But whatever do you suspect the duchess of doing?"

"I am not as concerned with her as I am with Lady Felicity and Lord Andrew. But she *is* Lady Felicity's bosom-friend. If Lady Felicity is up to something, chances are the duchess is involved."

"No, I am certain you are mistaken."

Nell put her hand on his arm. "Edward, do not forget—the duchess is Hartford's wife, and Hartford is still very much alive."

"Of course. I am in no danger of forgetting that fact. What are you suggesting?"

"Nothing. But I am your cousin. I know you—and I know what it is like to want and not be able to have. I am fortunate Lady Gaston is not possessive of her husband. I do not think Hartford is similarly inclined."

"Hartford is an old fool."

"Perhaps. But he is a duke and proud. I would not put it past him to insist on a duel if he felt his honor slighted."

"I am not afraid of him."

"I did not think you were. But it cannot reflect well on you to fight a man twice your age, even if you win. And if you kill him, a duke and Charlotte's husband. . . ." Nell squeezed his arm. "I just do not want to see you backed into a corner from which there is no gracious way out."

He covered her hand with his. "Don't worry. I won't do anything foolish. I promise."

She smiled slightly, a touch of melancholy in her voice. "Love is often foolish, Edward."

Robbie half listened to Meg and Parks argue about garden design. At least, that's what he thought the discussion was about. He was making no attempt to follow the conversation closely. He employed a perfectly competent head gardener at each of his estates and he let the man do his job. Of course, if any of his men took to torturing the bushes into the odd arrangements Tynweith favored, they would be looking for new employment in short order. He had no patience with obscene shrubbery.

He glanced at Parks. His friend was more animated than he'd seen him in years. And Meg was equally passionate. The two should make a match of it. They would bore anyone else to madness.

Speaking of bores. . . . Thank God Dodsworth was sitting on the other side of the carriage. Parks served as a wall—a hedge, more appropriately—between them. Dunlee and Tynweith had to suffer the detailed description of that palace Dodsworth was planning for his blasted horses.

He watched the trees bowl by. They should be at the castle shortly. He hoped Lizzie had taken his words to heart and would stay near Lady Beatrice or Meg. He would keep an eye on her, of course, but she'd made it abundantly clear last night she would not welcome his company.

Why did he always say the wrong thing to her these days? Hell, he didn't know what the right thing was anymore. Surely she saw that she'd not behaved sensibly in sitting by herself in the drawing room or going off on a ramble with only Meg as a companion?

It was clear she was in danger. Take that billiard game, for instance. God, that had been torture. He hated having to be in such proximity to Felicity. To seek her company voluntarily had tied his stomach in knots—especially after his close escape just the other day. How she could face him so calmly after she'd crawled naked into his bed was a mystery. The girl was brazen, utterly brazen. It was impossible to guess what such a creature would do. The rules of polite society were obviously beyond her ken.

And Lord Andrew was just as bad. Worse. It was one thing for a woman to try to trap a man into marriage, but quite another for a man to prey on a naïve young miss. *That* was reprehensible. The blackguard had been so damn sneaky. He'd managed to make every brush against Lizzie look accidental.

He should have thrashed the bastard right there by the billiard table.

He scowled at the innocent landscape. He felt so damn powerless. If Lizzie were his wife, he would have clear rights to protect her from any kind of insult. But she was not—could never be—his wife. And now she was not even his friend.

Why had she ripped up at him like that when he'd walked her to her room? He had only spoken the truth.

"Lord Tynweith," Meg said, "I've been meaning to ask you something."

Robbie looked away from the window. What momentous question could have caused Meg to focus on something other than vegetation?

"Yes, Miss Peterson?" Tynweith smiled politely.

"Lady Elizabeth and I were in need of exercise yesterday and walked over to the castle."

"I see. I hope you won't find today's outing sadly flat then."

"No, of course not." Meg shook her head, then paused and smoothed her skirt. "We didn't have much time to look around, but we did stumble on something that caused us some consternation."

"Really? I am sorry. What was the problem?"

"Your dungeon, Lord Tynweith. Did you know that it is most unusual?"

Tynweith raised an eyebrow. "You have frequented many dungeons, Miss Peterson? I do find that surprising."

"Now see here—" Parks began.

Meg frowned back at him, stopping him cold. Then she frowned at Tynweith. "No, of course I have not frequented many—any—dungeons. Why do you say so?"

"Well, one supposes that one must know what is usual in dungeons to find a particular one unusual."

Meg rolled her eyes. "All right, Lord Tynweith, let me say instead that we found your dungeon quite unsettling."

"Dungeons are not designed to be comfortable places, Miss Peterson. At least this one has not been occupied for centuries."

"There I believe you are wrong, my lord. Not only did it appear your dungeon had been used recently, it looked as if it were being employed to torture people. There were manacles on the walls, whips on the table, and other odd, distasteful looking objects lying about. What do you think of that?"

Tynweith closed his eyes and rubbed his forehead. "I think I need to speak to some people at the local inn, Miss Peterson."

"Well, I certainly hope you do so. A sturdy lock might also be in order."

"Perhaps you are correct."

"I'd say so, Tynweith." Lord Dunlee frowned. "Don't want any heinous activities occurring on your estate. Could prove awkward, don't you know."

"More than awkward, Tynweith." There was a note

of anger in Parks's voice. "I trust the ladies will not be able to view this dungeon on our outing today?"

"I will definitely warn them against venturing in that direction, and I will send a locksmith up after we return."

"Good. We wouldn't want their tender sensibilities lacerated."

"No indeed." Lord Dunlee nodded in agreement.

Mr. Dodsworth was curiously silent. Robbie examined the man as the carriage pulled to a stop. He looked extremely eager to exit the coach. Extremely eager and extremely red.

Who would have thought boring old Dodsworth might know any use for a whip other than to get a horse to go?

Chapter Thirteen

Lizzie watched Lord Dunlee and Lord Botton disappear into the tower. For some reason, she did not think they were headed up the stairs to view the battlements.

"It's too bad Tynweith had the lawn mowed," Meg said. "I'm certain he destroyed some lovely plant specimens."

"He couldn't very well hold a picnic in the weeds we saw here yesterday." Lizzie frowned. "I can't believe you mentioned the dungeon to him."

"Of course I did, and it was a good thing, too. I don't believe he was aware the place was being used for nefarious purposes. He said he would send out a locksmith when we return to put a stop to the business."

"Did he happen to say what the nefarious purposes were? Surely he didn't think the local people were being tortured?"

Sir George and Tynweith had just come out of the tower. They were sniggering.

"No, he did not say, but he wasn't shocked. I got the impression this had happened before. He appeared to believe people at the inn were using the room without his permission."

"Hmm." Now Robbie and Parks were going in. Surely *they* were headed for the battlements?

The only two men who had not rushed to examine something in the tower were Lord Andrew and Mr. Dodsworth. Lord Andrew was in the middle of what appeared to be an intense conversation with Lady Felicity. They were standing well beyond the eavesdropping range of Lady Dunlee—Lizzie could almost taste her frustration.

Mr. Dodsworth was standing by himself, watching Miss Hyde and Mrs. Larson put the finishing touches on the picnic preparations. His color was fluctuating oddly, reddening whenever more gentlemen entered the tower.

"Where is Lord Peter? I don't think I've seen him since yesterday." Meg snorted. "Not that I've missed him. I wish he'd go back to London."

"Well, you've gotten your wish. Lady Dunlee reported on the way over that he went back to Town. Said he had pressing business there, though she doubted that explanation. Petticoat business is what she said."

Robbie and Parks came out with Lord Dunlee and Lord Botton.

"Oh good. There's Mr. Parker-Roth." Meg grabbed Lizzie's arm and tugged her toward the group. "I want him to look at some plants I found. I think I may have stumbled across the castle's herb garden."

The men had stopped a distance away. Lord Botton was gesturing in an extremely animated manner.

"I tell you," he said as Lizzie and Meg came within earshot, "don't dismiss it until you've tried it. The switch—"

"Ladies, how lovely to see you." Robbie spoke quickly and loudly.

"What?" Lord Botton looked quite taken aback to be so rudely interrupted until he glanced over his shoulder at Lizzie and Meg. Then he turned an interesting shade of red and bowed slightly. "Oh, yes, lovely, um, indeed. Lovely day, isn't it? Lovely castle."

Lizzie nodded. All the gentlemen had a reddish hue to their complexions.

"What are you switching?" Meg asked.

"Conversational topics, Miss Peterson," Parks said. "Do you have a subject to suggest?"

Meg's face lit up. "Actually, I do. I've found an interesting clump of vegetation by what I believe was once the castle's kitchen. I think there may be a number of non-native species of herbs in the collection."

"Fascinating. However, I suspect that is a topic which will not hold the attention of everyone present."

"It won't?"

Lizzie covered her smile. Lord Botton was staring at Meg as if she were some exotic beast.

"Meg," Lizzie said, "you *know* you're prone to bore people once you get going."

Meg smiled slightly. "Perhaps."

"Why don't you and Miss Peterson go investigate these plants, Parks?" Robbie said. "I'm well enough acquainted with Miss Peterson to know she will suffer greatly if she cannot discuss this botanic bounty immediately."

"Very well. I confess I *would* like to see the specimens." Parks offered Meg his arm.

"Yes, do go enjoy yourselves." Lord Botton watched them walk off, then shook his head. "Plants!" His tone left little doubt as to his feelings. "I believe I shall have a word with Lady Beatrice. Coming, Dunlee? I see Lady Bea is chatting with your charming wife and daughter."

"Yes, um, I think I'll just trot over and speak to Dodsworth. He looks a bit lonely at the moment."

Lord Botton nodded. "Good idea. You might ask him about technique—which he prefers."

"I am not interested in switch—" Lord Dunlee

looked at Lizzie and coughed. "That is, I'm not interested in, um, er. . . . Perhaps I *will* join you, Lord
Botton."

"Splendid. If you'll excuse us, Westbrooke, Lady
Elizabeth?"

"Certainly. Don't let us keep you." Lizzie watched
them make their way across the castle yard. She
looked back at Robbie. His expression was guarded.

"Shall I escort you to your chaperone?"

Lizzie drew breath to tell him she most definitely
did *not* want to be escorted anywhere and he could
very well stop trying to act like a big brother, but she
stopped before she uttered the first word. She saw the
determination in his eyes. No matter what she said, he
was going to do what he thought was right.

It was annoying, it was maddening, but it was en-
dearing, too.

"Aren't you afraid I might learn what Lord Botton
was so keen to discuss?"

Robbie's ears turned red. His face assumed a
mulish expression. She could see he was not in the
mood to be teased. And she was only partially teasing.
She had not forgiven him for his highhandedness last
night.

"Why don't you escort me over to Meg and Parks?"
A gust of wind tried to steal her bonnet and sent the
servants scurrying to protect the place settings. She
looked up—the storm clouds were much closer. "It
looks as if the weather may not wait on Lord Tynweith's convenience."

"We need to get this done today, Andrew."

"Why? I'm enjoying myself. I think I almost got
Westbrooke to throw a punch last night in the billiards room, Fel. Wouldn't that have been something?
The cool-headed Lord Westbrooke losing control so
shockingly?"

Felicity frowned at Lord Andrew. "This is not a game."

"Of course it is. Life's a game." He waggled his finger at her. "Don't be so serious."

"This *is* serious, you nodcock. I've been stalking Westbrooke for going on four years now. I'm tired of the hunt—it's time to move in for the kill."

"So romantic, Fel."

"Romance is for totty-headed poets."

"What? You don't want hearts and flowers from Westbrooke?"

Felicity snorted. "What would I do with those? I want a title and pounds per annum—influence and money, precedence and property."

"So mercenary."

"As if you are not. Surely it is not merely Lady Elizabeth's lovely eyes that persuaded you to help me ruin her."

"No, but I am not motivated solely by filthy lucre—I expect to gain a great deal of enjoyment from the deed. I don't believe the lady will just stand still and take her punishment. She will struggle. She'll be angry and terrified. It will be quite a treat. And if I have to wed her afterward, even better. I'll have a lifetime to mortify her." He grinned. "I will definitely enjoy flaunting a very public parade of lovers before the bitch's horrified eyes—and then make her submit to me in bed like a good little wife."

Felicity felt a moment of compunction, but she ignored it as she would a touch of indigestion.

"You may do what you wish with Lady Elizabeth as long as you take her off somewhere—somewhere other than the dungeon—without raising Westbrooke's suspicions."

"Hmm. That might be a little tricky. She does not seem to care for my company."

"Well, you must come up with some ruse to get her away from the group."

"And I'm not certain Westbrooke will let her out of his sight. If I just stroll away from the table with her, I wager he'll be at my throat like a rabid dog."

"Can't you be discreet?"

"Sweetings, I don't think it is possible to be *that* discreet."

"Well, I can't think of everything." She took a deep breath. She was not going to get anywhere if she irritated Andrew. "Do you have any suggestions?"

"Perhaps the duchess can help."

"Perhaps. She's been oddly distracted today, though." Felicity shrugged. "With luck there will be general milling around after luncheon and the deed will be accomplished easily. We can only plan so much. We will have to hope luck smiles on us a little."

The wind whipped by, trying to dislodge her bonnet. She grabbed the brim and squinted up at the sky. "I do hope the weather holds. If the rain comes in, everyone will run for the carriages and our plans will be washed away as well."

Lizzie grabbed her napkin before it could go sailing across the table. The wind was making the picnic especially exciting.

"Have you had word from home, Lady Elizabeth?" Mrs. Larson saved the end of the tablecloth from covering a dish of sweetbreads. "Isn't the duchess expected to deliver any day now?"

"Not quite yet—the baby is not due for a few weeks."

"And all is well?"

"Yes, thank you. Sarah had no trouble when her first child was born, so we don't anticipate any difficulties this time, though my brother, the duke, will worry."

Mrs. Larson smiled. "Of course, and so he should."

Her eyes twinkled. "It is his fault the duchess finds herself in such a state, is it not?"

Lizzie smiled back at her. "Yes, I suppose it is."

"I was not blessed with children, but my sister, Lady Illington, often said she thought her husband suffered more than she did when she was brought to bed. He felt so responsible yet so helpless. At that point there was nothing he could do but wait and pray that all went well."

Lizzie laughed. "My brother was the same, only he made everyone around him suffer, too. He paced his study like a caged animal—like one of the poor lions at the Tower menagerie—until my aunt, Lady Gladys, let him into Sarah's room. The accoucheur was not happy, but James threatened to have him hanged— I believe he said he would hang him himself—if the man didn't stop bellowing at him and get back to helping Sarah produce his son."

Mrs. Larson laughed, and Lizzie smiled. It was funny now—it had not been so amusing at the time. She had never seen James so agitated. He had always been the rock in her life. Even when their insane cousin had threatened Sarah's life, he had not seemed so beside himself as he'd been when Sarah was in labor. She was almost glad she would miss it this time.

Perhaps his concern wasn't so surprising. Their mother had died giving birth to her. James did not want to lose Sarah in the same way.

Lizzie glanced down the table. Robbie would never know the anguish of birth nor would he know the joy of holding his own son or daughter in his arms.

If she married him, she would not either.

She turned back to her hostess. Impulsively, she leaned closer. "Mrs. Larson, I do not mean to be encroaching, but, well, I wonder if you would tell me— do you miss having children?" She looked down at her plate. She was appalled at her boldness. What must the other woman think of her?

"I ask because I'm considering the subject myself, you see. That is, it is time I thought of marriage, and, um, thoughts of children follow naturally. I hope you don't find the question offensive. I apologize—"

Mrs. Larson put her hand on Lizzie's. "Yes," she said, "I miss having children." She smiled slightly. "My sister says she envies me my peace, but I envy her the energy and benevolent chaos of her household." She sighed. "And I do confess to feeling a bit lonely on occasion. Oh, I have Sir George when his wife allows it, and Edward—Lord Tynweith. But it is not the same as having my own family."

"No, I can see that it would not be." Lizzie swallowed around a sudden lump in her throat. She could not bear the loneliness. She'd been so lonely growing up. James had been away at school and then off to war. Her mother was dead; her father might as well have been for all the attention he showed her. She'd had only Aunt Gladys, Aunt's companion Lady Amanda Wallen-Smyth, and Meg.

And Robbie.

She looked down the table at him again. He'd bent to retrieve Miss Hyde's napkin from the ground where the wind had blown it. He handed it to her with a flourish and a small bow. Miss Hyde smiled fleetingly and ducked her head as she took the cloth from his fingers.

Robbie's smile never reached his eyes.

Lud! Lizzie felt tears prick her own eyes and she looked away.

She had not noticed. . . .

How could she not have noticed?

Robbie joked and laughed—he was the clown of any gathering—but she had not seen real joy in his face for years.

How could it have taken her so long to notice?

If she were lonely, Robbie had no one—no parents,

no brothers, no sisters. Sarah, James's wife, was his only cousin. One could not count Theobald.

How lonely must he be?

"Do you ever regret marrying Mr. Larson?" she heard herself ask.

"Oh, no. Edward doesn't believe it, but I loved my husband. I mourned—I still mourn—his passing." Mrs. Larson paused, looked down at her hands folded on her lap, and then met Lizzie's gaze directly. "Really, Lady Elizabeth, who knows if I would have had children had I married another man? Or if those children would have lived past infancy? We have so little control of our destinies, don't you think?"

Lizzie nodded. "Yes, I suppose you are right."

"I believe I am." Mrs. Larson smiled. "I don't regret for a moment marrying the man I loved. We had twenty-five wonderful years together. Sir George, on the other hand, has two sons but no love." She spread her hands and shrugged. "I would have liked to have both, but forced to choose, I'd choose love." She grinned. "My sister says babies are cute, but exhausting, and older children are not so cute and more exhausting. They argue and fight and get dirty and sick. She loves them dearly, but she also loves for me to come play auntie."

Lizzie smiled. "I think you are very wise, Mrs. Larson."

Mrs. Larson laughed. "I don't know about wise. Old, yes. I hope I've learned something over the years."

Mrs. Larson turned to talk to Mr. Parker-Roth on her other side. Lizzie turned to Mr. Dodsworth. He was still strangely subdued, but he could have recited the breeding history of each of the horses in his stable for all she cared. Her heart felt light for the first time in a long while.

She was going to choose love also.

* * *

"You know what you are supposed to do?"

Charlotte nodded. How could she not? Felicity had been rattling off directions in her ear all through luncheon. It was giving her indigestion.

She looked down the table at Edward. She wanted to be sitting next to him. He caught her glance for a moment and she felt it low in her stomach. The area between her legs where he had spent so much time the night before began to throb.

Who would have thought the procreative process could be so engrossing? Certainly her activities with Hartford and Lord Peter had given no indication of it. But Edward . . . A shiver ran up her spine.

"Charlotte, are you paying attention? This is important."

"Yes, Felicity." The girl was most annoying. Pushy, petulant, self-centered. Why hadn't she noticed it before? She would have to cut the connection as soon as they returned to London. "You want me to send Westbrooke to look for you in the dungeon."

"No! He would never come looking for me. You are to tell him you think that is where Lady Elizabeth has gone. Lord Andrew will have taken her away, so Westbrooke will be anxious to find her. Instead he will find me."

"Yes, all right. I have it now."

Would she see Edward in London? They would have to be discreet. Hartford was a trifle possessive. Well, and she could not afford any rumors running through the *ton*.

They had discussed this last night, when they were resting between couplings. There could be no indication that they were trysting. If she did become pregnant, she wanted the world to think the child was Hartford's. She especially wanted Hartford's odious grandnephew to believe it. That noxious little worm would search for any reason to contest the succession.

She selected a comfit from the dish the footman had just placed at her elbow. She should be charitable. Her child would snatch a title and vast wealth from a fifty-five year old man who had spent his life waiting to be duke.

"And then . . . ?" Felicity could not look more annoyed. She was clearly losing patience. Charlotte admitted her mind had been wandering.

"And then . . . ?" Charlotte repeated. Edward was talking to Lady Dunlee now. He had the handsomest profile. How had she resisted him all these years?

He had frightened her.

She'd been attracted to him the moment she'd seen him enter Easthaven's ballroom all those years ago. She'd asked her mother who he was.

"Tynweith," her mother had said. *"A mere baron—and dangerous. Not a man you wish to know."*

But she had wished to know him. She had been thrilled when Lady Easthaven had presented him. She'd accepted his request to dance before her mother could object.

He was different from the other men she'd met. He was exciting, dangerous—and he spoke to something in her she did not recognize. When she was with him, she did not feel like the good, dutiful daughter of the Duke and Duchess of Rothingham. She felt daring, wild, alive. As if, instead of the predictable, well-planned life her parents had chosen for her, there were exciting possibilities to choose from.

And then he had taken her out into the garden.

She could have stopped him. She thought of stopping him. But she wanted to go with him. She wanted to be daring, to pretend a little longer she was the girl she saw reflected in his gaze.

He had kissed her. It was nothing compared to their activities of last night, but it had been much more than she'd ever experienced. It was her first kiss, and his hands and mouth had been all over her. He had been rough and urgent. It had been too much for her. The fear had overtaken the excitement and she had slapped him. From then on, her mother had seen to it that she stayed far away from him.

If she'd married him instead of chasing after Alvord and marrying Hartford. . . . But she wouldn't have. She'd not had the courage then to withstand her parents' expectations.

"Charlotte!" Felicity shook her arm, her voice sharp. "*Do* pay attention. Once Westbrooke enters the tower, wait about five minutes—not much more, I don't expect him to stay long, especially if he senses a trap— and gather Lady Dunlee and as many other guests as you can to tour the dungeon."

"I don't think Edward—I mean, Lord Tynweith— will approve."

"Edward?" Felicity's eyes narrowed.

Charlotte tried not to blush. "I'm sorry. I've been speaking to Mrs. Larson—she sometimes refers to her cousin by his Christian name."

Felicity looked suspicious, but did not pursue the topic. Obviously she had more important concerns.

"I don't care what Tynweith thinks. If he questions you, point out that all the men have already toured the room and the ladies want to see what the fuss is about. Don't worry. I didn't include anything truly shocking when I set the stage for this little play."

"All right."

"And be certain Lady Dunlee is at the front of the group. I want her to have a good view so she can report every interesting detail to the *ton*."

"Yes. I will encourage her to lead the way."

"Splendid. Now you won't forget what to do?"

"No, I will remember."

"Good. Look—Mrs. Larson and Lady Elizabeth are rising. Luncheon is over."

Charlotte stood with Felicity. The wind caught her bonnet, almost tearing it from her head. She put her hand on it. "I do believe the storm is coming."

"But it is not here yet."

"My lord," Mrs. Larson said, "when do you wish to depart?"

Edward looked at the sky. "I believe we can safely stay another half hour." He addressed the group at large. "If there are any other sights you would care to see, I suggest you do so now and return to the castle entrance in thirty minutes. I will have the carriages ready to take us back to Lendal Park then."

"Come on. You need to distract Westbrooke so Andrew can take Lady Elizabeth away." Felicity grabbed Charlotte's arm.

"What can I say to distract the earl?" Charlotte pulled back. Felicity tugged again.

"You have to think of something. The plan depends on it."

"Why me?"

"You are the only one available. I must go to the dungeon. Come on!" She tugged harder.

"Very well." Charlotte had no idea what she would say to Westbrooke. Fortunately, she was not put to the test. Lady Dunlee, dragging her daughter behind her, reached the earl first.

"Lord Westbrooke, my daughter has been dying to see the ruined chapel. Quite gothic, I do believe. Right out of one of Mrs. Radcliffe's novels—not that we encourage the dear girl to read such things, of course, but. . . ." Lady Dunlee shrugged. "Would you be so kind as to escort her so she may view it?"

Lord Westbrooke did not look thrilled, but he smiled and bowed.

"Perfect," Felicity said as Westbrooke walked off with Lady Caroline. "I could not have planned it better. Now if Andrew is paying attention—yes, there he goes."

Lord Andrew joined the group that included Lady Elizabeth, Miss Peterson, Mr. Parker-Roth, Sir George, and Mrs. Larson.

"This is it." Felicity's voice sounded tight with excitement. "I have to go." She shook Charlotte's arm. "Don't forget—as soon as Westbrooke gets back, send him to the dungeon."

"What if he doesn't return until it is time to leave?"

Felicity rolled her eyes. "He'll be back shortly, depend upon it. He won't want to have Lady Elizabeth out of his sight for long." She chuckled. "I'll wager he'll practically run Lady Caroline through the chapel ruins."

Charlotte nodded. "I can just see her bonnet from here. Its feather *is* bobbing rather briskly."

"I don't doubt it. That means I haven't much time." Felicity shook her arm once more. "Remember, send Westbrooke to the dungeon. Wait five minutes, then come after him with Lady Dunlee and the others."

"Yes, yes. I won't forget."

Charlotte watched Felicity hurry away past the group with Lord Andrew. In a moment, that group broke up. Miss Peterson and Mr. Parker-Roth went off to examine some vegetation. The other two couples started toward the tower. Felicity had already disappeared inside.

Charlotte sighed. She would prefer not to be part of this sordid plan. She truly no longer felt a desire for revenge. The anger she'd felt toward Alvord and his family had been burned away by her passion for Edward.

He was standing not far from the tower, talking with Lady Dunlee and Lady Beatrice. Could she approach him now? No. She would have to guard her emotions too closely in front of Lady Dunlee.

Tonight. She wrapped her arms around her waist. She would be with him tonight. He would come to her as soon as the house had settled. She shivered in anticipation. Her body remembered the feel of his hands so clearly. She bit her lip to keep from moaning.

Could they steal a kiss . . . or more . . . this afternoon? Surely all the ladies would retire to rest until dinner. The men could entertain themselves. They would expect Edward to have estate business to attend to. They would expect him to spend time in his study.

She could meet him there. They could couple on the rug in front of the hearth or in his large, leather chair with the footstool. Or they could push his papers aside and mate in the middle of his broad desk.

Shocking. She could never have conceived of such things twenty-four hours ago. If she had heard even whispers of such activities, she would have been horrified. Now . . .

It was amazing what a difference a few hours could make.

Now she could picture Edward's body in detail. His shoulders, his chest, the dark hair curling down over his belly. And the rest of him—his thighs, his buttocks, his lovely thick . . . Mmm.

Her breasts knew the feel of his mouth now—her nipples tightened with the memory. Her lips throbbed for his—and her nether lips swelled and throbbed, too. The dampness he'd promised her was back. She wanted—no, needed—him to fill her. Now. She could not wait. There must be a shadowy corner somewhere in these ruins. They had half an hour. The way she felt, it would take only half a second. She certainly could not wait until tonight.

"Hallo! Tynweith!"

Dear God! It couldn't be. He was in London. He wasn't expected—should not travel. . . .

Life could not be that cruel.

She turned to look at the castle entrance.

Her husband, the Duke of Hartford, had arrived.

Chapter Fourteen

"Do you suppose I might see the battlements, Mrs. Larson? I had hoped to visit them yesterday when Meg and I walked over, but I couldn't manage to open the door."

What Lizzie really wanted to do was talk to Robbie, but she had missed her chance. Lady Dunlee had been too quick. Robbie had barely gotten to his feet before the woman had trapped him into escorting her daughter.

Perhaps it was just as well. Now was probably not the time to discuss their future. Surely once Robbie knew she was willing to forgo children to wed him, he would propose.

Mrs. Larson smiled. "Certainly, Lady Elizabeth. You must see it—the view is quite striking. Do you know what the problem was with the door?"

"I think it was merely stuck. Unfortunately I didn't have the strength to force it, and there wasn't room on the step for Meg and me to push together."

"Then we shall definitely need the assistance of a strong male. Sir George, may I prevail upon you?"

"I would be delighted to lend my strength to the endeavor."

"As would I, if I may," Lord Andrew said, coming to

stand next to Lizzie. He was just a shade too close—not close enough to cause comment, but close enough to make her feel crowded. She edged away. Out of the corner of her eye, she saw him smile slightly. He knew exactly what he was doing.

Lizzie hoped Mrs. Larson would decline his offer, but she was already thanking him.

"Splendid, Lord Andrew. And Miss Peterson, Mr. Parker-Roth, would you care to join us as well?"

"Thank you, no." Meg grinned. "Lizzie dragged me up those stairs yesterday. If I only have half an hour left here, I would much rather examine the flora growing on the castle grounds. I was studying some very interesting plants before luncheon—I'd like to go back to them."

"Mr. Parker-Roth?"

"I confess to having a greater interest in the view at ground level as well. I'll accompany Miss Peterson if I may."

"Ah, but is Parks interested in viewing the vegetation or the virgin?" Lord Andrew murmured.

Lizzie looked at Mrs. Larson. She gave no sign of having heard Lord Andrew's outrageous comment.

Should *she* take the man to task? She glanced at his profile. He turned and lifted an eyebrow. His face was expressionless, but his eyes taunted her. He was daring her to make a scene.

She would not accommodate him.

"Very well," Mrs. Larson was saying. "The house party is not over for a few more days, so if you change your minds, I'm certain another outing can be arranged."

Meg and Parks left to examine the foliage. Mrs. Larson took Sir George's arm. Lord Andrew offered his to Lizzie—she ignored it. She stepped closer to Mrs. Larson. The wind whipped her skirts around her ankles.

Lady Felicity was already disappearing into the

tower. Surely she was not going to view the battlements as well?

"Hallo! Tynweith!"

"Oh dear." Mrs. Larson stopped. They all stared at the castle entrance. A short, elderly man leaned on a burly footman's arm.

"It looks as if the Duke of Hartford has arrived," Mrs. Larson said. "If you'll excuse me?"

Mrs. Larson hurried over to greet the duke. Lord Tynweith was already there. Lizzie glanced at Charlotte. She was standing perfectly still in the freshly mowed grass, staring at her husband.

"There's my lovely duchess." Hartford's voice was still loud, but it had a wobbly note Lizzie hadn't heard before. "Missed our Thursday night appointment, didn't I?"

Charlotte started walking slowly toward the duke. Her back was perfectly straight, her head high. Her expression was remote, but pleasant.

"Good afternoon, your grace." Her voice was calm. She held out her hand.

Hartford grabbed her around the waist, yanked her to him, and planted a loud kiss on her mouth.

She disentangled herself gently. Her cheeks were only slightly flushed.

"God, don't you love 'em when they act so cool, Tynweith?"

Lord Tynweith did not answer. Mrs. Larson put a hand on his shoulder.

"I'll send a servant to the house to have a room made up for you, your grace," she said.

"Don't bother. I'll just share the duchess's room." He laughed and winked, squeezing Charlotte's waist so she lurched in his hold. "And her bed, of course. Still need an heir, you know."

Tynweith's body jerked but he didn't speak.

"Yes, well . . ." Mrs. Larson smiled weakly.

"I believe I should see if I can be of help." Sir George left without a backward glance.

"Got my carriage here, of course," Hartford was saying. "I'll take my duchess along now and get to work. No time like the present, heh?" He took Charlotte's arm. "Come along, my dear. The sight of your cool little body is making me feel like a regular satyr." He laughed again. "Believe I'll see how well sprung the carriage really is."

The duchess smiled slightly and murmured her good-byes.

"The poor woman." Lizzie had never thought to feel compassion for Charlotte, but she did now. To be married to that oaf—it didn't bear thinking of. "Hartford may be a duke, but he is first and foremost an idiot."

"Now, Lady Elizabeth, don't be so harsh. His grace was so overjoyed to be reunited with the object of his affections, he was overcome by feelings of connubial bliss."

Lizzie snorted. "Affection, Lord Andrew? I don't think so. Lust, more like."

"Well, lust is a pleasant feeling. I hope I'm as lusty as Hartford when I've more than four score years in my dish." He offered his arm again. "Shall we continue to the battlements?"

"Perhaps now that the duke has left, Mrs. Larson and Sir George would like to accompany us."

"I think they have other matters to command their attention."

Lord Andrew was correct. Mrs. Larson had pulled Lord Tynweith aside and was speaking to him very intently, while Sir George escorted Lady Dunlee and Lady Beatrice out of earshot. Lady Dunlee was almost bent backward, trying to hear her host and hostess's conversation.

Tynweith's face mirrored the storm clouds beginning to gather above them.

Lizzie chewed on her lip. Should she go with Lord Andrew? She didn't like the man, but she had been looking forward to taking in the view from the battlements. There was something so exhilarating about being up high, especially on a stormy day, the clouds rushing in, the wind whipping at her face. She loved to go up to Alvord's battlements on days like this. She felt free there, as if all the restraints, all the rules and responsibilities, all her worries were blown away.

She especially needed that feeling now.

But did she want to put up with Lord Andrew's unpleasant company to get it?

"Well, Lady Elizabeth?"

Discretion was the better part of valor.

"Perhaps I will view the battlements on a nicer day when Meg and Mr. Parker-Roth return."

"Perhaps you are a pudding-heart."

"Lord Andrew!"

"Come, Lady Elizabeth, surely you are not afraid to be in my company for—what—fifteen minutes? What do you think I can accomplish in so short a time?"

"Well . . ." Put that way, her hesitancy did seem ridiculous.

"We have already determined it is a fine day for battlements going. You know Miss Peterson and Mr. Parker-Roth have no interest in ever climbing those stairs. Westbrooke is not available to act as your watchdog. You will have to stand on your own two feet—or slink away like a good little girl to hide behind propriety."

"I . . ."

"I don't bite, Lady Elizabeth."

"I didn't think you did, Lord Andrew."

"Then be brave—be daring—and walk sedately up the castle steps with me to take in the view of the surrounding countryside."

Daring. She had decided to be daring this Season, hadn't she? And really, what could happen? It was the middle of the day in the middle of a picnic. She looked up at the clouds. The storm would be here shortly. Lord Andrew would not risk soaking his expensive Weston coat and waistcoat to engage in any questionable activities. It was not as if she were a debutante or attending her first house party. This *was* her fourth Season.

Really, as Lord Andrew had said, what could happen in fifteen minutes? She should not let her imagination run away with her.

"Very well, my lord. I expect you to be on your best behavior, however."

"Of course, Lady Elizabeth."

The slow, slightly leering smile he gave her was not reassuring.

This dungeon was perfect.

Lady Felicity hummed as she lit the candles. She wanted to be certain all the spectators could see every detail of this particular play.

It was a good thing she had hidden away most of her supplies. Who would have thought Lady Elizabeth and Miss Peterson would go exploring? And that the men would take it into their heads to tour the dungeon?

Felicity giggled. And who would have thought staid Mr. Dodsworth was a devotee of the switch? It made sense, when one thought about it. Tess, the girl at the inn whom Dodsworth favored, had told her she had to shout "Go, Dobbin" each time she hit Dodsworth's lily white arse.

How lucky she'd discovered that old history of the castle in Tynweith's library. Without it, she'd never have been able to come up with this plan. When she'd mentioned it, Andrew had told her of the thriving business the local lightskirts had. Why he hadn't thought to mention such an interesting fact immediately was beyond her understanding. She shrugged. He was a typical male. His little brain was taken up with basic urges. It took a woman to devise a truly inspired plot.

She spread her collection on the table. She had a short hunting whip, a longer whip with a frayed leather lash, and bound bundles of birch twigs of assorted lengths. The girls at the inn had lent her their cat-o'-nine-tails, a particular favorite, they'd said, with men who liked to play military games. They'd also given her a few more exotic implements—a scold's bridle, spiked collars, and an iron device that looked like thumb screws.

There were some things even she didn't care to know.

She arranged the items in what she hoped was a convincing display.

Apparently the dungeon was notorious among the male portion of the *ton*. Andrew certainly knew all about it. It was one of the main attractions of Tynweith's parties. Tess had said Dodsworth accepted his invitation primarily to meet "My Lady Birch."

It was now Felicity's turn to meet the lady.

She took out a few of her hair pins and scattered them over the floor. Then she loosened the neck of her dress and jerked it down. She wished she had a mirror handy, but unfortunately the dungeon was not equipped with one. She would just have to hope she looked properly mauled.

She selected one of the smaller birch bundles and tested its weight in her hand. How would it feel against her skin? Her nipples tightened in expectation. She hadn't tried that game before. Too bad Andrew wasn't here.

Would raising a welt be enough or did she need to draw blood? She pulled her dress lower and hit her upper arm and breast, catching the nipple. She drew in a sharp breath as the birch twigs stung her skin. Very nice.

She hit herself again, harder. A crisscross of red

welts contrasted splendidly with her white skin. She did wish she had a mirror, but it couldn't be helped. Still, as best she could tell, she looked quite good. Lady Dunlee would have a host of details with which to regale the tabbies of the *ton*.

She tossed the switch at her feet and took the key the local girls had given her out of her pocket. She was right handed, so the left manacle would be best. She looked up to where it was hanging from the wall. There were two sets—one for men, one for women. The girls had said the women's pair wasn't high off the ground, but she would have to stretch. It would be more comfortable if she removed her arm from her sleeve.

Should she shed her dress entirely? It would look even more scandalous. But the dungeon was a bit damp and chilly. She wriggled her left arm out and shivered. That was enough. No need to be more uncomfortable than necessary.

She reached up, closed the manacle over her wrist, and locked it. Her raised arm made her breast with its bright red welts lift nicely out of her corset. Excellent. She tossed the key onto the table. It landed in plain sight.

She settled down to wait. It shouldn't be long. Charlotte would have sent Lord Westbrooke to the dungeon by now. He should be appearing at any moment. As soon as she heard his footstep in the corridor, she would moan and cry piteously. He would rush to her aid, and, if Charlotte played her role correctly, Lady Dunlee, Lady Beatrice, Mrs. Larson—all the house guests—would come in shortly to see him with his hands on her. Then it was just his word against hers.

Yes, he was an earl, but she was the daughter of an earl. Papa might be cut by the *ton*, but he still held the title. And how could Westbrooke deny the evidence? She was manacled to the wall, the key well out of her reach, her dress pulled down almost to her waist, and her breast red with his beating. She would be nicely panicked. She'd sob into Lady Dunlee's arms; tell her how Westbrooke had suggested this game, how she had been happy to please him—everyone knew she'd been pursuing him for years—but then his passions had become too intense for her.

Lady Dunlee would believe her, and that was all that mattered. Even if the other ladies doubted her veracity, the circumstances of the scene were damning by themselves. And it didn't hurt that no one really knew what Westbrooke's sexual preferences were. He was so secretive. For all they knew, he could be as enamored of flagellation games as Dodsworth.

The plan was foolproof. Westbrooke was as good as snared.

She shifted. Her left hand was beginning to tingle and feel numb. Her shoulder was starting to ache as well.

No matter. She would distract herself. She had plenty of delightful thoughts to take her mind off some minor discomfort.

She would spend the last few minutes before Westbrooke arrived planning the many ways she would spend his lovely money.

"Lord Westbrooke, could we pause a moment?"

Lady Caroline was panting. Her cheeks had passed a becoming pink and turned to bright red. Beads of perspiration dotted her forehead. Even the feather in her bonnet was drooping.

Robbie didn't care. He didn't want to see the damn ruined chapel. It looked like every other patch of weeds and decaying masonry to him. He wanted to be with Lizzie.

"Certainly, Lady Caroline."

He looked back at the rest of the party. There was

Lizzie, standing with Mrs. Larson, Meg, Parks, and Sir George.

Bloody hell! Lord Andrew had joined the group.

"Look, Lord Westbrooke. I think this is where the altar must have been." Lady Caroline had walked across the stone floor to a raised platform. "Can't you just imagine the knights praying here before they rode out to battle?"

"Battle?" He'd like to do battle. He'd like to run Lord Andrew through with a lance.

Meg and Parks separated from the group, going off to inspect some weeds no doubt. At least Andrew couldn't harm Lizzie with Mrs. Larson present.

"Oh, Lord Westbrooke, there are some words carved in this stone. I think it must be Latin."

Robbie grunted. Wouldn't the girl be done soon?

"Could you come see? Perhaps you can tell me what it says. I can't read Latin."

"Certainly, Lady Caroline." Of course she couldn't read Latin—he'd be surprised if she could read much English beyond that necessary to understand the fashion plates. Lady Caroline did not strike him as a scholar.

He took a last look at Lizzie and Lord Andrew. The man appeared to be behaving himself. How could he not? Mrs. Larson and Sir George were standing right there.

"Lord Westbrooke?"

"Coming."

He forced himself to turn away. He was being absurd. Yes, Tynweith's house parties had the reputation of being fast, but they were not really dangerous except perhaps for naïve young debutantes who had more hair than wit. Lizzie was not totty-headed. She would not go off alone with a man of Andrew's stamp.

"Over here, Lord Westbrooke. See? What does it say?" Lady Caroline actually looked excited. He smiled

and bent to examine the inscription. She was almost
pleasant when she dropped her society airs.

"Is it a blessing? A mention of an especially brave
knight?"

Robbie ran his fingers over the carving to be certain. *"Antonio erat hic."*

"Yes? What does it mean?"

"Anthony was here." Robbie grinned. "Sorry. I suspect some bored young schoolboy carved this when
he escaped his tutor one day. Perhaps one of Tynweith's ancestors. You can ask him if he has a forebear
by that name."

"Oh." Lady Caroline looked crestfallen for a
moment and then perked up. "Perhaps there are
crypts. Do you think there might be? Could a knight
be buried right under our feet?"

Robbie hated to disillusion her. "I doubt it. We can
look, but I suspect any bodies are buried at the village
church."

For the next few minutes, he helped Lady Caroline
brush aside dead leaves and encroaching ivy. Surpris-
ingly, the ivy was the only thing encroaching. He had
not been pleased with the girl when she'd burst into
Lizzie's room with Felicity, the two of them looking
for his naked self, but now she appeared to be truly
enthusiastic about exploring the ruin. When they disturbed a field mouse in a tangle of dried vines, she
screamed but did not try to leap into his arms.

He was almost in charity with her when he finally
persuaded her to return to the rest of the party.

His feelings of good will did not last long. Something had happened while they were poking around
the ruins. People were standing in tight knots, talking
and shaking their heads. He picked up his pace.

"Please, Lord Westbrooke, you go too fast."

"My apologies, Lady Caroline."

He tried to slow his steps so the girl's fat little legs
could keep up with him. He scanned the groups for

Lizzie. He did not see her. Lord Andrew was missing also, but so were the duchess and Lady Felicity.

"You missed all the excitement, my lord." Lady Dunlee was the first to greet him. She was standing with Lord Botton and Mr. Dodsworth. Her eyes gleamed with suppressed gossip.

"Excitement?"

"Indeed." Lord Botton spoke as Lady Dunlee was opening her mouth. "Hartford came to collect his wife. Took her back to Lendal Park. Was quite vocal about what he planned to do with her once he got her there." Botton giggled. "Said he planned to start on the way."

"In the carriage, while the horses were moving." Dodsworth's voice held a note of wonder. "He was going to f—"

"Mr. Dodsworth! Please!" Lady Dunlee put her arm around Lady Caroline. "There are ladies present— including an impressionable young lady."

Dodsworth had the grace to flush. "My pardon, Lady Dunlee, Lady Caroline. No insult intended. Forgot myself."

"Obviously." Lady Dunlee sniffed.

"Did Lady Elizabeth return with them?"

The group stared at Robbie as if he were mad.

"Be a bit in the way, don't you think?" Lord Botton coughed into his hand. "You did understand what the duke had in mind?"

"Bed play," Dodsworth said helpfully, "only not in a bed. In a carriage. Hartford was going to f—"

"Mr. Dodsworth!"

"Sorry, sorry. I just can't get over . . . It never occurred to me. . . . In a carriage. . . . Horses, you know . . . I just never thought . . . Perhaps I could finally . . ." He turned bright red. "Very stimulating thought, that's all."

Lady Dunlee narrowed her eyes. "Have you been drinking?"

"No! No more than anyone else, that is. I just—"

"If you will excuse me?" Watching Dodsworth tie himself in verbal knots or speculating on the duke's sexual preferences wasn't getting Robbie any closer to locating Lizzie. He spotted Parks and Meg. Perhaps they would know where Lizzie was. They had been with her not so many minutes ago.

"Parks."

"Westbrooke. You missed quite a spectacle."

"It was terrible." Meg looked ready to hit someone. Robbie stepped back slightly so he did not present a target. "That old man is despicable."

"That old man is a duke, Miss Peterson."

"I don't care, Mr. Parker-Roth. Duke or drayman, no one should be so rude. The poor duchess."

Meg was warming up for a long diatribe. Robbie was certain Hartford was lower than pond scum, but he didn't have time to listen to a verbal drubbing.

"I'm actually more concerned with Lizzie at the moment, Meg. I don't see her. Do either of you know where she is?"

"I believe Lady Elizabeth was going up to the battlements," Parks said.

Meg nodded. "Yes. We couldn't get the door opened yesterday."

"She and Mrs. Larson both wanted to go, I believe," Parks said. "Sir George and Lord Andrew are escorting them."

Panic grabbed Robbie's chest. "Mrs. Larson is standing over there with Tynweith, Parks."

"Hmm. So she is. And I see Sir George there, too. So that leaves . . ."

"Lord Andrew." Bloody hell. "If you'll excuse me?"

Lizzie did not care for preceding Lord Andrew up the stairs. He said he wished to be in a position to catch her if she stumbled. She believed he wished to observe her ankles.

She paused on the last turn. "We are almost to the top, my lord. Shall I step aside now and let you pass?"

"No, no, Lady Elizabeth. Please keep going."

"But you will need to be in front when we reach the door. It is stuck quite securely. You will want to use your complete strength to open it."

He smirked. "We'll see."

"What do you mean, 'we'll see'? I assure you, I could not get it to budge."

His smirk grew. "Lady Elizabeth, just because *you* cannot open the door, does not mean *I* cannot. I do not anticipate any difficulty. And this way I will not block your first view of the battlements."

Lizzie suppressed a strong urge to put her hands on Lord Andrew's shoulders and push hard. He would get a taste of her strength and she would get the opportunity to hear the satisfying sound of his conceited head hitting the steps all the way to the ground.

She turned and continued climbing.

"Here we are, my lord. How do you intend—oh!"

Lord Andrew stepped onto the stair right behind her and put both hands on the door. She was trapped by his body. More than trapped. He was pressed up against her—she felt his length all along her back. She did not like it. A whisper of panic fluttered along her spine.

Thankfully he made short work of the refractory door. One push and the job was done. She would have been exceedingly annoyed if she'd not been so happy to be free of him. She stepped quickly over the threshold and onto the battlements.

The wind whipped over her, stealing her breath and threatening to take her bonnet. She laughed, and the wind stole her laughter, too.

She loved this weather. The clouds, roiling masses of gray, hung so low she could almost touch them. She took a deep breath. The air was damp, chill, wild. She smelled the storm coming, tasted its flat, metallic flavor.

She leaned on the parapet. Eddies of dead leaves swirled around her skirts. In the distance, the village church steeple jutted up into the sky as if it would prick the storm clouds and let loose the rain. To the west, the brownish yellow walls of Lendal Park caught a stray ray of sunlight.

She straightened to take in the view from the other side of the tower and collided with a large, solid object.

"What?" She tried to turn, but found her way blocked by Lord Andrew's chest. The wind must have masked his footsteps. She twisted to see his face over her shoulder. "My lord, you are crowding me."

"That is my intention." He shoved her up against the parapet so her breasts flattened against the stone. She felt something sharp at the back of her neck, then the scrape of his fingers on her skin. There was a rending sound and her dress sagged.

"Lord Andrew!" She tried to push away from the wall—she couldn't. Her hands were trapped under her. She threw her hips back instead.

"Mmm. That feels good." His voice was thick. He thrust his hips forward and a hard ridge pushed into her bottom.

She froze—and felt her corset tighten briefly, then loosen. The wind whistled over her shift.

"What are you doing?!"

"Cracking you like a lobster so I can get to the tender meat inside." He grabbed her shoulders and jerked her around. He still had a knife in his right hand.

She tried not to panic, but her heart was pounding. It was difficult to get the air to speak.

"Lord Andrew, please. Stop."

He kept her imprisoned with his weight. She assessed her chances of getting to the door and down the stairs to safety. They were not good. There was no hope of arguing with a knife in such close quarters, and even if she did get free, she would have trouble navigating the old, winding stairs without tripping on her loosened clothing. Pitching headlong down those stone steps would be dangerous indeed.

She glanced at Andrew's face. Perhaps not as dangerous as staying here with this madman.

"You won't get away, sweetings, so don't hurt yourself trying." He chuckled. "I have much more amusing ways to hurt you."

"No." She was losing her battle with panic. Fear made it hard to get even one word out.

"Oh, yes." He tilted his head, studying her face. "It would be somewhat amusing to have you with your headgear on, but I think we will leave that treat for another day." He tugged on her ribbons, plucked her bonnet off, and threw it over the parapet. "Today I believe it will be more entertaining to see how you look with the wind in your hair."

Lizzie craned around to see her poor hat tossed by the winds to land on the grass outside the castle. If only they were above the courtyard. Then Robbie or Meg or one of the other guests would see her bonnet sailing through the air and come investigate.

Her movement was a mistake. The ridge throbbed against her belly.

"Nice." He tangled his hand in her hair, pulling the pins out and throwing them over the parapet as well. Her hair tumbled over her shoulders. The wind caught it and whipped it around her face. She pushed on his chest. Perhaps she could free herself now.

She couldn't.

He jerked her dress and corset down. She saw a moment of opportunity and brought her knee toward his crotch. He evaded her easily. Laughing, he pressed against her again. He caught the tip of his knife under the neck of her shift.

"No!"

"Yes." He pricked the fabric and tore it to her waist, exposing her breasts. He studied them. "Too small for my tastes, but I've seen worse."

"Lord Andrew, my brother will kill you."

"No, I think he will insist I marry you. But don't worry. I will graciously agree to do so—and then I shall have complete control of your property and your person. Won't that be fun?"

She bucked against him. He laughed thickly.

"Remember how I said I didn't bite?"

Whatever was he getting at? "Yes."

"I lied." He dropped his knife and bent his head, closing his teeth around her nipple.

Chapter Fifteen

Where the hell was Westbrooke?

Felicity stretched up on her toes to take some of the pressure off her arm. She'd lost all sensation in it. It might as well belong to another person—or to a corpse.

What if no one came? What if she were left here?

She looked at the key lying on the table. She'd thought she'd considered everything. It had seemed a good plan to put it there—more damning evidence when everyone found Westbrooke with her. She reached for it. Impossible. The little feeling she still had in her left arm presented itself as shooting pain. The key wasn't inches from her fingers, it was feet. No amount of stretching would work.

Damn it all, why had she tried to be so clever? She should have kept the bloody thing in her pocket.

Where the frigging hell *was* Westbrooke? He should have been here by now. Hadn't Charlotte sent him yet? No, the stupid bitch must have forgotten to play her part. Surely she would remember before everyone left? When she saw Felicity wasn't there to get in the carriages, Charlotte would recall her role.

She hoped. Charlotte had been behaving in an exceedingly odd manner since they'd arrived at the house party. She'd been nervous. On edge. And then today she'd been the opposite—dreamy, languid, as if her mind were somewhere else.

Where? Felicity frowned. Charlotte had cast more than one look at their host during luncheon. Was there something between those two? Perhaps. That miniature in Charlotte's room—that was certainly peculiar. And now that she pondered it, Charlotte did have the look of a woman who'd been thoroughly bedded recently. But Charlotte didn't like bed play. Or, she hadn't liked it. Had Tynweith changed her opinion?

Interesting. If dear Charlotte didn't do her part, Felicity would see to it that Hartford heard all the details of his wife's activities. The duke was very possessive. He would not take kindly to Tynweith's cuckolding him.

Damn.

If Charlotte didn't play her part, Felicity would be stuck in this dungeon for hours.

She noticed movement out of the corner of her eye and turned. A large black spider was crawling over her elbow. She jerked away. The spider kept crawling. She couldn't feel it. She reached up with her free hand and flicked the creature away. She couldn't feel the touch of her own fingers.

She could hear though. The silence was heavy, but there was a scrambling in the far corner of the room. What the hell was that? She squinted. Did she see the gleam of a rat's eyes?

She moaned. She had to get out of here.

She forced herself to take a deep breath. If she called out now, anyone might come to her aid. Mrs. Larson or Lord Dunlee. The plot would be ruined.

She could not let her emotions run away with her. Tynweith had said the party would only stay another half hour. At least ten minutes must have passed since then—more like fifteen. She didn't have much longer to wait. She just had to be patient.

* * *

"I could kill the man."

"Edward, please. Get hold of yourself."

"But he's a frigging idiot, Nell. You heard him." Tynweith fought to keep his voice down. He could see Lady Dunlee's avid expression as clearly as Nell could.

"Yes, I heard him. He's despicable—but he is also a duke *and* her grace's husband. You have no rights here, Edward."

"I've the right of any gentleman to see that ladies are treated with respect!"

"Shh. Yes, of course. But if you acted on that right, you would cause severe speculation as to your motives— you have never bestirred yourself to defend any other lady's feelings."

"I've never seen them violated so publicly."

"And what is more, I don't believe Charlotte would thank you. She went with Hartford. She didn't ask for your aid."

"No, she didn't." That had galled him. After last night she must know she could turn to him for protection.

Yet Hartford had not offered her injury, really. He'd merely wanted to exercise his marital rights. He'd been beyond boorish to publicly humiliate Charlotte by advertising his intentions, but that had been his only real sin. Some would not call it a sin at all.

Nell was right. He would have looked extremely odd leaping to Charlotte's defense. More than odd— suspicious.

Charlotte wanted the world to think any child she might get as the result of this house party's activities was Hartford's. This afternoon's little drama was perfect for her purposes. If she were found to be increasing, all the *ton* would congratulate the duke, especially after Lady Dunlee spread the story of his arrival, as she was sure to do.

This was for the best—but he hated it. To think of

the old man pawing Charlotte's body, putting himself between her lovely thighs . . .

God, it made him want to puke.

"Are you all right, Edward?"

"Yes." He turned away from Nell. "Where is everyone? We should be returning."

"No, Edward. Not yet."

"Why not? The storm is coming. No one wants to get wet. I can't imagine anyone cares if we leave a few minutes early."

"Charlotte may care."

"What?"

"Think, Edward. If you rush everyone back, we may arrive only shortly after the duke and duchess—sooner if you spring the horses as I can tell you are in the mood to do."

"So?"

"So you will embarrass the duchess further. You'll give Hartford another opportunity to entertain our guests with his crude remarks. And if he has engaged in any . . . activities in his coach, the duchess's person may show some signs of it—her clothing or hair might be disarranged." Nell put her hand on his shoulder. "I think she would prefer not to have an audience, don't you?"

"Damn." Nell was right. Charlotte would be mortified. He wouldn't add to her burdens for anything.

"Very well." He took Nell's hand and put it on his arm. "Then I am going to have to keep you from Sir George for a while longer, I'm afraid. I need you to prevent me from killing someone—and to tell me when an adequate amount of time has passed so I can haul this collection of cod's heads back to Lendal Park."

Robbie strode toward the tower. He wanted to run, but that would have focused everyone's attention on his behavior and created a scandal. Lizzie was probably fine. Lord Andrew was a blackguard. He might make Lizzie uncomfortable, but as far as Robbie knew, the man had not added raping ladies to his list of sins.

Of course, there was always a first time.

He stepped over the threshold into the dim light of the tower and paused to give his eyes time to adjust. He would not help Lizzie by falling down the old stairs and breaking his neck. He—

What was that? Damn, it sounded like a woman's moan coming from the dungeon. But Parks had been clear that Lizzie had wanted to see the battlements. That made sense. Lizzie loved heights. She would have no interest in the dungeon unless Andrew dragged her there.

God, is that what the bastard had done? The room held some nasty instruments of torture. Even if Andrew used only the switch. . . . No, he couldn't bear to think of Lizzie's soft white skin marred by a lash. He started for the dungeon. He stopped with his foot on the top step.

All was quiet now. Could he have imagined the sound?

If he'd actually heard Lizzie, shouldn't he have heard Andrew's voice, too?

It made no sense. He listened. Nothing.

His nerves *were* stretched tight. Perhaps the noise had been a product of his worry—or perhaps Andrew had muffled Lizzie's mouth. Bloody hell.

It would take only a moment to run down to the dungeon. But if Lizzie were on the battlements, that was a moment too long.

He did not have the luxury of indecision.

"Stop! That hurts." Lizzie pushed against Lord Andrew's shoulders. She screamed, but the sound was whipped away by the wind. Andrew laughed.

"God, I'd hoped I could get you to do that." He squeezed her breasts hard and laughed again. "I doubt anyone can hear you, but please, scream all you want. I find the sound invigorating." He grabbed her bottom and pulled her tight against him. "See? I am bursting with vigor. Can you feel it?"

She felt too much. Only her thin shift protected her from his touch. She felt the rough ridge of his pantaloons against her belly; the heat of his palms, of each of his fingers on her bottom. She pushed against his shoulders again. He pulled her tighter still, trapping her hands between them. He whispered in her ear.

"Do you know what will happen, Lady Elizabeth, when I unbutton my pantaloons and lift the hem of your shift?"

He paused. Did he really expect an answer? She shook her head. She was afraid she did know. She remembered Meg's talk of breaching and blood. She remembered Robbie naked in her room. He had been large, but she had not felt threatened. Now she did.

"I will ram my cock up inside you, my dear, and in doing so I will answer one of the burning questions of this house party—were you really alone in your bed when Felicity came looking for Westbrooke, or were you entertaining a very naked earl?" He bit her earlobe. He was holding her so tightly she did not have room to flinch. "Is the prim and proper sister of the Duke of Alvord still a virgin or is she merely mutton dressed as lamb? I can hardly wait to find out."

He covered her mouth with his. She kept her teeth clenched—until he twisted her nipple. She gasped with the pain, and his tongue plunged in to gag her.

She fought to control her panic. She needed to keep her wits about her. Surely Lord Andrew must loosen his grip at some point in this process. When he went to open his breeches or pull up her shift, then perhaps she would have a chance to escape.

Perhaps not. She felt his hand creeping up her leg,

taking her shift with it. He moved his hips back only enough to get the thin cloth up to her waist, keeping her trapped with his chest. She felt the cold, rough stone of the parapet against her bottom.

"The amusing thing is I can never really know you *are* a virgin, can I? Only that you *were* a virgin. Because in making the discovery, I disprove the statement." He grinned. "No matter. I assure you, whatever your state at this moment, you will most definitely not be a virgin shortly."

She felt him fumble with his buttons.

She screamed again.

Robbie took the worn steps two at a time.

What if he'd guessed wrong? What if Lizzie *was* in the dungeon? He should have gone there first. He was wasting precious seconds coming up here.

But Meg had said Lizzie wanted to see the battlements. There was no reason for her to go down to the dungeon. She and Meg had seen that room yesterday—and there was no pleasant view there.

No, Lizzie would definitely have chosen the battlements.

If she'd had the choice. If Andrew had wanted her in the dungeon, her wishes would have been irrelevant. She'd be no match for a man's strength.

Robbie took a deep breath. He was letting his imagination run amok. Lord Andrew might not be his choice of escort for Lizzie—hell, the blackguard wasn't his choice to be within sixty kilometers of Lizzie—but the man had never been accused of hurting a lady. Lizzie was safe. He hoped.

Who had made that moaning sound in the dungeon?

Perhaps it was just the wind—or perhaps he'd imagined it. He would not have thought that possible before this damn house party, but now he was not so certain.

He'd not been sleeping well. This morning it had felt as if he'd not slept at all, but he had. He'd dreamt of Lizzie.

She'd been naked. He'd seen her reflection just as he had that first night. He'd watched her hands move slowly down her curves—over her sweet breasts, narrow waist, flat belly—to the dark blond triangle at the juncture of her thighs. In his dream, he hadn't held her away when she'd come to him. He'd pulled her tight against his body, felt her breasts flatten against his chest, her belly cradle his heat. In his dream, he took her to bed and slid his length into her wet, warm depths.

He had woken hard as a rock.

He wouldn't think about it. Thinking only brought him misery, and in any event, he had finally reached the top of the stairs.

He took a deep breath. He was a gentleman. He must not rush madly out onto the battlements as if he thought Andrew were raping Lizzie. How absurd. He was just there to lend Lizzie support if she wished it, and to be sure Andrew's behavior did not cross the line. If Lizzie were actually here, of course, and not down in the dungeon. It was quite possible he would find no one on the other side of this door.

He pushed. The door stuck a moment, held back perhaps by the wind whistling on the other side. He pushed harder and it swung open.

Lizzie's panicked scream lanced his ears.

Shock held him frozen for a second. Lord Andrew had Lizzie trapped against the parapet. He had one hand on her naked waist, the other on his buttons.

Red, elemental anger unlike anything Robbie had felt before rushed through him.

He was going to kill the bastard.

* * *

"Is it time, Nell? Can we go back now? I swear if I hear Lady Dunlee say one more word about Hartford and Charlotte I will strangle the woman."

Nell smiled and patted Tynweith's arm. "You have been very patient. Yes, I think we can go, Edward. You told everyone thirty minutes. It must be close to that now. And the storm is almost upon us."

"Splendid." Tynweith looked up at the sky. It did look as if the heavens would open at any second. He stopped a passing footman. "William, please tell the coachmen to get the carriages ready to depart."

"Yes, my lord."

William hurried to the gatehouse where the coachmen were treating their thirst with a few pints of ale. Tynweith strode over to his guests.

"As you can see, the weather is threatening. I've called for the coaches. If we are fortunate, we'll arrive at Lendal Park before the first raindrops fall."

"Good. I'd hate to have this bonnet ruined." Lady Dunlee smiled. "And I do want to see how Hartford is getting on." She covered her mouth and tittered as if she were a young girl. "That is, if he has finished with his other, um, pursuits."

Tynweith gritted his teeth. Why didn't Dunlee rein in his wife? He glanced at the man. He was studying the clouds.

"Yes, well, the carriages should be ready in just a moment. If you would all proceed to the gatehouse?" Tynweith turned to lead the way.

"Lord Tynweith!" Lady Beatrice's voice was sharp.

"Yes?" He paused and looked back. What was the woman's problem? He wanted to leave now.

"Lady Elizabeth is missing. We cannot leave her here."

Tynweith wanted to shout at the woman to keep track of her charges. Instead he smiled.

"No, indeed. Do you know where she is?"

Lady Beatrice frowned. "I am not certain. Meg, do you know where Lizzie went?"

"I believe she's on the battlements."

"That's right." Nell nodded. "We were going up together and then I got distracted by other concerns. I believe Lord Andrew may be there as well."

"And Lord Westbrooke," Miss Peterson said. "He went up in search of Lizzie a few minutes ago."

"And they have not yet returned?" Lady Dunlee shook her head. "Whatever can they be doing up there? I'm not certain it's quite proper for Lady Elizabeth to be alone with two gentlemen."

"Oh, for God's sake, Clarissa," Lady Beatrice said, "I'm sure she's just looking at the view."

"Oh? And which view would that be?"

"The view of the countryside, of course." Lady Beatrice appeared to bite her tongue hard. Tynweith suspected she would like to describe in detail her feelings concerning Lady Dunlee. "Lizzie *is* in her fourth Season. She's not some bird-witted debutante. She can take care of herself."

"If you say so." Lady Dunlee smirked. "Shall we go see?"

"Please, lead the way."

"Ladies, I'll just send a footman. There's no need for you both to climb the stairs." Tynweith did not want to wait for the women to haul their substantial selves up all the steps to the battlements. He wanted to leave the blasted ruins as soon as possible. He wanted to leave now.

"No, thank you, Lord Tynweith." Lady Dunlee kept walking. "If anything of an unfortunate nature has occurred, Lady Elizabeth will want the support of another woman."

Lady Beatrice just rolled her eyes and kept pace.

"Perhaps I should go along as well," Nell said.

"But no one else, mind," Tynweith muttered. "There's not room on those stairs for a parade."

"Of course."

"And hurry them along, will you?"

Nell just smiled and left. Tynweith consulted his watch and the sky. He sighed. It looked very much as if he were going to get wet. Perhaps the rain would cool his temper.

"Scream all you like, sweetings," Lord Andrew whispered in Lizzie's ear. He squeezed her breast again. "No one can hear you. In fact—urgh."

Lord Andrew's cravat suddenly tightened like a noose. His eyes widened, and his hands flew up to grab the cloth as his body jerked back.

"Robbie!"

Robbie didn't acknowledge her—she wondered if he'd heard her. His face had lost all trace of good humor. His eyes, his mouth, were chiseled stone. He looked murderous. He twisted his left hand tighter and Andrew's face turned purple, eyes bulging. His hands fluttered over his cravat, plucking ineffectually at the cloth. He looked as if he would pass out at any moment.

Robbie decided to help him. He cocked back his right fist and slammed it into Andrew's face. There was a very unpleasant crunching sound and a lot of blood.

"Bastard." Robbie hit him once more, catching him under the chin, knocking his lower jaw into his upper, snapping his head back. He let his limp body fall to the floor and turned to her.

His eyes still held murder.

"Robbie, I . . ."

"Why the hell did you come up here with that, that . . ." Robbie's jaw clenched. "Why did you come up here with *him*? Don't you have *any* sense?"

There was too much residual anger in his voice. She did not think he would hurt her, but she was still a little afraid of him. She was not tempted to brangle with him now.

"I'm sorry. I . . ."

"Sorry? *Sorry?* He was going to rape you, Lizzie."

A sob caught in her throat. "I know."

"Bloody hell." His hands were on her then, but not roughly. They skimmed over her bare shoulders, her bruised breasts, her sore and bleeding nipple.

"He bit you."

She nodded. She couldn't speak. Her throat was clogged with tears.

"Damn bastard." Robbie's voice was harsh, but his touch was gentle. He gathered her up, cradled her securely against his chest. She shuddered and rested her cheek on his waistcoat. She breathed in his scent. Her heart slowed.

She felt safe, sheltered by Robbie's hard body and strong arms.

"Robbie." She lifted her head to look at him—and caught movement from the corner of her eye. Andrew.

"Robbie!"

"What?"

"Behind you."

He turned. Andrew had staggered to his feet and was leaning against the parapet about ten feet away. Blood streamed from his nose and his eyes had swollen to slits, but he had his knife out and pointed at them. His battered lips twisted.

"Move away from Lady Elizabeth, Westbrooke."

Robbie shifted so Lizzie was behind him. "Why should I do that?"

"Because I am very skilled at knife throwing. I can put this blade in your chest with my eyes closed."

"Handy. Your eyes *are* almost closed, aren't they?"

"Robbie." Lizzie touched his back. Her heart was pounding again. Andrew would do as he said, she had no doubt on that score. "Robbie, move. I can't bear to have you hurt."

Andrew's voice sharpened. "Listen to Lady Elizabeth, Westbrooke. Move now if you want to continue living."

Robbie shrugged. "If you put it that way, I guess I have no choice."

Robbie stepped to the right. Lizzie straightened. Her heart was in her throat. She willed herself to breathe slowly. She might be half naked, but she was not going to cower in front of Lord Andrew. She met his gaze as calmly as she could.

He laughed. "So brave. You deserve better than Westbrooke. Didn't you know he was a milksop, Lady Elizabeth? He's as henhearted as—"

The rest of the sentence was lost in an agonized scream. Another knife had appeared, this one protruding from Andrew's right arm. Andrew's weapon clattered to the ground.

"Did I neglect to mention that I, too, am somewhat skilled with a blade?" Robbie asked.

Andrew snarled and grabbed at his arm.

"Get his knife, Robbie."

"My pleasure." Robbie picked up the weapon. "I'll take this back, too, if you don't mind," he said as he pulled his own knife out of Andrew's arm. Blood soaked the man's shirtsleeve.

Lizzie's knees started shaking. She leaned against the parapet. Her head throbbed. She couldn't see. . . .

"Lizzie, are you all right?"

She gulped air. Robbie's arms came around her.

"I was just light-headed for a moment. I'm all right now."

"You're certain?"

"Yes, I'm . . ."

A feminine scream erupted from the doorway. Lady Dunlee stood there, flanked by Lady Beatrice and Mrs. Larson. She raised her lorgnette.

"Taking in the view, Beatrice?" she said. "I don't believe it was just the view Lady Elizabeth was taking in."

Chapter Sixteen

"Exactly what are you implying, Clarissa?"

Lady Dunlee waved her lorgnette at Lizzie. "Let us just say, Beatrice, that one of these gentlemen must marry Lady Elizabeth immediately."

Robbie put his coat over Lizzie's shoulders. He hoped Lady Bea would deny Lady Dunlee's assertion, but he was not surprised when he saw her nod in agreement. Appearing in one's shift—and not even all of one's shift—in the company of two men was not a misstep easily remedied.

"That's ridiculous!" Lizzie's voice wavered slightly. "Nothing happened."

Lady Dunlee put her lorgnette back to her eyes. Even he stared. Lizzie flushed and pulled Robbie's coat closer around her.

"Nothing *permanent* happened."

"On the contrary, miss, something permanent *did* happen. If—" Lady Beatrice looked at Lady Dunlee. Lady Dunlee examined the lace on her sleeve. "*When* word of this gets out, your reputation will be as shredded as your clothing."

"No. Why should word get out?" Lizzie sounded desperate. "Mrs. Larson, you won't say a thing, will you?"

"Of course not."

"And Lady Dunlee, surely you can refrain from spreading the story?"

Robbie turned his snort into a cough. Lady Dunlee was smiling slightly and examining her lace again. He would bet she could no more keep this tale under her bonnet than she could stop breathing.

"Ladies, perhaps we should continue this discussion in the carriages." Mrs. Larson smiled and gestured toward the door. "I'm certain Lady Elizabeth would appreciate leaving this location, and I do believe the storm will be upon us at any moment."

Lady Beatrice and Lady Dunlee ignored her.

"I am afraid you are correct, Clarissa," Lady Bea said. "Lady Elizabeth must be betrothed now and married as soon as may be." She crossed her arms under her sizable breasts. It was clear no one was leaving until the matter was resolved to her satisfaction. "Gentlemen?"

Robbie heard Lizzie draw in a sharp breath that ended on a sob.

He couldn't look at her. His stomach clenched in a tight, hard knot, and familiar hot shame pooled in his gut.

How could he marry Lizzie? How could he condemn her to a life without children, without passion?

How could he tell her . . . Panic seized his chest. He struggled to breathe.

He couldn't tell her.

"I will be happy to offer for Lady Elizabeth," Lord Andrew said. The words came out slightly mumbled—the man's lips were swollen and he was missing at least two teeth. "After all, it is my fault she finds herself in this state. I let my animal instincts get the better of me."

He grimaced in a way that was perhaps intended as a smile.

"I have no excuse except that I have worshiped

Lady Elizabeth for years—I was crushed when she turned down my earlier offer."

Robbie waited for Lady Beatrice to put the bastard in his place. Instead she nodded.

Good God. She couldn't mean to . . . She wouldn't let Lizzie wed. . . .

"No." Lizzie almost shouted the words. "I will not marry Lord Andrew."

"Lizzie, you don't have a choice—"

"I do have a choice, Lady Beatrice. James would never force me to wed that snake."

"Perhaps not, but even the duke cannot repair the damage you've done to your reputation today. If you don't wed, you'll be condemning yourself to live in the country, at Alvord, a spinster for the rest of your life."

"My Aunt Gladys never married, and she spent many a Season in Town." Lizzie sounded defiant, but Robbie heard the thread of panic in her voice.

"Your Aunt Gladys never appeared naked in public with two gentlemen, miss."

"I'm not"—Lizzie's voice dropped to a whisper—"naked."

Lady Dunlee snorted. "You're near as can be."

"I really think we should postpone this discussion until everyone is calmer." Mrs. Larson gestured toward the stairs again. "I suggest we leave now. I do believe it is going to rain at any moment."

Everyone ignored her.

"Very well, Lord Andrew." Lady Beatrice threw Robbie a look before she considered the other man. "Since you have offered—"

"You cannot mean to let Lizzie marry that blackguard." Panic made Robbie's voice tighter than he would like.

"Have you another suggestion, Lord Westbrooke? The girl needs a husband."

"I do not need a husband."

Robbie looked at Lizzie. She was staring straight ahead, chin up, hands clutching his coat.

She had been so innocently wanton when she'd drunkenly pursued him in her bedroom. She'd been so purely passionate in Tynweith's shrubbery. If she married Lord Andrew—no, the thought was too obscene to contemplate. He could not condemn her to a life with that bastard. The man *might* give her children, but he would definitely give her pain. The possibility of motherhood could not outweigh the certainty of abuse. Lord Andrew would break her spirit.

"I will marry Lizzie," Robbie said as the storm clouds finally opened.

Lizzie sat dripping in a carriage with just Lady Beatrice and Meg for company. Everyone else had squeezed into the other vehicles to give her privacy.

"Lizzie, are you really going to marry Robbie?"

Lizzie didn't know the answer to that question. Lady Beatrice did.

"Of course she is, Meg. She has no other option. I tell you, I was a bit concerned when Lord Andrew offered and Westbrooke stood there like a block."

A bit concerned? Mindless panic was what Lizzie had felt. To be bound to that despicable man for life, to be compelled to tolerate his most intimate touch. . . . She could not have borne it.

And yet it would have been her own fault if she'd been so condemned.

She looked out the window. She didn't see the rain and the passing scenery—she saw Lord Andrew's face, his eyes hot, his mouth cruel, as he'd tried to open his breeches. She felt his weight on her, pinning her to the stone parapet. She could not have stopped him. If Robbie had not arrived when he did, she'd have been . . . Lord Andrew would have . . .

She pressed her head against the carriage wall.

It was all her fault. She had to be daring. She had to insist on visiting the battlements even after Mrs. Larson and Sir George had left the party—even when she knew Lord Andrew would be her only escort.

Robbie was right. Apparently she had no sense whatsoever. She'd been in the billiard room. She knew Lord Andrew was not to be trusted.

She sniffed, swallowing tears. She had not known, she truly had not imagined, that anyone could be so evil.

And now poor Robbie was being made to pay for her stupidity. It was obvious he had not wanted to offer for her—he had done so only to save her from Lord Andrew.

Perhaps there was a way out. They would get engaged. Then after the worst of the scandal had subsided, she would call it off.

She would jilt Robbie. She squeezed her eyes shut. She would jilt him, and by doing so cause a second scandal. He would be embarrassed. She would be disgraced. No one would ever marry her. Lady Beatrice was right—she'd be consigned to Alvord to live her days out as a spinster aunt.

She took a deep breath, letting it out slowly.

She would have to marry Robbie.

Have to? It was no burden for her—she had wished for it for years, just not in this way. She loved him.

She would make it up to him. She would be the best wife a man could have. Whatever he wanted, she would do. If he wanted her to stay in the country, she would. If he wanted to keep a mistress—several mistresses—she would not complain. She would see to it that he never regretted today's chivalry.

Everything would be all right. She had enough love for them both. She—

A new thought intruded.

What if Robbie were in love with someone else?

* * *

Damn, it had been quite a day—and it wasn't near over yet. Lord Tynweith poured himself a generous glass of brandy and sprawled in his favorite chair by the fire. He'd retreated to his sitting room to hide until dinner.

Who would have thought Lord Andrew was such a bounder? Almost raping a fellow house guest—that really was bad *ton*. He'd confined the man to his room and stricken him from any future guest lists. At least he wouldn't be seducing young ladies any time soon. Scaring them, perhaps. Westbrooke had done a thorough job of rearranging the man's face.

He sipped his brandy thoughtfully. Who would have guessed Westbrooke was so handy with his fives? As far as he knew, the earl didn't frequent Gentleman Jackson's to practice his boxing form. And apparently he knew how to use a knife as well. Tynweith shook his head. The things one learned about people when one spent a little time with them.

He snorted. Lady Dunlee certainly had learned a lot, and it was clear she was bursting to return to London and educate the rest of society. God, even soaking wet, the woman had been veritably twitching with excitement. And she would have plenty of juicy tidbits for the ravening tabbies. Nell had said the scene on the battlements was shocking, and Nell was not easily shocked.

One good thing about all this—Westbrooke had finally overcome whatever odd scruples had been holding him back from offering for Lady Elizabeth. Still, according to Nell, he hadn't leapt at the opportunity; it had only been the distasteful prospect of seeing the girl tied to Lord Andrew that had impelled him to action.

Tynweith chuckled. Unless he missed his guess, Lord Westbrooke would be impelled to other action immediately. Lady Beatrice had had a very determined look on her face when she'd climbed out of the carriage. He suspected she wanted Lady Elizabeth wed before Lady Dunlee could draw her first gossipy breath in a London ballroom.

He scowled at the fire. Damn Lady Dunlee. Her eyes had gleamed like a feral dog's when Hartford had come bumbling through the castle gatehouse.

He got up to pour himself more brandy. With luck, Lady Elizabeth's scandal would be so delicious, Lady Dunlee would not think to regale the gabble grinders with her account of Hartford's bizarre arrival.

He swirled the amber liquid in the bottom of his glass. The thought he'd been avoiding finally intruded.

How was Charlotte?

He'd truly wanted to murder Hartford this afternoon. Thank God Nell had been there to stop him. She'd been right, of course. He would have done no one good by making a scene, least of all Charlotte.

He tossed off the contents of his glass. The brandy burned his throat and caused his eyes to water. He wouldn't think of Charlotte.

He couldn't think of anything else.

He went to his window. He was jumpy. He could not sit still.

He had thought to visit Charlotte's bed tonight. He had thought about it every second from the moment he'd left her room this morning to the moment Hartford had appeared in the ruins. He'd thought about the silkiness of her hair, the taste of her skin, the warm wetness of her passage. . . .

He was going mad, like a man dying of thirst who'd been given one small sip of water and then been held back from the well.

He looked out over the green lawns, the gardens. He needed a wife, an heir. . . .

Damn.

He strode back to the fire.

He had not seen Charlotte since she'd left with

Hartford. Nor had he seen the duke. That was . . . what? Two hours ago? Was the old satyr still at it?

He slashed at the logs in the fireplace. Sparks shot into the air. He must remember this was what Charlotte wanted. As repulsive as the thought of Hartford mounting her was, it was what she wanted. What she needed. A means to an end.

If she left Lendal Park enceinte, she would be happy.

He stabbed the logs once more. He didn't believe that. He couldn't. He had woken her to passion. She had melted in his arms. The Marble Duchess had turned molten at his touch. She needed him as much as he needed her.

He turned away from the fire. Enough. Thinking about it only tied his stomach in knots. As Nell pointed out, he had no rights here. Charlotte was a married woman.

He would go downstairs. Perhaps he could interest Westbrooke in a game of billiards. The earl seemed as morose as he. They would be a good pair.

He stepped into the corridor. He had to pass Charlotte's room. He walked briskly. He was not going to think of her in bed with that wizened old man. Hartford would never cause her to scream with passion, but if he did, Tynweith definitely did not want to hear it.

So why was he slowing his steps outside her door?

There *was* a sound coming from her room. An odd sound.

He paused. There was no one else in the hall—no one would notice if he put his ear to the door. . . .

He heard it again. A faint noise, but urgent. He pressed his ear to the wood.

"Help."

Bloody hell! What could Hartford be doing? He listened further. There was no answering male voice.

"Help." Again, a little louder with a sob this time.

He didn't care if Hartford *was* Charlotte's husband—

he could not ignore a plea for assistance under his own roof.

He shoved on the door. Thankfully it opened easily. There was no one in the sitting room.

"Charlotte, it's Edward. Are you all right?"

"Edward. Oh, God. Edward. In here. Please . . ."

Charlotte's voice came from the bedroom. Tynweith reached the door in two strides.

"Good God!"

He stared at Hartford's shriveled arse. The duke was stretched out on top of Charlotte. He wasn't moving.

Charlotte's panicked eyes met his.

"Help me, Edward. I'm trapped. I think . . . Oh, God. I think he's dead."

"My lord, may I say I am delighted—" Collins's grin collapsed abruptly into a frown. "That is . . . I mean . . . it *is* true you are to marry Lady Elizabeth, is it not?"

Robbie gripped the windowsill more tightly. He'd like to be out in the storm again. The wind and biting rain matched his mood exactly. No point in depressing his valet, though. The man must be merry as a grig at the news of his impending nuptials—his wedding Lizzie meant Collins could finally make Betty an honest woman.

He turned away from the window and attempted a smile. He had to force his lips to move—it was probably not a very convincing performance. Damn. He used to be quite skilled at pretending good spirits.

"Yes, Collins, you are correct. Lady Elizabeth and I plan to wed." Immediately, if Lady Beatrice had anything to say to the matter. She'd already sent word to James—or would once the storm had passed. Even she recognized sending a man out on the road in this downpour was lunacy.

She'd informed him in no uncertain terms that he was to ride for a special license tomorrow.

"My lord, you are dripping on the carpet. You need to get out of those wet clothes or you will catch your death."

There was an idea. He could save Lizzie by sticking his spoon in the wall—but only after wedding her. Dying at this point would condemn her to marry Andrew.

"You need a warm bath, my lord. I'll arrange for it at once."

"I'm not some hothouse flower, Collins. A little cold and wet won't kill me."

"It pays to be cautious, my lord."

Robbie pulled his sodden shirt over his head while Collins made the necessary preparations for a tub and hot water. Surely the man wasn't going to coddle him until he tied the knot with Lizzie? That would drive him mad.

Another reason to wed quickly, he supposed. Annoying solicitude was not acceptable grounds for murder.

He shivered out of his breeches. A bath *would* be nice. It wouldn't warm the cold terror gripping his heart, but it should take the chill out of his flesh.

What the hell was he going to do? Lady Beatrice had been correct—the scandal would be horrific if Lizzie didn't marry posthaste. She had been, for all intents and purposes, naked on the battlements, and once the heavens opened, the rain had soaked the remaining scraps of her shift to transparency.

Now if Lady Dunlee could be persuaded to be discreet. . . .

"What are you laughing at, my lord?"

Collins was frowning harder. Not surprising. Robbie's laughter had not been prompted by humor. The thought of Lady Dunlee being discreet was ludicrous.

He might as well ask the rain pelting the window not to wet anything.

"Nothing. Is the bath ready?"

"Yes, my lord."

"Splendid."

Robbie sank into the warm tub. The water stung his cold skin and made his numb toes ache as they came back to life. He closed his eyes for a moment. It did feel good.

"Hand me the soap, Collins, and take yourself off."

"My lord, I'd be happy to help with your bath."

"Well, I'd not be happy for your help. Go away."

Robbie sighed and sank lower in the tub as he heard the door close. What was he going to do?

Marrying Lizzie was a dream come true—a nightmare.

He dunked his head, then took the soap and started lathering his hair.

After the disaster at the Dancing Piper, MacDuff and his chums had taken every opportunity to twit him.

"Challenge Westbrooke to a duel with swords—he's got only a little weapon."

"Fallen off any good mounts lately, Westbrooke?"

"Let me know if you visit Fleur again, Westbrooke. I'll come behind to give the poor girl satisfaction."

He had learned how to deal with the twits. He'd laughed and pretended their words did not hurt. Their interest in taunting him faded eventually.

His anxiety didn't. When he went home at the end of term, he decided the problem was much like falling off a horse—you just needed to get right back on and ride again. So he tried. Nan had helped him lose his virginity; he reasoned she'd be an excellent choice to cure him of his nerves.

It hadn't worked. Nan had been happy to go off to the abandoned hermit's cottage with him. She'd been quite enthusiastic, even. She'd done her best to encourage

him. And she'd even been kind when he'd lost his . . .
courage at the crucial moment.

*"Don't worry, love. These things 'appen, though mostly
to older gents. Just finish me with yer finger and we'll call it
a day."*

Damn. He'd gotten some soap in his eye—that was
why it was tearing. He scrubbed his arms.

What the bloody hell was he going to do on his wedding night?

Tynweith waited for the last of the house guests to
assemble in the drawing room. Charlotte had stayed
upstairs with her maid. Well, and Hartford was upstairs, too, in a manner of speaking.

Poor Charlotte. She'd been quite shaken when
he'd found her. Not surprising. She'd been trapped
under the duke—literally a dead weight—for a good
little while. Apparently he had died in medias res.

She was more composed now, but still not ready to
face the likes of Lady Dunlee. Tynweith clenched his
hands into fists and then carefully relaxed each finger.
Lady Dunlee was just entering the room. She'd be in
alt with this new morsel of tittle-tattle. He drew a deep
breath.

"If I may have your attention?"

The desultory chatter died down. It was clear his
guests expected an announcement of interest. All eyes
focused on him—some, like Lady Dunlee's, sharp and
hungry; others, slightly amused. Lord Westbrooke
stood off to the right, his face pleasantly expressionless. Lady Elizabeth, hands folded in her lap, sat next
to Lady Beatrice, as far from the earl as possible.

He cleared his throat. This was harder than he'd
expected.

"I've asked you all here—"

"But we aren't all here," Lady Caroline interrupted.

"Yes, I know. The duchess did not feel up to appearing as you will understand when I tell you—"

"But what about Lady Felicity?" Lady Caroline frowned. "I've been thinking about her all afternoon. I haven't seen her since luncheon."

Tynweith surveyed the room. Lady Caroline was correct. Felicity *was* absent. Had *he* seen her since luncheon? She'd been talking to Charlotte at table, but she had not been with her when Hartford arrived, had she? Where had she gone?

"Our departure *was* rather hurried given the storm and other, um, events," he said. "Perhaps she was in one of the other carriages?"

"She wasn't in ours," Lady Beatrice said.

"And if she wasn't in ours," Lady Caroline said, "she wasn't in any, because your coach carried only men, didn't it, Lord Tynweith?"

"Yes. Well, it's not far to walk. Perhaps she came home earlier."

"So where is she now? Shouldn't she be here? I thought everyone was supposed to be here." Lady Caroline leaned forward, displaying her plump breasts a little too completely. "Perhaps she fell in the ruins and is still there, calling vainly for help."

"I don't think . . ." He tried to remember the scene at the castle as they were boarding the carriages. *Had* Felicity been there? He could not be certain. His mind had been on Charlotte—and everything had been so chaotic with the storm and Lady Elizabeth's scandal.

"I did send the locksmith over to secure the dungeon door. He would have found Lady Felicity if she were there. She is probably resting in her room or strolling the grounds. I will have someone sent to check on her immediately." He looked at Flint who bowed and disappeared. His butler would have the girl here shortly.

"Perhaps it is best if Lady Felicity doesn't hear this

particular announcement." Lady Dunlee cast a glance at Westbrooke. "I believe she will not take it well."

"No, uh . . ." Surely Felicity would not be upset at Hartford's passing? And why was Lady Dunlee looking at the earl?

Comprehension dawned.

"Oh, no. That is not the announcement I was preparing to make."

Lady Dunlee stared at him as if he had lost his mind. He was beginning to feel that perhaps he had.

"The announcement I have to make—the very *sad* announcement—is that the Duke of Hartford expired in bed this afternoon."

He should have left the location of the duke's demise out of the sentence. Lord Botton sniggered. Even Sir George was beset by a coughing fit. Tynweith rushed to cover the sounds.

"Obviously, this is a great shock to us all and especially to the duchess. To honor her feelings and the duke's memory, I'm afraid I must bring this house party to a premature close. I must ask you all to leave in the morning. I am sorry, but to continue with entertainments when one of the oldest peers of the Realm has died would not be proper."

"Very true," Lord Dunlee said. "Very well put, Tynweith. My wife, my daughter, and I will prepare to depart early tomorrow."

"Thank you. I am sorry—yes, Flint?" The butler was gesturing from the door. Everyone turned to look.

"My lord, I have some unfortunate news to report."

"Well, go ahead, man." There was no point in being overly discreet at this point. Felicity's absence had already been noted—better to have the truth than wild speculations.

"First, Lord Andrew has taken leave of the premises."

Tynweith nodded. Just as well. He hadn't decided what to do with the man anyway. Chances were Alvord would like Lord Andrew's guts for garters, but the duke could find the blackguard himself if he wished. "And?"

"And I regret to inform you that Lady Felicity has not been seen at Lendal Park since the carriages left for the ruins this morning."

"Oh, poor Felicity!" Lady Caroline actually wrung her hands.

Damn. Could Felicity have wandered off and gotten hurt in the ruins? Shouldn't the locksmith have found her? Apparently not.

"Send a footman to the castle immediately, Flint."

"Yes, my lord. I—"

"Thank you, Dickey. You were wonderful."

"That's Lady Felicity's voice!" Lady Caroline led the charge into the entry hall with her mother close behind. Lady Dunlee managed to squeeze through the door first—and came to an abrupt halt.

"Oh, my." She sounded breathless with scandal.

"What is it?" Tynweith pushed to the front of the crowd.

Lady Felicity was indeed standing in the entry hall. Her hair was falling down her back and her dress was almost falling off her person. She was clinging to the arm of a very burly, very embarrassed locksmith.

Lady Dunlee had another tasty morsel to add to her gossip stew.

Chapter Seventeen

"I don't see why I need to marry Robbie so quickly."
Lizzie swallowed her panic. She was back in her room
at Lady Beatrice's town house. They had left Lendal
Park two days ago. Robbie had ridden ahead and pro-
cured a special license. In less than thirty minutes, she
would say her vows in Lady Beatrice's drawing room
and become the Countess of Westbrooke.

She felt like throwing up.

"You don't?" Lady Beatrice paused in stroking the
large orange cat in her lap. Queen Bess meowed her
disapproval and butted her head against Lady Bea's
hand. Lady Bea resumed stroking. "How long have
you been acquainted with Lady Dunlee? I have no
doubt the woman is already entertaining her intimates with every detail she observed on Tynweith's
battlements—and probably a few she didn't."

"That's the honest truth," Betty said as she pinned
up a lock of Lizzie's hair. "That woman would gossip
about God Almighty if she could."

Lizzie frowned at Betty in the mirror; Betty smiled
back and tweaked her hair.

"Ouch."

"So sorry, my lady."

"You just want to move to Westbrooke House."

Betty grinned. "Very true, my lady. Me and Collins have waited years for this day."

Lizzie grunted. At least someone was happy. "But Lady Bea, wouldn't our engagement be enough to scotch the rumors?"

"Perhaps in the regular way of things, but there is nothing regular about this situation. You are the Duke of Alvord's sister, one of—if not *the*—most prominent woman your age in society, and you were seen practically as bare as the day you were born in the company of two men by one of London's biggest gossips. The story of Westbrooke's naked excursion to your bedchamber is sure to be discussed as well. No, if you are not securely wed to the earl before you step over the first society threshold, you'll be given the cut direct by every woman of the *ton*—and probably garner the unpleasant attentions of all the rakes as well."

Lizzie's stomach twisted. "Surely not!"

"I would be willing to wager on it. This house party will be discussed for the rest of this Season and probably many Seasons to come. The pattern card of respectability, Lady Elizabeth, ruins her reputation, and the old satyr, Hartford, cocks up his toes. Not to mention Lady Felicity's encounter with the local locksmith. Much too delicious a plateful of scandal for the tabbies to ignore. The only way to curtail their feast is to flash a wedding ring at them."

Lizzie gripped her hands in her lap and willed the little she had been able to eat to stay where it belonged. She feared Lady Beatrice was correct.

"And there are two more reasons for you to wed quickly—Lady Felicity and Lord Andrew. Felicity had a somewhat less than rational reaction to your engagement announcement."

That was an understatement. Lizzie rubbed the space between her eyebrows. She was developing a crashing headache to go with her unsettled stomach. Lady Dunlee had taken it upon herself to inform Felicity of

Robbie's betrothal the moment she saw the girl standing in Tynweith's entry hall, leaning on the arm of the locksmith who'd discovered her in the ruined castle. Fortunately the man had good reactions. He'd caught Felicity's fist before it could connect with Lizzie's eye.

"Felicity will not relinquish her ambitions gracefully, nor will she relish being a laughingstock," Lady Beatrice said. "Everyone knows she's been pursuing Westbrooke—and she knows everyone knows. And I cannot like the fact that Lord Andrew is likely lurking somewhere in London. He has proven himself no gentleman." She shook her head, causing the orange plume in her hair to bob. "I'd say there was every reason to rush your nuptials. Once the knot is tied, there is little Felicity or Andrew can do."

"And you love Robbie," Meg said, leaning forward to touch Lizzie's arm. "It is not as if you are rushing into marriage with a stranger."

"It is just so . . . sudden." Lizzie sniffed back tears. This was not the way she had imagined her wedding. Not that she needed—or wanted—a big ceremony at St. George's, Hanover Square—not at all. She had never thought to marry in London. No, when she'd dreamt of the day, she had pictured the church at Alvord with her family there—James and Sarah. Aunt Gladys. And Robbie, but a Robbie wildly in love with her, not this resigned, reserved man who was marrying her only to save her reputation.

"I wish James were here." Lizzie bit her lip. She hadn't meant to say that out loud.

Lady Beatrice got up, dumping an annoyed Queen Bess on the floor, and patted Lizzie's shoulder. "I know. He would be, of course, if Sarah weren't on the verge of being brought to bed. He'll come visit as soon as he can—or you and Robbie can visit him later when you are at Westbrooke."

Lizzie sighed. "Can't we go there now?"

"We discussed this. It is best you remain in London

and go about for a few weeks to stifle the rumors. Then, when all the *ton* has seen you, you can leave for the country. Then your departure will not look like a retreat."

"There." Betty smiled and stepped back. "All done, my lady. Ye do look beautiful."

"Very true." Lady Beatrice consulted her watch. "The earl should be here at any moment. There is only one task left to do." She cleared her throat and looked at Meg. "Meg, you may go get ready."

"I *am* ready, Lady Bea."

"Then you may go see that everything is in order downstairs and keep Lord Westbrooke company should he arrive early."

"But—"

"*Go,* Meg. I have some words of a private nature to share with Lizzie."

"Oh."

Meg looked as shocked as Lizzie felt. Words of a *private* nature? Surely she didn't mean . . . ?

She did. As soon as the door closed behind Meg, Lady Bea settled her sizable bulk in a chair close to Lizzie and put her hand on Lizzie's arm.

"My dear, I know your mother died when you were born. Has your aunt or your sister-in-law ever spoken to you about the marriage bed?"

Lizzie wished the floor would open and swallow her up.

"No. Those conversations usually occur right before, um. . . ."

"Exactly. Right before the wedding—and the wedding night, of course. And since you will be wed in about"—Lady Bea consulted her watch—"fifteen minutes, I believe I had best give you a hint of what to expect, if you will allow it."

"Um." What could an elderly spinster possibly know about the intimate relations of marriage?

Lady Beatrice took Lizzie's inarticulate response as assent.

"The main thing, my dear, is not to be afraid. The marriage act may seem very odd at first, but you will soon become accustomed to it and I daresay enjoy it." Lady Bea frowned. "Some women have the misguided notion that ladies of the *ton* cannot or should not experience pleasure in carnal relations. Balderdash! A lady can be as passionate as a lightskirt. The basic equipment is the same. It's what's up here"—she tapped her head—"that matters."

"Yes. Of course." Lizzie could barely get the words out. Embarrassment was strangling her. Surely Lady Beatrice . . . The woman had never married. . . . How could she know . . . ?

"Now, there may be a little pain, a little blood, tonight when Lord Westbrooke breaches your maidenhead, but you must not be concerned. It is just a momentary discomfort. After that I'm certain everything will be splendid. The earl is a handsome man. He must know his way around a woman's body. You are in good hands"—Lady Beatrice smiled archly—"literally."

"Um. Yes. Of course. Thank you." Lizzie had not been looking forward to facing Robbie, but she would face a den of lions to escape any more of this conversation. "Do you suppose it is time to go downstairs?"

Lady Beatrice chuckled. "Eager, are you? Well, if I were forty years younger, I might have my eye on the earl, too."

Lizzie stared at Lady Beatrice in horror as the older woman consulted her watch once more.

"Good evening, Alton." Robbie handed his hat to Lady Beatrice's butler, a tall thin man with a shock of white hair. He looked like a University don, but rumor was he sprang from the London stews. Robbie believed it. The man's demeanor was all that was proper, but his eyes were as sharp as a lancet. Made a man worry he'd be bled of all his secrets.

Robbie looked away quickly. He did not want Alton bleeding *him*.

"Good evening, my lord." Was there a note of humor in the man's voice? "May I extend my sincere felicitations on your impending nuptials?"

"Yes. Of course. Thank you." Robbie glanced back. Those damn eyes were watching him still. The man couldn't know, could he? Surely he couldn't tell Robbie was . . . ?

Ridiculous. Alton might be preternaturally perceptive, but he was not a mind reader.

He bit his lip. Lizzie would have no need to read minds—she could read the limp evidence of his failing clearly if he visited her bed tonight. How was he going to keep his secret from her? God. His head throbbed from trying to find an answer to that question. He'd thought of nothing else in the last two days.

"If you'll step into the drawing room, my lord? You will find Miss Peterson there with the parson."

Robbie nodded and tried not to appear as if he were fleeing the entry hall.

Hell, Alton should look to his own secrets. There'd been rumors about him and Lady Beatrice for years, reportedly even back to when he was a young footman in Knightsdale's service and Lady Beatrice was not yet out. People said he was the reason she'd never married. And when Knightsdale had finally given up on her and let her set up her own household, she'd chosen an elderly, deaf, and very nearsighted cousin as her companion, and Alton as her butler. That had been before Robbie was born. The companion had long since departed for the hereafter, but Alton was still in residence.

Why hadn't Charles insisted his aunt use the Knightsdale town house to launch his sister-in-law?

It had a better location and a much more appropriate butler.

Robbie repressed a snort. Most likely Lady Beatrice flat out refused. And Knightsdale House *was* an incredibly dark and depressing place. Charles's father had been rather dark and depressing himself.

Robbie stepped into the drawing room and was assaulted by a battalion of roses.

"Oof!"

Meg's face appeared on the other side of the flowers. She grinned. "Sorry. I was just rearranging things. Lizzie should be down at any minute." She lowered her voice and leaned closer. "Lady Beatrice sent me downstairs so she could have *the talk* with Lizzie."

"Ah, yes." He hoped his face wasn't as red as the blossoms Meg was transporting. "And Reverend Axley?"

Meg gestured with her head. "By the peonies."

"Parks?"

"I don't—ah!" She looked over his shoulder, and her face lit up like a thousand candles. "He just arrived."

Robbie felt Parks's hand on his shoulder. "Good evening, Miss Peterson. Ready to step into parson's mousetrap, Westbrooke?"

"As ready as I will ever be." He would be more than ready if only he didn't have his mortifying secret. There was no other woman he would rather marry.

"Good. The bridegroom is here." Lady Beatrice appeared in the doorway. "Come along, Lizzie. It is time to get married."

Lady Beatrice moved and Lizzie stepped into view. God.

She was beautiful. No, that word was inadequate. She was ethereal. Heavenly. He would certainly feel he'd reached heaven if he could truly make her his wife. As it was, he feared he was facing hell. To have her in his home, in the countess's bedroom next to his, to know everyone including Lizzie expected him to come to her bed—hell could not be worse.

Her white ball gown clung to her sweet curves like water. He wanted to run his hands over the silk, and then strip away the fabric to touch the silk of her skin. The image of her naked before her glass in Tynweith's guest room flashed into his memory in tantalizing detail and his recalcitrant organ surged to life. Damn. If only . . .

Reverend Axley cleared his throat. "Shall we begin?"

The words of the wedding service washed over Robbie. He had heard them many times before. At James's wedding—also a hurried affair held in a drawing room—and at Charles's. He had never thought to hear them spoken for him. He had given up all hope of marriage years ago.

What was he going to do tonight?

He glanced down at Lizzie. She was unusually pale. He took her hand in his. Her fingers felt like ice. He rubbed their backs with his thumb, and she angled a fleeting smile up at him before turning back to the minister.

If only . . . But there was no point in wishing he were a normal man. No amount of wishing had made his shy little member brave before. It was cowering in his breeches now, like the tail of a frightened dog, limp and droopy, at the thought of bedding Lizzie— or rather, failing Lizzie. Damn it.

The minister was frowning at him. God, what had he missed? The man would expect him to pay attention at his own wedding.

"Your vows, my lord? You need to reply . . . ?"

"I do. Yes. Of course I do."

He had no choice. He could not condemn Lizzie to wed that bastard, Lord Andrew. Even a marriage to him was better than that. Nor could he expose her to the *ton's* vitriol. No, their marriage was the only solution—which was the only reason he was standing here.

He heard her murmur her vows.

At least now he would have the right to protect her if Lord Andrew or any other man made improper advances. Not that he expected anyone would. He might not be the Duke of Alvord, but he was not insignificant. He had some power. And more than one rake might take note of Lord Andrew's rearranged countenance.

He snorted. Reverend Axley and Lizzie both gave him a startled look. He smiled back at them.

The cowardly bastard had probably gone to ground somewhere until the evidence of his beating faded.

He shook his head. He had never felt such anger as he had when he'd seen that blackguard assaulting Lizzie. He hadn't known himself.

"You do not have the ring, my lord?" Reverend Axley frowned at Robbie.

He frowned back. "Of course I have the ring. Why would you think I didn't?"

"I'm sorry, my lord, but you shook your head when I asked you. I understood—"

"No, I'm sorry. I was woolgathering."

"Woolgathering, my lord?" The reverend's eyebrows jumped halfway up his forehead. "At your wedding?"

"Well, yes. Not precisely woolgathering, I suppose. Daydreaming, more like."

"Ah." Reverend Axley gave him a knowing look and a wink. "I see. Not much longer to wait, my lord, for those activities."

"No, uh, that is. . . ." The man thought . . . ? But the minister was frowning again. Best not to argue the matter.

He took Lizzie's hand. Her fingers trembled slightly. Her lovely eyes were huge. He felt another stab of guilt. They should be sparkling with happiness, not shadowed by sadness and worry.

He felt like a beast. She should have a wedding

dress and veil, hundreds of guests filling St. George's, James giving her away, her Aunt Gladys crying in the congregation—not this hurried little ceremony. He didn't care for such stuff, of course. If he were capable of consummating this marriage, he'd say his vows naked on a dung heap, but Lizzie should have better.

Well, it was not really his fault. Circumstances in the person of Lord Andrew had put them in this situation. They must make the best of it.

He slid his ring slowly onto her finger and looked up into her eyes. They held a question he had not the courage to answer. Impulsively, he lifted her hand to his lips and kissed it.

She smiled, and it was as if the sun had come out from behind the clouds.

Lizzie climbed into Robbie's carriage. Her stomach shivered with nerves. She glanced at her new husband.

He was sitting as far from her as possible, staring straight ahead, his mouth in a thin line, his jaw clenched, his arms crossed tightly over his chest. He might as well hang a sign on his neck: WARNING—DO NOT APPROACH.

If she didn't say something, they would ride to his town house in silence.

What did one say to a new husband who was clearly not happy to be wed? Thank you?

"Are you all right?" she asked.

He frowned in the dim light. "Of course I'm all right. Why wouldn't I be all right?"

"I don't know. You seem"—sad? He wouldn't care to hear that—"quiet."

"I'm tired." He shifted position slightly. "Yes, tired. It's been a long day—a long few days. I think I shall go to bed—" He coughed. "That is, I shall go to *sleep* early. If you don't mind."

Was he trying to tell her he would not be

visiting her room tonight? She felt a mix of relief and disappointment.

"No, of course I don't mind. I am tired, too. It *has* been a very exhausting few days."

"Yes indeed." Robbie nodded. "Very exhausting. Early to bed—uh, sleep—would do wonders for us both, I'm certain."

"Yes."

Silence again. She heard the clop of the horses' hooves; the creak of the carriage. The Watch shouted the hour and some drunken men shouted back at him.

Robbie cleared his throat. "I am sorry about the wedding."

Lizzie felt her stomach drop to her slippers. Not that she was surprised—she knew he hadn't wanted to marry her.

"I'm sorry, too. You do know I never meant to trap you?"

He frowned at her. "What are you talking about? You didn't trap me—Lord Andrew did."

She drew in a sharp breath. So he *did* feel trapped.

He ran his hand through his hair. "That didn't come out quite right. What I meant was, I'm sorry you had such a rushed, disappointing ceremony. You must have wished for more."

"No. It was fine. I didn't wish for more." *I just wish you loved me.* She bit her lip. She hadn't said those words, had she? No. She must not have. Robbie had not recoiled in horror.

She should ask him now if he loved someone else.

She couldn't. Her throat seized up at the thought.

He grunted and settled back into silence.

What else could they talk about?

"Do you think Lord Andrew is in Town?"

That was an inspired choice.

"Yes, I'm afraid he might be. You'd think he'd go home to lick his wounds, but as far as I can tell he hasn't. I've inquired at all his father's properties. There has been no sign of him." He reached out as if to touch her, then let his hand fall back to his lap. "I know Felicity came back to Town. That girl has no shame."

"Surely she will not bother you now? We are wed—there is nothing she can do."

"I wouldn't be so certain. She and Andrew are both harboring a goodly dose of anger. At a minimum I expect some nasty rumors to circulate."

The coach slowed to a stop and a footman opened the door.

"My lord, we've arrived. Mr. Bentley has assembled the staff to welcome Lady Westbrooke."

"Thank you, Thomas."

Lady Westbrooke? Robbie's mother had died years ago. Why would . . .

"Oh."

Robbie smiled. "I'm sure you'll get used to your new title quickly."

"Yes. Of course." Not if Lord Westbrooke remained the stiffly reserved man helping her down from the carriage. She did not feel like Lady Westbrooke at all.

She smiled and nodded at Mr. Bentley, the butler, and Mrs. Bentley, Robbie's housekeeper, and the rest of the servants lined up to meet her.

"Mrs. Bentley, if you'll show Lady Westbrooke to her room?"

"Certainly, my lord."

She'd thought Robbie would take her upstairs, but he was talking to his butler. Perhaps it was just as well. She was feeling a little teary. He would not care to see her turn into a watering pot.

Mrs. Bentley had bright brown eyes and a wide, warm smile. "You must be exhausted, my lady."

"Yes, I am rather tired." And panicked. It hit her suddenly as she walked up these unfamiliar stairs. She was a wife now, no matter how unwanted. Her life had changed irreversibly.

She took a sustaining breath.

Mrs. Bentley touched her arm lightly. "Are you all right, my lady?"

"Yes, thank you. Just a little overwhelmed."

"You poor thing." Mrs. Bentley patted her hand. "You'll settle in quickly. We are all delighted to welcome you." She leaned a little closer. "If you'll forgive me for saying so, the master has been a bit blue-deviled these last years. We—Mr. Bentley and I—think you are just what he needs."

Lizzie flushed. "Thank you."

Mrs. Bentley nodded and continued up the stairs. "I had the countess's rooms aired as soon as we got word of the wedding. I think you will find them quite comfortable. Your maid is there now, putting away your things."

Lizzie felt a thread of relief. At least there would be one thing unchanged—Betty would still fuss at her and argue with her. She stumbled slightly. She would, wouldn't she? The girl was now wed to Robbie's valet. That would not change her too much, would it?

Apparently not. At least Lizzie didn't notice any difference when she entered her bedchamber. Betty was hanging her favorite ball gown in the wardrobe. She closed the door when she saw Lizzie and grinned.

"Oh, my lady, isn't this a lovely room?"

"Yes, Betty, very lovely."

It *was* a beautiful room, decorated in blues and golds. She walked over to the window and pushed back the heavy curtains. The moon lit the back garden, bathing the fountain and trellises with pale light.

"Let me brush out yer hair, my lady. Ye want to be ready when Lord Westbrooke arrives."

Lizzie sat down at the dressing table. "I don't

believe Lord Westbrooke will be coming tonight, Betty. He is very tired."

Betty snorted. "Don't ye believe that for a minute, my lady. Men are *never* too tired for bed play. He'll be up shortly, ye'll see."

Would he? Betty seemed so certain—but Robbie had been clear, hadn't he?

Lizzie's stomach twisted. She really didn't know what she wanted.

Collins was whistling, damn him.

"I thought you'd come up earlier, my lord." He tilted his head at the door to the countess's room and grinned.

Robbie turned away to put his cravat pin on his bureau. Lizzie was on the other side of that door.

He would not think about it.

"I had to speak to Bentley. I've had men looking for Lord Andrew, you know."

Collins grunted. "Any luck finding the bastard?"

"No, but I'm not surprised. I expect he'll stay away from society functions until his face heals." Robbie pulled off his cravat. "I just don't want him bothering Lizzie."

Collins helped him out of his coat. "Surely the man won't trouble the new Lady Westbrooke."

"I sincerely hope he will not, but he didn't have a shred of compunction about troubling her before. The Duke of Alvord is not someone most men would want as an enemy."

Collins shrugged. "Ah, but now Lady Elizabeth is your wife, my lord." He grinned again. "I know you'll keep a very close eye on her." He winked.

Robbie gritted his teeth. If Collins didn't leave soon, he was going to plant his fist in the middle of that knowing grin.

It wasn't Collins's fault. The man was newly married

himself and obviously enjoying every moment of his wedded bliss. He merely anticipated the same joys for Robbie.

"That will be all for tonight, Collins."

Could the man's grin get any wider?

"Have a very"—Collins looked at the door to the countess's room again—"pleasant night, my lord."

Robbie let out a long breath the moment his valet left.

He looked at the connecting door. Lizzie was on the other side. She was probably in bed, dressed in her nightgown. Was it the high-necked virginal gown she'd had at Tynweith's house party or something new, something diaphanous? Mmm. Something that skimmed her lovely breasts and floated over the blond curls at the apex of her thighs, something he could slide slowly up her beautiful body. . . .

Was she waiting for him? Surely she had taken his hint? But what if she expected him to come to her?

She was in a strange room in a strange household. She had suffered through Lord Andrew's attack, the resulting scandal, and then that hurried wedding. Her emotions must be disordered. He should go to her. Talk to her.

Kiss her.

Part of him leapt at the thought.

He put his hand on the door.

He wanted to give her many kisses, too many to count. He wanted to bury his face in her hair, to kneel between her thighs, to. . . .

Right. And when he was there, ready to enter her, what would happen? This enthusiastic part of him that was almost bursting from his pantaloons would wilt like the shy little flower it was.

Then would Lizzie laugh at him as Fleur had? Or would she pity him? Which was worse?

God, they were both awful. Better to go to his study and get roaring drunk.

Chapter Eighteen

"You look terrible."

"Thank you, Fel. I'm quite aware of the fact. I feel terrible, too."

"I've not seen you at any parties recently."

"Do you think I want to advertise the fact Westbrooke rearranged my face for me?"

"No, I don't suppose you do." Felicity leaned back against the tree trunk. Lord Palmerson had an exceptionally large, dark garden. Some very interesting activities could be conducted in complete privacy here. She studied Andrew in the dim light. His face might be an unpleasant rainbow of bruises but the other portions of his anatomy appeared to be completely functional. She reached for the fall of his pantaloons.

He moved his hips back.

"Shy, Andrew?"

"No. I merely am not in the mood to be distracted. Aren't you angry at the way things turned out? Trapping Westbrooke and compromising Lady Elizabeth were your ideas, after all."

Felicity shrugged. "I'm not happy, of course, but what can I do? Westbrooke's married."

"Ah, but perhaps not happily. I'd swear something is wrong between Westbrooke and his wife."

"How do you know? You've been playing least in sight ever since we got back to London."

Andrew snorted—and winced. "As you say, my face is not a thing of beauty at the moment. But I have my spies. You've seen Westbrooke and Lady Elizabeth, too, Fel. They are not together much, are they?"

"Well, no, but it is not good *ton* for husbands and wives to live in each other's pockets."

"But newlyweds, Fel? They've only been married two weeks. And the few times they are together, they aren't. Surely you've noticed how far apart they stand and how carefully they don't look at each other? Quite a contrast to the longing glances they used to litter *ton* gatherings with."

Andrew had a point. She'd been busy looking for another matrimonial quarry, so hadn't been studying Westbrooke any longer. Now that she thought on it . . . Yes, she had noticed a certain distance between them. A certain chill. And Lady Elizabeth . . .

"You're right. The new Lady Westbrooke looks like she hasn't had a good swiving."

"Exactly. Something is keeping Westbrooke out of her bed."

"Interesting." Felicity grinned. She'd certainly like to make that couple's lives miserable if she could. "What do you suggest?"

"Rumors usually work well. See that the new Lady Westbrooke hears some juicy gossip about Westbrooke's sexual exploits."

"He doesn't have any sexual exploits, Andrew—at least none I've been able to discern. The man is either incredibly discreet or a eunuch."

Andrew had a fleeting look of disgust on his battered face that quickly turned into a grimace. "They don't have to be *true*, Felicity. Innuendo often works best. Vague whisperings that can't be confirmed or denied. Little drops of verbal acid that eat away at lovely Lady Westbrooke's confidence. We want her to feel unease, to worry, to doubt. Then her imagination will take over, and we can sit back and enjoy the farce."

"Perhaps she'll turn to you for comfort?"

Andrew snorted and winced again. "Bloody little hope of that—but I do know some delightfully devious men who look like angels, but most certainly aren't. They would be happy to cuckold Westbrooke."

"Ooo, do I know them?"

"I'm certain you do, but they don't play with unmarried ladies."

"Ah. Another compelling reason to get a husband." Felicity leaned forward and put her hand on Andrew's fall again. This time he flinched, but did not pull back. She smiled and stroked him. A lovely hard ridge grew under her hand.

"I'll be delighted to go back to the party and drop a few hints," she said, "but first . . . Well, I'd hate to waste the convenient darkness, wouldn't you?"

"Something is wrong between Lizzie and Westbrooke, Billy."

Lady Beatrice lay in bed and surveyed her butler. After all these years, he still made her heart beat faster. She frowned.

"I shouldn't let you into my bed, you know, until you promise to make an honest woman of me."

Alton sighed. "Bea, we have been through this almost every day since you seduced me in the Knightsdale attic. I cannot marry you."

"I don't see why not."

"You would if you weren't so pigheaded. I am not of your class—I'm just about as far from your class as possible. You are the sister and aunt of a marquis—I'm the bastard of a whore and who knows what? A sailor at best. Furthermore, I am your butler. Society would be scandalized."

"Oh, pshaw! Society is a bunch of totty-headed, stiff-rumped fools. They can go to the devil."

"Bea, it is easy for you to say that now, but wait until the first door is slammed in your face. You'll feel differently then."

Bea sat up with that. "How dare you tell me how I will feel? You're more of a stickler than any of the patronesses of Almack's. I don't give the snap of my fingers for such stuff. I only go to the routs and balls because I'm bored." She stretched out her arms to him. "Say yes, Billy. We can go to the Continent until the worst of the fuss dies down." She grinned. "We may as well add to the gossip orgy Tynweith's party has provided."

Alton scooped Queen Bess off his pillow. She meowed her usual protest and stalked over to her own bed.

"I don't believe her highness wishes us to marry."

"Nonsense." Bea wrapped her arms around his neck. "She loves you—and you love her. She looked very well fed when I got home from Lendal Park."

Alton grunted. "Cook has a soft spot for the creature."

Bea chuckled. "Cook says the same thing about you." She nuzzled his neck. "Did you miss me?"

"You know that I did. I have already shown you—many times."

"Show me again."

Alton was an extremely accomplished lover. He had been good when he was a young man and he'd only gotten better over the years. He knew exactly what she liked, knew just how to tease her until she was wild for him.

Well, and she knew what he liked, too. She ran her tongue over an exquisitely sensitive part of his anatomy and smiled when she heard his quick intake of breath.

Afterward, she rested her head on his chest and returned to her original concern.

"Billy, there is something wrong between Lizzie and Westbrooke."

"So you said. They are newly married, Bea. It will take them a while to settle into life together."

"No, it's more than that. Lizzie still has the look of a virgin about her."

"Bea! You are being fanciful. How can Lady Westbrooke still be a virgin?"

"I don't know, but I mean to find out."

"You can't meddle in their affairs."

"I certainly can. And so can you."

"What?!" Alton stiffened.

"Yes. You must talk to Lord Westbrooke."

"He is not going to talk to the butler, especially about personal matters."

"You were a spy during the war with Napoleon. You can gain his confidence."

"Spying was different—"

"It was not. You were getting information for a good cause. This is a good cause, too. You'll be helping continue Westbrooke's line and make two young people happy."

"Bea—"

"Please, Billy? We will invite them for an intimate dinner. You will get Westbrooke drunk. Then he will confide in you."

"He won't."

"He will." Bea shook Alton's arm. "He looks desperate to me. He needs the advice of a man of your experience."

"I don't think—"

"And I will not be idle. I will see what I can learn from Lizzie. Together, I'm certain we can solve this problem."

"We can't—"

"We *can*. We must. Please?"

Billy had never been able to say no when she used

that particular note of need in her voice. She was not surprised when he sighed heavily.

"Oh, very well."

"I knew I could count on you."

She proceeded to thank him *very* thoroughly indeed.

"Thank you for escorting me to Lady Beatrice's dinner party, Robbie." Lizzie sat, hands folded, on one side of the carriage. Robbie occupied the other.

"You are my wife, Lizzie. If you want something, you need only ask."

I want you in my bed. Lizzie pressed her lips tightly together. She hadn't said that out loud, had she? No. Robbie was still in his seat. If she'd spoken, he would have leapt from the moving coach.

They'd been married almost a month, and still he had not visited her room. He'd stopped attending most social events with her. She was surprised he'd agreed to come tonight, though Lady Bea's invitation had quite pointedly demanded his presence.

They were strangers inhabiting the same house.

She'd waited for him on their wedding night, even though he'd hinted he wouldn't come. Betty had convinced her he would, but Betty had been wrong. She'd waited every night since.

She smiled ruefully. Betty was furious. *"It's not natural,"* she said every time she looked at the connecting door. Lizzie was certain Betty had shared her feelings with Collins who must have mentioned the topic to Robbie.

Did he hate her?

She smoothed the fabric of her skirt. She had been twisting it into knots. Betty would castigate her if she came back with her beautiful new dress ruined.

What did it matter? She could dress in servants' castoffs for all Robbie cared.

She sniffed as quietly as possible, casting a glance at her husband. He had his head back against the squabs, his eyes closed.

And then there were the rumors inundating society all of a sudden. She had never heard a whisper concerning Robbie's sexual exploits in all the years she'd been in Town, and now she encountered giggles and knowing looks every time she approached a group of women.

Did Robbie really have several mistresses and a few choice widows he visited regularly? No wonder he was tired.

Well, there was only one way to find out the truth of the matter. She must ask him.

Her hands started to shake. She gripped her skirt again.

Perhaps she should wait until they were returning? Then she could flee to her bedchamber for a good cry. If she broached the subject now, she would have to maintain her composure under Lady Beatrice's eagle eye all through dinner.

No. If she waited, she would lose her courage. She only had a thimbleful in any case.

"Robbie." Her voice broke. She cleared her throat and tried again. "Robbie, I've been meaning to speak with you about . . . about a . . ." She cleared her throat once more. "I've been meaning to speak to you about . . . ack." Her throat closed up tight.

"Are you all right?"

"No. I am not all right." She sat up straighter and clasped her hands very tightly together. "I need to speak with you. Well, I've been meaning to apologize."

Robbie smiled wryly. "Lizzie, I'm certain you have nothing to apologize for."

"No, I do. If I hadn't been such a flat, so buffle-headed as to go up in the tower with Lord Andrew, you would not have been compelled to wed me."

"You could not have foreseen that blackguard would attack you."

"Well, no, I suppose not. But I knew he was not to be trusted. I knew it was unwise to be alone with him."

Robbie held up his hand. "Enough. Do not torture yourself. It serves no purpose."

"But I feel badly for having ruined your life."

"You have not ruined my life, for God's sake."

"But . . . that is, I meant to ask . . . do you love someone else, Robbie? Is our marriage keeping you from her?"

Robbie's voice was tight. "I do not love someone else."

"And your mistresses and widows? I realize . . . I mean I . . . well, I have heard rumors recently and I would prefer to know the truth. Not that I have any grounds to ask you to stop frequenting the women—"

"There are no mistresses or widows. I have heard the rumors, too. They are ridiculous—and just began circulating after our marriage. I suspect Lady Felicity and Lord Andrew are the authors of the tales."

Lizzie nodded. "That thought had occurred to me also, so why . . ." She took a deep breath and grabbed her courage tightly in both hands. She would never get this close to an answer again. "So why do you not visit my bed?"

Robbie made an odd noise that sounded like "gaag."

"Are *you* all right?"

He grunted.

"I'm certain I should not be raising the issue, but I can see no benefit in roundaboutation. You need an heir, do you not?"

Robbie made another odd noise. Lizzie took that as assent.

"Exactly. And I am completely willing to assist you in that endeavor."

"Lizzie." Robbie ran a finger under his cravat and

cleared his throat. "Lizzie, I told you I could not have children. That is why I did not offer for you before."

"Well, yes, I know that is what you said, but you never explained *how* you had ascertained that fact. Is it because your mistresses have not conceived? I am not sure that is conclusive evidence. I think you should try again."

"Lizzie!"

The light was too dim to be able to say for certain, but she thought Robbie had turned a bright shade of red.

"No, this is too important a subject to ignore." Lizzie looked down. Her skirt was a wrinkled mess. Part of her wondered what Lady Bea would say when she saw it. The other part was in full out panic. Her heart was beating so wildly, it felt like it would leap from her breast.

She had to get an answer now. She would never have the courage to revisit this subject.

"I have spent many hours recently considering the topic. I know you did not choose me—"

"Lizzie, for God's sake—"

"—but you are, unfortunately, stuck with me. I know, also, that I am not a great beauty, but neither am I a total antidote. Couldn't you just close your eyes and pretend I was someone else? Couldn't the task be accomplished that way?"

"Lizzie!" Robbie grabbed her shoulders and shook her so hard her head flopped back. "Don't say such things. You are lovely, beautiful, a diamond of the first water. You are all any man—all I—could want. If I could have chosen, I would have chosen you."

"So why . . . ?"

"Because—"

"My lord?"

Lizzie turned. Robbie's footman stood at the open door of the carriage, waiting for them to descend.

* * *

Thank *God* Thomas had opened the carriage door when he had. Robbie smiled at Lady Beatrice as he stepped into her drawing room. Still, it was only a temporary reprieve. He had to talk to Lizzie soon— sooner now he knew she was blaming herself for his behavior. God! Hearing her denigrate herself. . . . The words had stabbed him through the heart.

"Are you feeling quite the thing, Lizzie?" Lady Beatrice inspected Lizzie through her lorgnette and then turned the blasted thing in his direction. Her beady little eyes studied his face.

He kept himself—barely—from running a finger around the top of his cravat.

"I'm fine, Lady Beatrice." Lizzie's voice was subdued. The black fog of melancholy that had enveloped him since his marriage thickened.

"And you, Lord Westbrooke?" Lady Beatrice lowered her lorgnette and raised an eyebrow. "You seem a trifle down pin as well."

"I am perfectly fine." He tried to inject some ice into his tone. Lady Beatrice did not look impressed.

"Hmm. You sound as if you've caught a chill. Have some brandy. Alton, give the man some brandy."

Robbie could have sworn Alton threw Lady Bea a sharp look before he poured.

"Might as well fill three glasses. I'll have one, and I'm certain Lizzie here could do with a little liquid warmth, heh, miss?"

"I, um . . ." Lizzie glanced at Robbie. "Well, yes, all right. Thank you."

Robbie took a glass from the butler. Where were all the other invitees?

Suddenly he had a very bad feeling about this dinner party.

"Whom else are you expecting, Lady Beatrice?" He sipped his brandy. Hopefully it would steady his nerves. "Where is Meg?"

"Meg went to the theater." Lady Beatrice smiled coyly. "Didn't I tell you? You and Lizzie are my only guests."

The sip had been a bad idea. The liquid shot up his nose. He choked.

Alton kindly pounded him on the back.

He wiped his streaming eyes. When he could see again, he saw Lady Beatrice grinning at him.

"I merely wished to spend some time with the newlyweds. Frankly, as I say, neither of you is exactly glowing with joy. Why?"

Fortunately he did not have anything in his mouth now, though he might strangle on his tongue. Instinctively, he looked for support from the only other male in the room. Alton gave him a commiserating smile. The man had shared the same household, if not the same bedroom, with Lady Beatrice for over forty years. He must be used to her odd starts.

"Lady Beatrice, please." Lizzie sounded quite fierce. She was glaring at the woman. "Our marriage is none of your concern."

"Now don't get on your high ropes, girl. Of course it is my concern. I was your chaperone. I feel responsible. Something obviously is not right between you two."

Robbie was going to expire of mortification right here in Lady Beatrice's drawing room. "You are to be commended for your concern, ma'am, but I really must protest your intrusion into our private affairs."

"Hmm." The woman stared at him. He kept his face politely blank. He had had years of perfecting his society mask.

Suddenly she smiled. "Very well. I'll change the subject. Alton, is dinner ready?"

"I shall inquire." The butler gave Lady Beatrice another speaking look. She grinned back at him.

Bloody hell, they looked like an old married couple.

"I have heard a number of unpleasant rumors recently," Lady Beatrice said. "Ridiculous mutterings about you, Lord Westbrooke. If one believed them all, one would think you never got out of bed—and never slept either."

His ears were red, he knew it. "But of course the rumors *are* ridiculous—and I am not certain you have changed the subject."

Lady Beatrice shrugged. "We are now discussing the latest *on dits*, a perfectly common society topic." She turned to Lizzie. "Do *you* think the stories groundless?"

"Of course. We just discussed them in the carriage coming here. There were no rumors before we married. To have so many spring up after we wed—it is rather obvious that Lady Felicity and Lord Andrew are behind them."

Lady Bea nodded. "My thoughts exactly. And, if you'll pardon my saying so—"

"Do we have a choice?"

Lady Beatrice frowned at Robbie. "Stop muttering—and no, you do not have a choice. As I was saying, the rumors are really too outlandish to be believed. Those two would have done much better to have chosen one tale to spread. That would have been much more believable."

"Thank you."

"I told you to stop muttering, sir."

Robbie gritted his teeth. Growling would be equally unwelcome, he assumed.

"So it is not these foolish stories coming between you?"

"No!"

Robbie and Lizzie spoke together as Alton opened the door.

"Dinner," he said, "is served."

"Splendid. Come along."

Lady Beatrice took Alton's arm. The man froze and glowered at her.

"Oh, don't be such an old stick, Billy. It's just family, after all. You will join us for dinner."

Robbie swore he could hear "Billy's" teeth grinding.

"My lady, I am the butler. A butler does not sit down with the mistress—and, as to family, neither Lord Westbrooke nor Lady Westbrooke is the least bit related to you."

"Pshaw." She shook his arm. "I need your help. I'm certain Lord Westbrooke will welcome another male at table."

Lady Beatrice was one hundred percent correct about that.

"Join us, Alton," Robbie said. "It is a trifle irregular, but I dare say most things about Lady Beatrice are."

Instead of glaring, the old harridan grinned at him.

"Exactly. You may as well get used to eating with company, Billy, since I do mean to marry you."

Robbie could almost see the steam coming out of Alton's ears. So the rumors were true about them. He wasn't surprised, not after seeing them together. And much as he'd love to witness Lady Beatrice getting a blistering set down from her butler, he'd much rather have another male at the dinner table. At this point gender meant much more than class.

"Please, Alton. Perhaps you can keep Lady Beatrice in line."

The man sighed. "I have not been able to do so heretofore."

Lady Beatrice patted Alton on the arm. "Don't take it to heart, Billy. My brother George said the same, though nowhere near as civilly."

The meal was torture. Alton sat stiffly, clearly uncomfortable. Lizzie spent most of her time studying her plate. Robbie clutched his wine glass as a drowning man would cling to a handy piece of flotsam.

Without warning, Lady Beatrice speared a bean and pointed her fork at him. "Before you wed, Westbrooke, you scandalized society with the longing looks you cast at Lizzie."

Robbie's mouth dropped open. Fortunately it was empty at that moment.

"He did?" Lizzie halted her fork's progression from her plate to her lips. She blinked at Lady Beatrice.

"You mean to tell me you didn't notice?"

Lizzie blushed and shook her head. "No, I never did."

Lady Beatrice rolled her eyes. "Well, you were the only member of the *ton* who didn't. But that's beside the point. The important thing is now everyone is noticing the lack of those looks. They are beginning to speculate. You do not want the *ton* speculating, I assure you."

"Oh." Lizzie began to mutilate her lobster patty.

Damn. Robbie hated to see Lizzie unhappy.

"Lady Beatrice, for God—"

Lady Beatrice raised her eyebrow.

"—goodness sake. We are married now. Longing looks are quite inappropriate."

"Indeed. I completely agree. They should be replaced by lustful looks, by I-can't-wait-to-get-back-into-bed-with-you looks."

"Lady Beatrice!"

"Don't 'Lady Beatrice' me, Lord Westbrooke. *Have* you two been to bed?"

Robbie opened his mouth, but nothing came out. He felt, he was sure, just like a beached fish.

"Hmm. I wouldn't think you'd need pointers, boy, but if you do, ask Billy. He's quite the virtuoso between the sheets."

Chapter Nineteen

"Let's leave the men to their port, Lizzie."

"Surely that isn't necessary, Lady Beatrice? We are such a small gathering." Frankly, Lizzie felt it was time to go home. Robbie and Mr. Alton had been imbibing rather freely. She gave Robbie a speaking look. He grinned drunkenly back at her and took another swallow of wine.

"Go 'long, Lizzie. Billy and I'll be fine, won't we, Billy?"

Mr. Alton nodded carefully.

"See?" Lady Beatrice leaned over and whispered in Lizzie's ear. "We'll leave 'em alone. Give Billy a chance to talk some sense into that cod's head you married."

"I don't know. . . ." The odds of either man formulating a sensible thought at this point were remote.

"I do." Lady Beatrice stood. "If you'll excuse us, gentlemen?"

The men lurched to their feet.

"Cert'ly." Robbie hiccupped. Mr. Alton inclined his head.

Lady Beatrice led Lizzie back to the small drawing room.

"Have a seat by the fire, dear, and I will get us something to drink."

"I don't see the tea tray." Lizzie perched on the edge of her chair. Did she want to have this conversation? Surely it would be better to collect Robbie and call for the carriage.

But what if Lady Beatrice could help?

No, she couldn't discuss her marital troubles. She'd be betraying Robbie's confidence.

If only Thomas hadn't opened the coach's door when he had. If they'd had five more minutes—not even that—one more minute, Robbie might have told her why he'd been avoiding her bed.

Could she get him to talk to her again?

"Blech! Who wants tea? Brandy's what we need."

"Lady Beatrice, I really don't think. . . ."

"Good. Don't think." Lady Beatrice handed her a glass of brandy and settled herself into the comfortable chair across from her. "Feel. Talk. Tell me what the problem is between you and your new husband."

"There is no problem."

Lady Beatrice snorted and raised an eyebrow. Lizzie looked down and pleated her skirt.

"Well, perhaps there is a problem, but we are just wed. We will work it out with time."

Lady Beatrice snorted again. Lizzie looked up.

"It's not as if Robbie *wanted* to marry me."

"Oh, please! Has he or has he not come to your bed? Given his reaction at dinner, I would say the answer is no."

She stared at Lady Bea. Surely Robbie would not want her to reveal such an intimate detail.

Her silence was answer enough.

"Just as I thought."

"Lady Beatrice, there has hardly been time—"

"Lizzie, a determined man can get his—" Lady Bea paused and coughed. "Trust me, there has been plenty of time. We need to discover why Lord Westbrooke has not made use of the many hours at his disposal."

"Perhaps he doesn't find me attractive enough for

such activities." There, she had said it. A huge weight lifted off her shoulders. She took a large swallow of brandy and savored the burning warmth.

"My dear, any female is attractive when a man is thinking with his"—Lady Beatrice coughed again. "Ahem. In any event you are being foolish beyond permission. I was not lying earlier—Westbrooke *did* amuse the *ton* with his longing looks. The man definitely finds you attractive. There must be something bothering him. Perhaps Billy can ferret it out."

Lizzie's stomach leapt to her throat, putting her evening's dinner at dangerous risk of reappearance. "Surely Mr. Alton would not discuss . . . ?"

"Surely he would—that is his mission tonight."

"Oh." Robbie did not like people prying into his affairs. He would be furious. He would never talk to her now. "He can't. That is, I do not think that would be wise. Robbie—"

Lady Beatrice swept away Lizzie's objections with a wave of her hand. "Fiddle-faddle. We must find out what is troubling the earl for his own good. The future of the Westbrooke title depends on it, does it not?"

Lizzie flushed. "Well, there is Cousin Theobald."

Lady Beatrice made a face. "That creature? Please! Perhaps if we sprinkled snuff . . . never mind. Theobald is not an option." She poured them both more brandy. "Don't you *want* Westbrooke in your bed?"

"Uh." Heat swept through her. She looked at the fire. It had not suddenly blazed hotter. "Yes. That is, I would like to have children."

"But you would like to have Westbrooke, too, correct? Naked. Kissing you, touching you, licking—"

"Yes, yes." If she heard any more, she'd spontaneously combust. "I'm certain it is terribly shocking, but yes."

"Lose that notion immediately, miss. If you care for a man—especially if you're married to him—nothing you do is too shocking. Well, not in a bad way at least."

She leaned forward and tapped Lizzie on the knee. "I think you need to shock the earl into action, Lizzie."

"Really?" Lizzie shook her head, trying to clear the throbbing from her ears. She took another sip of brandy. This was a very unsettling conversation. Still, if Lady Beatrice could show her how to get close to Robbie . . . well, she would do anything to accomplish that goal.

"Yes. You have already waited for him to make the first move and he has not done so. You must take matters into your own hands." Lady Bea grinned. "Literally."

"Oh?" Lizzie took another sip of brandy.

"Yes. You must seduce him."

Lizzie choked. The brandy burned her nose.

"Seduce Robbie?"

"It should not be difficult." Lady Beatrice sat back. "I will send word to the mantua-maker first thing in the morning. I told you you should have included that lovely silk nightgown in your trousseau."

Lizzie took another gulp of brandy. "The *red* nightgown?"

"Exactly."

"Oh, no. I couldn't wear that. It's scandalous! I would die of embarrassment."

Lady Beatrice leveled a stern gaze at her over her brandy glass. "Would you rather die a virgin?"

Put that way . . .

"No."

"I didn't think so."

If something so simple could solve her problem— well, it was worth a try. "All right. I will wear the red nightgown."

"Good. It should be ready by tomorrow night— I will tell Elise to put everything else aside." Lady Beatrice chuckled. "Not that there is much work to be done on such a slip of cloth."

Lizzie *would* die of embarrassment. She would have

o send Betty away. She would never be able to don
uch a scandalous outfit in her maid's presence.

"And then you must go in to Robbie—you cannot
ait for him to come to your room."

Go uninvited into Robbie's room? Her stomach
hivered.

"But I think . . . I believe he doesn't spend much
ime there."

"He does sleep there though, doesn't he? Or has he
eft the house entirely?"

"No. No, I believe he does still come to, um, bed,
ust very late at night."

Lady Beatrice shrugged. "That's no matter then.
ou just climb into his bed and wait." She grinned.
You will be a splendid surprise for him."

"I don't know. . . ."

"Courage. You must be determined to get what you
want."

"Well . . ."

"It is best for him, too, remember. He needs an
eir."

"Yes."

They sipped their brandy in silence. A log popped
nd sizzled in the fire.

Could she do it? Could she wear that scandalous
ed gown and climb into Robbie's bed?

What was the worst that could happen? Robbie
might be vexed, but all he could do was send her back
o her own room.

Lady Beatrice must have read her mind.

"Lizzie, you must not let Westbrooke send you away.
This is your chance. Fight for him."

"But how?"

"Tempt him. Tantalize him."

Lizzie swallowed more brandy. "Perhaps I will
merely annoy him."

"Oh, I sincerely doubt that." Lady Bea leaned close
nd dropped her voice. "You will be able to tell how

interested he is by the size of his male organ. If he say he wants you to leave, but his pantaloons are bulging he is lying."

Lizzie dropped her jaw. "It's a *good* thing if his, ah . . if it's swollen?"

Lady Beatrice blinked. "You've seen a male organ?

Lizzie flushed. "At the house party . . . Robbie . . . thought he had bumped himself on the windowsill. . . .

"Thank God! I feared the man was impotent, but i his cock can crow. . . ." Lady Beatrice grinned. "This i an excellent sign. You must not be afraid to touch i my dear, with your fingers or your lips." She winked "Or your tongue."

"Touch it?" Lizzie frowned. "Are you certain?"

Lady Beatrice leaned forward and clicked he brandy glass against Lizzie's. "Lady Westbrooke, I hav never been more certain of anything in my life."

Robbie took another swallow of port.

"So, Billy, are you going to marry the old harridan— I mean, Lady Beatrice?"

Alton frowned at his glass. "No. It is completely im possible. You may be certain I've told Lady Beatric that a thousand times."

Robbie slid lower in his chair. "Oh, I don't know Don't see why you can't tie the knot. It isn't as if the ol girl's going to affect the succession. Charles has an hei and is working on more—and Lady Bea is well beyond the age of motherhood." That was an understatement She was almost beyond the age of grandmotherhood "People will talk, of course, but then, people have beer whispering about the two of you for years."

Alton sighed. "I know. I should never have taken this position. I should have left Knightsdale's service the moment I saw which way the wind blew."

"Now, now." Robbie patted Alton on the back. "Nc

use crying over spilt milk. What's done is done. I'm
sure you're a comfort to Lady Bea in her old age."

Alton spewed port over the tablecloth.

"Old age? The woman's only a few years past sixty."

"That's right." Why was Alton looking at him as if he
were daft? The man must be close to sixty-five himself—
had at least one foot in the grave. "I suppose there may be
some who think you'd be marrying her for her money,
but as you are even older than she . . . well, it's not as if she
will predecease you. You are a companion for her declin-
ing years—I'm certain everyone will think so."

Alton appeared to be gasping for breath.

"I say, you aren't having an apoplexy or anything
are you?"

Alton covered his eyes with one hand and waved at
Robbie with the other.

"No, no. I just . . . I merely . . . poor *old* Lady Beatrice." He emitted a noise that sounded suspiciously
like a snigger.

"Are you certain you're all right?"

"Yes. I'm fine." Alton dropped his hand. There was
an odd gleam in his eye. "I'm so happy we're having
this talk. Have some more port."

"Thank you."

Alton filled Robbie's glass to the brim.

"You really believe Beatrice won't suffer if we wed?"

"Well." Robbie contemplated his glass. He couldn't
lie. "There will be some doors closed to her, but I
doubt she'd wish to attend affairs at those homes
anyway. She doesn't strike me as a woman who is extremely high in the instep."

"You're right there. Old Bea doesn't have much patience for a good bit of the *ton*."

"Exactly." Robbie nodded. The port was making
him feel very mellow. Expansive.

"But what of her nephew, the marquis? He certainly
can't like it."

"Charles? He's not one to worry overmuch about a

man's pedigree. Didn't want to be a peer himself."
Robbie leaned back in his chair and grinned at Alton.
"'Course you'll always be welcome at Westbrooke—
you and Bea."

"Generous of you." Alton refilled his glass.

"Least I can do. Lizzie don't care." Robbie sighed
and stared at his port. "Lizzie's a real brick."

Alton grunted. "Sounds like a favorite hound."

"No. Love her. God, I wish I could . . . damn." He cradled a mouthful of port on his tongue while he thought.
He swallowed. "Thing is, she deserves better than me."

"What? A duke or a marquis?"

"No. Don't mean rank. To hell with rank. Who
cares about rank? Lizzie don't. No, it's . . . I can't . . ."
He drained his glass and held it out to Alton. The
man generously filled it again.

"The damnable thing is . . . well, you must know.
You're old, right?"

Alton arched an eyebrow.

"Exactly." Robbie leaned closer. "Secret, don't you
know? Can't bear to tell Lizzie. Well, I did tell her I
can't have children, but she doesn't understand. You
would, I'm sure. At your age, you must have the same
problem. Not that it matters to you." Robbie closed his
eyes briefly. "But I'm not yet thirty."

"And that problem would be . . . ?"

"Cock won't fight."

"Ah."

"It's limper than a damned stewed carrot."

"I see." Alton cleared his throat. "Always?"

"Well, no. It's worse, really. The damn thing gets as
hard as an iron poker until it's time to do the deed.
Then it cowers like a frightened maiden."

Alton nodded. "And you've never . . . ?"

"Twice. But then . . . let's just say I had a bad experience."

"Hmm." Alton stared into his port. The man looked
damn inscrutable. "I believe I can help you."

"You can?!" Robbie almost knocked over his glass. No, wait. Stupid. How could an elderly man help him? "I don't mean any insult, but really . . . I assume it's been years since you. . . ."

"Actually, no. It's been since this morning."

Robbie did slosh his port onto the tablecloth then. "*What?* This morning? As in today? As in twelve hours ago?"

Alton consulted his timepiece. "Ten hours, actually." He grinned. "*And* twelve."

"Twice? At your age?"

Alton shrugged. "Lady Bea is quite inspiring."

"Damn." Robbie drummed his fingers on the table. Twice in two hours—and the man was ancient. And Lady Beatrice was . . . well, Lady Beatrice. "What's your secret?"

Alton looked around and then leaned close. "A potion," he whispered.

"A potion?" Robbie whispered back.

Alton nodded. "A cordial."

"Oh." Robbie drew a circle on the tablecloth with his spilled port. "Do you think . . . is there any hope . . . ?"

Alton nodded. "Definitely. I will have Bea make some up for you."

"Tonight?"

"Not tonight, I'm afraid. There are a few ingredients she does not have on hand."

Damn. "Then when?"

Alton smiled. "Tomorrow. I'll have it sent round as soon as it's done. And then tomorrow night . . ." He grinned. "Magic. Trust me. One glass of this cordial and you'll be a new man. Works every time."

"So I'll be able to . . . ?" Robbie could not believe his nightmare might have an end.

Alton nodded. "Multiple times—though you do not want to overdo it at first. Spare Lady Westbrooke any discomfort. Virgins, you know."

God, if it really worked . . . It *must* be magic if it could invigorate a man as old as Alton.

"You promise?"

"You have my word."

Robbie felt a weight lift off his shoulders.

"Splendid. Splendid. I cannot wait."

"You told him *what?*" Lady Beatrice bolted upright in bed. Queen Bess hissed and jumped down from her place on Alton's pillow.

Alton pulled his shirt over his head. "I told him you would make him a cordial." He dropped the shirt on the floor and grinned. "Said it worked for me."

Lady Beatrice snorted. "*You* have never had a performance problem."

"No, but Westbrooke doesn't know that." Alton laughed and shed his breeches. "Young fool thinks anyone over forty must be in his dotage. I'm certain he cannot imagine an ancient specimen such as I having sexual congress at all. He just about fell off his chair when I said I was still capable."

"Hmm. More than capable." Lady Beatrice reached out and stroked the most capable part of his anatomy. "Much more." She ran her fingers up and down, smiling at his sharp intake of breath. "I wasn't lying when I said you were a virtuoso." She replaced her fingers with her tongue. "Mmm."

Alton stroked her hair and laughed shakily. "It's not as if I have any competition. We were children when we began this game."

She smiled up at him, tugging on his hips. "I knew what I wanted even then, and I have never been disappointed. If only you would get over your stubbornness and marry me, my life would be complete."

"I doubt that."

She stopped smiling and straightened, getting up on her knees so she could look him in the eye. "Do not doubt it. It is true. I went off to that stupid house party in the hopes you would miss me."

He cupped her cheek. "I did miss you, Bea. Terribly. I miss you every time you leave." He rubbed his thumb over her bottom lip. "But if you married me, you would not be invited to any more such parties."

"Do you think I care?" She pulled back out of his grasp. "I spent most of my time at Tynweith's pining for you—when I wasn't dodging Lord Botton, that is."

"That poltroon was there?"

"He was. And I will tell you he is a very difficult man to evade. It is like trying to slip out of an octopus's grasp. Every time you think you're free, another tentacle latches on."

"Damn. If I had been there, he would not have been so bold."

"Exactly." She stroked his chest. "I need you to protect me, Billy."

Alton snorted. "I doubt that."

"I *want* you to protect me."

"Bea—"

She put her hand over his mouth. "No. Listen. I'm tired of living in sin. I know people will talk, but I'd rather have them whisper we are wed than I am keeping you."

Alton grasped her fingers. "They don't say that!"

"Clarissa, Lady Dunlee does. Oh, not in my hearing, of course. She's all false smiles to my face."

"I'll kill the woman."

"No. Marry me instead." She drew little patterns on his chest. "Can't you understand? I only go about now because of Lizzie and Meg. I'd be happy to be done with it. I have a few friends who will still accept me, and I don't care for the rest."

"Bea, you can't know that anyone will stand by you. You may think they will—they may even think they will—but when they are faced with the fact of your wedding, when they are asked to greet the butler as your husband—"

She grabbed his arms and shook him. "I don't care. Everyone—even my nephew Charles—could turn against me and I still would not care."

"Bea—"

"Billy, I am not a girl any more." She snorted. "I have not been a girl for ages. I know my own mind. I want you as my husband. Will you marry me?"

Alton opened his mouth . . . and then closed it. He smiled slightly. "Perhaps. Once you've got Meg settled, then . . . well, perhaps."

Bea whooped and tugged him so he fell down next to her on the bed. "Billy Alton, I'm going to hold you to that."

Alton laughed, catching her hands from where they had wandered. "I only said 'perhaps,' Bea."

She grinned. "That's the closest you've come to 'yes' in over forty years, Billy. It's only a small step from there to the altar."

"But—"

"Shh." She put her finger on his lips. "I'm tired of arguing. There are many more enjoyable things to do with our tongues."

She bent her head and proceeded to demonstrate quite thoroughly.

Much later Bea sighed and twined her fingers in the hair on Alton's chest. "That was lovely."

He stroked her breast. "Hmm. Especially for an old man."

"*I* don't think you're old."

"I don't feel old when I'm with you." He kissed her leisurely. Her hand moved down his stomach. He caught her fingers before they got into too much trouble and put them back on his chest.

"Bea, about Westbrooke."

"Hmm?"

"I think—stop that." He tugged her fingers back again. "Love, I do need *some* time to recover, you know."

Bea sighed. "All right. So what about Westbrooke?"

"I think my idea about the potion might just work. I believe his problem is in his head, not his. . . ." He coughed.

"But a cordial? I'm not a charlatan. . . . or a witch."

"Of course not—you are merely a very wise woman."

"I am that." Bea smiled. "Perhaps I can come up with something." She let her fingers drift down Alton's body again. "I just need a little inspiration."

Chapter Twenty

Robbie stared up at his bed canopy. His head felt as if a cavalcade were pounding through it—and his mouth tasted as foul as the pavement left behind the horses. He'd had far too much port last night.

He closed his eyes, but that just made the riders pick up their pace.

Why had he agreed to go with Lizzie to Lady Beatrice's? He should have suspected a trap. He'd felt the woman's lorgnette surveying him at every *ton* gathering since his wedding.

He should have turned tail the moment he'd stepped over her threshold and seen there were no other guests.

A memory tried to push into his awareness but he suppressed it.

What had the women talked about after they'd left the table? Lady Bea had given him an exceedingly odd look when he and Lizzie had taken their leave. It had been very pointed—he'd been too drunk to notice anything more subtle than a sledgehammer.

The niggling memory tried to surface again. He ignored it.

And Lizzie'd kept darting glances at him in the carriage all the way home. Drunken glances. She'd had too much to drink as well. Poor thing. She was probably feeling worse than he now. Hopefully she was not casting up her accounts in her room.

What *had* she and Lady Beatrice discussed?

He smiled. Alton had said—

The memory he'd been assiduously ignoring roared into his consciousness. Surely he hadn't . . . ?

He turned over and buried his face in his pillow.

He had.

He'd told Alton his secret.

He'd been drunk as an Emperor and he'd chattered like a bloody magpie.

What the hell was he going to do now?

"My lord?"

"Go away, Collins."

"But—"

"Collins, if you wish to remain in my employ, you will depart now."

"But—"

"Now."

"Very well." Collins sniffed. "I have a bottle here for you. It was just delivered from Lady Beatrice. Where should I put it?"

"On the bureau."

Robbie smiled grimly into his pillow when he heard the door close. Thank God. He could not bear Collins's eyes on him.

He could not bear anyone's gaze.

Would Alton keep his confidence? The man must know how unpleasant the *ton* could be. And really, telling Robbie's tale would hurt Lizzie as well. Lady Bea would not like that.

Surely the man would not breathe a word of his mortifying secret.

Except to Lady Beatrice. Damn. But Alton had said she could help.

It would be worth even extreme mortification if he could be cured of his affliction.

Was this the cordial? He'd best get up and see.

A small, unremarkable bottle sat on his bureau. He picked it up. Heavy, dark blue glass. He worked loose the stopper and sniffed. Brandy and something else. He put it to his lips.

No. He replaced the cork as he looked at the door to Lizzie's room.

Tonight. He would hide in his study now, gathering his courage.

He hoped to God Lady Bea *was* a witch.

Lizzie glanced at her wardrobe. The package had arrived that afternoon. She hadn't opened it, but she knew what it was. The scandalous nightgown.

"Collins says his lordship has been hiding in his study all day." Betty put the finishing touches on Lizzie's hair. "Hugging a brandy bottle, I don't doubt."

Lizzie bit her lip. What if Robbie didn't come up to his room this evening? What if he stayed in his study all night, too drunk to move?

What if she put on that scandalous nightgown and waited in his bed only to be discovered by Collins?

Her stomach twisted into a tight knot.

Courage. She must be daring. She had to fight for what she wanted—and she wanted Robbie.

She would go to this dreadful soiree at Lord Palmerson's and smile while the *ton* tittered about her absent husband. Then she would come home and seduce that husband any way she could.

"There ye go, my lady. All ready. Too bad his idiot lordship won't go with ye."

"I'm sure Lord Westbrooke has other concerns."

Betty snorted. "Don't know what they could be. Nodcock's got a beautiful wife waiting for him. He—"

"Betty." Lizzie gave her maid a quelling glance. "Thank you. I will not be late."

"No need to hurry back, more's the pity," Betty muttered as Lizzie closed the door.

She ignored Betty's words. If her plans were successful tonight, she would not have to go out alone again. She would not have to sleep alone again.

She *had* to be successful.

She started down the stairs. There was a commotion in the entry hall. She heard Mr. Bentley's voice and then a loud, angry reply. James? She picked up her skirts and ran the rest of the way. Her brother stood just inside the door glaring at the butler.

"James!" What was he doing here? Surely nothing had happened to Sarah? "What is it?"

"Lizzie."

He smiled and opened his arms. She threw her own arms around his waist and hugged him hard. Then she pulled back and studied his face.

"How is Sarah? You have only good news, I hope?"

His smile widened to a self-satisfied grin.

"Sarah is fine. She sent me to bring word she's safely delivered another son."

"That's wonderful! I can hardly wait to see him."

James frowned. "You won't have to wait. I'm taking you back with me after I beat my former friend senseless. Where is your worthless husband?"

"James, you are scandalizing Robbie's butler."

James glared at Mr. Bentley. "And why should I care?"

Lizzie grabbed his arm and pulled him toward the front door. "Come with me to the Palmerson soiree. We can talk in the carriage."

James dug in his heels. "We have no need to talk. You will pack your things and come home with me now."

"Back to Alvord? You are leaving tonight?"

"Not tonight. First thing in the morning."

She smiled at Mr. Bentley who was trying very hard to look impassive. "Tell Lord Westbrooke I've gone out with the duke, will you? I shall not be terribly late."

"You shall not be late at all—you will not be back." James scowled at her. "Go pack your things."

"We will discuss this in the carriage."

"Fine." James nodded. "My coach is just outside."

"Oh, no, your grace. I am not taking the chance you will kidnap me. We are taking the Westbrooke equipage."

"Lizzie—"

She pushed James out the door.

"James, you can just get it through your thick skull that I am not deserting Robbie."

"Not deserting Robbie? If even half the rumors I've heard are true, that cur does not deserve your loyalty."

"Of course the rumors aren't true." She took Thomas's hand to climb into the Westbrooke carriage. "I'm certain Lord Andrew and Lady Felicity are behind all the tittle-tattle."

"Ah, Lord Andrew." James's tone grew even colder. "I would like to get my hands on that blackguard."

James's eyes were as cold as his voice. Lord Andrew had best hope he did not encounter the Duke of Alvord.

"Tell me about Sarah and the baby. What did you name him?"

"David Randolph. He's a lusty little fellow. He—" James stopped. "Oh, no. You are not going to divert me. You will tell me everything that occurred at that blasted house party."

"No, I won't."

James glared at her. "Yes, you will. I should never have let you go to London with Lady Beatrice as your chaperone—"

"Stop. Everything is fine."

"Everything is *not* fine. I can tell you are not happy. I saw it in your eyes when you came down the stairs."

A lump blocked her throat. She swallowed. "We can talk about that later."

"Lizzie—"

"Later, James. Now tell me how Will likes his new brother."

James's lips formed a tight line. She didn't think he would answer, but finally he sighed.

"Very well. We will not discuss the house party— now. But I intend to have the complete story from you later."

Lizzie chose not to bait the bear and remind him she was a married woman. She smiled sweetly.

"So, about Will—and Sarah and young David Randolph . . . ? Was it an easy labor this time?"

"I suppose so, but I do wish babies could enter the world in a less nerve-racking way."

It did not take James long to warm to his subject. He happily discussed his family for the remainder of the ride to Palmerson House.

"Lady Beatrice, my brother has just arrived."

"Good evening, your grace." Lady Beatrice smiled at James—and then grinned at Lizzie in a most unusual way.

"Good evening, Lady Beatrice." James's tone was frosty, but at least he didn't give the woman the cut direct. He turned to greet Meg.

"Do you have good news, your grace?" Meg asked. "The duchess is well?"

James finally smiled. "Very well. She is delivered of a second son."

"Congratulations!" Lady Beatrice lifted a glass of champagne from a passing footman and handed it to James. "This calls for a toast."

Meg leaned over and whispered in Lizzie's ear. "I don't suppose your brother came to Town merely to give you the good news?"

"Of course not. He's heard the stupid rumors—and he wants to discuss Tynweith's house party."

Meg inclined her head toward some potted palms. "Felicity is busy spreading more tales."

"I see." Lizzie narrowed her eyes. She had had enough—more than enough. "If you'll excuse me?"

"Of course. Would you care for my assistance?"

"No. I can handle this myself."

She made her way across the room, pausing on the other side of the foliage. Felicity and Lady Rosalyn Mannerly had their heads close together.

"I go into the country for a few weeks," Lady Rosalyn said, "and I miss all the juicy tidbits. Hartford cocked up his toes at Tynweith's house party?"

"Yes, but that wasn't the most interesting occurrence."

Lady Rosalyn laughed. "No indeed. The story that he got his notice to quit while astride the duchess is quite amusing. And equally titillating is the new rumor that Tynweith is haunting Hartford House. Betting has him offering for the duchess as soon as she is out of mourning."

"I'm sure he will." Felicity's voice had an edge to it. "And you've heard about the new Lady Westbrooke?"

"Oh, yes," Lady Rosalyn said. "Lady Elizabeth, that pattern card of respectability, was naked with not one but two men. Too delicious."

The women sniggered.

Felicity dropped her voice lower. "Westbrooke is not happy with his fate."

"No?"

"Not at all. Haven't you noticed? They are rarely together and when they are—well, let's just say the earl does not look enchanted with his bride."

Lady Rosalyn's shocked whisper carried clearly to Lizzie's ears. "I hear she has not unbent enough to open her legs for him."

Lizzie closed her eyes in mortification.

"I don't doubt plenty of other women have been willing to console him," Felicity said.

"So he's been climbing into other beds?"

"That is what I've heard." Felicity giggled. "Many, many beds."

This had gone far enough. Lizzie stepped around the palm fronds.

"Good evening, Lady Felicity."

"Ack!"

"And Lady Rosalyn—how . . . interesting to see you."

"Lady Westbrooke." Lady Rosalyn smirked. "How do you find married life?"

"Wonderful." Lizzie summoned her memory of Robbie naked in her room at Lendal Park. That should give her the proper glow.

"Is Lord Westbrooke here tonight?" Lady Felicity threw a significant glance at Lady Rosalyn.

"No. He's at home." Lizzie lowered her lashes slowly. "Waiting."

"I see." Lady Rosalyn's eyes darted to Lady Felicity. "So . . . rumors of Westbrooke's dissatisfaction with his marriage are greatly exaggerated?"

Lizzie forced herself to laugh. "Oh my, yes. Not that I should speak of such things, of course—especially with unmarried spinst—I mean, ladies."

Both the women glared at her.

Lady Rosalyn forced a thin smile. "If you'll excuse me? I promised Lord Framley I'd have a word with him." She nodded and left so quickly the palm fronds bobbed and swayed.

Lizzie turned to look at Lady Felicity.

"There have been some very odd rumors circulating

through the *ton* recently. Rumors concerning my marriage and my husband's behavior."

"Really? How unfortunate." Felicity smiled slightly. "You should not be surprised. When couples marry so quickly under such . . . interesting circumstances. . . ." Felicity shrugged. "Well, rumors are rather inevitable, are they not?"

"I don't think so. In fact I think someone has gone out of her way to spread these tales." Lizzie leaned close and spoke quietly and distinctly. "As Countess of Westbrooke I would be extremely displeased to think anyone so mean spirited as to try to damage my marriage."

"I don't know what you mean."

"Good. You might share my sentiments with Lord Andrew."

Felicity's eyes strayed toward the garden. "Lord Andrew? He's not even in London."

"I'm happy to hear that. Now if you'll excuse me? I believe I've spent enough time here—the company is sadly insipid, don't you agree?" Lizzie smiled in a way she hoped was knowing. She must have succeeded, because Felicity's gaze sharpened to dagger points.

She stopped by James on her way out.

"I have the headache. I am going home."

"Good. I don't want to stay either. I'll take you to Alvord House."

"No, James. I'm going *home*—to my husband. You may call in the morning."

"Lizzie—"

She put her hand on his arm.

"James, you are right. I'm not happy—now. But I will be truly miserable if I walk away from Robbie at this point. I have to try to make my marriage work."

"That's Westbrooke's job."

"That is both our jobs. I need to talk to Robbie." She smiled and squeezed his arm. "But thank you for caring so much."

"I will see you in the morning."

Lizzie nodded. She stepped away and paused.

"If you are feeling at loose ends . . . if you would like to bash something . . . I believe if you hurry, you might find Lord Andrew in Palmerson's garden."

James's face lit up. "Really? Splendid!"

Chapter Twenty-One

"My lady! We did not expect you home so soon." Mr. Bentley shot a nervous glance over Lizzie's shoulder.

She smiled. "My brother decided to stay at the soiree and then go on to Alvord House. He won't be calling here until the morning."

The butler's shoulders visibly relaxed. "Very good, my lady."

It was Lizzie's turn to feel nervous. "Is Lord Westbrooke still in his study?"

"No, I believe he went upstairs above an hour ago."

"I see. Thank you. Good night, then."

She climbed the stairs to her room. She had to seduce Robbie tonight. If she didn't, James would drag her back to Alvord tomorrow and everything would become much more complicated.

It was time for action—daring action.

Betty was tidying her dressing table when she came in. She almost dropped the rouge pot when she saw Lizzie.

"My lady, yer home so early. Are ye all right?"

"I'm fine, Betty. I just . . ." She looked at the voluminous nightgown Betty had laid out on her bed—the nice, virginal, long sleeved, high-necked nightgown.

Daring, be bold and daring.

"I won't be needing that tonight."

"Ye won't? Ye wear it every night."

"Not tonight." She walked resolutely to the wardrobe and pulled out the small bundle. She had not had the courage to open it when it had arrived this afternoon. She had thought she wouldn't have the courage to open it in front of Betty.

If she were going to wear it for Robbie, she had best get over her shyness.

It was very small and very light. Was there *any* fabric inside? Surely the mantua-maker had not made a mistake and sent her an empty parcel?

She tore away the wrappings. Red silk spilled over her fingers.

Betty lifted it out of her limp grasp and held it up.

"Ooh! I'm guessing his lordship won't be needing Collins's services for a long while."

Robbie sprawled in his big chair by the fire, clad only in his dressing gown. He'd sent Collins away as soon as he could. He wanted to be alone.

No, that was a lie. He wanted to be with Lizzie.

He picked up the blue cordial bottle from the table by his elbow and read the note again: *Take at bedtime.*

God, this had better work. If it could animate a man Alton's age. . . . Well, perhaps there was hope.

He poured the liquid into a glass. It was amber colored like brandy. He rolled a little around on his tongue. It tasted like brandy, too, though it did have an unusual sweetness to it.

He swallowed and looked at the connecting door. James had come for Lizzie tonight. Bentley had assured him she'd been adamant in refusing to return to Alvord, but James could be damn persuasive. And, really, why would she stay? She was not happy. She was trapped in an empty marriage to a man who could not make her his wife in truth. It was a hellish situation.

But, if she left. . . . God! He took another swallow of cordial.

If she left, what would he do?

She'd been part of his life forever—the plaguey little sister of his friend, the young girl trying so hard to be brave while her brother was away fighting Napoleon, the beautiful woman who'd graced the *ton*'s ballrooms. She was sweet and bright and funny. How could he live without her?

How could he live *with* her? They could never go back to the way things had been. There would always be this empty bed between them.

What the bloody hell was he going to do?

Drink Lady Beatrice's concoction and pray it worked.

He took another sip and closed his eyes, resting his head against the back of his chair. Did he hear a scratching on the connecting door? Ridiculous! He was letting his imagination run away with him.

He should talk to Lizzie. It was the least he could do. Explain that the problem was his. That there was nothing lacking in her.

He slumped lower in his chair, cradling his glass against his chest. She'd been so beautiful, so eager and passionate in her room that first night at Lendal Park. Any man would be lucky to have her. He would be lucky if he *could* have her.

He kept his eyes closed, reveling in his very explicit memories, and took another sip. Mmm. The cordial must be working. His skin—a particular section of his skin—had grown extremely sensitive. He felt the silk of his dressing gown brush against it.

He was also hallucinating. He'd swear his clothing had parted, exposing his shy little organ—which was rapidly becoming not so shy and not so little—to the cool air. And then something warm and soft touched him ever so lightly. Little glancing touches from his root to his tip.

He spread his legs. He was as hard as iron now and very hot. He kept his eyes firmly closed. He did not want to risk dispelling this sensual pleasure. This was better than any of his dreams.

The light dry touches turned into little wet licks. Heat pooled in his groin. He moaned.

"Am I hurting you?"

His eyes flew open. Lizzie knelt on the floor between his legs, her face as red as the fire.

Not a dream or hallucination.

He grew even harder. Amazing. He was suddenly less worried he would wilt than explode.

"No. No, you are not hurting me."

"The swelling is not a bad thing?"

"Definitely not."

She wrapped her hand around him. "Does this hurt?"

"No." He spread his legs farther. To see her delicate fingers around his shaft—his very hard shaft—was a dream come true. Well, only part of his dream. His fickle little organ could still . . .

He felt it start to shrink and he quickly took another sip of cordial.

He would not worry about the past or the future. He would concentrate on the present moment.

Lizzie kissed the tip of his poor organ and it swelled with delight at the attention.

It was a very lovely, a very splendid moment.

"This is such an odd part of you, you know. When I first touched it, it was small and soft—and now look at it."

He looked at it. It looked wonderful—long and thick and hard. Eminently capable of accomplishing its marital duty. He tossed off the rest of Lady Bea's cordial.

"I believe it is time to adjourn to my bed."

Lizzie stood up.

He dropped his glass on the floor.

"What in God's name do you have on?" Robbie was staring at her body.

She flushed and crossed her arms over her chest.

No, she was going to be daring tonight. Hiding was not daring.

She forced herself to open her arms and turn in a slow circle. The red silk nightgown fluttered over her skin, caressing, teasing, making her crave a firmer touch. Robbie's.

"Do you like it?"

"Like it? It is completely, totally scandalous."

"Oh." She dropped her arms. Perhaps the nightgown *was* too revealing. Well, there was no perhaps about it. The red bits of fabric were translucent. They accentuated rather than covered her nakedness. She flushed and brought her hands up—

Robbie was out of his chair and pulling them away before she could blink.

"It is shocking and scandalous and enticing and maddening. Just never wear it in another man's sight."

"Of course not. I would never . . . um . . ."

Robbie was *looking* at her. He had his hands on her shoulders, just as he'd had that first night at Lendal Park, and he was holding her away again, but this time his eyes were not focused on her face. Not at all. They were studying her throat, her breasts, her waist, her . . . um. Her nipples hardened into tight little pebbles and a certain part of her felt very hot. Damp.

Needy.

"Please, Robbie."

"Hmm?"

He was studying a particular part of her very intently. She moved to break his concentration.

"What?" He looked slightly dazed.

Daring, she should be daring.

"It is quite all right to touch, you know."

"Really?" One corner of his mouth tilted up in a smile.

"Yes." The word was little more than a whisper.

He touched her then, carefully, almost reverently, his eyes watching everything he did. His face was so intent, so . . . hungry.

His hands slid under the scraps of silk to cradle her breasts. His fingers stroked her, circled around her nipples, rubbed them. She drew in a sharp breath. Her temperature soared; she felt a wash of moisture flood the empty place between her thighs. Her knees threatened to buckle.

He ran his hands down her sides, spanning her waist and going lower. His thumbs skimmed over the thatch of hair there. She flexed her hips, inviting him to explore that part of her anatomy. It was crying for his touch.

Instead, his hands slid back up to her breasts, to her aching nipples. His thumbs flicked over them and heat spiraled low in her stomach.

This was far better than what she had imagined when she'd stood naked before her mirror at Lendal Park. Only one detail needed improvement—a major detail. Robbie had far too much clothing on. She could not see his lovely male organ—it was hiding in the voluminous folds of his dressing gown.

She reached for his belt and tugged.

Ah. She loved his body. She moved closer, and this time he let her. She pushed aside his dressing gown, slid her arms around his waist, buried her face in his chest, and hugged him tightly.

His arms came around her to hug her back.

"I love you, Robbie," she whispered. "I love you whether you can give me children or not."

He tilted her face up. The passion in his eyes had dimmed to a dark sadness. She felt the ridge against her belly shrink and soften slightly.

"Lizzie, I love you, too. More than I can say. But I don't know . . ."

A muscle jumped in his cheek. She reached up to stroke it.

"Just tell me, Robbie. Please?"

His hold on her loosened. He was withdrawing. No! She would not let him. She tightened her arms.

"Tell me. I love you. Whatever it is, it will not change my love." Her eyes were wet. She pressed her face into his chest. She felt him lower his head.

"I cannot. . . . I do not know if I can . . ."

He shuddered. She stroked his back and waited.

"I have not been able to . . . be with a woman for years."

His male organ was no longer pressing against her belly.

"It does not matter, Robbie."

"It *does* matter." He pushed her away, turning to face the fire.

She wrapped her arms around him from behind. "It does not matter."

"It does." His voice was shaky, as if he might be suppressing tears. "It's a damnable coil. I'm so sorry you are chained to me."

"Well, I am not sorry." She rubbed her cheek on his back. What could she do for him? She hated the sadness in his voice.

Her fingers wandered below his waist and found his poor little organ. It leapt at her touch.

She smiled. She knew what she needed to do. She stroked him and he drew in a sharp breath.

"I did . . . I have this cordial . . ." He was panting slightly. "I don't know if it will work . . ."

"Then we will just have to try and see, won't we?"

He took her fingers away from where they'd been playing and turned to face her. "But what if it doesn't work? You need—"

"Do not tell me what I need. I know what I need— I need you." She reached for his dressing gown. "I need you naked in bed this instant."

It was time to be very daring indeed.

"Lizzie—"

"Do not say another word, sir. I have decided that I am going to seduce you. I expect you to be a gentleman and allow me to have my wicked way with you."

His useless organ began to feel not quite so useless.

"Well, if you put it that way . . ."

"I do indeed. You do not have to lift a finger." She looked down and something else lifted slightly. The minx grinned at him. "I am going to take charge of everything."

It couldn't hurt to play along.

"Your wish is my command."

"Excellent." She tugged his dressing gown off him and dropped it on the floor. Cool air touched his heated skin.

"Now that I have you suitably naked, you need to help me off with this silly nightgown."

Did Lizzie's voice waver slightly? "There is nothing silly about it. It is vastly attractive."

"Perhaps, but it is very much in the way at the moment."

"Hardly very much . . . there's not enough there for that."

"True, but anything is too much." She took a deep breath, causing her breasts to rise delightfully. "I want my skin against yours—nothing in between." She smiled up at him. "Don't you think that is a good plan?"

"Yes." Definitely. All of him thought so.

He began to hope this would work.

"Are you thinking, Robbie?"

"What?"

"You are not to be thinking or planning or most importantly worrying. You are just to do as you are told, understand? Now, please remove my nightgown."

"My pleasure." He took the hem. The silk of the cloth was nothing compared to the silk of Lizzie's skin. He flattened his palms on her thighs, taking his time. Over her hips, her waist. She raised her arms. Her breasts rose invitingly. He stopped to drop a kiss on one nipple.

"Ack!"

"Hmm?" He pushed the gown up higher so he could see her face. "You didn't like that?"

She pulled her arms free. "I *loved* it. I would like much more of the same."

She took his hand and pulled him toward his bed. His shy little organ was going along quite enthusiastically. In fact, it was leading the way.

She pushed him to sit on the edge of the mattress, then spread his knees and stood between them. She cupped his jaw and put her mouth on his. He waited to see what she would do.

She licked the seam of his lips.

She pulled back and looked him in the eye. "Open your mouth, sir."

He grinned and did so. She resumed her explorations.

Her tongue was small and agile. Her hands stroked his cheeks, his hair, his shoulders, his back, and finally the part of him that was most enjoying this game.

"Are you thinking about anything, Robbie?"

"Huh?" Her fingers glided up and down his length.

They felt beyond wonderful. He blinked at her. She had a very self-satisfied smirk on her face.

"Have I animated your animal instincts? Do I have you mindless with lust?"

He laughed. "I am most assuredly moving in that direction."

"Splendid." She paused. Her smile wavered. "Um, what should I do now?"

Was his little wanton running out of ideas?

"Perhaps I should do something. I'd like to taste your lovely breasts. They are dangling here so invitingly."

"They are too little to dangle."

"Really?" He drew his finger down the slope of one perfect globe. "If you say so. May I taste one—or both—anyway?"

She flushed.

"Very well. Taste away."

He cupped her breasts and put his mouth to one nipple. He circled it with his tongue, licked, and sucked.

Lizzie moaned. Her hands were now gripping his shoulders. He ran one hand down her stomach and dipped his finger in the opening between her thighs. It was delightfully wet.

"Oh." She pushed away from him. She was very flushed. Her bosom heaved in the most entrancing way. "Lie down, sir. I believe it is time to proceed to the next step in my plan of seduction."

"Yes, my lady."

He stretched out in the middle of his bed. She knelt beside him and just looked at him, all of him. Her gaze was torture—he needed her touch. He needed to touch her. He reached for her, but she scooted back.

"Not yet." She was studying his groin. Damn. He had no problem with stiffness at the moment. He was so stiff that he ached.

"Soon?" he croaked.

She kissed his belly and moved lower.

"Soon," she said, and put her mouth over him.

Oh, God. He spread his legs to give her more free-dom to roam. Her delicate touch was driving him mad. Her hand cupped his sack while her mouth . . . her tongue. . . . He was going to explode.

She sucked on him and his hips lifted off the bed.

She laughed. "Amazing." She dipped her head again.

No. Enough. He was not going to spill his seed out-side her beautiful body, and if he didn't stop her im-mediately that was a definite possibility.

He flipped her onto her back.

"My turn."

He was so much stronger than she. Not that she wanted to struggle with him. She had enjoyed playing the game—more than enjoyed. But she was ready for him to take the lead now. She had reached the limits of her imagination.

His hands moved over her.

Um. She could feel her imagination expanding.

Oh.

Oh my.

He was kissing her breasts. And licking them. She arched up to encourage him to concentrate on her nipples. He laughed, sending little puffs of air across the sensitive peaks.

"Hmm. You are giving me ideas, Lizzie."

"Good!"

He laughed again and flicked her with his tongue.

"Ah!"

He repeated the action.

She twisted on the bed. The cool air made her nip-ples tighten unbearably.

He bent his head once more. This time she caught him and held him where she wanted him.

"Such a demanding wife you are."

"Yes. I—oh!"

He sucked on her and she thought she would die. She ran her hands through his hair, over his shoulders, down his back.

Now another part of her was demanding attention. Fortunately, his hands were moving in the correct direction, though not swiftly enough. She spread her legs, arched her hips.

He pushed down gently on her belly, dropping her back to the bed. He moved up to kiss her.

"So impatient, Lizzie."

She could barely speak. Her breath came in short gasps.

"Yes. I'm done with being patient." She wiggled under his hand. "Hurry up!"

"And what exactly do you want?"

"I don't know!" She wanted to wail—perhaps she did wail. She arched her back, but his hand low on her belly kept her hips down. She was aching there. The space between her legs was wet and empty. She needed him now.

"Touch me."

"Still giving orders. I think I will be in charge for a while." He kissed her nose. "I *am* touching you."

She could weep with frustration. "No, you are not. Not in the correct location. Stop playing with me. I need you—desperately—to touch me there."

"Hmm? I wonder where 'there' is." He spread his fingers so they just grazed the hair below her belly. "Here, perhaps?"

"Yes! No. Lower."

"Lower? Here?" His finger was just a shade too high.

She tried to flex her hips, to bring the aching part up to his touch. She could not move.

"Lower. Please. Lower."

"Lower?" He kissed her slowly and thoroughly. He grinned down at her. "Here?"

Finally. The tip of his finger found her. She squeaked and he kissed her again.

His finger felt wonderful—but it wasn't moving. It needed to move. She wiggled her hips and he laughed.

"You know, I have a splendid idea."

"What?"

He lifted himself off her before she could grab him. His wonderful finger left, too.

"Robbie, that is not—"

She emitted a very unladylike scream. He had replaced his finger with his mouth. His tongue. His very mobile, very clever, wonderful tongue.

The force of her pleasure caused her to sit bolt upright.

He had died and gone to heaven. He had Lizzie's taste in his mouth; he was surrounded by her smell; he had just brought her to screaming ecstasy.

She flopped back on the bed. Her knees relaxed, opening even further. He studied her beautiful center, giving it one last, long lick.

She shuddered.

He moved back over her body, positioning himself to enter her.

He hesitated. Could he? Would he—

"Are you thinking again?"

Lizzie's voice was still weak from pleasure. He smiled. God, he loved her.

Suddenly he loved her even more. She reached down and took him in her hands, gently cupping his sack, stroking him, rubbing him over her wetness.

"Now, Robbie. Please. I want you. I'm ready. Come in."

She pulled him forward, flexed her hips . . .

He slid deep inside her.

God. Dear God. He sent his Maker a fervent prayer of thanks.

She was wet and tight and hot around him. He lay on her, supporting most of his weight on his arms. He felt her breasts flattened against his chest, smelled her sweet scent of lemon and woman.

"Did I hurt you?"

"No." She flexed her hips again and wiggled. He gasped. "Stop talking and *move.*"

A breathy laugh escaped him.

"My pleasure."

It was. Such pleasure as he'd never felt before. In and out. He felt her tightening around him. In and out. He couldn't wait. In—

He exploded. Pulse after exquisite pulse, his seed leaving him, filling her; his hope for a son, a daughter, a future. His love given to his love.

Did he feel her contracting around him? He didn't know. He couldn't tell where he ended and Lizzie began.

He collapsed onto her, tears wetting his face.

She must have dozed a little. Robbie had lifted himself off her. She missed his weight.

She turned her head. He was lying next to her, watching her.

"That was wonderful." She stroked his hair and kissed him languidly. "I feel splendidly married."

He smiled slowly. "You are definitely married now, my love." He kissed her back. "I hope you didn't mind me taking over at the end."

"Not at all." She grinned. "You did a brilliant job."

"Thank you." He stroked her breast. "You cannot imagine what a gift you have given me."

"Mmm." Suddenly she didn't feel so languid. In fact, she was full of energy, eager to repeat the fascinating activities in which they had just engaged.

She slid her hand down his body. He caught it before it reached its destination.

"Lizzie, aren't you sore?"

She took stock of her body and shrugged.

"Only a little—and I know what will make me feel better."

"I don't—"

She brought her other hand more quickly to her target. He was growing nicely.

"I do—and I'd say you are interested, too."

He laughed. "Of course I am."

A drop of moisture formed at his tip. She spread it over him with her finger.

"Why did you wait so long to do this?"

He smoothed her hair off her face. "I thought I could not do it. Whenever I tried, the important part of me grew limp and useless."

She touched his heart and forehead. "*These* are the important parts of you." She smiled and gently hugged the part that was growing so large. "Though this is nice, too."

His eyes closed. "Yes." There was a tremor in his voice. "Thank God for crazy Lady Beatrice."

"What do you mean?"

"She's the one who made up the cordial I took this evening. Mmm. Keep doing what you are doing."

"I don't think Lady Beatrice's silly potion had anything to do with what just happened."

"No? I can't say for—uh!"

She pushed him onto his back and straddled him.

"As I said, I think Lady Beatrice's cordial was quite

beside the point. I believe it was my inspired performance that did the trick."

Robbie cupped her breasts and slid his hands down
to her hips. "You know, you may be correct."

"Of course I am." She laughed and leaned forward
to kiss him once again.

And here's a sneak peek at
Sally MacKenzie's next novel,
THE NAKED GENTLEMAN . . .

Chapter One

Viscount Bennington was a terrible kisser.

Meg repressed a sigh. What a pity. She had been willing to overlook his receding hairline, large nose, and frequent petulance, but this was too much. How could she wed a man whose lips felt like two fat slugs? They were trailing wetly over her cheek toward her right ear at the moment.

She should strike him from her list of potential suitors.

Still, he *did* have one of the largest plant collections in England. She would dearly love to have daily access to all that botanical wealth.

The slugs had diverted to her jaw.

How important could kissing be? Only a small portion of one's married life was devoted to the amatory arts after all. Chances were Viscount Bennington had a mistress or two. He'd only look to her for an heir. Once that task was accomplished, he would leave her alone.

She could do it. More than one woman had suffered through the activities of the marriage bed by lying still and thinking of England. She'd spend the time mentally cataloguing Bennington's vast gardens.

His lips wandered to a spot behind her ear. She

would need a handkerchief to dry her face when he was finished slobbering over her.

She drew in a deep breath, but stopped when her lungs were only half full.

He smelled. The odor was quite pronounced at these close quarters. Thankfully he was only a few inches taller than she, so she did not have her nose squashed against his waistcoat.

And he should have a word with his valet about the state of his linen. There was a thin line of dirt on his collar and cravat.

Eww! He'd stuck his tongue in her ear.

That did it. He could own the Garden of Eden and she would still have to eliminate him from her list of possible husbands.

"My lord!" She shoved against his thin chest.

"Hmm?" His mouth moved down to the base of her neck and fastened there, just like a leech.

"Lord Bennington, please." She shoved again. None of the other men she'd taken into the shrubbery had been this bold. "You must stop . . . eep!"

His hands had slid down to her hips. He pulled her tightly against him. She felt an ominous bulge in his pantaloons.

She shoved harder. She might as well be pushing against a stone wall. Who would have guessed such a short, scraggy man would be so immovable?

"My lord, you are making me uncomfortable."

He pressed his bulge more tightly against her. "And *you* are making *me* uncomfortable, sweetings." His voice was oddly thick. His mouth returned to her skin. He nipped her shoulder.

"Ouch! Stop that."

The man was a viscount. A gentleman. Surely he would not do anything untoward in Lord Palmerson's garden, just yards away from a crowded ballroom.

He was not stopping. Now he was licking the place he had bitten. Disgusting.

"My lord, return me to Lady Beatrice this instant!"

He grunted and returned his mouth to her throat.

Should she scream? Would anyone hear her over the music? If she waited for the quiet between sets. . . . Perhaps another couple had chosen to stroll in the cool night air and would come to her assistance.

Lord Bennington nuzzled her ear. "Don't be alarmed, Miss Peterson. My intentions are completely honorable."

"Honorable? I—" Meg paused. "Honorable as in 'marriage' honorable?"

"Of course. What did you think?"

What *did* she think? Yes, he was somewhat revolting, but should a little dirt and slobber eliminate him from matrimonial consideration? This was her goal, to be wed or engaged before the Season ended. The Season was barely underway and here she was already on the verge of a respectable—no, a brilliant—offer. A vicar's daughter nabbing a viscount? The society gossips would have their tongues working overtime to spread the news.

He *did* have all those lovely plants. A greenhouse and garden in London and acres of vegetation in Devon.

Really, how many times would she have to put up with his attentions if she married him? Papa and Harriet were extremely attached to each other, and her sister and her friend Lizzie spent a great deal of time with their husbands, but most married couples of the *ton* rarely saw each other. If she were lucky, she would conceive quickly, maybe even on her wedding night. Then she and Bennington could go their separate ways.

She could endure a few moments of inconvenience to get the key to his greenhouse, couldn't she? There was no one else who had such a wealth of plants. Well, no one but Mr. Parker-Roth, and he clearly wasn't interested in marrying her.

She moistened her lips. Could she say yes? It was

past time she wed. She wanted a home of her own. A garden. Children.

Children with Lord Bennington's overwhelming nose?

"My lord, I don't—"

"Come, Miss Peterson. You won't get another offer. Surely you know that."

"Lord Bennington!" He might be a viscount, but that did not give him license to be insulting.

"The other men haven't mentioned marriage, have they?"

"The other men?" Had he noticed her excursions into the shrubbery? Surely not. She'd been very discreet. "I'm not certain what you mean. I thought since we share an interest in horticulture, exploring Lord Palmerson's garden with you would be stimulating."

He chuckled and flexed his hips. His annoying bulge dug into her. "Very stimulating."

Something was definitely stimulated. Who would have thought such a short man would have such a large, um . . .

"My lord . . ."

"At this rate, you are more apt to lose your reputation than win a husband, Miss Peterson. Men talk, you know."

It was a very good thing the garden was dark. Meg felt her cheeks burning. Surely he didn't think . . . ?

"Lord Bennington, I assure you—"

"Oh, I know you didn't do anything but exchange a few kisses. Lord Farley said you were quite untutored. Thought he might have been your first. Was he?"

"Lord Bennington! Please. I would like to return to the ballroom *now.*"

"I imagine at your advanced age you are a little curious." He laughed. "Probably a little desperate, too."

"My lord, I am only twenty-one."

"Right. Well past the age when you might expect to grab a husband, hmm?"

"Not at all."

"Come now, Margaret. I may call you Margaret, mayn't I? I believe we're sufficiently acquainted to dispense with the proprieties."

His left hand landed on her bodice.

She grabbed his wrist. Somehow he had managed to shed his gloves. "No, we are definitely not sufficiently acquainted."

"You are just suffering from maidenly fears, sweetings." His fingers brushed across the tops of her breasts.

"Lord Bennington!"

"Call me 'Bennie.' All my intimates do."

"I couldn't possibly. Remove your hand this instant."

He moved it to her shoulder.

"I'm thirty-six. It's time I thought of getting an heir. Your family is respectable. Your father is connected to the Earl of Landsdowne, isn't he?"

"He is Lord Landsdowne's uncle, but the earl doesn't concern himself with us." She looked through the leaves toward the beckoning light. Did she see movement in the shadows? She hoped someone was nearby to assist her if necessary.

The viscount's fingers stroked her skin. She clenched her teeth.

"But your sister is the Marchioness of Knightsdale. I'm certain she concerns herself with you. Didn't she raise you after your mother died?"

"Yes. The ballroom, my lord. It is past time we returned." His palms were unpleasantly damp.

"And the Countess of Westbrooke is your good friend."

"Yes, yes." Had the man made a study of all her connections? "The ballroom, Lord Bennington. Please escort me back to the ballroom. If you wish to discuss my family further, we can do so there."

"And both the earl and the marquis are close

friends of the Duke of Alvord—in fact, the earl is the duchess's cousin."

"Lord Bennington . . ."

"I would like to be connected to all that power and wealth. Any one of those men could finance an expedition to the jungles of South America without a second thought."

"Jungles? South America?" Had the man lost his mind?

"I want to send my own men out to find exotic plants, Margaret."

"I see." She would like that, too, but she couldn't imagine anyone she knew financing such an undertaking. "An expedition such as you describe is very expensive. Mr. Parker-Roth was telling me—"

Bennington's hand tightened on her shoulder.

"My lord, you are hurting me."

"You know Parker-Roth?"

"Slightly. I met him at a house party last year." Meg shifted position. "Please, Lord Bennington, you will leave a bruise."

He loosened his fingers. "My pardon. I just cannot abide the man. He's a neighbor of mine. Spends most of his time in the country."

"Ah." So that was why she hadn't seen him—not that she'd been looking, of course.

"It's disgusting the way everyone fawns over him when he does attend a Horticultural Society meeting. *He* has plenty of money—he sends his brother all over the globe, looking for plant specimens."

"I see." Lord Bennington's hold on her had slackened. Would he let her go now? "Shall we return to the ballroom, my lord?"

"But you haven't given me your answer."

"Answer?"

"Yes. Will you marry me or not?"

Lord Bennington was frowning at her, all signs of passion gone. She found it quite easy to make up her mind.

"I am very sorry, my lord. I am fully aware of the great honor you'd do me, but I believe we would not suit."

The frown deepened.

"What do you mean, we would not suit?"

"We will not . . . suit." What did the man want her to say? That she thought he was a hideous oaf and she had had a huge lapse in judgment in even speaking to him?

"You brought me into this dark garden and yet you are turning down my offer?"

"I really did not expect an offer of marriage, my lord."

"What kind of an offer did you expect? Are you looking for a slip on the shoulder, then?"

"My lord! Of course not. I was not expecting an offer *now*. I mean, I was not expecting an offer of anything—any offer at all. I just wished to take a turn about the garden."

"Miss Peterson, I was not born yesterday. You lured me into this darkened corner for a reason. Was it just to steal a kiss? Are you that starved for amorous activity?"

"Lord Bennington!" Had the man actually said "amorous" with regard to her?

"You are not going to use me to satisfy your urges."

Urges! Her only urge was to get back to the light and sanity of the ballroom.

The viscount was becoming markedly agitated. She really had not anticipated such a reaction. The other men had been completely amiable when she'd suggested they go back inside. Lord Bennington was almost hissing.

"You chose to come into the garden with me, so now you'll pay the price. When I'm finished with you, your wealthy relatives and friends will beg me to wed you."

"Lord Bennington, be reasonable. You are a gentleman."

"I am a man, Miss Peterson. Surely your sister has

warned you it is highly unwise to be alone with a man in an isolated place."

Emma had warned her of many things—perhaps she should have listened to this particular lecture. At least she would be spared Emma's jobation this time—her sister was safely ensconced in Kent with her sons. If she could just get away from Bennington, all would be well. She had learned her lesson. She would not be visiting any shadowy shrubbery again.

The viscount stuck his hands into her coiffure, sending pins flying everywhere. Her hair cascaded over her shoulders.

"Lord Bennington, stop immediately!"

He grunted. His hands were on her bodice again. She jerked her knee up, but she missed her target.

"Playing that game, are you?"

"My lord, I will scream."

"Please do. The scandal will be delightful. How much do you suppose the marquis will pay to keep it quiet?"

"Nothing."

"Oh, Miss Peterson, you *are* naïve."

He mashed his mouth on hers, parting her lips. His tongue slithered between her teeth like a snake, threatening to choke her. She did the only thing she could think of.

She bit down hard.

John Parker-Roth—Parks to his friends—stepped out of the heat and noise of Lord Palmerson's ballroom into the cool quiet of the garden.

Thank God. He drew in a deep breath. He could still smell the stench of London, but at least he wasn't choking any longer on the foul mix of perfume, hair oil, stale breath, and sweat that permeated the air inside. Why his mother wanted to subject herself to that crush of humanity was beyond him.

He chose a path at random. Palmerson's garden was large for Town. If he could ignore the cacophony of music and conversation spilling out of the house and the general clamor from the street, he could almost imagine he was back in the country.

Almost. Damn. Had the plants Stephen sent arrived yet? He should be home to receive them. If they traveled all the way from South America to die waiting to be unpacked at the Priory. . . . It didn't bear consideration.

Would MacGill follow his instructions exactly? He'd written them down in detail and gone over each point with the man, but the pigheaded Scot always thought he knew best. All right, usually he did. MacGill was a bloody fine head gardener, but still, these plants required careful handling.

He wanted to be there himself. *Why* had his mother insisted on dragging him to Town now?

He blew out a pent up breath. He knew why—the blasted Season. She *said* it was to get more painting supplies and to catch up with her artist friends, but she didn't fool him. She wanted him wed.

He'd heard Palmerson had a good specimen of *Magnolia grandiflora*. He'd see if he could find it. With luck it would be in the farthest, darkest corner of the garden. He wouldn't put it past his mother to come out here looking for him, dragging her latest candidate for his hand behind her.

Why the hell couldn't she accept the fact he did not want to marry? He'd told her time after time. Was it such a hard message to understand?

Apparently it was. And now she sighed and got that worried frown every time she looked at him.

He batted aside a drooping vine. The fact of the matter was there was no need for him to marry. He didn't have a title to pass on. The Priory could go to Stephen or Nicholas, if Father didn't outlive them all. He was very happy with his life. He had his work—his plants and his gardens. He had an accommodating widow in the village—not that he visited her much anymore. Frankly, he'd rather be working in his rose beds than Cat's bed. The roses were less trouble.

No, a wife would just be an annoyance.

Damn it, was that rustling in the shrubbery? That would make this evening complete—stumbling over some amorous couple in the bushes. He veered away from the suspect vegetation.

The problem was Mother firmly believed marriage was necessary for male contentment. He took a deep breath and let it out slowly. God give him patience. Didn't she ever open her eyes and look around the bloody ballrooms to which she'd been dragging him? *She* might be happily married, and Father might be content, but most husbands and wives were not.

He had no interest in stepping into parson's mousetrap. Maybe if Grace had—

No. He would not entertain such a ridiculous notion. He'd decided that years ago. Grace had made her choice, and she was happy. Last he'd heard, she had two children. She'd been in the ballroom just now. He'd seen her laughing up at her husband at the end of the last set.

The noise from the bushes was getting louder. Wonderful. Were the lovers having a spat? That was the last thing he wanted to witness. He would just—

"You *bitch!*"

Good God, that was Bennington's voice. The man had the devil's own temper. Surely he wouldn't—

"My lord, please." The girl's voice held a thread of fear. "You are hurting me."

He strode forward without another thought.

She must not panic. Bennington was a gentleman.

He looked like a monster. He stared at her through narrowed eyes, nostrils flaring, jaw hardened. His hands gripped her upper arms. She was certain his fingers would leave bruises.

"You *bitch!*"

"My lord, please." She moistened her lips. Fear made it hard to get her breath. He was so much stronger than she, and the garden was so dark.

He was a viscount, a peer, a gentleman. He wouldn't really harm her, would he?

She had never seen a man so angry.

"You are hurting me."

"Hurting you? Ha! I'll show you hurting."

He shook her so her head flopped on her neck like a rag doll's, then he yanked her bodice down, tearing the fabric. He grabbed her breast and squeezed. The pain was excruciating.

"Bite me, will you? How would you like me to bite your—"

A well-tailored sleeve appeared at his throat.

He made a gagging sound, releasing her to claw at the black silk cutting across his neck.

"You bastard." Mr. Parker-Roth jerked Lord Bennington back, spun the viscount around, and slammed his fist into the man's jaw, sending him backward into a holly bush. Meg would have cheered if she hadn't been trying so hard not to cry. She pulled on her bodice, but the cloth was torn too badly to cover her. She crossed her arms over her chest.

"Parker-Roth." Bennington spat out the name along with some blood as he extracted himself from the prickly vegetation. "What the hell is the matter with you? The lady invited me into the garden."

"I'm certain she didn't invite you to maul her."

"A woman who goes off alone with a man . . ."

". . . is not asking to be raped, Bennington."

The viscount opened his mouth, then closed it abruptly. His jaw swelled and he had blood on his cravat. "I wasn't going to . . . I wouldn't, of course . . . I merely lost my temper." He glanced at Meg. "My humble apologies, Miss Peterson. I will do the proper thing, of course, and speak to your brother-in-law in the morning, then travel down to Kent to see your father."

"No!" She swallowed and took a deep breath. She would not shout. She spoke slowly and distinctly, "I will not marry you. I would not marry you even if you were the last man in England—no, the last man in all the world."

"Now, Margaret—"

"You heard Miss Peterson, Bennington. I believe she was quite clear as to her sentiments. Now do the *proper* thing and take yourself off."

"But—"

"I will be happy to assist you in finding the back gate—in fact I would be delighted to kick your miserable arse out into the alley."

"Margaret . . . Miss Peterson."

"Please, Lord Bennington, I assure you there is nothing you can say to persuade me to entertain your suit."

"You are merely overset. I was too impassioned, perhaps."

"*Perhaps?*" She pressed her lips together. She would *not* have a fit of the vapors here in Palmerson's garden.

He frowned at her, and then sketched a small bow. "Very well, I will leave since you insist." He turned and paused. "I do apologize most sincerely."

Meg nodded. He did sound contrite, but she just wanted him gone. She closed her eyes, listening to his steps fade away. She could not bear to look at the man still standing beside her.

Why had *Parks* been the one to find her in such an embarrassing situation? What must he think of her?

Perhaps he would just go away and let her expire in solitude.

She felt a gentle touch on her cheek.

"Miss Peterson, are you all right?"

She shook her head.

"I'm so sorry you had to endure Bennington's attentions. You shouldn't have. . . . Well, he is not the sort of man you should. . . . He has a terrible temper."

That was supremely evident.

"You can't go back to the ballroom like this. With whom did you come?"

She forced herself to speak. "Lady Beatrice."

"I shall fetch her. Will you be all right alone?"

"Y-yes." She bit her lip. She would *not* cry—well, not until he left.

He made an odd noise, a short exhalation that sounded both annoyed and resigned.

"Oh, for God's sake, come here."

His hands touched her shoulders, urging her gently toward him. She resisted for only a heartbeat.

The first sob escaped as her face touched his waistcoat. She felt his arms, warm and secure, come around her, felt his hand lightly touch her hair. A tight knot in her chest loosened.

She sobbed harder.

The girl was Miss Margaret Peterson—Meg, Westbrooke had called her. He'd met her at Tynweith's house party last spring. He'd liked her. She'd seemed quite levelheaded—very knowledgeable about garden design and plants in general. He'd enjoyed talking to her.

And looking at her.

All right, he *had* enjoyed looking at her. She was very attractive. Slim, but with generous curves in all the right places. Warm brown eyes with flecks of gold and green. Silky brown hair.

He tangled his fingers in that hair, massaging the back of her head. She felt very nice in his arms. It had been too long since he'd held a woman.

Much too long if he was feeling amorous urges toward a lady who was blubbering all over his cravat.

He would pay Cat a visit as soon as he got back to the Priory, right after he checked on that plant shipment.

He patted her shoulder. Her skin was so smooth, soft . . .

He dropped his hand to the safety of her corseted back.

What had she been thinking, coming out into Palmerson's dark garden with a man of Bennington's stamp? Was she no better than she should be? She *had* been a guest at Tynweith's scandalous house party.

And had behaved perfectly properly there. She had gone into the garden with him, but always in the daylight and always to discuss a particular planting.

She made a peculiar little sound, a cross between a sniff and a hiccup.

"Are you all right, Miss Peterson?"

She nodded, keeping her head down.

"Here—take my handkerchief."

"Thank you."

She still would not meet his eyes.

"You can't go back to the ballroom, you know." There was enough light to see one slender white shoulder was completely exposed, as was the lovely curve of her breast, the darker shadow of a nipple . . .

He moved his hips back to save her the shock of his sudden attraction.

Damn, he had *definitely* been too long without a woman.

"I'm sorry to be such a watering pot. I've thoroughly soaked your clothing."

"You had an upsetting experience." He cleared his throat. "You do know you shouldn't be alone with a man in the darkened shrubbery, don't you?"

"Yes, of course." She stepped a little away from him. "None of the others so forgot themselves."

"Others? There have been others?"

* * *

Meg flushed. Parks looked so shocked.

"I'm not a debutante."

"No, but you are young and unmarried."

"Not so young. I'm twenty-one."

Parks lifted an eyebrow. Meg felt a spurt of annoyance. Was the man criticizing her?

"Lady Beatrice has not commented on my behavior."

He lifted the eyebrow higher. Suddenly she wanted to grab his spectacles and grind them under her heel. She was so tired of people looking at her in just that way.

"Ohh, you are as bad as the rest of the priggish, nasty beasts in that ballroom."

She spun on her heel, took a step—and caught her foot on a root.

"Aaa!" She was falling face first toward the holly bush Bennington had recently vacated.

Strong hands grabbed her before she collided with the prickly greenery and hauled her up against a rock-hard chest. She shivered. The cool night air raised goose bumps on her arms and . . .

She looked down. Her breasts had fallen completely out of her dress.

"Ack!"

"What's the matter?"

"Close your eyes!"

"What?"

Oh, lud, was that the crunch of shoes on gravel? Someone was coming this way! She had to hide.

There was no place to hide. She twisted around and plastered herself up against Parks. Perhaps God would work a miracle and make her invisible.

The Almighty was not interested in assisting her this evening.

"Halooo! Mr. Parker-Roth . . . is that you? I didn't know you were in Town."

"Oooh." Meg muffled her moan in Parks's cravat. It

couldn't be. . . . Please, not Lady Dunlee, London's biggest gossip!

She felt Parks's arms tighten around her. His response rumbled under her cheek.

"I've recently arrived, Lady Dunlee. Good evening, my lord."

"Good evening, Parker-Roth. We were just taking a turn in the garden, but, um . . ." Lord Dunlee cleared his throat. "I, um, believe it's time we returned to the ballroom."

"Just a minute." Lady Dunlee's voice was sharp. "Who's that with you in the shrubbery, sir? I can't see."

"My dear, I think we interrupt the gentleman."

Lady Dunlee snorted. "Obviously. The question is, what exactly are we interrupting?"

Meg closed her eyes. She was going to die of embarrassment.

"That's Miss Peterson, isn't it? My word, I had no idea you two were quite so . . . friendly."

Discover the Romances of
Hannah Howell